*Critical acclaim for* Hostage:

'Another terrific stand-alone novel . . . What makes *Hostage* so enjoyable is the way he builds on the basic premise . . . Blistering' Peter Guttridge, *Observer*

'[Crais] matches his canny plotting with characterisation of a rare order' *Crime Time*

'Warning: don't sit down to read just a little bit of this book. Be sure you have a large block of time in front of you or you *will* lose sleep . . . Full of surprise and creative plotting' George Easter, *Deadly Pleasures*

'The suspense is kept up throughout' Susanna Yager, *Saturday Telegraph*

'Intense and driven, *Hostage* has the propulsiveness of an action movie – its characters developed, its scenarios paid off in spades' *Waterstone's Books Quarterly*

Robert Crais is the bestselling author of the Elvis Cole detective novels. He lives in Los Angeles. His website address is http://www.robertcrais.com.

# Hostage

Robert Crais

ORION

An Orion paperback

First published in Great Britain in 2001
by Orion
This paperback edition published in 2002
by Orion Books Ltd,
Orion House, 5 Upper St Martin's Lane,
London WC2H 9EA

A CIP catalogue record for this book
is available from the British Library.

ISBN 0 75284 787 2

Typeset by Deltatype Ltd, Birkenhead, Merseyside
Printed and bound in Great Britain by
Clays Ltd, St Ives plc.

To Frank, Toni, Gina, Chris, and Norma;
And to Jack Hughes, who enriched our lives.
For twenty years of friendship and laughter,
tacky though it may be.

# PROLOGUE

*The man in the house was going to kill himself. When the man threw his phone into the yard, Talley knew that he had accepted his own death. After six years as a crisis negotiator with the Los Angeles Police Department's SWAT team, Sergeant Jeff Talley knew that people in crisis often spoke in symbols. This symbol was clear: Talk was over. Talley feared that the man would die by his own hand, or do something to force the police to kill him. It was called suicide by cop. Talley believed it to be his fault.*

*'Did they find his wife yet?'*

*'Not yet. They're still looking.'*

*'Looking doesn't help, Murray. I gotta have something to give this guy after what happened.'*

*'That's not your fault.'*

*'It is my fault. I blew it, and now this guy is circling the drain.'*

*Talley crouched behind an armored command vehicle with the SWAT commander, a lieutenant named Murray Leifitz, who was also his negotiating team supervisor. From this position, Talley had spoken to George Donald Malik through a dedicated crisis phone that had been cut into the house line. Now that Malik had thrown his phone into the yard, Talley could use the public address megaphone or do it face-to-face. He hated the megaphone, which made his voice harsh and depersonalized the contact. The illusion of a personal relationship was important; the illusion of trust was everything. Talley strapped on a Kevlar vest.*

Malik shouted through the broken window, his voice high and strained.

'I'm going to kill this dog! I'm going to kill it!'

Leifitz leaned past Talley to peek at the house. This was the first time Malik had mentioned a dog.

'What the fuck? Does he have a dog in there?'

'How do I know? I've got to try to undo some of the damage here, okay? Ask the neighbors about the dog. Get me a name.'

'If he pops a cap, we're going in there, Jeff. That's all there is to it.'

'Just take it easy and get a name for the dog.'

Leifitz scuttled backward to speak with Malik's neighbors.

George Malik was an unemployed housepainter with too much credit card debt, an unfaithful wife who flaunted her affairs, and prostate cancer. Fourteen hours earlier, at two-twelve that morning, he had fired one shot above the heads of the police officers who had come to his door in response to a disturbance complaint. He then barricaded the door and threatened to kill himself unless his wife agreed to speak to him. The officers who secured the area ascertained from neighbors that Malik's wife, Elena, had left with their only child, a nine-year-old boy named Brendan. As detectives from Rampart Division set about locating her, Malik threatened suicide with greater frequency until Talley was convinced that Malik was nearing the terminal point. When the Rampart detectives reported what they believed to be a solid location obtained from the wife's sister, Talley took a chance. He told Malik that his wife had been found. That was Talley's mistake. He had violated a cardinal rule of crisis negotiation: He had lied, and been caught. He had made a promise that he had been unable to deliver, and so had destroyed the illusion of trust that he had been building. That was two hours ago, and now word had arrived that the wife had still not been found.

'I'm gonna kill this fuckin' dog, goddamnit! This is her goddamned dog, and I'm gonna shoot this sonofabitch right in the head, she don't start talkin' to me!'

Talley stepped out from behind the vehicle. He had been on the scene for eleven hours. His skin was greased with sweat, his head throbbed, and his stomach was cramping from too much coffee and stress. He made his voice conversational, yet concerned.

'George, it's me, Jeff. Don't kill anything, okay? We don't want to hear a gun go off.'

'You liar! You said my wife was gonna talk to me!'

It was a small stucco house the color of dust. Two casement windows braced the front door above a tiny porch. The door was closed, and drapes had been pulled across the windows. The window on the left was broken from the phone. Eight feet to the right of the porch, a five-member SWAT Tactical Team hunkered against the wall, waiting to breach the door. Malik could not be seen.

'George, listen, I said that we'd found her, and I want to explain that. I was wrong. We got our wires crossed out here, and they gave me bad information. But we're still looking, and when we find her, we'll have her talk to you.'

'You lied before, you bastard, and now you're lying again. You're lying to protect that bitch, and I won't have it. I'm gonna shoot her dog and then I'm gonna blow my brains out.'

Talley waited. It was important that he appear calm and give Malik the room to cool. People burned off stress when they talked. If he could reduce Malik's level of stress, they could get over the hump and still climb out of this.

'Don't shoot the dog, George. Whatever's between you and your wife, let's not take it out on the dog. Is it your dog, too?'

'I don't know whose fuckin' dog it is. She lied about

3

everything else, so she probably lied about the dog. She's a natural-born liar. Like you.'

'George, c'mon. I was wrong, but I didn't lie. I made a mistake. A liar wouldn't admit that, but I want to be straight with you. Now, I'm a dog guy myself. What kind of dog you got in there?'

'I don't believe you. You know right where she is, and unless you make her talk to me, I'm gonna shoot this dog.'

The depths to which people sank in the shadowed crevasses of desperation could crush a man as easily as the weight of water at the ocean floor. Talley had learned to hear the pressure building in people's voices, and he heard it now. Malik was being crushed.

'Don't give up, George. I'm sure that she'll talk to you.'

'Then why won't she open her mouth? Why won't the bitch just say something, that's all she's gotta do?'

'We'll work it out.'

'Say something, goddamnit!'

'I said we'll work it out.'

'Say something or I'm gonna shoot this damned dog!'

Talley took a breath, thinking. Malik's choice of words left him confused. Talley had spoken clearly, yet Malik acted as if he hadn't heard. Talley worried that Malik was dissociating or approaching a psychotic break.

'George, I can't see you. Come to the window so I can see you.'

'STOP LOOKING AT ME!'

'George, please come to the window!'

Talley saw Leifitz return to the rear of the vehicle. They were close, only a few feet apart, Leifitz under cover, Talley exposed.

Talley spoke under his breath.

'What's the dog's name?'

Leifitz shook his head.

'They say he doesn't have a dog.'

4

'OPEN YOUR GODDAMNED MOUTH RIGHT NOW OR I'M SHOOTING THIS DOG!'

Something hard pounded in the center of Talley's head, and his back felt wet. He suddenly realized that illusions worked both ways. The Rampart detectives hadn't found Malik's wife because Malik's wife was inside. The neighbors were wrong. She had been inside the entire time. The wife and the boy.

'Murray, launch the team!'

Talley shouted at Murray Leifitz just as a loud whip-crack echoed from the house. A second shot popped even as the tactical team breached the front door.

Talley ran forward, feeling weightless. Later, he would not remember jumping onto the porch or entering through the door. Malik's lifeless body was pinned to the floor, his hands being cuffed behind his back even though he was already dead. Malik's wife was sprawled on the living-room sofa where she had been dead for over fourteen hours. Two tac officers were trying to stop the geyser of arterial blood that spurted from the neck of Malik's nine-year-old son. One of them screamed for the paramedics. The boy's eyes were wide, searching the room as if trying to find a reason for all this. His mouth opened and closed; his skin was luminous as it drained of color. The boy's eyes found Talley, who knelt and rested a hand on the boy's leg. Talley never broke eye contact. He didn't allow himself to blink. He let Brendan Malik have that comfort as he watched the boy die.

After a while, Talley went out to sit on the porch. His head buzzed like he was drunk. Across the street, police officers milled by their cars. Talley lit a cigarette, then replayed the past eleven hours, looking for clues that should have told him what was real. He could not find them. Maybe there weren't any, but he didn't believe that. He had blown it. He had made mistakes. The boy had been here the entire time, curled at the feet of his murdered mother like a loyal and faithful dog.

Murray Leifitz put a hand on his shoulder and told him to go home.

Jeff Talley had been a Los Angeles SWAT officer for thirteen years, serving as a Crisis Response Team negotiator for six. Today was his third crisis call in five days.

He tried to recall the boy's eyes, but had already forgotten if they were brown or blue.

Talley crushed his cigarette, walked down the street to his car, and went home. He had an eleven-year-old daughter named Amanda. He wanted to check her eyes. He couldn't remember their color and was scared that he no longer cared.

# Part One
## THE AVOCADO ORCHARD

# CHAPTER 1

**Bristo Camino, California**
Friday, 2:47 P.M.

DENNIS ROONEY

It was one of those high-desert days in the suburban communities north of Los Angeles with the air so dry it was like breathing sand; the sun licked their skin with fire. They were eating hamburgers from the In-N-out, riding along in Dennis's truck, a red Nissan pickup that he'd bought for six hundred dollars from a Bolivian he'd met working construction two weeks before he had been arrested; Dennis Rooney driving, twenty-two years old and eleven days out of the Antelope Valley Correctional Facility, what the inmates called the Ant Farm; his younger brother, Kevin, wedged in the middle; and a guy named Mars filling the shotgun seat. Dennis had known Mars for only four days.

Later, in the coming hours when Dennis would frantically reconsider his actions, he would decide that it hadn't been the saw-toothed heat that had put him in the mood to do crime: It was fear. Fear that something special was waiting for him that he would never find, and that this special thing would disappear around some curve in his life, and with it his one shot at being more than nothing.

Dennis decided that they should rob the minimart.

'Hey, I know. Let's rob that fuckin' minimart, the one on the other side of Bristo where the road goes up toward Santa Clarita.'

9

'I thought we were going to the movie.'

That being Kevin, wearing his chickenshit face: eyebrows crawling over the top of his head, darting eyeballs, and quivering punkass lips. In the movie of Dennis's life, he saw himself as the brooding outsider all the cheerleaders wanted to fuck; his brother was the geekass cripple holding him back.

'This is a better idea, chickenshit. We'll go to the movie after.'

'You just got back from the Farm, Dennis, Jesus. You want to go back?'

Dennis flicked his cigarette out the window, ignoring the blowback of sparks and ash as he considered himself in the Nissan's sideview. By his own estimation, he had moody deep-set eyes the color of thunderstorms, dramatic cheekbones, and sensuous lips. Looking at himself, which he did, often, he knew that it was only a matter of time before his destiny arrived, before the special thing waiting for him presented itself and he could bag the minimum-wage jobs and life in a shithole apartment with his chickenshit brother.

Dennis adjusted the .32-caliber automatic wedged in his pants, then glanced past Kevin to Mars.

'What do you think, dude?'

Mars was a big guy, heavy across the shoulders and ass. He had a tattoo on the back of his shaved head that said BURN IT. Dennis had met him at the construction site where he and Kevin were pulling day work for a cement contractor. He didn't know Mars's last name. He had not asked.

'Dude? Whattaya think?'

'I think let's go see.'

That was all it took.


The minimart was on Flanders Road, a rural boulevard that linked several expensive housing tracts. Four pump islands framed a bunkerlike market that sold toiletries, soft drinks, booze, and convenience items. Dennis pulled up behind the building so they couldn't be seen from inside, the Nissan bucking as he downshifted. The transmission was a piece of shit.

'Look at this, man. The fuckin' place is dead. It's perfect.'

'C'mon, Dennis, this is stupid. We'll get caught.'

'I'm just gonna see, is all. Don't give yourself a piss enema.'

The parking lot was empty except for a black Beemer at the pumps and two bicycles by the front door. Dennis's heart was pounding, his underarms clammy even in the awful dry heat that sapped his spit. He would never admit it, but he was nervous. Fresh off the Farm, he didn't want to go back, but he didn't see how they could get caught, or what could go wrong. It was like being swept along by a mindless urge. Resistance was futile.

Cold air rolled over him as Dennis pushed inside. Two kids were at the magazine rack by the door. A fat Chinaman was hunkered behind the counter, so low that all Dennis could see was his head poking up like a frog playing submarine in a mud puddle.

The minimart was two aisles and a cold case packed with beer, yogurt, and Cokes. Dennis had a flash of uncertainty, and thought about telling Mars and Kevin that a whole pile of Chinamen were behind the counter so he could get out of having to rob the place, but he didn't. He went to the cold case, then along the rear wall to make sure no one was in the aisles, his heart pounding because he knew he was going to do it. He was going to rob this fucking place. As he was walking back to the truck, the Beemer pulled away. He went to the passenger window. To Mars.

'There's nothing but two kids and a Chinaman in there, the Chinaman behind the counter, a fat guy.'

Kevin said, 'They're Korean.'

'What?'

'The sign says "Kim." Kim is a Korean name.'

That was Kevin, always with something to say like that. Dennis wanted to reach across Mars and grab Kevin by the fucking neck. He pulled up his T-shirt to flash the butt of his pistol.

'Who gives a shit, Kevin? That Chinaman is gonna shit his pants when he sees this. I won't even have to take it out, goddamnit. Thirty seconds, we'll be down the road. He'll have to wipe himself before he calls the cops.'

Kevin squirmed with a case of the chicken-shits, his nerves making his eyes dance around like beans in hot grease.

'Dennis, please. What are we going to get here, a couple of hundred bucks? Jesus, let's go to the movie.'

Dennis told himself that he might have driven away if Kevin wasn't such a whiner, but, no, Kevin had to put on the goddamned pussy face, putting Dennis on the spot.

Mars was watching. Dennis felt himself flush, and wondered if Mars was judging him. Mars was a boulder of a guy; dense and quiet, watchful, with the patience of a rock. Dennis had noticed that about Mars on the job site; Mars considered people. He would watch a conversation, say, like when two of the Mexicans hammered a third to throw in with them on buying some tamales. Mars would watch, not really part of it but above it, as if he could see all the way back to when they were born, see them wetting the bed when they were five or jerking off when they thought they were alone. Then he would make a vacant smile like he knew everything they might do now or in the future, even about the goddamned tamales. It was creepy, sometimes, that expression on his face, but Mars thought that Dennis had good ideas and usually went along. First time they met, four days ago, Dennis felt that his destiny was finally at hand. Here was Mars, charged with some dangerous electrical potential that

crackled under his skin, and he did whatever Dennis told
him.

'Mars, we're gonna do this. We're robbing this fuckin'
store.'

Mars climbed out of the truck, so cool that even heat
like this couldn't melt him.

'Let's do it.'

Kevin didn't move. The two kids pedaled away.

'*No one's here, Kevin!* All you have to do is stand by the
door and watch. This fat fuck will cough right up with the
cash. They're insured, so they just hand over the cash.
They get fired if they don't.'

Dennis grabbed his brother's T-shirt. The Lemonheads,
for chrissake. His fucking brother was a lemonhead. Mars
was already halfway to the door.

'Get out of the truck, you turd. You're making us look
bad.'

Kevin wilted and slid out like a fuckin' baby.


JUNIOR KIM, JR.
KIM'S MINIMART


Junior Kim, Jr., knew a cheese dip when he saw one.

Junior, a second-generation Korean-American, had put
in sixteen years behind a minimart counter in the
Newton area of Los Angeles. Down in Shootin' Newton
(as the LAPD called it), Junior had been beaten, mugged,
stabbed, shot at, clubbed, and robbed forty-three times.
Enough was enough. After sixteen years of that, Junior,
his wife, their six children, and all four grandparents had
bailed on the multicultural melting pot of greater LA, and
moved north to the far less dangerous demographic of
bedroom suburbia.

Junior was not naïve. A minimart, by its nature, draws
cheese dips like bad meat draws flies. Even here in Bristo
Camino, you had your shoplifters (mostly teenagers, but

often men in business suits), your paperhangers (mostly women), your hookers passing counterfeit currency (driven up from LA by their pimps), and your drunks (mostly belligerent white men sprouting gin blossoms). Lightweight stuff compared to LA, but Junior believed in being prepared. After sixteen years of hard-won inner-city lessons, Junior kept 'a little something' under the counter for anyone who got out of hand.

When three cheese dips walked in that Friday afternoon, Junior leaned forward so that his chest touched the counter and his hands were hidden.

'May I help you?'

A skinny kid in a Lemonheads T-shirt stayed by the door. An older kid in a faded black wife-beater and a large man with a shaved head walked toward him, the older kid raising his shirt to show the ugly black grip of a pistol. 'Two packs of Marlboros for my friend here and all the cash you got in that box, you gook motherfucker.'

Junior Kim could read a cheese dip a mile away.

His face impassive, Junior fished under the counter for his 9mm Glock. He found it just as the cheese dip launched himself over the counter. Junior lurched to his feet, bringing up the Glock as the black-shirted dip crashed into him. Junior hadn't expected this asshole to jump over the counter, and hadn't been able to thumb off the safety.

The larger man shouted, 'He's got a gun!'

Everything happened so quickly that Junior wasn't sure whose hands were where. The black shirt forgot about his own gun and tried to twist away Junior's. The big guy reached across the counter, also grabbing for the gun. Junior was more scared now than any of the other times he had pulled his weapon. If he couldn't release the safety before this kid pulled his own gun, or wrestled away Junior's, Junior knew that he would be fucked. Junior Kim was in a fight for his life.

Then the safety slipped free, and Junior Kim, Jr., knew that he had won.

He said, 'I gotcha, you dips.'

The Glock went off, a heavy 9mm explosion that made the cheese dip's eyes bulge with a terrible surprise.

Junior smiled, victorious.

'Fuck *you*.'

Then Junior felt the most incredible pain in his chest. It filled him as if he were having a heart attack. He stumbled back into the Slurpee machine as the blood spilled out of his chest and spread across his shirt. Then he slid to the floor.

The last thing Junior heard was the cheese dip by the door, shouting, 'Dennis! Hurry up! Somebody's outside!'

### MARGARET HAMMOND,
### WITNESS

Outside at the second pump island, Margaret Hammond heard a car backfire as she climbed from her Lexus.

Margaret, who lived across the street in a tile-roofed home that looked exactly like a hundred others in her development, saw three young white males run out of the minimart and get into a red Nissan pickup truck, which lurched away with the jumpy acceleration that tells you the clutch is shot. It headed west toward the freeway.

Margaret locked the pump nozzle to fill her tank, then went into the minimart to buy a Nestlé's Crunch chocolate bar, which she intended to eat before she got home.

Less than ten seconds later, by her own estimation, Margaret Hammond ran back into the parking lot. The red Nissan had disappeared. Margaret used her cell phone to call 911, who patched her through to the Bristo Camino Police Department.

\*

Their voices overlapped, Kevin grabbing Dennis's arm, making the truck swerve. Dennis punched him away.

'You killed that guy! You *shot* him!'

'I don't know if he's dead or what!'

'There was fucking blood everywhere! It's all over you!'

'Stop it, Kevin! He had a fuckin' gun! I didn't know he would have a gun! It just went off!'

Kevin pounded the dash, bouncing between Dennis and Mars like he was going to erupt through the roof.

'We're fucked, Dennis, *fucked*! What if he's *dead?!*'

'*SHUT UP!*'

Dennis licked his lips, tasting copper and salt. He glanced in the rearview. His face was splattered with red dew. Dennis lost it then, certifiably freaked out because he'd eaten human blood. He swiped at his face, wiping the blood on his jeans.

Mars touched him.

'Dude. Take it easy.'

'We've gotta get away!'

'We're getting away. No one saw us. No one caught us. We're fine.'

Mars sat quietly in the shotgun seat. Kevin and Dennis were wild, but Mars was as calm as if he had just awakened from a trance. He was holding the Chinaman's gun.

'Fuck! Throw it out, dude! We might get stopped.'

Mars pushed the gun into his waistband, then left his hand there, holding it the way some men hold their crotch.

'We might need it.'

Dennis upshifted hard, ignoring the clash of gears as he threw the Nissan toward the freeway two miles ahead. At least four people had seen the truck. Even these dumb Bristo cops would be able to put two and two together if they had witnesses who could tie them to the truck.

'Listen, we gotta think. We gotta figure out what to do.'

Kevin's eyes were like dinner plates.

'Jesus, Dennis, we gotta turn ourselves in.'

Dennis felt so much pressure in his head that he thought his eyes were swelling.

'No one's turning themselves in! We can get outta this! We just gotta figure out what to do!'

Mars touched him again.

'Listen.'

Mars was smiling at nothing. Not even looking at them.

'We're just three guys in a red truck. There's a million red trucks.'

Dennis desperately wanted to believe that.

'You think?'

'They've got to find witnesses. If they find those two kids or the woman, then those people have to describe us. Maybe they can, but maybe they can't. When the cops get all that sorted out, then they have to start looking for three white guys in a red truck. You know how many red trucks there are?'

'A million.'

'That's right. And how long does all that take? The rest of the day? Tomorrow? We can be across the border in four hours. Let's go down to Mexico.'

The vacant smile was absolutely sure of itself. Mars was so calm that Dennis found himself convinced; it was as if Mars had run this path before and knew the turns.

'That's a fucking plan, Mars. That's a *plan*! We can kick back for a few days, then come back when everything blows over. It always blows over.'

'That's right.'

Dennis pushed harder on the accelerator, felt the transmission lag, and then a loud BANG came from under the truck. The transmission let go. Six hundred dollars. Cash. What did he expect?

'Mother*FUCK*ing piece of *SHIT!*'

The truck lost power, bucking as Dennis guided it off the road. Even before it lurched to a stop, Dennis shoved open the door, desperate to run. Kevin caught his arm, holding him back.

'There's nothing we can do, Dennis. We're only making it worse.'

'Shut up!'

Dennis shook off his brother's hand and slid out of the truck. He searched up and down the road, half expecting to see a highway patrol car, but the cars were few and far between and those were mostly soccer moms. Flanders Road from here to the freeway cut through an area of affluent housing developments. Some of the communities were gated, but most weren't, though most were hidden from the road by hedges that masked heavy stone walls. Dennis looked at the hedges, and the walls that they hid. He wondered if escape lay beyond them.

It was like Mars read his mind.

'Let's steal a car.'

Dennis looked at the wall again. On the other side of it would be a housing development filled with cars. They could crash into a house, tie up the soccer mom to buy some time, and *drive*.

Dennis didn't think about it any more than that.

'Let's go.'

'Dennis, please.'

Dennis pulled his brother out of the truck.

They crashed into the hedges and went up the wall.

OFFICER MIKE WELCH,
BRISTO CAMINO POLICE

Officer Mike Welch, thirty-two years old, married, one child, was rolling code seven to the Krispy Kreme donut shop on the west side of Bristo Camino when he got the call.

'Unit four, base.'

'Four.'

'Armed robbery, Kim's Minimart on Flanders Road, shots fired.'

Welch thought that was absurd.

'Say again, shots fired. Are you kidding me?'

'Three white males, approximately twenty years, jeans and T-shirts, driving a red Nissan pickup last seen west on Flanders Road. Get over there and see about Junior.'

Mike Welch was rolling westbound on Flanders Road. Junior's service station was straight ahead, less than two miles. Welch went code three, hitting the lights and siren. He had never before in his three years as a police officer rolled code three other than when he pulled over a speeder.

'I'm on Flanders now. Is Junior shot?'

'That's affirm. Ambulance is inbound.'

Welch floored it. He was so intent on beating the paramedics to Kim's that he was past the red truck parked on the opposite side of the road before he realized that it matched the description of the getaway vehicle.

Welch shut his siren and pulled off onto the shoulder. He twisted around to stare back up the street. He couldn't see anyone in or around the truck, but there it was, a red Nissan pickup. Welch waited for a gap in traffic, then swung around and drove back, pulling off behind the Nissan. He keyed his shoulder mike.

'Base, four. I'm a mile and a half east of Kim's on Flanders. Got a red Nissan pickup, license Three-Kilo-Lima-Mike-Four-Two-Nine. It appears abandoned. Can you send someone else to Kim's?'

'Ah, we can.'

'I'm gonna check it out.'

'Three-Kilo-Lima-Mike-Four-Two-Nine. Rog.'

Welch climbed out of his car and rested his right hand on the butt of his Browning Hi-Power. He didn't draw his weapon, but he wanted to be ready. He walked up along the passenger side of the truck, glanced underneath, then walked around the front. The engine was still ticking, and the hood was warm. Mike Welch thought, sonofabitch, this was it, this was the getaway vehicle.

'Base, four. Area's clear. Vehicle is abandoned.'

'Rog.'

Welch continued around to the driver's-side door and looked inside. He couldn't be sure that this was the getaway vehicle, but his heart was hammering with excitement. Mike Welch had come to the Bristo police department after seven years as a roofing contractor. He had thought that police work would be more than writing traffic tickets and breaking up domestic disturbances, but it hadn't worked out that way; now, for the first time in his career, he might come face-to-face with an actual felon. He looked either way up and down the road, wondering why they had abandoned the truck and where they had gone. He suddenly felt frightened. Welch stared at the hedges. He squatted again, trying to see under the low branches, but saw nothing except a wall. Welch drew his gun, then approached the hedges, looking more closely. Several branches were broken. He glanced back at the truck, thinking it through, imagining three suspects pushing through the hedges. Three kids on the run, shitting their pants, going over the wall. On the other side of the wall was a development of expensive homes called York Estates. Welch knew from his patrol route that there were only two streets out unless they went over the wall again. They would be hiding in someone's garage or running like hell out the back side of the development, trying to get away.

Welch listened to the Nissan's ticking engine, and decided that he was no more than a few minutes behind them. His heart rate increased. He made his decision. Welch burned rubber as he swung out onto the road, intent on cutting them off before they escaped the development, intent on making the arrest.

*

Dennis dropped from the wall into a different world, hidden behind lush ferns and plants with leathery green leaves and orange trees. His impulse was to keep running, haul ass across the yard, jump the next wall, and keep going, but the siren was right on top of them. And then the siren stopped.

Kevin said, 'Dennis, *please*, the police are gonna see the truck. They're gonna know who we are.'

'Shut up, Kevin. I *know*. Lemme think!'

They were in a dense garden surrounding a tennis court at the rear of a palatial home. A swimming pool was directly in front of them with the main house beyond the pool, a big-ass two-story house with lots of windows and doors, and one of the doors was open. Just like that. Open. If people were home, there would be a car. A Sony boom box beside the pool was playing music. There wouldn't be music if no one was home.

Dennis glanced at Mars, and, without even looking back at him, almost as if he had read Dennis's mind again, Mars nodded.

JENNIFER SMITH

Sixty feet away through the open door, Jennifer Smith was thoroughly pissed off about the state of her life. Her father was behind closed doors at the front of the house, working. He was an accountant, and often worked at home. Her mother was in Florida visiting their Aunt Kate. With her mom in Florida and her dad working, Jen was forced 24/7 to ride herd on her ten-year-old brother, Thomas. If her friends wanted to go to the Multiplex, Thomas had to go. If she lied about going to Palmdale so she could sneak down to LA, Thomas would tell. Jennifer

Smith was sixteen years old. Having a turd like Thomas grafted to her butt 24/7 was wrecking her summer.

Jen had been laying out by the pool, but she had come in to make tuna fish sandwiches. She would have let the turd starve, but she didn't mind making lunch for her father.

'Thomas?'

He hated it if you called him Tommy. He didn't even like Tom. It had to be Thomas.

'Thomas, go tell Daddy that lunch is ready.'

'Eat me.'

Thomas was playing Nintendo in the family room.

'Go tell Daddy.'

'Just yell. He'll hear you.'

'Go get him or I'll spit in your food.'

'Spit twice. It turns me on.'

'You are *so* gross.'

Thomas paused the Nintendo game and looked around at her. 'I'll get him if you ask Elyse and Tris to come lay out.'

Elyse and Tris were her two best friends. They had stopped coming over because Thomas totally creeped them out. He would wait in the house until everyone was lying by the pool, then he would appear and offer to rub oil on them. Even though everyone said ooo, yuck, go away, he would sit there and stare at their bodies.

'They won't lay out with you here. They know you watch.'

'They like it.'

'You are *so* gross.'

When the three young men stepped inside, Jen's first thought was that they were gardeners, but all the gardeners she knew were short, dark men from Central America. Her second thought was that maybe they were older kids from school, but that didn't feel right either.

Jennifer said, 'May I help you?'

The first one pointed at Thomas.

'Mars, get the troll.'

The biggest one ran at Thomas, as the first one charged into the kitchen.

Jennifer screamed just as the first boy covered her mouth so tightly that she thought her face would break. Thomas tried to shout, but the bigger boy mashed his face into the carpet.

The third one was younger. He hung back near the door, crying, talking in a loud stage whisper, trying to keep his voice down.

'Dennis, let's go! This is crazy!'

'Shut up, Kevin! We're here. Deal with it.'

The one holding her, the one she now knew as Dennis, bent her backwards over the counter, mashing the sandwiches. His hips ground against hers, pinning her. His breath smelled of hamburgers and cigarettes.

'Stop kicking! I'm not going to hurt you!'

She tried to bite his hand. He pushed her head farther back until her neck felt like it would snap.

'I said stop it. Relax, and I'll let you go.'

Jennifer fought harder until she saw the gun. The bigger boy was holding a black pistol to Thomas's head.

Jennifer stopped fighting.

'I'm going to take my hand away, but you better not yell. You understand that?'

Jennifer couldn't stop watching the gun.

'Close the door, Kevin.'

She heard the door close.

Dennis took away his hand, but kept it close, ready to clamp her mouth again. His voice was a whisper.

'Who else is here?'

'My father.'

'Is there anyone else?'

'No.'

'Where is he?'

'In his office.'

'Is there a car?'

Her voice failed. All she could do was nod.

'Don't yell. If you yell, I'll kill you. Do you understand that?'

She nodded.

'Where's his office?'

She pointed toward the entry.

Dennis laced his fingers through her hair and pushed her toward the hall. He followed so closely that his body brushed hers, reminding her that she was wearing only shorts and a bikini top. She felt naked and exposed.

Her father's office was off the entry hall behind wide double doors. They didn't bother to knock or say anything. Dennis pulled open the door, and the big one, Mars, carried in Thomas, the gun still at his head. Dennis pushed her onto the floor, then ran straight across the room, pointing his gun at her father.

'Don't say a goddamned word! Don't fucking move!'

Her father was working at his computer with a sloppy stack of printouts all around. He was a slender man with a receding hairline and glasses. He blinked over the tops of the glasses as if he didn't quite understand what he was seeing. He probably thought they were friends of hers, playing a joke. But then she saw that he knew it was real.

'What are you doing?'

Dennis aimed his gun with both hands, shouting louder.

'Don't you fucking move, goddamnit! Keep your ass in that chair! Let me see your hands!'

What her father said then made no sense to her.

He said, 'Who sent you?'

Dennis shoved Kevin with his free hand.

'Kevin, close the windows! Stop being a turd!'

Kevin went to the windows and closed the shutters. He was crying worse than Thomas.

Dennis waved his gun at Mars.

'Keep him covered, dude. Watch the girl.'

Mars pushed Thomas onto the floor with Jennifer, then

24

aimed at her father. Dennis put his own gun in the waistband of his pants, then snatched a lamp from the corner of her father's desk. He jerked the plug from the wall, then the electrical cord from the lamp.

'Don't go psycho and everything will be fine. Do you hear that? I'm gonna take your car. I'm gonna tie you up so you can't call the cops, and I'm gonna take your car. I don't want to hurt you, I just want the car. Gimme the keys.'

Her father looked confused.

'What are you talking about? Why did you come here?'

'*I want the fucking car, you asshole! I'm stealing your car! Now, where are the keys?*'

'That's what you want, the car?'

'Am I talking fucking Russian here or what? DO YOU HAVE A CAR?'

Her father raised his hands, placating.

'In the garage. Take it and leave. The keys are on the wall by the garage door. By the kitchen. Take it.'

'Kevin, go get the keys, then come help tie these bastards up so we can get outta here.'

Kevin, still by the windows, said, 'There's a cop coming.'

Jennifer saw the police car through the gaps in the shutters. A policeman got out. He looked around as if he was taking his bearings, then came toward their house.

Dennis grabbed her hair again.

'Don't fucking say a word. Not one fucking word.'

'Please don't hurt my children.'

'*Shut up.* Mars, you be ready! Mars!'

Jennifer watched the policeman come up the walk. He disappeared past the edge of the window, then their doorbell rang.

Kevin scuttled to his older brother, gripping his arm.

'He knows we're here, Dennis! He must've seen me closing the shutters!

'Shut up!'

The doorbell rang again.

Jennifer felt Dennis's sweat drip onto her shoulder and wanted to scream. Her father stared at her, his eyes locked onto hers, slowly shaking his head. She didn't know if he was telling her not to scream, or not to move, or even if he realized that he was doing it.

The policeman walked past the windows toward the side of the house.

'He knows we're here, Dennis! He's looking for a way in!'

'He doesn't know shit! He's just looking.'

Kevin was frantic, and now Jennifer could hear the fear in Dennis's voice, too.

'He saw me at the window! He knows someone's here! Let's give up.'

'Shut up!'

Dennis went to the window. He peered through the shutters, then suddenly rushed back to Jennifer and grabbed her by the hair again.

'Get up.'

MIKE WELCH

Officer Mike Welch didn't know that everyone in the house was currently clustered less than twenty feet away, watching him through the gaps in the shutters. He had not seen Kevin Rooney or anyone else when he'd pulled up. He'd been too busy parking the car.

As near as Welch could figure, the people from the red Nissan had jumped the wall into these people's backyard. He suspected that the three suspects were blocks away by now, but he hoped that someone in this house or the other houses on this cul-de-sac had seen them and could provide a direction of flight.

When no one answered the door, Welch went to the side gate and called out. When no one responded, he returned to the front door and rang the bell for the third and final time. He was turning away to try the neighbor when the heavy front door opened and a pretty teenage girl looked out. She was pale. Her eyes were rimmed red.

Welch gave his best professional smile.

'Miss, I'm Officer Mike Welch. Did you happen to see three young men running through the area?'

'No.'

Her voice was so soft he could barely hear her. Welch noted that she appeared upset, and wondered about that.

'It would've been five or ten minutes ago. Something like that. I have reason to believe that they jumped the wall into your backyard.'

'No.'

The red-rimmed eyes filled. Welch watched her eyes blur, watched twin tears roll in slow motion down her cheeks, and knew that they were in the house with her. They were probably standing right on the other side of the door. Mike Welch's heart began to pound. His fingers tingled.

'Okay, miss, like I said, I was just checking. You have a good day.'

He quietly unsnapped the release on his holster and rested his hand on his gun. He shifted his eyes pointedly to the door, then mouthed a silent question, asking if anyone was there. She did not have time to respond.

Inside, someone that Mike Welch could not see shouted, 'He's going for his gun!'

Loud explosions blew through the door and window. Something hit Mike Welch in the chest, knocking him backward. His Kevlar vest stopped the first bullet, but another punched into his belly below the vest, and a third slipped over the top of his vest to lodge high in his chest. He tried to keep his feet under him, but they fell away. The girl screamed, and someone else inside the house screamed, too.

Mike Welch found himself flat on his back in the front

27

yard. He sat up, then realized that he'd been shot and fell over again. He heard more shots, but he couldn't get up or duck or run for cover. He pulled his gun and fired toward the house without thinking who he might be hitting. His only thought was to survive.

He heard more shots, and screaming, but then he could no longer hold his gun. It was all he could do to key his shoulder mike.

'Officer down. Officer down. Jesus, I've been shot.'

'Say again? Mike? Mike, what's going on?'

Mike Welch stared at the sky, but could not answer.

# CHAPTER 2

Friday, 3:24 P.M.

JEFF TALLEY

Two-point-one miles from York Estates, Jeff Talley was parked in an avocado orchard, talking to his daughter on his cell phone, his command radio tuned to a whisper. He often left his office in the afternoon and came to this orchard, which he had discovered not long after he had taken the job as the chief of Bristo Camino's fourteen-member police department. Rows of trees, each tree the same as the last, each a measured distance from the next, standing without motion in the clean desert air like a chorus of silent witnesses. He found peace in the sameness of it.

His daughter, Amanda, now fourteen, broke that peace.

'Why can't I bring Derek with me? At least I would have someone to hang with.'

Her voice reeked of coldness. He had called Amanda because today was Friday; she would be coming up for the weekend.

'I thought we would go to a movie together.'

'We go to a movie every time I come up there. We can still go to the movies. We'll just bring Derek.'

'Maybe another time.'

'When?'

'Maybe next time. I don't know.'

She made an exaggerated sigh that left him feeling defensive.

'Mandy? It's okay if you bring friends. But I enjoy our alone time, too. I want us to talk about things.'

'Mom wants to talk to you.'

'I love you.'

She didn't answer.

'I love you, Amanda.'

'You always say you want to talk, but then we go sit in a movie so we can't talk. Here's Mom.'

Jane Talley came on the line. They had separated five months after he resigned from the Los Angeles Police Department, took up residence on their couch, and stared at the television for twenty hours a day until neither of them could take it anymore and he had moved out. That was two years ago.

'Hey, Chief. She's not in the greatest mood.'

'I know.'

'How you doing?'

Talley thought about it.

'She's not liking me very much.'

'It's hard for her right now. She's fourteen.'

'I know.'

'She's still trying to understand. Sometimes she's fine with it, but other times everything sweeps over her.'

'I try to talk to her.'

He could hear the frustration in Jane's voice, and his own.

'Jeffrey, you've been trying to talk for two years, but nothing comes out. Just like that, you left and started a new life and we weren't a part of it. Now you have this new life up there and she's making a new life down here. You understand that, don't you?'

Talley didn't say anything, because he didn't know what to say. Every day since he moved to Bristo Camino he told himself that he would ask them to join him but he hadn't been able to do it. He knew that Jane had spent the past two years waiting for him. He thought that if he asked right now she would come to him, but all he managed to do was stare at the silent, immobile trees.

Finally, Jane had had enough of the silence.

'I don't want to go on like this anymore, just being separated. You and Mandy aren't the only ones who need to make a life.'

'I know. I understand.'

'I'm not asking you to understand. I don't care if you understand.'

Her voice came out sharp and hurt, then both of them were silent. Talley thought of her on the day they were married; against the white country wedding gown, her skin had been golden.

Jane finally broke the silence, her voice resigned. She would learn no more today than yesterday; her husband would offer nothing new. Talley felt embarrassed and guilty.

'Do you want me to drop her at your house or at the office?'

'The house would be fine.'

'Six o'clock?'

'Six. We can have dinner, maybe.'

'I won't be staying.'

When the phone went dead, Talley put it aside, and thought of the dream. The dream was always the same, a small clapboard house surrounded by a full SWAT tactical team, helicopters overhead, media beyond the cordon. Talley was the primary negotiator, but the nightmare reality of the dream left him standing in the open without cover or protection while Jane and Amanda watched him from the cordon. Talley was in a life-or-death negotiation with an unknown male subject who had barricaded himself in the house and was threatening suicide. Over and over, the man screamed, 'I'm going to do it! I'm going to do it!' Talley talked him back from the brink each time, but, each time, knew that the man had stepped closer to the edge. It was only a matter of time. No one had seen this man. No neighbors or family had been found to provide an ID. The subject would not reveal his name. He was a voice behind walls to everyone except Talley, who knew with a numbing dread that the man in the house was himself. He had become the subject in the house, locked in time and frozen in place, negotiating with himself to spare his own life.

In those first weeks, Brendan Malik's eyes watched him from every shadow. He saw the light in them die over and over, dimming like a television with its plug pulled, the spark that had been Brendan Malik growing smaller, falling away until it was gone. After a while, Talley felt nothing, watching the dying eyes the same way he would watch *Wheel of Fortune*: because it was there.

Talley resigned from the LAPD, then sat on his couch for almost a year, first in his home and later in the cheap apartment he had rented in Silver Lake after Jane threw him out. Talley told himself that he had left his job and his family because he couldn't stand having them witness his own self-destruction, but after a while he grew to believe that his reasons were simpler, and less noble: He believed that his former life was killing him, and he was scared. The incorporated township of Bristo Camino was looking for a chief of police for their fourteen-member police force, and they were glad to have him. They liked it that he was SWAT, even though the job was no more demanding than writing traffic citations and speaking at local schools. He told himself that it was a good place to heal. Jane had been willing to wait for the healing, but the healing never quite seemed to happen. Talley believed that it never would.

Talley started the car and eased off the hard-packed soil of the orchard onto a gravel road, following it down to the state highway that ran the length of the Santa Clarita Valley. When he reached the highway, he turned up his radio and heard Sarah Weinman, the BCPD dispatch officer, shouting frantically over the link.

'. . . *Welch is down. We have a man down in York Estates . . .*'

Other voices were crackling back at her, Officers Larry Anders and Kenn Jorgenson talking over each other in a mad rush.

Talley punched the command freq button that linked him to dispatch on a dedicated frequency.

'Sarah, one. What do you mean, Mike's down?'

'Chief?'

'What about Mike?'

'He's been shot. The paramedics from Sierra Rock Fire are on the way. Jorgy and Larry are rolling from the east.'

In the nine months that Talley had been in Bristo, there had been only three felonies, two for nonviolent burglaries and once when a woman had tried to run down her husband with the family car.

'Are you saying that he was *intentionally* shot?'

'Junior Kim's been shot, too! Three white males driving a red Nissan pickup. Mike called in the truck, then called a forty-one fourteen at one-eight Castle Way in York Estates, and the next thing I know he said he'd been shot. I haven't been able to raise him since then.'

Forty-one fourteen. Welch had intended to approach the residence.

Talley punched the button that turned on his lights and siren. York Estates was six minutes away.

'What's the status of Mr. Kim?'

'Unknown at this time.'

'Do we have an ID on the suspects?'

'Not at this time.'

'I'm six out and rolling. Fill me in on the way.'

Talley had spent the last year believing that the day he became a crisis negotiator for the Los Angeles Police Department had forever changed his life for the worse.

His life was about to change again.

*

Jennifer had never heard anything as loud as their guns; not the cherry bombs that Thomas popped in their backyard or the crowd at the Forum when the Lakers slammed home a game-winning dunkenstein. The gunfire in movies didn't come close. When Mars and Dennis started shooting, the sound rocked through her head and deafened her.

Jennifer screamed. Dennis slammed the front door, pulled her backwards to the office, then pushed her down. She grabbed Thomas and held tight. Her father wrapped them in his arms. Layers of gun smoke hung in shafts of light that burned through the shutters; the smell of it stung her nose.

When the shooting was done, Dennis sucked air like a bellows, stalking back and forth between the entry and office, his face white.

'We're fucked! That cop is *down!*'

Mars went to the entry. He didn't hurry or seem scared; he *strolled.*

'Let's get the car before more of them get here.'

Kevin was on the floor beside her father's desk, shaking. His face was milky.

'You shot a cop. You shot a cop, Dennis!'

Dennis grabbed his brother by the shirt.

'Didn't you hear Mars? He was going for his gun!'

Jennifer heard a siren approaching behind the shouting. Then Dennis heard it, too, and ran back to the windows.

'Oh, man, they're coming!'

Jennifer's father pulled her closer, almost as if he was trying to squeeze her into himself.

'Take the keys and go. The keys are on the wall by the garage. It's a Jaguar. Take it while you still can.'

Dennis stared through the open shutters like prison bars, watching the street with fearful expectation. Jennifer wanted them to run, to go, to get out of her life, but

Dennis stood frozen at the windows as if he was waiting for something.

Mars spoke from the entry, his voice as calm as still water.

'Let's take the man's car, Dennis. We have to go.'

Then the siren suddenly seemed to be in the house, and it was too late. Tires screeched outside. Dennis ran to the front door. The shooting started again.

## TALLEY

York Estates was a walled development that had been named for the legendary walled city of York in England, a village that was protected from the world by a great stone wall. The developers built twenty-eight homes on one-to three-acre sites in a pattern of winding streets and cul-de-sacs with names like Lancelot Lane, Queen Anne Way, and King John Place, then surrounded it by a stone wall that was more decorative than protective. Talley cut his siren as he entered from the north, but kept the lights flashing. Jorgenson and Anders were shouting that they were under fire. Talley heard the pop of a gunshot over the radio.

When he turned into Castle Way, Talley saw Jorgenson and Anders crouched behind their car with their weapons out. Two women were in the open door of the house behind them and a teenaged boy was standing near the cul-de-sac's mouth. Talley hit the public address key on his mike as he sped up the street.

'You people take cover. Get inside your homes!'

Jorgenson and Anders turned to watch him approach. The two women looked confused and the boy stood without moving. Talley burped his siren, and shouted at them again.

'Get inside *now!* You people *move!*'

Talley hit the brakes hard, stopping behind Jorgenson's

unit. Two shots pinged from the house, one snapping past overhead, the other thumping dully into Talley's windshield. He rolled out the door and pulled himself into a tight ball behind the front wheel, using the hub as cover. Mike Welch lay crumpled on the front lawn of a large Tudor home less than forty feet away.

Anders shouted, 'Welch is down! They shot him!'

'Are all three subjects inside?'

'I don't know! We haven't seen anyone!'

'Are civilians in the house?'

'I don't know!'

More sirens were coming from the east. Talley knew that would be Dreyer and Mikkelson in unit six with the ambulance. The shooting had stopped, but he could hear shouts and screaming inside the house. He flattened on the street and called to Welch from under the car.

'Mike! Can you hear me?'

Welch didn't respond.

Anders shouted, his voice frantic.

'I think he's dead!'

'Calm down, Larry. I can hear you.'

Talley had to take in the scene and make decisions without knowing who or what he was dealing with. Welch was in the middle of the front lawn, unmoving and unprotected. Talley had to act.

'Does this house back up on Flanders Road?'

'Yes, sir. The truck is right on the other side of the wall that runs behind the house, that red Nissan! It's the suspects who hit Kim's.'

The sirens were closer. Talley had to assume that innocents were inside. He had to assume that Mike Welch was alive. He keyed his transceiver mike.

'Six, one. Who's on?'

Dreyer's voice came back.

'It's Dreyer, Chief. We're one minute out.'

'Where's the ambulance?'

'Right behind us.'

'Okay. You guys set up on Flanders by the truck in case these guys go back over the wall. Send the ambulance in, but tell them to wait at Castle and Tower. I'll bring Welch to them.'

Talley broke the connection, then pushed himself up to a crouch.

'Larry, did you guys fire on the house?'

'No, sir.'

'Don't.'

'What are you going to do?'

'Stay down. Don't fire at the house.'

Talley climbed back into his car, keeping his head low and the driver's door open. He backed up, then powered into the yard, maneuvering to a stop between Welch and the house to use the car as a shield. Another shot popped the passenger-side window. He rolled out of the car almost on top of Welch. Talley opened the rear door, then dragged Welch to the car. It was like lifting two hundred pounds of deadweight, but Welch moaned. He was alive. Talley propped him upright in the open door, then lifted for all he was worth to fold Welch onto the backseat. He slammed the door, then saw Welch's gun on the grass. He went back for it. He returned to the car and floored the accelerator, fishtailing across the slick grass as he cut across the yard and into the street. He sped back along the cul-de-sac to the corner where the ambulance was waiting. Two paramedics pulled Welch from the rear and pushed a compress onto his chest. Talley didn't ask if Welch would make it. He knew from experience that they wouldn't know.

Talley stared down the length of the cul-de-sac and felt himself tremble. The first flush of panic was passing, and now he had time to think. Now he had time to acknowledge that what was happening here was what had cost him so much in Los Angeles. A hostage situation was developing. His mouth went dry and something sour flushed in his throat that threatened to make him retch.

He keyed the mike again to call his dispatcher. He had exactly four units on duty and another five officers off. He would need them all.

'Chief, I pulled Dreyer and Mikkelson off the minimart. We've got no one on the scene now. It's totally unsecured.'

'Call the CHP and the Sheriffs. Tell them what's going on and request a full crisis team. Tell them we've got two men down and we have a possible hostage situation.'

Talley's eyes filled when he realized that he had used that word. Hostage.

He remembered Welch's gun. He sniffed the muzzle, then checked the magazine. Welch had returned fire, which meant that he might have wounded someone in the house. Maybe even an innocent.

He shut his eyes hard and keyed the mike again.

'Tell them to hurry.'


JENNIFER

Jennifer whispered, 'Daddy.'

Her father held her head, whispered back.

'Shh.'

They snuggled closer. Jennifer thought her father might be trying to pull them through the floor, that if he could just make the three of them small enough they would disappear. She watched Mars peering through the shutters, his wide back hunched like an enormous swollen toad. When Mars glanced back at them, he looked high.

Kevin threw a *TV Guide* at him.

'What's wrong with you? Why'd you start shooting?'

'To keep them away.'

'We could've gotten out the back!'

Dennis jerked Kevin toward the entry.

'Get it together, Kev. They found the truck. They're already behind us.'

38

'This is bullshit, Dennis! We should give up!'

Jennifer wanted them to run. She wanted them to get away, if that's what it took; she wanted them *out*.

The words boiled out of her before she could stop them.

'We don't want you here!'

Her father squeezed her, his voice soft.

'Be quiet.'

Jennifer couldn't stop.

'You have no right to be here! No one invited you!'

Her father pulled her closer.

Dennis jabbed a finger at her.

'Shut up, bitch!'

He turned and shoved his brother into the wall so hard that Jennifer flinched.

'Stop it, Kevin! Go through the house and lock all the windows. Lock the doors, then watch the backyard. They're gonna come over that wall just like we did.'

Kevin seemed confused.

'Why don't we just give up, Dennis? We're caught.'

'It's going to be dark in a few hours. Things will change when it gets dark. Go do it, Kev. We're going to get out of this. We will.'

Jennifer felt her father sigh before he spoke. He slowly pushed to his knees.

'None of you are going to get out of this.'

Dennis said, 'Shut the fuck up. Go on, Kevin. Watch the back.'

Kevin disappeared toward the rear through the entry.

Her father stood. Both Dennis and Mars aimed their guns at him.

Jennifer pulled at his legs.

'Daddy! Don't!'

Her father raised his hands.

'It's okay, sweetie. I'm not going to do anything. I just want to go to my desk.'

Dennis extended his gun.

'Are you fuckin' nuts?! You're not going anywhere!'

'Just take it easy, son.'

'Daddy, don't!'

Her father seemed to be moving in a dream. She wanted to stop him, but she couldn't. She wanted to say something, but nothing came out. He walked stiffly, as if he was prepared to take a punch. It was as if this man in the dream wasn't her father, but someone she had never before seen.

He went behind his desk, carefully placing two computer disks in a black leather disk case as he spoke. Dennis followed along beside him, shouting for him to stop, shouting that he shouldn't take another step, and pointing the gun at his head. Dennis looked as scared as she felt.

'I'm warning you, goddamnit!'

'I'm going to open my desk.'

'*I'll fuckin' kill you!*'

'Daddy, *please!!!*'

Jennifer's father held up a single finger as if to show them that one tiny finger could do them no harm, then used it to slide open the drawer. He nodded toward the drawer, as if to show Dennis that nothing would hurt him. Her father took out a thick booklet.

'This is a list of every criminal lawyer in California. If you give up right now, I'll help you get the best lawyer in the state.'

Dennis slapped the book aside.

'Fuck you! We just killed a cop! We killed that Chinaman! We'll get the fuckin' death penalty!'

'I'm telling you that you won't, not if you let me help you. But if you stay in this house, I can promise you this: You'll die.'

'*Shut up!*'

Dennis swung his gun hard and hit her father in the temple with a wet thud. He fell sideways like a sack that had been dropped to the floor.

'*No!*'

Jennifer lunged forward. She pushed Dennis before she realized what she was doing.

*'Leave him alone!'*

She shoved Dennis back, then dropped to her knees beside her father. The gun had cut an ugly gouge behind his right eye at the hairline. The gouge pulsed blood, and was already swelling.

'Daddy? Daddy, wake up!'

He didn't respond.

'Daddy, *please!*'

Her father's eyes danced insanely beneath the lids as his body trembled.

'Daddy!'

Tears blurred her eyes as unseen hands lifted her away. The nightmare had begun.

# CHAPTER 3

Friday, 3:51 P.M.

TALLEY

Talley wanted to stay with Welch, but he didn't have the time. He had to stabilize the scene and find out what was going on inside the house. He requested a second ambulance to stand by in case there were more casualties, then climbed back into his car and once more drove into the cul-de-sac. He brought his unit so close to Anders's vehicle that the bumpers crunched. He slipped out and hunkered behind the wheel again, calling over to Anders and Jorgenson.

'Larry, Jorgy, listen up.'

They were young guys. Men who would work as carpenters or salesmen if they weren't working as suburban policemen. They had never seen anything like what was now developing on Castle Way, and neither had any of Talley's other men. They had never pulled their guns. They had never made a felony arrest.

'We've got to evacuate these houses and seal the neighborhood. I want all the streets coming in here blocked.'

Anders nodded vigorously, excited and scared.

'Just the cul-de-sac?'

'All the streets coming into the neighborhood. Use Welch's unit to get back to the corner, then go from house to house here on the cul-de-sac through the backyards. Climb the walls if you have to, and move everyone out the same way. Don't expose yourself or anyone else to this house.'

'What if they won't leave?'

'They'll do what you say. But don't let anyone come out the front of their homes. Start with the house directly behind us. Someone could be wounded in there.'

'Right, Chief.'

'Find out who lives here. We need to know.'

'Okay.'

'One more thing. We might have one or more perps still on the loose. Have the other guys start a house-to-house. Warn everyone in the neighborhood to be on the lookout.'

Anders duckwalked to Welch's unit, the first car in the line, then swung it around in a tight turn and accelerated out of the cul-de-sac.

The first few minutes of any crisis situation were always the worst. In the beginning, you rarely knew what you were dealing with, and the unknown could kill you. Talley needed to find out who he was dealing with, and who was at risk in the house. Maybe all three perpetrators were in the house, but he had no way of knowing. They might have split up. They might have already murdered everyone inside. They might have killed the occupants, shot up the street, then committed suicide. Jeff Talley might be staring at a lifeless house.

Talley keyed his mike to talk to his other cars.

'This is Talley. Clear the freq and listen. Jorgenson and I are currently in front of the house at one-eight Castle Way in York Estates. Anders is evacuating the residents of the surrounding houses. Dreyer and Mikkelson are at the rear of the property on Flanders Road near a red Nissan pickup. We believe that one or more of the people who shot Junior Kim and Mike Welch are in the house. They are armed. We need an ID. Did Welch run the plates on that truck?'

Mikkelson came back.

'Chief, two.'

'Go, two.'

'The truck is registered to Dennis James Rooney, white male, age twenty-two. He has an Agua Dulce address.'

Talley pulled out his pad and scratched down Rooney's name. In another life he would dispatch a unit to Rooney's address, but he didn't have the manpower for that now.

His radio popped again.

'Chief, Anders.'

'Go, Larry.'

'I'm with one of the neighbors. She says the people in the house are named Smith, Walter and Pamela Smith. They've got two kids. A girl and a boy. Hang on. Okay, it's Jennifer and Thomas. She says the girl is about fifteen and the boy is younger.'

'Does she know if they're in the house?'

Talley could hear Anders talking with the neighbor. Anders was so anxious that he was keying his mike before he was ready. Talley told him to slow down.

'She says the wife is in Florida visiting a sister, but she believes that the rest of the family is at home. She says the husband works there in the house.'

Talley cursed under his breath. He had a possible three hostages inside. Three killers, three hostages. He had to find out what was happening inside the house and cool out the shooters. It was called 'stabilizing the situation.' That's all he had to do. He told himself that over and over like a mantra: *That's all you have to do.*

Talley took a deep breath to gather himself, then another. He keyed his public address system so that he could speak to the house. In the next moment he would engage the subjects. In that instant, the negotiation would begin. Talley had sworn that he would never again be in this place. He had turned his life inside out to avoid it, yet here he was.

'My name is Jeff Talley. Is anyone in the house hurt?'

His voice echoed through the neighborhood. He heard a

police car pull up at the mouth of the cul-de-sac, but he did not turn to look; he kept his eyes fixed on the house.

'Everyone in the house relax. We're not in a hurry here. If you've got wounded, let's get them tended to. We can work this out.'

No one answered. Talley knew that the subjects in the house were now under incredible stress. They had been involved in two shootings, and now they were trapped. They would be scared, and the danger level to the civilians would be great. Talley's job was to reduce their stress. If you gave the subjects time to calm down and think about their situation, sometimes they realized that their only way out was to surrender. Then all you had to do was give them an excuse to give up. That was the way it worked. Talley had been taught these things at the FBI's Crisis Management School, and it had worked that way every time until George Malik had shot his own son in the neck.

Talley keyed the mike again. He tried to make his voice reasonable and assuring.

'We're going to start talking sooner or later. It might as well be now. Is everyone in there okay, or does someone need a doctor?'

A voice in the house finally answered.

'Fuck you.'


### JENNIFER

Her father's eyes flickered as if he were dreaming, back and forth, up and down. He made a soft whimpering sound, but his eyes didn't open. Thomas hunched beside her, whispering.

'What's wrong?'

'He's not waking up. He should be awake, shouldn't he?'

45

This wasn't supposed to be happening; not in her house, not in Bristo Camino, not on this perfect summer day.

'Daddy, *please!*'

Mars knelt beside her to feel her father's neck. He was large and gross. She could smell him. Sweat and vegetables.

'Looks like brain damage.'

Jennifer felt a rush of fear and nausea, then realized that he was toying with her.

'Fuck you.'

Mars blinked uncomfortably, as if she had surprised and embarrassed him.

'I don't do things like that. They're bad.'

Mars walked away.

Her father's wound pulsed steadily, but the bleeding had almost stopped, the clotted blood and injured flesh swelling into an ugly purple volcano. Jennifer stood, and faced Dennis.

'I want to get some ice.'

'Shut up and sit your ass down.'

'*I'm getting some ice. He's hurt.*'

Dennis glared at her, his face red and angry. He glanced at Mars, then at her father. Finally, he turned back to the shutters.

'Mars, take her into the kitchen. Make sure Kevin isn't fucking off back there.'

Jennifer left without waiting for Mars, and went to the kitchen. She saw Kevin hiding behind the couch in the family room so that he could see the French doors. She wanted the backyard to be crowded with police officers and vicious police dogs, but it was empty. The pool was clean and pure, the raft that she had been enjoying less than thirty minutes earlier motionless on the water, the water so clear that the raft might have been floating on air. Her radio sat on the deck beside the pool, but she couldn't hear it. It had all happened so fast.

Jennifer opened the cabinet beneath the sink. Mars kicked it shut.

'What are you doing?'

He towered over her, his groin only inches from her face. She slowly stood to her full height. He was still a foot taller, and so close that it hurt to look up. Jennifer smelled the sour vegetables again. It took all of her strength not to run.

'I'm getting a washcloth. Then I'm going to open the freezer for the ice. Is that all right with you?'

Mars edged closer. His chest brushed the tips of her breasts. She did not let herself look away or step back, but her voice was hoarse.

'Get away from me.'

Mars stared down at her, his eyes unfocused, almost as if he couldn't see her. A vacant smile played at his lips. He swayed, his chest massaging gently against her breasts.

She still would not let herself step back. She summoned her strength again, and spoke clearly.

'*Get away from me.*'

The vacant smile flickered, then his eyes focused as if he could once more see her.

She opened the cabinet again without waiting for him to answer, found a cloth, then went to the freezer for ice. It was a huge black Sub-Zero, the kind with a freezer drawer on the bottom. She pulled it open, then scooped ice into the washcloth. Most of it spilled onto the floor.

'I need a bowl.'

'So get one.'

Mars walked away as she got the bowl. He went into the family room, and asked if Kevin had seen anything. She couldn't hear Kevin's answer.

Jennifer chose a green plastic Tupperware bowl, then saw the paring knife on the counter, left from when she diced a slice of onion for the tuna. She glanced at Mars, but Mars was still with Kevin. She was terrified that if

47

she reached for the knife they would see her, and then she thought that even if she had the knife what would she do with it? They were older and stronger. She glanced up again. Mars was staring at her. She averted her eyes, but saw from the corner of her eye that he stayed with Kevin. Her shorts didn't have pockets and her suit top didn't have enough material to cover the knife. Even if she took it, what would she do with it? Attack them? Puh-lease. Mars came back to the kitchen. Without thinking about it, she pushed the knife behind the Cuisinart mixer her mom kept on the counter.

Mars said, 'What's taking so long?'

'I'm ready.'

'Hang on.'

Mars went to the refrigerator and pulled it open. He took out a beer, twisted off the cap, and drank. He took a second bottle and tipped it toward her.

'You want one?'

'I don't drink beer.'

'Mommy won't know. You can do anything you want right now, and Mommy won't know.'

'I want to go back to my father.'

She followed him back to the office, where Mars gave the second beer to Dennis at the shutters. Jennifer joined Thomas at their father beside the desk. She scooped ice from the bowl into the washcloth, then made an ice pack and pressed it to her father's wound. She cringed when he moaned.

Thomas edged closer and spoke so softly that she could barely hear him.

'What's going to happen?'

Mars's voice cut across the room.

*'Shut up!'*

Mars was staring at her. Slowly, his gaze moved down along the lines of her body. She flushed again, forcing herself to concentrate on her father. She knew he was playing with her, just as he had before.

The phone rang.

Everyone in the room looked at the phone, but no one moved. The ringing grew louder and more insistent.

Dennis said, 'Jesus Christ!'

He stalked to the desk and scooped up the phone, but the ringing continued.

'What the fuck is this? Why won't it stop?'

Thomas said, 'It has more than one line. Press the blinking light.'

Dennis stabbed the blinking light, then slammed down the phone. The ringing stopped.

Dennis went back to the shutters, grumbling about rich people having more than one line.

The phone rang again.

'*Fuck!*'

The public address voice from the street echoed through the house.

'Answer the phone, Dennis Rooney. It's the police.'


### TALLEY


Hunkered behind the front wheel of his radio car, Talley listened to the ringing in his ear as a helicopter appeared. It spiraled down for a closer look until Talley could see that it was from one of the Los Angeles television stations. They would have heard about Kim and Welch by monitoring police frequencies. If the helicopters were here, the vans and reporters would be close behind. Talley covered the phone and twisted around to see Jorgenson.

'Where are the Sheriffs?'

'Inbound, Chief.'

'Get back on the horn and request air cover. Tell them we have news choppers coming in.'

The phone inside the house was still ringing. Talley thought, *Answer the phone, you sonofabitch.*

'Tell Sarah to call the phone company. Get a list of all

49

the lines to the house and have them blocked except through my cell number. I don't want these guys talking with anyone on the outside except for us.'

'Okay.'

Talley was still giving orders when the phone stopped ringing and a male voice answered.

'Hello?'

Talley waved Jorgenson quiet, then took a breath to center himself. He did not want his voice to reveal his fear.

'Is this Dennis Rooney?'

'Who are *you?*'

'My name is Jeff Talley. I'm with the Bristo Police Department, out here behind the car in front of you. Is this Dennis Rooney?'

Talley specifically did not identify himself as the chief of police. He wanted to appear to have a certain degree of power, but he also did not want to be seen as the final authority. The negotiator was always the man in the middle. If Rooney made demands, Talley wanted to be able to stall by telling him that he had to check with his boss. That way Talley remained the good guy. He could build a bond with Rooney through their mutual adversity.

'That cop was going for his gun. That Chinaman pulled a gun, too. No one wanted to shoot him. It was an accident.'

'Is this Dennis Rooney? I want to know with whom I'm speaking.'

'Yeah. I'm Rooney.'

Talley felt himself relaxing. Rooney wasn't a raving lunatic; he didn't start off by screaming that he was going to murder everyone in the house.

Talley made his voice firm, but relaxed.

'Well, Dennis, I need to know whether or not anyone in there needs a doctor. There was an awful lot of shooting.'

'We're cool.'

'We can send in a doctor, if you need it.'

'I said we're cool. Aren't you listening?'

Rooney's voice was strained and emotional. Talley expected that.

'Everyone out here is concerned about who's in there with you, Dennis, and how they're doing. Do you have some people in there with you?'

Rooney didn't answer. Talley could hear breathing, then a muffled sound as if Rooney had covered the phone. He would be thinking it through. Talley knew that thinking things through logically would be hard for Rooney during these next few minutes. Rooney would be pumping on adrenaline, frantic, and scared. Finally, he came back on the line.

'I got this family. That isn't kidnapping, is it? I mean, they were already here. We didn't grab'm and take'm someplace.'

Rooney's answer was a good sign; by showing concern for the future, he revealed that he did not want to die and feared the consequences of his actions.

'Can you identify them for me, Dennis?'

'You don't need to know that. I've told you enough.'

Talley let that slide. The Sheriff's negotiator could press for their names later.

'Okay, you're not going to tell me their names right now. I hear that. Will you at least tell me how they're doing?'

'They're fine.'

'How about your two friends? You don't have a man dying on you, do you?'

'They're fine.'

Talley had gotten Rooney to admit that all three gunmen were in the house. He muted the phone and turned to Jorgenson.

'All three subjects are in the house. Tell Larry to call off the house-to-house.'

'Rog.'

Jorgenson radioed his call as Talley returned to Rooney.

51

Overhead, a second helicopter joined the first and positioned itself in a hover. Another news crew.

Talley said, 'Okay, Dennis, I want to explain your situation.'

Rooney interupted him.

'You been asking me questions, now I've got a question. I didn't shoot that Chinaman. He pulled a gun and we were wrestling and his own gun went off. That Chinaman shot himself.'

'I understand, Dennis. There'll probably be a security camera. We'll be able to see what happened.'

'The gun just went off, is what I'm saying. It went off and we ran and that's what happened.'

'Okay.'

'So what I want to know is, that Chinaman, is he okay?'

'Mr. Kim didn't make it, Dennis. He died.'

Rooney didn't respond, but Talley knew that images of shooting his way out and possibly even of suicide would be kaleidoscoping through his head. Talley had to give him a vent for the pressure.

'I won't lie to you, Dennis; you guys are in trouble. But if what you said about the struggle is true, that could be a mitigating circumstance. Don't make things worse than they already are. We can still work our way out of this.'

Kim having pulled a gun would mitigate nothing. Under California law, any death occurring during the commission of a felony was murder, but Talley needed to give Rooney some measure of hope. It did.

Rooney said, 'What about the police officer? He went for his gun, too.'

'He's still alive. You caught a break there, Dennis.'

'Don't you forget I've got these people in here. Don't you guys try to rush the house.'

Some of the edge had gone from Rooney's voice.

'Dennis, I'm going to ask you right now to let those people go.'

'No way.'

'You're ahead of the game as long as they're not hurt. The police officer is alive. You said Mr. Kim pulled a gun on you. Just let those people walk out.'

'Fuck that. They're the only thing keeping you from blowing us away. You'll kill us for shooting that cop.'

'I know you're feeling that way right now, Dennis, but I'm going to give you my word about something. We're not going to storm the house. We're not coming in there by force, okay?'

'You'd better not.'

'We're not. But I want you to know what you're facing out here. I'm not telling you to threaten you; I'm telling you to be straight up. We have officers surrounding the house, and this neighborhood is locked down. You can't escape, Dennis; that just isn't going to happen. The reason I'm out here talking to you is that I want to get out of this thing without you or the people in that house getting hurt. That's my goal here. Do you understand that?'

'I understand.'

'The best thing you can do to help yourself is to let those people go, Dennis. Let them go, then surrender, everything nice and peaceful and orderly. If you're cooperative now, it will look better for the judge later. Do you see that?'

Rooney didn't respond, which Talley took as a positive sign. Rooney wasn't arguing. He was thinking. Talley decided to terminate the contact and let Rooney consider his options.

'I don't know about you, Dennis, but I could use a break. You think about what I said. I'll call back in twenty minutes. If you want to talk before that, just shout, and I'll phone you again.'

Talley closed the phone. His hands were shaking so badly that he dropped it. He took another deep breath and then another, but they didn't help to steady him.

Jorgenson said, 'Chief? You okay?'

Talley waved that he was fine.

The helicopters were still up there. They had set up on fixed points in a hover. That meant they were using their cameras.

Talley put the phone in his pocket, told Jorgenson to call if anything changed, then backed his car out of the cul-de-sac. One conversation with a scared twenty-two-year-old kid, and Talley wanted to vomit. Larry Anders was waiting at the intersection along with two more of his officers: Scott Campbell and Leigh Metzger. Campbell was a retired Bakersfield security officer who signed on with Bristo to supplement his pension. Metzger was a single mother who had spent eight years on the San Bernardino Police Department as an instructional officer. She had almost no street time. Seeing them gave Talley no confidence.

'Jesus, Larry, are the goddamned Sheriffs coming here on foot? Where are they?'

'Sarah's been on the phone with them, Chief. She says you should call.'

Talley felt his stomach clench.

'What's wrong?'

'I don't know. She also says that the newspeople want to know what's happening. They've got reporters at the minimart, and they're on their way here.'

Talley rubbed his face, then checked his watch. It had been fifty-three minutes since Junior Kim was shot. Fifty-three minutes, and his world had collapsed to the size of a subdivision.

'When the newspeople get here, let them into the development, but don't let them come here to the cul-de-sac.'

'Ah, there's an empty lot by King and Lady, something like that. Can I put them over there?'

'Perfect. And don't let them wander around. I'll get over there in a few minutes and make a statement.'

Talley went to his car, telling himself that everything was fine. He had established contact, found out that all three subjects were in the house, and no one was shooting. He opened his car and felt the heat roll out as if from an oven. He was so drained that he didn't care. He radioed his office.

'Give me some good news, Sarah. I need it.'

'The Highway Patrol is sending six patrol units from Santa Clarita and Palmdale. They should be about ten minutes out, and inbound now.'

Patrol units.

'What about a tactical squad and the negotiation team? We need to get those people deployed.'

Talley sounded strident, but he didn't care.

'I'm sorry, Chief. Their response team is hung up in Pico Rivera. They said they'll get here as soon as possible.'

'That's just fucking great! What are we supposed to do until then?'

'They said you'll have to handle it yourself.'

Talley held the mike in his lap without the strength to lift it.

'Chief? You still there?'

Talley pulled the door shut, started the engine, and turned on the air conditioner. Anders and Campbell looked over when they heard the engine start, then seemed confused when he didn't pull away. He turned the vents so they blew the cold air into his face. Talley shook so badly that he pushed his hands under his legs, feeling frightened and ashamed. He dug his fingers into his thighs and told himself that this wasn't Los Angeles, that he was no longer a negotiator, that the lives of the people in the house did not rest with him. He only had to hang on until the Sheriffs took over, and then he could go back to his orchard and the perfect peace of its stillness. It was only a matter of minutes. Of seconds. He told himself that anyone could hang on for seconds. He told himself that, but he didn't believe it.

## CHAPTER 4

Friday, 4:22 P.M.

DENNIS

Dennis slapped down the phone, livid with an anger he could barely contain, shouting, 'Fuck *you*!'

Talley thought he was an idiot, all that shit about wanting a peaceful resolution and promising not to storm the house. Dennis knew the score when it came to cops: A cop was down, so somebody had to pay. The bastards would probably assassinate him the first chance they got without ever giving him a chance to stand trial. That bastard Talley probably wanted to pull the goddamned trigger himself. Dennis was so pissed off that he felt sick to his stomach.

Mars said, 'What did they want?'

'What do you think they want, Mars? Jesus, they want us to give up.'

Mars shrugged, his expression simple.

'I'm not giving up.'

Dennis glared at the two kids huddled around their old man, then stalked out of the office. He needed to figure a way out of this fucking house, and away from the police. He needed a plan. Walking made it easier to think, like he could get away from the fear of being trapped; a big-ass house like this, and it felt as if the weight of it was crushing his breath away. If he threw up, he didn't want to do it in front of Mars.

Dennis crossed through the kitchen, searching for the garage. He found the keys on a Peg-Board in the pantry just like the man had said, and shoved open the door to the garage. A gleaming Jaguar sedan and Range Rover were waiting, neither more than a couple of years old. Dennis checked the gas in the Jaguar, and found the tank full. If his truck had broken down only five minutes sooner, if they had found this house only five minutes sooner, if they had driven away in this sweet Jaguar only five minutes sooner, they wouldn't be sweating out a murder count. They wouldn't be trapped.

Dennis smashed his fist into the steering wheel, shouting, 'SHIT!'

He closed his eyes.

Chill, dude.

Don't lose it.

There has to be a way out.

'Dennis?'

Dennis opened his eyes and saw Kevin in the door, squirming like he had to pee.

'You're supposed to be watching for the cops.'

'I need to talk to you. Where's Mars?'

'He's watching the front like you're supposed to be watching the back. Get out of here.'

Dennis shut his eyes tight. The cops were watching the front and back of the house, but it was a big house; there had to be a window or door that the cops couldn't see. The house was surrounded by trees and bushes and walls, all of which blended and merged with the heavy cover of the surrounding houses. When night came, the shadows between the houses would fall like heavy black coats. If he created a diversion – say, he dressed up the hostages to look like Mars, Kevin, and himself, tied them into the Jaguar, then used the remote control to raise the garage door – all the cops would be watching the garage as he slipped out the other side of the house and away through the shadows.

'Dennis?'

'We're looking at murder charges, Kevin. Let me *think*.'

57

'It's about Mars. We've got to talk about what happened.'

Kevin wore the pussy face again, the mewly lurching eyebrows and don't-kick-me expression that made Dennis want to punch him. Dennis hated his younger brother and always had; hated the suffocating weight of having to carry him through life. He didn't need the prison shrink to tell him why: Kevin was their past; he was their weak ineffectual mother who abandoned them, their brutal meth-head father who beat them, their pathetic and embarrassing place in life. Kevin was the shadow of their future failure, and Dennis hated him for it.

Dennis got out of the Jaguar and slammed the door.

'We've got to find a way out of here, Kevin, that's what we've got to do. It's that simple. We look for a way out of this goddamned house because I am *not* going back to jail.'

Dennis pushed past his brother, unable even to look at him. Kevin followed along behind. They went through a kitchen, then along a wide hall past a formal dining room to a den with lush leather couches and a beautiful copper bar. Dennis imagined himself serving drinks to beautiful guests who had stepped out of television commercials and porno tapes. He would be a player if he lived in a house like this. He would have become the man of his destiny.

They reached the master bedroom at the rear of the house. It was a huge room with sliding glass doors that looked out at the pool, this one room bigger than the apartment Dennis and Kevin shared. Dennis wondered if there was a bathroom window or some other way to sneak out.

Kevin plucked at his arm.

'Dennis, *listen*.'

'Look for a way out.'

'Mars lied about that cop who came to the door. That cop never pulled his gun. You didn't have to shoot him.'

Dennis grabbed Kevin's shirt.

'Stop it! We didn't have any choice!'

'I was standing right there. I was watching him, Dennis. He put his hand on his gun, but he didn't pull it. I'm telling you that cop never drew.'

Dennis let go of Kevin's shirt and stepped back, not knowing what to say.

'You just didn't see, is all.'

'I was *there*. Mars lied.'

'Why would he do that?'

'Something's wrong with that guy, Dennis. He *wanted* to shoot that cop.'

Dennis's throat felt tight. He was pissed off, thinking this was just like his fuckup brother, dishing out another helping of shit onto a plate that was already overflowing.

'You don't know what you're talking about. We're surrounded by cops and we're looking at a homicide charge. We've got to find a way out of this, so just *stop*.'

Three doors opened off the bedroom. Dennis thought they might lead to closets or bathrooms with maybe a window on the side of the house, but that isn't what he found.

Clothes hung on racks with shoes filling shoe stands beneath the clothes like any other large closet, but this room had something more: A bank of small black-and-white televisions filled the near wall; Mars and the two kids could be seen on one of the screens; another showed the cop car sitting out front in the cul-de-sac; the Jaguar and the Range Rover were revealed in the garage; every room, bathroom, and hall inside the house was visible, as well as views of the outside of the house, the pool, poolhouse, and even the area behind the poolhouse. Every inch of the property seemed to be watched.

'Kevin?'

Kevin came up behind him, and made a hissing sound. 'What is this?'

'It's a security system. Jesus, look at this stuff.'

Dennis studied the view of the master bedroom. The camera appeared to be looking from the upper left ceiling corner above the door through which he had just entered. Dennis went out and looked up into the corner. He saw nothing.

Still inside the room, Kevin said, 'Hey, I can see you.'

Dennis rejoined his brother. The monitors were above a long keyboard set with button pads, LED windows, and red and green lights. Right now, all of the lights glowed green. Rows of buttons were lined along the right side of the keyboard, the buttons labeled MOTION SENSORS, INFRARED, UPSTAIRS LOCKS, DOWNSTAIRS LOCKS, and ALARMS. Dennis felt creeped out. He turned back to the door and slowly pushed it. The door swung easily, but with a feeling of weight and density. A heavy throwbolt was set into the door so that it could be locked tight from the inside. Dennis rapped on the door with his knuckles. Steel.

He turned back to his brother.

'What the fuck is going on here? They've got this place stitched up like a bank.'

Kevin was on his knees at the back of the closet, partially buried by a wall of hanging clothes. He slowly rocked back on his heels, then turned around holding a white cardboard box about the size of a shoe box. Dennis saw that the wall behind the clothes was like a small metal garage door that could be raised or lowered. It was raised, and more white boxes were stacked behind it.

Kevin held out the box.

'Look.'

The box was filled with hundred-dollar bills. Kevin pulled out a second box, then a third. They bulged with money. Dennis opened a fourth box. Money.

Dennis and Kevin looked at each other.

'Lets get Mars.'

Jennifer was worried. Her father's breathing was raspy. His eyes jerked spastically beneath their lids like eyes do when someone is having bad dreams. She placed a pillow from the couch beneath his head, and sat beside him, holding the ice to his head. The bleeding had stopped, but the wound was red and inflamed, and an ugly bruise was spreading across his face.

Thomas nudged her knee, and whispered.

'Why won't he wake up?'

She glanced at Mars before she answered. Mars had pulled her father's desk chair across the room and was sitting so that he could watch the police.

'I don't know.'

'Is he going to die?'

Jennifer was worried about that, too, though she didn't want to say. She thought that her father might have a concussion, though the only thing she knew about concussions for real was that the catcher on her high school baseball team had gotten a concussion during a game when he had blocked home plate and a bigger player had bowled him over. Tim had to go to the hospital that night and missed two days of school. Jennifer was scared that her father needed a doctor, too, and might get worse without medical attention.

'Jen?'

Thomas nudged her again, his voice an insistent whisper.

'Jen?'

She finally answered, and tried to look upbeat.

'I think he has a concussion. That's all it is.'

The phone on her father's desk rang. Mars glanced over, but made no move to answer it. The phone stopped ringing just as Dennis and Kevin reappeared from the rear of the house. Dennis walked over and stared down at her father, then her. The expression on his face creeped her out. Kevin was staring, too.

Dennis squatted beside her.

'Your old man, what's he do for a living?'

'He's an accountant.'

'He does taxes for other rich people, he handle their money, what?'

'Duh. That's what accountants do.'

Jennifer knew she was taunting him, and she was ready for his anger, but Dennis seemed to consider her. Then he glanced at Thomas before smiling.

'What's your name?'

'Jennifer.'

'What's your last name?'

'Smith.'

'Okay, Jennifer Smith. And your old man?'

'Walter Smith.'

Dennis looked at Thomas.

'How about you, fat boy?'

'Eat me.'

Dennis grabbed Thomas's ear.

Thomas blurted out his name.

'Thomas!'

'Fat boy Thomas, you give me shit, I'm gonna beat your ass. Are we clear on that?'

'Yes, sir.'

Dennis let go of Thomas's ear.

'That's a good fat boy.'

Jennifer wished that he would just leave them alone, but he didn't. He smiled at her and lowered his voice.

'We're going to be here a while, Jennifer. Where's your bedroom?'

Jennifer blushed furiously, and Dennis smiled wider.

'Now don't think nasty thoughts on me, Jennifer. I didn't mean it like that. You look cold, wearing just the bikini top. I'll bring you a shirt. Cover up that fine body.'

She averted her eyes and blushed harder.

'It's upstairs.'

'Okay. I'll bring you something.'

Dennis told Mars to come with him, and then the two of them left. Kevin went to the window.

The phone rang again, but Kevin ignored it. The ringing went on forever.

Thomas nudged her knee again.

When she looked at him, his face was deathly white with pink blotches at the corners of his mouth. That was the face he got when he was angry. She knew he didn't like being called a fat boy.

He nudged her again, wanting to say something. She made sure that Kevin wasn't watching them, then mouthed the word more than spoke it.

'What?'

Thomas leaned close and lowered his voice even more. The pink spots at his mouth burned brightly.

'I know where Daddy has a gun.'

# CHAPTER 5

Friday, 5:10 P.M.

GLEN HOWELL

Glen Howell closed his cell phone after fifteen rings. He didn't like that. He was expected, and he knew that this person always answered his phone, and was irritated that now, him running late like this, the sonofabitch would pick *now* not to answer. In Glen Howell's world, lateness was not tolerated and excuses were less than useless. Punishment could be severe.

Howell didn't know why the streets leading into York Estates were blocked, but the traffic was at a standstill. He figured it had to be a broken gas line or something like that for them to close the entire neighborhood, backing up traffic and wasting everyone's time. Rich people didn't like to be inconvenienced.

The window on his big S-class Mercedes slid down without a sound. Glen craned out his head, trying to see the reason for the delay. A lone cop was working the intersection, waving some cars away. He let a television news van through. Glen raised the window again, the heavy tint cutting the glare. He took the .40-caliber Smith & Wesson from his pocket and put it in the glove box. He had a valid California Concealed Weapon Permit, but thought it best not to draw attention to himself if he had to get out of the car.

Glen checked his watch again for the fourth time in five minutes. He was already ten minutes late. At this rate, he would be still later. Three of the cars ahead of him turned away, one car was let through, and then it was his turn. The cop was a young guy, tall and rectangular with a protruding Adam's apple.

Glen lowered the window. The heat ballooned in, making him wish he was back in Palm Springs, instead of being an errand boy. He tried to look professional and superior, working the class distinctions, rich successful business dude, lowly uneducated public servant.

'What's going on, Officer? Why the roadblock?'

'Do you live here in the neighborhood, sir?'

Glen knew that if he lied, the cop might ask to see his driver's license for the address. Glen didn't want to get caught in a lie.

'I have a business appointment. My associate is expecting me.'

'We've got a problem in the neighborhood, so we've had to close the area. We're only admitting residents.'

'What kind of problem?'

The cop looked uncertain.

'Do you have family in the development, sir?'

'Just my friends, like I said. You're making me worried about them, Officer.'

The cop frowned, and glanced back along the row of cars behind Glen.

'Well, what it is, we've got robbery suspects in one of the houses. We've had to evacuate several of the homes, and close off the development until we can secure the area. It could take a while.'

Glen nodded, trying to look reasonable. Ten seconds, he already knew that he couldn't flash a hundred at this guy to buy his way in. He would never go for it.

'Listen, my client is expecting me, Officer. It won't take long. Really. I just need a few minutes, then I'm gone.'

'Can't let you in, sir, I'm sorry. Maybe you could phone your party and have them come meet you, if they're still inside. We've had people going door to door, telling people to stay indoors or offering to escort them out. I can't let you in.'

Glen worked on staying calm. He smiled, and stared past the patrol car like he was thinking. His first impulse in any confrontation was to use his gun, put two hot ones square in the other guy's forehead, but he had a handle on that. Years of therapy had taught him that, even though he had an anger-based personality, he could control it. He controlled it now.

'Okay. That might work. Can I park over here to call?'

'Sure.'

Glen pulled his car to the side, then called the number again. This time, he let it ring fifteen times, but still didn't get an answer. Glen didn't like this. With all the cops around, his guy might have developed a case of the quivering shits and was laying low, or maybe he'd been forced from his home. He might even have a bunch of cops in his home, using it as a command post or something. Glen laughed out loud at that one; no fucking way. Glen figured the guy must've been evacuated, in which case he would probably call Palm Springs to arrange another meet location, and Palm Springs would phone Glen. The cop would probably know which families had been evacked, or could find out, but Glen didn't want to draw attention to his man by asking.

Glen wheeled around in a slow U and headed back up the street, still thinking about it, when he saw that another television news van had joined the line. Glen decided to take a flyer, and lowered his window when he reached the van. The driver was a balding guy with a rim of hair behind his ears and loose skin. A trim Asian woman with pouty lips perched in the passenger seat. Glen guessed her for the on-air talent, and wondered if the puffy lips were natural or man-made. Women who injected shit into their lips creeped him out. He decided that she was probably a spitter.

Glen said, 'Excuse me. They wouldn't tell me what's

going on, just that some people in the neighborhood are being evacuated. Do you guys know anything about this?'

The woman twisted in her seat and leaned forward to see past the driver.

'We don't have anything confirmed, but it looks like three men were fleeing the scene of a robbery and took a family hostage.'

'No shit. That's terrible.'

Glen couldn't give less of a shit except that it was ruining his day. He wondered if he could talk the reporter into letting him come along.

'Do you live in the neighborhood?'

Glen knew that she was angling for something, and began to relax. If she thought he had something that she wanted, she might be willing to get him inside.

'I don't live here, but I have friends in there. Why?'

The line of cars had moved forward, but the news van stayed where it was. The reporter flipped through a yellow pad.

'We've got unconfirmed reports that there are children involved, but we can't get anyone to tell us anything about the family. It's a family named Smith.'

The big Mercedes sensed the heat. The air conditioner blew harder. Glen didn't feel it.

'What was the name again?'

'Mr. and Mrs. Walter Smith. We've heard they have two children, a boy and a girl.'

'They're being held hostage? These three guys have the Smiths?'

'That's right. Do you know them? We're trying to find out about the kids.'

'I don't know them. Sorry.'

Glen rolled up the window and pulled away. He drove slowly so as not to attract attention. He had the strange sensation of being removed from his body, as if the world had receded and he was no longer a part of it. The a.c. was roaring. Walter Smith. Three assholes had crashed into

Walter Smith's home, and now the place was surrounded by cops and cameras, and their whole fucking neighborhood was sealed.

Three blocks later, Glen pulled into a parking lot. He took his gun from the glove box and put it back in his pocket. He felt safer that way. He opened his phone again, and dialed another number. This time, his call was answered on the first ring.

Glen spoke four words.

'We have a problem.'


### Palm Springs, California
5:26 P.M.

SONNY BENZA

Oxygen was the key. Sonny took a deep breath, trying to feed his heart. He was forty-seven years old, had high blood pressure, and lived in fear of the stroke which had claimed his father at fifty-five.

Benza stood in the games room of his mansion perched on a ridge above Palm Springs. Outside, his two kids, Chris and Gina, home from school, were splashing in the pool. Inside, Phil Tuzee and Charles 'Sally' Salvetti pulled an extra television next to the big screen, sweating like pigs, 36 inches, a Sony. They were rushed and frantic, anxious to get the set on. Between the big-screen projection TV with the picture-in-picture function and the Sony, they could watch all three major Los Angeles television stations. Two showed aerial views of Walter Smith's house, the third some pretty-boy talking head outside a gas station.

Sonny Benza still refused to believe it.

'What do we know? Not this TV bullshit. What do we know for *sure?* Maybe it's a different Walter Smith.'

Salvetti wiped the sweat from his forehead, looking pale under the Palm Springs tan.

'Glen Howell called it in. He's at the house, Sonny. It's *our* Walter Smith.'

Tuzee made a patting motion with his hands, trying to play the cooler.

'Let's everybody take it easy. Let's relax and walk through this a step at a time. The Feds aren't knocking on the door.'

'Not yet.'

Phil Tuzee was close to pissing himself. Sonny put his arm across Tuzee's shoulders, giving the squeeze, being the one in control.

'We got, what, ten or fifteen minutes before that happens, right, Phil?'

Tuzee laughed. Just like that, they were calmer. Still worried, still knowing they had a major cluster fuck of a problem, but the first bubble of panic had burst. Now, they would deal with it.

Benza said, 'Okay. What exactly are we dealing with here? What does Smith have in the house?'

'It's tax time, Sonny. We have to file the corporate quarterlies. He has our records.'

The bristly hairs on the back of Benza's head stood.

'You're sure? Glen hadn't made the pickup?'

'He was on his way to do that when this shit went down. He gets there and finds the neighborhood blocked off. He says Smith doesn't answer his phone, which you know he would do if he could, and then he gets the story from some reporters. Three assholes broke into Smith's house to hide from the cops, and now they're holding Smith and his family hostage. It's our Walter Smith.'

'And all our tax stuff is still in that house.'

'Everything.'

Benza stared at the televisions. Stared at the house on the screens. Stared at the police officers crouched behind bushes and cars, surrounding that house.

Sonny Benza's legitimate business holdings included sixteen bars, eight restaurants, a studio catering company, and thirty-two thousand acres of vineyards in central California. These businesses were profitable in their own right, but they were also used to launder the ninety million dollars generated every year by drug trafficking, hijackings, and shipping stolen automobiles and construction equipment out of the country. Walter Smith's job was to create false but reasonable profit records for Sonny's legitimate holdings which Benza would present to his 'real' accountants. Those accountants would then file the appropriate tax returns, never knowing that the records from which they were working had been falsified. Benza would pay the appropriate taxes (taking every deduction legally allowable), then be able to openly bank, spend, or invest the after-tax cash. To do this, Walter Smith held the income records of all Benza businesses, both legal and illegal.

These records were in his computer.

In his house.

Surrounded by cops.

Sonny went over to the big glass wall that gave him a breathtaking view of Palm Springs on the desert floor below. It was a beautiful view.

Phil Tuzee followed him, trying to be upbeat.

'Hey, look, it's just three kids, Sonny. They're gonna get tired and come out. Smith knows what to do. He'll hide the stuff. These kids will walk out and the cops will arrest them, and that's that. There won't be any reason for the cops to search the house.'

Sonny wasn't listening. He was thinking about his father. Frank Sinatra used to live down the street. It was the house that Sinatra had remodeled to entertain JFK, spent a couple of hundred thousand to buff out the place so he and The Man could enjoy a little poolside poon as they discussed world affairs, sunk all that money into his nest only to have, after the checks were signed and the work was done, JFK blow him off and refuse to visit. Story goes that Sinatra went fucking nuts, shooting through the walls, throwing furniture into the pool, screaming that he was gonna take out a hit on the motherfucking President of the United States. Like what did he expect, Kennedy to be butt-buddies with a mobbed-up guinea singer? Sonny Benza's home was higher up the ridge than Frank's old place, and larger, but his father had been impressed as hell with Sinatra's place. First time his father had come out to visit, he'd walked down to Sinatra's place and stood in the street, staring at Sinatra's house like it held the ghost of the Roman Empire. His father had said, 'Best move I ever made, Sonny, turning over the wheel to you. Look how good you've done, living in the same neighborhood as Francis Albert.' The Persians who lived there now had gotten so freaked out by Sonny's dad, they had called the police.

'Sonny?'

Benza looked at his friend. Tuzee had always been the closest to him. They'd been the tightest when they were kids.

'The records don't just show our business, Phil. They show where we get the money, how we launder it, and our split with the families back east. If the cops get those records, we won't be the only ones who fall. The East Coast will take a hit, too.'

The breath flowed out of Phil Tuzee as if he were collapsing.

Sonny turned back to the others. They were watching him. Waiting for orders.

'Okay. Three kids like this, the cops will give'm time to chill, they'll see they're caught and that the only way out is to give up. Two hours tops, they'll walk out, hands up, then everybody goes to the station to make their statements. That's it.'

Hearing it like that made sense.

'But that's a best-case scenario. Worst case, it's a

bloodbath. When it's over, the detectives go in for forensic evidence and come out with Smith's computer. If that happens, we go to jail for the rest of our lives.'

He looked at each man.

'If we live long enough to stand trial.'

Salvetti and Tuzee traded a look, but neither of them added anything because they knew it was true. The East Coast families would kill them.

Tuzee said, 'Maybe we should warn them. Call old man Castellano back there to let'm know. That might take off some of the edge.'

Salvetti raised his hands.

'Jesus, no fuckin' way. They'll go apeshit and be all over us out here.'

Sonny agreed.

'Sally's right. This problem with Smith, we've got to get a handle on it fast, solve the problem before those bastards back in Manhattan find out.'

Sonny looked back at the televisions and thought it through. Control and containment.

'Who's the controlling authority? LAPD?'

Salvetti grunted. Salvetti, like Phil Tuzee, was a graduate of USC Law who'd worked his way through school stealing cars and selling cocaine. He knew criminal law.

'Bristo is an incorporated township up by Canyon Country. They have their own police force, something like ten, fifteen guys. We're talking a pimple on LA's ass.'

Tuzee shook his head.

'That doesn't help us. If the locals can't handle this, they'll call in the Sheriffs or maybe even the Feds. That's all we need, the Feebs rolling in. Either way, there'll be more than a few hick cops to deal with.'

'That's true, Phil, but it will all be processed back

through the Bristo PD office because it's their jurisdiction. They've got a chief of police up there. It's his crime scene even if he turns over control.'

Sonny turned back to the televisions. A street-level camera was showing the front of the house. Sonny thought he saw someone move past a window, but couldn't be sure.

'This chief, what's his name?'

Salvetti glanced at his notes.

'Talley. I saw him being interviewed.'

The television shifted its shot to show three cops hunkered behind a patrol car. One of them was pointing to the side of the house like he was giving orders. Sonny wondered if that was Talley.

'Put our people on the scene. When the Feds and Sheriffs come in, I want to know who's running their act, and whether they've ever worked OC.'

If they had experience working Organized Crime, he would have to be careful who he deployed to the area.

'It's already happening, Sonny. I've got people on the way, clean guys, not anyone they would recognize.'

Benza nodded.

'I want to know everything that comes out of that house. I want to know about the three turds who started this mess. That bastard Smith might start talking just to cut a break for himself or his family. He might let them in on everything.'

'He knows better than that.'

'I want to know it, Phil.'

'I'm on it. We'll know.'

Sonny Benza watched the three cops hunkered behind the patrol car, the one he believed to be the chief of police talking on a cell phone. He had never murdered a police officer because killing cops was bad for business, but he would not hesitate to do so now. He would do whatever it took to survive. Even if it meant killing a cop.

'I want to know about this guy Talley. Find out

73

everything there is to know about him, and every way we can hurt him. By the end of the day, I want to own him.'

'We'll own him, Sonny.'

'We better.'

# Part Two
## THE FLY

# CHAPTER 6

Friday, 6:17 P.M.

TALLEY

Two of Talley's night-shift duty officers, Fred Cooper and Joycelyn Frost, rolled up in their personal cars. Cooper was breathless, as if he had run from his home in Lancaster, and Frost hadn't even taken the time to change into her uniform; she had strapped her vest and Sam Browne over a sleeveless cotton top and baggy shorts that showed off legs as pale as bread dough. They joined Campbell and Anders in the street.

Talley sat motionless in his car.

When Talley rolled to a barricade-hostage situation with SWAT, his crisis team had included a tactical team, a negotiating team, a traffic control team, a communications team, and the supervisors to coordinate their actions. The negotiating team alone included a team supervisor, an intelligence officer to gather facts and conduct interviews, a primary negotiator to deal with the subject, a secondary negotiator to assist the primary by taking notes and maintaining records, and a staff psychologist to evaluate the subject's personality and recommend negotiating techniques. Now Talley had only himself and a handful of untrained officers.

He closed his eyes.

Talley knew that he was in the beginning moments of panic. He forced himself to concentrate on the basic things that he needed to do: secure the environment, gather information, and keep Rooney cool. These three things were all he had to do until the Sheriffs took over. Talley began a mental list; it was the only way he could keep his head from exploding.

Sarah called him over his radio.

'Chief?'

'Go, Sarah.'

'Mikkelson and Dreyer got the security tape from the minimart. They said you can see these guys plain as a zit on your nose.'

'They inbound?'

'Five out. Maybe less.'

Talley felt himself relax as he thought about the tape; it was something concrete and focused. Seeing Dennis Rooney and the other subjects would make it easier to read the emotional content in Rooney's voice. Talley had never bet a hostage on his intuition, but he believed there were subtle clues to emotional weakness – or strength – that an astute negotiator could read. It was something he knew. It was familiar.

His four officers were staring at him. Waiting.

Talley climbed out of his car and walked up the street. Metzger had a look on her face, the expression saying it was about goddamned time.

They needed a house in which to view the tape. Talley set Metzger to that, then divided more tasks among the others: Someone had to find out if the Smiths had relatives in the area, and, if so, notify them; also, they had to locate Mrs. Smith in Florida. The Sheriffs would need a floor plan of the Smith house and information on any security systems that were involved; if none were available from the permit office, neighbors should sketch the layout from memory. The same neighbors would be questioned to learn if any of the Smiths required life-sustaining medications.

Talley began to grow comfortable with the familiarity of the job. It was something that he'd done before, and he had done it well until it killed him.

By the time Talley finished assigning the preliminary tasks, Mikkelson and Dreyer had arrived with the tape. He met them at a large Mediterrean home owned by a bright sturdy woman who originally hailed from Brazil. Mrs. Peña. Talley identified himself as the chief of police and thanked her for her cooperation. She led them to the television in a large family room, where she showed them how to work the VCR. Mikkelson loaded the videotape.

'We watched the tape at Kim's to make sure we had something. I left it cued up.'

'Did you pull up anything on Rooney from traffic or warrants?'

'Yes, sir.'

Dreyer opened his citation pad. Talley saw that notes had been scrawled across the face of a citation, probably while they were driving.

'Dennis James Rooney has a younger brother, Kevin Paul, age nineteen. They live together over in Agua Dulce. Dennis just pulled thirty days at the Ant Farm for misdemeanor burglary and theft, knocked down from felony three. He's got multiple offenses, including car theft, shoplifting, drug possession, possession of stolen goods, and DUI. The brother, Kevin, did juvenile time on a car theft beef. At one time or another, both were in foster care or were wards of the state. Neither graduated from high school.'

'Any history of violent crimes?'

'Nothing in the record but what I said.'

'When we're done here, I want you to talk to their landlord. Guys like this are always behind on the rent or making too much noise, so the landlord has probably had to jam them. I want to know how they reacted. Find out if they threatened him or flashed a weapon or rolled over and made nice.'

Talley knew that a subject's past behavior was a good predictor of future behavior: People who had used violence and intimidation in the past could be expected to react with violence and threats in the future. That was how they dealt with stress.

'Find out from the landlord if they have jobs. If they work, ask their employers to come talk to me.'

'Got it.'

Mikkelson stepped away from the VCR.

'We're ready, Chief.'

'Let's see it.'

The screen flickered as the tape engaged. The bright color image of a daytime Spanish-language soap opera was replaced by the soundless black-and-white security picture of Junior Kim's minimart. The camera angle revealed that the camera was mounted above and to the right of the cash register, showing Junior Kim and a small portion of the clerk's area behind the counter. The counter angled up the left side of the frame, the first aisle angled along the right. The camera gave a partial view of the rest of the store. Small white numbers filled a time-count window in the lower right of the screen.

Mikkelson said, 'Okay. Here they come. The guy we think is Rooney entered a few minutes ago, then left. Here where the tape picks up, it's maybe five minutes later.'

'Okay.'

A sharp-featured white male matching Dennis Rooney's description opened the door and walked directly to Junior Kim. A larger white male with a broad face and wide body entered with him. The second man's hair was shaved down to his scalp in a fuzz cut.

'Is that Rooney's brother?'

'The third guy is about to come in. The third guy looks like Rooney.'

A third white male stepped inside before Mikkelson finished. Talley knew the third man was Rooney's brother from the resemblance, though Kevin was shorter, thinner, and wearing a Lemonheads T-shirt. Kevin waited by the door.

Talley studied their expressions and the way they carried themselves. Rooney was a good-looking kid, with eyes that were hard but uncertain. He walked with an arrogant, rolling gait. Talley guessed that he was posturing, but couldn't yet tell if Rooney was posturing for others or himself. Kevin Rooney shuffled from foot to foot, his eyes flicking from Dennis to the gas islands outside the store. He was clearly terrified. The larger man had a wide flat face and expressionless eyes.

'We have an ID on the big guy?'

'No, sir.'

'Was the camera hidden?'

'Hanging off the ceiling big as a wart on a hog's ass, and these guys didn't even bother to wear masks.'

Talley watched the video without a feeling of connection. During his time on LAPD he had seen three or four hundred such videos, all showing robberies gone bad just the way this one was about to go bad, and only one out of twenty perpetrators had bothered to don a mask. Mostly, they didn't care; mostly, they didn't think about it; geniuses didn't go into crime. Only the first tape had shocked him. He was still a probationary officer, twenty-two years old and fresh from the academy. He had watched a thirteen-year-old Vietnamese girl walk into a convenience store just like this one, shoot the elderly African-American clerk in the face at point-blank range, then turn her gun on the only other person in the store, a pregnant Latina named Muriel Gonzales who was standing next to her. The pregnant woman had fallen to her knees, thrusting her hands up as she begged for her life. The Vietnamese shooter touched the gun to Muriel Gonzales's forehead and let off a shot without hesitation, then calmly walked around behind the counter and cleaned out the cash register before walking out of the store. When she reached the door, she hesitated, then returned to the counter, where she stole a box of Altoids. After that she stepped over Muriel Gonzales and left.

Seeing those murders had left Talley so shaken that he had spent the next two months thinking about resigning.

The events in Kim's Minimart happened as quickly: Rooney lifted his shirt to expose a gun, then vaulted over the counter. Kim stood with a gun of his own. Talley was relieved that Rooney had told the truth about Kim having a gun. It wouldn't help Rooney in court, but Talley could use what he was seeing to play on Rooney's sense of being the victim of bad luck. That was all Talley cared about right now, finding things he could use to manipulate Dennis Rooney.

The struggle between Rooney and Junior Kim lasted only seconds, then Kim staggered backward, dropped his pistol, and slumped against the Slurpee machine. Rooney was clearly surprised that Kim had been shot. He jumped back over the counter and ran to the door. The larger man didn't move. Talley found that odd. Kim had just been shot and Rooney was running, but the third man just stood there. Junior Kim's pistol had landed on the counter. The third man tucked it into his waist, then leaned over the counter, resting his weight on his left hand.

Mikkelson said, 'What's he doing?'

'He's watching Kim die.'

The big man's pasty Pillsbury Doughboy face creased. Mikkelson said, 'Jesus, he's smiling.'

Talley's back and chest prickled. He stopped the tape, then rewound it until the unknown subject leaned forward on his hand.

'We need to confirm that the younger guy is Kevin Rooney, and we need to ID the third subject. Make hard-copy prints from the tape. Show them to Rooney's landlord, his neighbors, and the people at his job. We might get a fast ID on the third guy that way.'

Mikkelson glanced at Dreyer uncertainly.

'Ah, Chief, how do we make prints from the tape?'

Talley cursed under his breath. In Los Angeles, an

officer would take the tape to the Scientific Investigations Division in Glendale, then return an hour later with however many prints were needed. Talley thought that the Palmdale PD probably had the necessary equipment to do that job, but Palmdale was a long drive in Friday-night traffic.

'You know the computer store in the mall?'

'Sure. They sell PlayStations.'

'Call first. Tell them we have a VHS videotape and ask if they know how to grab and print a frame. If they can, take it there. If they can't, call the camera store in Santa Clarita. If *they* can't help, call Palmdale.'

Talley pointed out the unknown subject's hand resting on the counter. He turned to Cooper and Frost.

'See here where he put his hand? I want you two to meet the Sheriff's homicide team at Kim's, and tell them about this. They'll be able to lift a good set of prints.'

'Yes, sir.'

Talley told them to get to it, then headed back out to the street and climbed into his car. He considered his impressions of Rooney from the videotape and from their conversation. Rooney wanted to be 'understood,' but he also wanted to be seen in exaggerated heroic terms: Tough, manly, and dominant. Talley decided that Rooney was a low-self-esteem personality who craved the approval of others while seeking to control his environment. He was probably a coward who covered his lack of courage with aggressive behavior. Talley decided that he could use Rooney's needs to his advantage. He checked his watch. It was time.

Talley opened his phone and punched the redial button. The phone in Smith's house rang. And rang. On the tenth ring, Rooney still hadn't answered. Talley grew worried, imagining a mass murder though he knew it was more likely that Rooney was just being a dick. He radioed Jorgenson.

'Jorgy, anything happening at the house?'

Jorgenson was still hunkered behind his car in the body of the cul-de-sac.

'Nada. It's quiet so far. I would've called you if I heard anything.'

'Okay. Stand by.'

Talley pressed the redial button again. This time he let the phone ring an even dozen times before he closed the phone. He went back on the radio.

'You hear anything from the house?'

'I thought I heard the phone ringing.'

'See any movement?'

'No, sir. It's quiet as a clam.'

Talley wondered why Rooney was refusing to answer the phone. He had seemed agreeable enough during their first contact. Talley keyed his radio again.

'Who's on with the CHiPs?'

The California Highway Patrol officers had been used to supplement his own people on the perimeter of the house. They worked off their own communication frequency, distinct from the Bristo freq.

'I am.'

'Tell them to advance to the property lines. I don't want them exposed to fire, but I want Rooney to see them. Put them at the east and west walls, and at the back wall.'

'Rog. I'll take care of it.'

If Rooney wouldn't answer the phone, Talley would force Rooney to call him.

DENNIS

The money changed things. Dennis couldn't stop thinking about the money. It no longer was enough to escape; he was frantic to take the money with him. Dennis brought Mars to the closet, letting him see the boxes of cash that crowded the closet floor. Dennis laid his hands on the cash to savor the velvety feel. He lifted a pack of

84

hundred-dollar bills to his nose and riffled the bills, smelling the paper and ink and the sweet human smell of cash. He tried to guess the number of bills in the pack. Fifty, at least; maybe a hundred. Five thousand dollars. Maybe ten thousand. Dennis couldn't stop touching the money, feeling it; softer than any breast, silkier than a woman's thigh, sexier than the finest ass.

He grinned up at Mars so wide that his cheeks cramped.

'There's gotta be a million dollars here. Maybe more. Look at it, Mars! This place is a bank!'

Mars barely glanced at the money. He went to the back of the little room, looking at the ceiling and the floor, tapping the walls, then studied the monitors. He pushed the boxes aside with his feet.

'It's a safety room. Steel door, reinforced walls, all the security; it's like a bunker. If anyone breaks into your house, you can hide. I wonder if they have sex in here?'

Dennis was irritated that Mars showed so little interest in the cash. Dennis wanted to dump the cash into a huge pile and dive in naked.

'Who gives a shit, Mars? Check out this cash. We're rich.'

'We're trapped in a house.'

Dennis was getting pissed off. This was the life-altering event that Dennis had always known was waiting for him: This house, this money, here and now – this was his destiny and his fate; the moment that had drawn him all the years of his life, plucked at him to take chances and commit outrageous acts, made him the star in the movie of his own life – all along it had been pulling him forward to the here and now, and Mars was harshing his mellow. He shoved a pack of cash into his pocket and stood.

'Mars, listen, we're going to take this with us. We'll put it in something. They must have suitcases or plastic bags.'

'You can't run with a suitcase.'

'We'll figure it out.'

'It's going to be heavy.'

Dennis was getting more pissed off. He slapped Mars in the chest. It was like slapping a wall, but Mars averted his eyes. Dennis had learned that Mars would go along if you knocked the shit out of him.

'We can carry it, we can even stuff it up our asses, but we're not leaving here without it.'

Mars nodded, rolling over just as Dennis knew he would.

'I'm glad you found the money, Dennis. You can have my share.'

Mars was depressing him. Dennis told Mars to go back to the office to make sure Kevin wasn't fucking up. When Mars left, Dennis felt relieved; Mars was fucking weird and getting weirder. If he didn't want the money, Dennis would keep it all for himself.

He searched through the other closets in the bedroom until he found a black Tumi suitcase, the kind with a handle and wheels. Dennis filled it with packs of hundreds; worn bills that had seen a lot of use, not a crisp new note among them. When the suitcase was full, Dennis wheeled it into the bedroom and parked it on the bed. Mars was right: He didn't know how he was going to get out of here lugging that big-ass case. He wouldn't be able to sneak out a window and run through backyards, but they had two cars and three hostages. Dennis refused to believe that he had come this close to his destiny to let it slip away.

Dennis returned to the office and found Mars watching the television. Mars turned up the volume.

'It's on every channel, dude. You're a star.'

Dennis saw himself on television. The newspeople had cut one of Dennis's old booking photos into the upper right corner of the screen. It was a shot that made him look like Charles Manson.

The picture changed to an aerial view of the house they were in. Dennis saw police cars parked in the street and two cops hunkered behind the wheels. A hot newschick was saying how Dennis had recently been released from the Ant Farm. Dennis found himself grinning again. Something smoky rushed through Dennis's veins just as it did when he got away with stealing a car: part anger and rage, part rush, part a groovy feeling like the whole fucking world was giving him high fives. Here he was with a million bucks for the taking, here he was on television. It was the big FUCK YOU to his parents, to his teachers, to the cops, to all the shitbirds who had kept him down. FUCK! YOU! He had arrived. He felt real. It was better than sex.

'Yeah! Fuckin' YEAH!'

He went to the door.

'Kevin! Come see this!'

The phone rang, spoiling the magic of the television. That would be Talley. Dennis ignored it, and returned to the television. The helicopters, the cops, the reporters – everyone was here because of him. It was *The Dennis Rooney Show*, and he had just figured out the ending: They would use the kids as hostages and boogie to the border in that big flashy Jaguar with the helicopters broadcasting every moment of the trip on live TV.

Dennis slapped Mars on the arm.

'I got it, dude. We'll use the Jaguar. We'll take the cash and the two kids, and leave their father here. The cops won't mess with us if we have those kids. We can boogie straight down to TJ.'

Mars shrugged blandly, his voice as quiet as a whisper.

'That won't work, Dennis.'

Dennis grew irritated again.

'Why not?'

'They'll shoot out the tires, and then a police sniper will put a bullet in your head from a hundred yards away.'

'Bullshit, Mars. O. J. Simpson drove around for *hours*.'

'O. J. Simpson didn't have hostages. They won't let us

leave with these children. They'll kill us, and we won't even see it coming.'

The picture shifted again to an aerial view of the minimart surrounded by Highway Patrol cars. The view slowly orbited the cars. The movement made Dennis feel sick, like riding in the backseat of a car. He watched the cops crouched behind their cars, and worried that Mars was right about the snipers. That was just the kind of chickenshit double cross the cops would pull.

Dennis was still thinking about it when Kevin screamed from his position by the French doors.

'Dennis! There's cops all over the place out here! *They're coming!*'

Dennis forgot the snipers and ran to his brother.


TALLEY

Talley was in the cul-de-sac, waiting behind his car, when Dennis began shouting from the house. Talley let him rant, then opened his phone and called.

Dennis answered on the first ring.

'You fuck! You tell those fuckin' cops to move back! I don't like'm this close!'

'Take it easy, Dennis. Are you saying that you don't like seeing the officers on the perimeter?'

'Stop saying whatever I say back to me! You know what I mean!'

'I do that to make sure I understand you. We can't afford to misunderstand each other.'

'If these bastards try to come in here, people are gonna die! Everybody's gonna die!'

'No one is going to hurt you, Dennis. I told you that before. Now give me a minute to see what's going on out here, okay?'

Talley hit the mute button on his phone.

'Jorgy, are you on with the perimeter?'

88

'Yes, sir.'

'Are they on the walls where we placed them?'

'Yes, sir. We've got two north on Flanders, and two more in each of the rear yards on either side. They're on the wall.'

Talley turned off the mute.

'Dennis, I'm checking into it, okay? Tell me what you see.'

'I see fuckin' cops! I'm looking right at'm. They're too close!'

'I can't see them from out here behind my car. Help me, okay? Where are they?'

Talley heard muffling sounds, as if Rooney was moving with the phone. Talley wondered if it was a cordless. Like all hostage negotiators, he hated cordless and cell phones because they didn't anchor the subject. You could fix a hardwired phone's location. Then you knew the subject's location whenever you had him on the line. If you launched a tactical breach, knowing the subject's location could save lives.

Rooney said, 'All the way around, goddamnit! These bastards over here at this white house. They're right on the goddamn wall! You make them get back!'

Talley hit the mute button again. The white house was a sprawling contemporary to Talley's left. A brushed-steel gate crossed the front drive. The house on the east side to Talley's right was dark gray. Talley counted to fifty, then opened the cell line again.

'Dennis, we got a little problem here.'

'Fucking right we got a problem. Make'm get back!'

'Those officers are Highway Patrolmen, Dennis. I'm with the Bristo Camino Police Department. They don't work for me.'

'Bullshit!'

'I can tell you what they're going to say.'

'Fuck what they say! If they come over that wall, people are going to die! I've got hostages in here!'

'If I tell these guys that you're being cooperative, they'll be more inclined to cooperate with you. You understand that, don't you? Everyone out here is concerned that the civilians in there with you are okay. Let me speak with Mr. Smith.'

'*I told you they're fine.*'

Talley sensed that everything inside wasn't as Rooney claimed, and that concerned him. Most hostage takers agreed to let their hostages say a few words because they enjoyed taunting the police with their control of the hostage; it made them feel powerful. If Rooney wouldn't let the Smiths talk, then he must be frightened of what they might say.

'Tell me what's wrong, Dennis.'

'Nothing's wrong! I'll let the sonofabitch talk when I get good and goddamned ready. I'm in charge of this shit, not you!'

Dennis sounded so stressed that Talley backed off. If anything was wrong in the house, he didn't want to make the situation worse. But having pressed Rooney for a concession, he had to get something or he would lose credibility.

'Okay, Dennis, fair enough for now, but you've still got to give me something if you want the patrolmen to back off. So how about this: You tell me who you have in there. Just tell me their names.'

'You know who owns the house.'

'We heard that those kids might have some friends over.'

'If I tell you, will you get these assholes to back off?'

'I can do that, Dennis. I just got word from their commander. He'll go along.'

Rooney hesitated, but then he answered.

'Walter Smith, Jennifer Smith, and Thomas Smith. There's no one else in here.'

Talley muted the phone again.

'Jorgy, tell the CHiPs to back off the wall. Tell them to

find a position with a view of the house, but they can't be on the wall. Have them do it now.'

'Rog.'

Talley waited as Jorgenson spoke into his mike, then he went back to his phone.

'Dennis, what do you see?'

'They're pulling back.'

'Okay. We made it work, me and you. We did something here, Dennis. Way to go.'

Talley wanted Rooney to feel as if they had accomplished something together. Like they were a team.

'Just keep them away. I don't like them that close. They come over that wall, people are going to die in here. Do you understand what I'm saying? I'm not a guy you can fuck with.'

'I'll give you my word about that right now. We're not coming in there. We won't come over that wall unless we think you're hurting someone. I want to be up front about that. If it looks like you're going to hurt those people, we'll come in without warning.'

'I'm not going to hurt anyone if you stay away. That's all there is to it.'

'That's the way to play it. Just be cool.'

'You want these people, Talley? You want them safe and sound? Right now?'

Talley knew that Rooney was about to make his first demand. It could be as innocent as a pack of cigarettes or as outrageous as a phone call from the President.

'You know that I do.'

'I want a helicopter with a full tank of gas to take us to Mexico. If I get the helicopter, you get these people.'

During his time with SWAT, Talley had been asked for helicopters, jet aircraft, limousines, buses, cars, and, once, a flying saucer. All negotiators were trained that certain demands were non-negotiable: firearms, ammunition, narcotics, alcohol, and transportation. You never allowed a subject the hope of escape. You kept him isolated. That was how you broke him down.

Talley responded without hesitation, making his voice reasonable, but firm, letting his tone assure Rooney that the refusal wasn't the end of the world, and wasn't confrontational.

'Can't do that, Dennis. They won't give you a helicopter.'

Rooney's voice came back strained.

'I've got these people.'

'The Sheriffs won't trade for a helicopter. They have their rules about these things. You could ask for a battleship, but they won't give you that, either.'

When he spoke again, Rooney sounded weaker.

'Ask them.'

'It can't even land here, Dennis. Besides, Mexico isn't freedom. Even if you had a helicopter, the Mexican police would arrest you as soon as it landed. This isn't the Old West.'

Talley wanted to change the subject. Rooney would brood about the helicopter now, but Talley thought that he could give him something else to think about.

'I saw the security tape from the minimart.'

Rooney hesitated, as if it took him a moment to realize what Talley was saying, then his voice was anxious and hopeful.

'Did you see that Chinaman pull a gun? Did you see that?'

'It played out just the way you said.'

'None of this would've happened if he hadn't pulled that gun. I damn near shit my pants.'

'Then none of this was premeditated. That's what you're saying here, right? That you didn't premeditate what happened?'

Rooney wanted to be seen as the victim, so Talley was sending the subtle message that he sympathized with Rooney's situation.

'We just wanted to rob the place. I'll admit that. But, fuck, here comes the Chinaman pulling a gun. I had to defend myself, right? I wasn't trying to shoot him. I was just trying to get the gun away so he couldn't shoot *me*. It was an accident.'

The adversarial edge disappeared from Rooney's voice. Talley knew that this was the first indication that Rooney was beginning to see Talley as a collaborator. Talley lowered his voice, sending a subtle cue that this was just between them.

'Can the other two guys hear me?'

'Why do you want to know that?'

'I understand that they might be there with you, so you don't have to respond to what I'm about to say, Dennis. Just listen.'

'What are you talking about?'

'I know you're worried about what will happen to you because the officer was shot. I've been thinking about that, so I've got a question. Was anyone else in there shooting besides you? Just a yes or no, if that's all you can say.'

Talley already knew the answer from Jorgenson and Anders. He let the question hang in the air. He could hear Rooney breathe.

'Yes.'

'Then maybe it wasn't your bullets that hit the officer. Maybe it wasn't you who shot him.'

Talley had gone as far as he could. He had suggested that Rooney could beat the rap by shifting the blame to one of the other subjects. He had given Rooney a doorway out. Now, he had to back off and let Rooney brood over whether or not to step through.

'Dennis, I want to give you my cell phone number. That way you can reach me whenever you want to talk. You won't have to shout out the window.'

'That'd be good.'

Talley gave him the number, told Rooney that he was

going to take another break, then once more backed his car out of the cul-de-sac. Leigh Metzger was waiting for him on the street outside of Mrs. Peña's home. She wasn't alone. Talley's wife and daughter were with her.

### Santa Monica Hospital Emergency Room
### Santa Monica, California
Fifteen years ago

*Officer Jeff Talley, shirtless but still wearing his blue uniform pants even though they are ripped and streaked with blood, notices her calves first. He is a sucker for shapely calves. Talley is sitting on a gurney in the emergency room, his torn hand packed in a bowl of ice to reduce the swelling and kill the pain while he waits for them to take him to X-ray. His partner, a senior patrol officer named Darren Consuelo, is currently locking Talley's gun, radio, Sam Browne, and other equipment in the trunk of their patrol car for safekeeping.*

*The nurse comes out of a door across the room, lost in whatever she's scribbling on the clipboard, dressed in white with a pale blue apron, her dark hair pulled back into a ponytail. The calves get him first because they are not hidden by the clunky white stockings that nurses often wear; they are sleek, strong, and fiercely brown from much time in the sun. She has legs like a gymnast or sprinter, which Talley likes. He checks her out: tight ass, trim body, shoulders broad for her small stature. Then he sees her face. She appears to be about his age, twenty-three, twenty-four, something like that.*

*'Nurse?'*

*He winces when she glances over, trying to look like he's suffering intense pain. In truth, his hand is numb.*

*She recognizes the LAPD pants and shoes, smiles encouragingly.*

*'How's it going, Officer?'*

*She is not a beautiful woman, but she is pretty with healthy clean skin, and an expression of kindness that moves him. Her eyes glow with a warmth that fills him.*

'Ah, Nurse –'

*He reads her name tag. Jane Whitehall.*

'Jane . . . they were supposed to bring me to X-ray, but I've been out here forever. Think you could check for me?'

*He makes the grimace again, impressing her with his suffering.*

'I know they're backed up tonight, but I'll see what I can do. What's wrong?'

*He lifts his hand from the pink ice. The fleshy pad on the inside of his third finger is ripped and torn. The edges of the laceration are blue from the cold, but the bleeding has mostly stopped.*

*Nurse Whitehall grimaces sympathetically.*

'Ow. That's nasty.'

*Talley nods.*

'I chased a rape suspect into a backyard in Venice, where the guy sicced his pit bull on me. I'm lucky I've still got a hand.'

*Nurse Whitehall carefully places his hand back into the ice. Like her eyes, her touch is warm and certain.*

'Did you catch him?'

'Yes, ma'am. He went down hard, but he went down. I always get my man.'

*He smiles, letting her know that he is kidding her, and she returns his smile. Talley thinks that he is making great headway, and is about to tell her that he has just been accepted to become a Special Weapons and Tactics officer when Consuelo comes plopping around the corner with a Diet Coke and two PayDay candy bars. Consuelo, like always, smells of cigarettes.*

'Jesus, you're still sittin' there? Haven't they snapped the picture yet?'

*Talley takes the Diet Coke, wishing that Consuelo*

*would go back to the candy machine. He wants to be alone with the nurse.*

'They're backed up. You can hang out in the coffee shop, you want. I'll find you when I'm done here.'

*Nurse Whitehall smiles politely at Consuelo.*

'I'll see where we are with the X-ray.'

*Consuelo grunts, gruff and pissed off about having to spend his day in the emergency room.*

'While you're back there, snag a load of klutz pills for this guy, extra strength.'

*Quickly, Talley says,* 'I'll find you in the coffee shop.'

*Nurse Whitehall cocks her head, clearly wondering what Consuelo means.*

'Were you with him when the pit bull attacked?'

'That what he told you happened to his hand?'

*Talley feels the flush creep up his neck. He meets Consuelo's eyes with a silent plea for help.*

'Yeah, Consuelo was there. When we collared the rapist in Venice.'

*Consuelo bursts out laughing, spraying peanuts and caramel all over the gurney.*

'A rapist? A pit bull? Jesus, lady, this dumb putz slammed his finger in the car door.'

*Consuelo walks away, gurgling his smoker's laugh.*

*Talley wants to crawl under the gurney and disappear. When he looks at Nurse Whitehall again, she is staring at him.*

*Talley shrugs, trying to make a joke.*

'I thought it was worth the shot.'

'That really how you hurt your hand, you caught it in a car door?'

'Not very heroic, is it?'

'No.'

'Well, there you go.'

*Nurse Whitehall walks three steps away, stops, turns back, and looks at him with an expression of profound confusion.*

'I must be out of my mind.'

She kisses him just as two doctors and another nurse step off the elevator. Talley pulls her close, kissing her deeply, just as he does again that night after their date at the Police Academy's Rod and Gun Club, and every night thereafter. From the instant he sees the warmth in her eyes, Jeff Talley is in love.

Three months and one day later, they marry.


## TALLEY

Talley felt embarrassed and angry with himself. He had been so consumed that he had forgotten about Jane and Amanda. He checked the charge on his cell phone battery, then pocketed the phone and joined them.

Amanda looked like her mother: both were short, though Amanda was a bit taller, and both were thin. They shared what Talley felt was their most telling feature: faces so expressive that they were open doors to their hearts. Talley had always been able to see whatever Jane felt; in the beginning when the feelings were good, this was good; but toward the end, the open reflections of pain and confusion added to a load he found impossible to bear.

Talley kissed his daughter, who was as responsive as a wet towel.

'Sarah told us that there are men with guns barricaded in a house! Where are they?'

Talley pointed toward the cul-de-sac.

'Just around the corner and up that street. You see the helicopters?'

The helicopters made it hard to hear.

Amanda's eyes were wide and excited as she looked around at the police cars, but Jane looked drawn with dark rings circling her eyes. Talley thought that his wife looked tired. He felt a stab of guilt and shame.

'You been working overtime?'

'Not so much. Two nights a week.'

'You look tired.'

'Does it make me look older, too?'

'Jesus, Jane, I didn't mean it like that. I'm sorry.'

She closed her eyes and nodded, her expression saying that they were covering familiar ground.

Rather than stand outside, Talley brought them into the house. Mrs. Peña's kitchen was filled with the rich smells of brewing coffee and cheese enchiladas. She had put out pitchers of water and cans of soft drinks, insisting that the officers help themselves, and now she was cooking.

Talley introduced Jane and Amanda to Mrs. Peña, then led them into the family room. The big television was playing live coverage of the scene. Amanda went to the television.

'Sarah said they have hostages.'

'They have a father and two children. We think that's all, but we don't know. One of the kids is a girl. About your age.'

'This is *so* cool. Can we go see the house?'

'No, we can't go up there.'

'But you're the chief of police. Why not?'

Jane said, 'It's a crime scene, Mandy. It's dangerous.'

Talley turned to his wife.

'I should've called, Jane. This thing broke just after we spoke, then everything was happening so fast that I didn't even think of it. I'm sorry.'

Jane touched his arm.

'How are *you* doing?'

'I think the guy's going to come around. I've been on the phone with him; he's scared, but he's not suicidal.'

'I'm not asking about the situation, Chief. I mean *you*.'

She glanced at her hand on his arm, then looked up at him again.

'You're shaking.'

Talley stepped away just enough so that her hand fell.

He glanced past her at the big television. He could see Jorgenson hunkered behind his radio car.

'The Sheriffs are taking over as soon as they get here.'

'But they're not here. You are. I know what this does to you.'

'They'll be here when they get here. I'm the chief of police, Jane. That's it.'

She stared at him the way she did when she was looking for meaning beyond his words. It used to infuriate him. Where Jane's face was a mirror to every emotion she felt, his face was flat and plain and revealed nothing. She had often accused him of wearing a mask, and he had never been able to explain that it wasn't a mask. It was a tightly held control that kept him from falling apart.

He looked away again. It hurt to see her concern.

'All right, Jeff. I'm just worried about you, is all.'

Talley nodded.

'You guys should have dinner up here before you head back. Let some of the traffic bleed out. Maybe that Thai place. You like that place, don't you?'

Jane grew serious, then nodded.

'We could do that. There's no point in rushing home.'

'Good.'

'I don't want to just drop her off at your place so she has to sit there all alone, so how about she and I go eat, then we'll both stay over. We'll rent a movie. If this thing blows over tonight, you and Mandy could be laughing about it tomorrow this time.'

Talley felt embarrassed. He nodded, but the nod was a stall because he didn't know what to say. He noticed that Jane had dyed her hair a new color. She had colored it the same rich chestnut for as long as Talley could remember, but now it was a deep red so dark that it was almost black. Her hair was cut shorter, too, almost a boy cut. Talley realized then that this woman deserved more than he would ever be able to give her. He told himself that if

99

he cared for her and for whatever they once had, he had to set her free, not curse her with a man whose heart had died.

'What?'

He looked away again.

'You and I need to talk.'

She didn't say anything for a moment, just stared up at him until a faint smile touched the corners of her mouth. He could tell that she was frightened.

'All right, Jeff.'

'The Sheriffs will be here soon. When they get set up, I'll hand off the phone, and then I should be able to leave.'

She nodded.

Talley wanted to tell her then. He wanted to tell her that she was free, that he wouldn't hold her back any longer, that he finally knew that he was beyond redemption, but the words wouldn't come and their absence left him feeling cowardly.

He told Metzger to escort his wife and daughter out of the development, then he went back to his car to wait for the Sheriffs in the dimming light.

### Santa Clarita, California
### Six miles west of Bristo Camino
### Chili's Restaurant
7:02 P.M.

GLEN HOWELL

Glen Howell didn't have to warn his people to keep their voices down; they were surrounded by middle-class vanilla families come to sop up cut-rate frozen shrimp and fried cheese on their Friday night out; people Glen Howell thought of as zombies; irritated men and women at the end of another pointless week, pretending that their screaming, out-of-control, overfed children weren't monsters. Welcome to suburbia, Howell thought, and you can stuff it up your ass.

Howell didn't let the four men and two women get booze, or food that was made to order. He didn't have time to hustle after the parolee cooks in the kitchen, and booze would put his people to sleep. He needed them sharp. Howell had called in each of the six himself, running each name past Sonny Benza personally. They were longtime associates who could do what needed to be done without drawing attention to themselves, and they could do it quickly. From what Howell was learning, speed was going to be everything. Speed, and a total domination of the local scene. He accepted the fact that he would not sleep again until this was over.

Ken Seymore, who had spent the past two hours pretending to be a reporter from the *Los Angeles Times*, was saying, 'They requested a full crisis response team from the L.A. County Sheriff's Department. The Sheriffs are on the way now, but there's been some kinda problem, so they've been delayed.'

Duane Manelli fired off a question. Manelli spoke in abrupt bursts, the way an M16A2 coughed out three-shot groups.

'How many people is that?'

'In the Sheriff's team?'

'Yeah.'

When Duane Manelli was eighteen years old, a state judge had given him the choice between going into the service or pulling twenty months for armed robbery. Manelli had joined the army, and liked it. He spent twelve years in the service, going airborne, ranger, and finally special forces. He currently ran the best hijack crew in Sonny Benza's operation.

Seymore found his notes.

'Here's what we're looking at: A command team, a negotiating team, a tactical team – the tac team includes a perimeter team, the assault team, snipers, and breachers – and an intelligence team. Some of these guys might double up on what they do, but we're looking at about thirty-five new bodies on the scene.'

Somebody whistled.

'Damn, when those boys roll, they roll.'

LJ Ruiz leaned forward on his elbows, frowning. Ruiz was a quiet man with a thoughtful manner who worked for Howell as an enforcer. He specialized in terrorizing bar owners until they agreed to buy their booze from distributors approved by Benza.

'What's a breacher?'

'If they gotta blow open a door or a window or whatever, the breachers set the charge. They go to a special school for that.'

Howell didn't like that many more policemen coming in, but they had expected it. Seymore had reported that, so far, the federal authorities hadn't been requested, but Howell knew that the odds of this would increase as time passed.

Howell asked when the Sheriffs would arrive.

'Cop I talked to, he said they'll be here in three hours, maybe four tops.'

Howell checked his watch, then nodded at Gayle Devarona, one of the two women at the table. Like Seymore, she had pretended to be a news reporter in order to openly ask questions. If the questions were too blatant to ask, she used her skills as a thief.

'What's up with the local cops?'

'We got sixteen full- and part-time employees, fourteen police officers and two full-time office people. I got their names here, and most of the addresses. I could've gotten the others, but I had to come here.'

Seymore laughed.

'Bitch, bitch, bitch.'

'Fist yourself.'

Howell told them to knock it off. Bullshit took time.

Devarona tore a single sheet from a yellow legal pad and passed it across the table to Howell.

'I got the names from the Bristo police office. The addresses and phones I got from a contact at the phone company.'

Howell scanned a neatly hand-printed list. Talley's name was at the top, along with his address and two phone numbers. Howell guessed that one was the house phone, the other a cell.

'You get any background on these people, see what we have to deal with?'

She went through what she had, which made Bristo sound like a burial ground for retired meter maids and retards. Not that bad, really, but Howell thought that they'd caught a break. He knew of small towns in Idaho where half the population had pulled time on LAPD's Robbery-Homicide Division and the other half were retired FBI. Try to fuck around up there, they'd hand you your ass. Howell checked his watch again. By midnight tonight, he could and would have credit checks and military records (if any) of each of these officers, as well as information about their families.

'What about Talley?'

Sonny Benza had specifically told him to zero in on Talley. You cut off the head, the body dies.

She said, 'I got what I could. Single, ex-LAPD. The condo he lives in is provided by the city.'

Seymore interrupted.

'Those cops I talked to out at Smith's place, they said Talley was a hostage negotiator in LA.'

Devarona scowled, like she hated him stepping on her goods.

'His last three years on the job. Before that, he was SWAT. There's a picture of him on the wall in their office, Talley in an assault suit, holding the big gun.'

Howell nodded at these last two bits of information. They were the first interesting things that he'd heard. He wondered how a SWAT-qualified crisis negotiator ended up crossing school kids in Beemerland. Maybe the free condo.

Devarona said, 'He was on LAPD a total of fourteen years, then he resigned. The woman I talked to didn't want to say, but I'd make him for a stress release. Something's hinky about why he hung it up.'

Howell made a note to pass that up to Palm Springs. He knew that Benza had people on the Los Angeles Police Department. If they turned something rotten on Talley, they might be able to use it as leverage. He had one last question about Talley.

'He work as a detective down there?'

'I asked about that. The girl didn't know, but it's still a good notion to follow up.'

When Devarona finished, Howell waited for more, but that was it. Everyone had given what they had. All in all, Howell couldn't kick. Start to finish, they'd had maybe two hours to get it together. Now there was more to do. He considered the sixteen names on Devarona's list. The list of bankers, lawyers, private investigators, and police officers owned by Sonny Benza and his associates was far longer; that list numbered in the hundreds, and all of those names could be brought to bear for the task at hand.

'Okay, get the rest of the addresses, then divide up the names and start digging. Gayle, you're on credit and finances. We get lucky, one of these clowns is gonna be in so deep that he's drowning. Maybe we can toss him a life preserver. Duane, Ruiz, find out where these people play. Some married doof is gonna keep a whore on the side; one of these turds is gonna like chasing the dragon with a fruit. Shovel dirt and find the skeletons. Ken, you're back at the house with the reporters. If anything breaks, I want to know about it before God.'

Seymore leaned back, irritated. Howell always got pissed off when he did that.

'Don't start with the faces, goddamnit. If you've got something to say, say it.'

'We're going to need more people. If this thing drags out a few days, we're gonna need a lot more.'

'I'm on it.'

Now Seymore leaned forward, and lowered his voice still more.

'If things get wet, we're going to need people who can handle that end.'

Wet work was blood work. Howell had already thought of that and had already made the call.

'The right people are on their way. You worry about your job. I got my side covered.'

Howell checked his watch again, then copied Talley's address and phone numbers on the bottom of the sheet. He tore off his copy, then stood.

'I want updates in two hours.'

Howell put Talley's address in his pocket as he walked out to his car. Not just anyone would murder a chief of police with an army of cameras and newspeople around. He needed someone special for a job like that.

# CHAPTER 7

## Newhall, California Sundown
Friday, 7:39 P.M.

MARION CLEWES

His name was Marion Clewes. He was waiting in a donut shop in Newhall, California, twelve miles west of Bristo Camino in an area where all of the signs were in Spanish. Marion was the only person in the shop other than the woman behind the counter who spoke no English and seemed uneasy about his being there. Even at sundown, the unairconditioned shop was hot, leaving her skin filmed with grease. It was a filthy place, with coffee rings on the broken Formica tables and a sticky floor. Marion didn't mind. He could feel the weight of the air, heavy with grease and cinnamon. He took a seat at a table facing the door to wait for Glen Howell.

Marion was used to meeting Howell in places like this. Howell was never comfortable with him, and was probably afraid of him. He suspected that Howell didn't even like him, but that was okay. They paid him well for doing what he enjoyed, and he did these things with a merciless dependability.

Marion stared at the woman. She crossed and recrossed her arms until she disappeared behind the fryer, frantic to escape his gaze. He shifted his stare to the parking lot. A fly droned past his ear. It was a black desert fly, fat with juice and thorny with coarse hair, kicking off green highlights in the cheesy fluorescent lights. It buzzed low over the table in an S-shaped course, swung slowly around, and landed in a sprinkle of sugar. Marion slapped it. He waited, holding his hand in place, feeling for movement. When Marion raised his hand, the fly oozed sideways, legs kicking, trying to walk. Marion watched it. The best it could do was drive itself in a pathetic circle. Marion examined his hand. A smear of fly goo and a single black leg streaked his third finger. He touched his tongue to the smear and tasted sugar. He watched the fly push itself in the circle. Gently, he held it in place with his left index finger, and used his right index fingernail to break away another leg. He ate it. Hmm. One by one, he broke away the fly's legs and ate them. One wing was damaged, but the other beat furiously. He wondered what the fly was thinking.

Headlights flashed across the glass.

Marion glanced up to see Howell's beautiful Mercedes pull to a stop. It was a lovely car. Marion watched Howell get out of the car and come inside. Marion pushed the fly to the side as Howell took a seat opposite him.

'There's a woman in the back. I don't think she speaks English, though.'

'This won't take long.'

Howell spoke softly, getting down to business. He placed a slip of yellow paper on the table in front of Marion.

'Talley lives here. It's a condo. I don't have anything about what the place is like or if there's security or anything like that.'

'It doesn't matter.'

'Here's the drill: We have to own this guy – that's straight from the top – and we don't have a lot of time to mess around. I need you to find something we can use to twist him.'

Marion put the address away. He had done this kind of thing before, and knew what was needed. He would look for weakness. Everyone held their weakness close. He would copy bank account numbers; he would search for pornography and drugs, old love letters and sex toys, prescription medications and computer files. Maybe a lab report from a personal physician describing heart disease or phone records to another man's wife. It could be anything. There was always something.

'Is he there now?'

'Don't you listen to the news?'

Marion shook his head.

'He's not home, but I can't tell you when he will or won't get back there. So be ready for that.'

'What if he walks in on me?'

Howell averted his eyes, reached a decision, then looked back.

'If he's got you, kill him.'

'Okay.'

'Listen, we don't want him dead. We want to control him. We need to use him. But if you're caught, well, fuck it. Cap his ass.'

'What about later? After he's used?'

'That's up to Palm Springs.'

Marion accepted that. Sometimes they were kept alive because they could be used over and over, but most times he was allowed to finish the job. The finishing was his favorite part.

Howell said, 'You have my pager number and my cell?'

'Yes.'

'Okay. Page me when you're done. Whether you find something or not, keep me in the loop.'

'What if there's nothing in his home?'

'Then we'll hit his office. That'll be harder. He's the chief of police.'

Howell got up without another word.

Marion watched the beautiful Mercedes slide away into the deepening twilight, then looked back at the fly. Its legless body lay on its side, still. Marion touched it. The remaining wing fluttered.

Marion said, 'Poor fly.'

Marion carefully pulled out the remaining wing, then left to do his job.

# CHAPTER 8

Friday, 7:40 P.M.

TALLEY

The helicopters over York Estates switched on their lights to become brilliant stars. Talley didn't like losing the sun. The creeping darkness changed the psychology of hostage takers and police officers alike. Subjects felt safer in the dark, hidden and more powerful, the night allowing them fantasies of escape. Perimeter guards knew this, so their stress level would rise as their efficiency decayed. Night laid the foundation for overreaction and death.

Talley stood by his car, sipping Diet Coke as his officers reported. Rooney's employer, who believed that he could identify the unknown subject, had been located and was inbound; Walter Smith's wife had not yet been found; Rooney's parole officer from the Ant Farm had been identified but was in transit to Las Vegas for the weekend and could not be reached; ten large pizzas (half veggie, half meat) had just been delivered from Domino's, but someone had forgotten napkins. Information was coming in so fast that Talley began to lose track, and it would come faster. He cursed that the Sheriffs hadn't yet arrived.

Barry Peters and Earl Robb trotted up the street from their radio car. Robb was carrying his Maglite.

'We're set with the phone company, Chief. PacBell shows six hard lines into the house, four of them listed, two unlisted. They blocked all six in and out like you wanted. No one else can call in on those numbers, and the only number they can reach calling out is your cell.'

Talley felt a dull relief; now he didn't have to worry that some asshole would get the Smiths' number and convince Rooney to murder his hostages.

'Good, Earl. Did we get more bodies from the Highway Patrol?'

'Four more CHiPs and two cars from Santa Clarita.'

'Put them on the perimeter. Have Jorgenson do it, because he knows what I told Rooney.'

'Yes, sir.'

Robb trotted away as Peters turned on his Maglite, lighting two floor plan sketches that had been made on typing paper.

'I worked these out with the neighbors, Chief. This is the upstairs, this is the downstairs.'

Talley grunted. They weren't bad, but he wasn't confident that they were accurate; details like window placement and closet location could be critical if a forced entry was required. Talley asked about architectural drawings.

'These are the best I could do; there wasn't anything at the building commission.'

'There should be. This is a planned community. Every house plan in the development should be on file.'

Peters looked upset and embarrassed.

'I'm sorry, Chief. I called both the Antelope Valley and Santa Clarita building commissions, but they don't have anything, either. You want me to try something else?'

'The Sheriffs are going to need those plans, Barry. Get hold of someone from the mayor's office or one of the council people. Sarah has their home and work numbers. Tell them we need access to the permit office right away. Pull the permits you find and check the contractors. Somebody had to keep a set of file plans.'

As Peters hustled away, Larry Anders's car rolled around the corner and pulled to a stop beside Talley. A slim, nervous man climbed from the passenger side.

'Chief, this is Brad Dill, Rooney's employer.'

'Thanks for coming, Mr. Dill.'

'Okay.'

Talley knew that Dill owned a small cement-contracting business based in Lancaster. Dill had weathered skin from working in the sun and small eyes that kept glancing somewhere else. He had trouble maintaining eye contact.

'You know what's going on here, Mr. Dill?'

Dill glanced up the street past Talley, then inspected the ground. Nervous.

'Okay, the officer told me. I just want to say I didn't know anything about this. I didn't know what they were going to do.'

Talley thought that Dill probably had a criminal record.

'Mr. Dill, those two didn't know what they were going to do until they did it. Don't worry about it. You're here because you've worked with them and I'm hoping you can help me understand them. You see?'

'Okay. Sure. I've known Dennis for almost two years now, Kevin a little less.'

'Before we get into that, I want you to identify these guys. Officer Anders says you also know the third subject?'

'Okay. Sure. That would be Mars.'

'Let's look at the pictures. Larry, do you have them?'

Anders returned to the car and brought back the two 8 × 10 prints that had been made from the security tape. He had to return to his car a second time for his Maglite. Soon they would have to move into one of the houses. Talley wondered if Mrs. Pena would let them use hers.

'Okay, Mr. Dill. Let's take a look. Can you identify these people?'

The first picture showed a slightly fuzzy Kevin Rooney by the front door; Dennis and the third man were clearly visible in the second print. Talley was pleased with the prints. Anders had done a good job.

'Okay. Sure. That's Kevin, he's Dennis's kid brother.

And that one is Dennis. He just come back from the Ant Farm.'

'And you know the third man?'

'That would be Mars Krupchek. He come on the job about a month ago. No, wait, not quite four weeks, I guess. Him, I don't know so well.'

Anders nodded along with Dill, confirming what he had heard earlier.

'I called Krupchek in to Sarah on the drive, Chief. She's running his name through DMV and the NCIC.'

Talley questioned Dill about how Dennis behaved on the job. Dill described a temperamental personality with a penchant for overstatement and drama. Talley grew convinced that his original impression was correct: Rooney was an aggressive narcissist with esteem problems. Kevin, on the other hand, showed evidence of concern for others; where Dennis would show up for work late and expend little effort on the job, Kevin showed up on time and was willing to help others; he was a passive personality who would take his cues from the stronger personalities in his sphere of influence. He would never drive an action, but would instead react to whatever was presented to him.

Talley paused to consider if he was missing an obvious avenue of questioning. He took the Maglite from Anders to look at the photograph of Kevin, then decided to move on to Mars Krupchek. He had been concerned about Mars since he had seen the unknown subject lean over the counter to watch Junior Kim die. Talley noticed something on the 8 × 10 of Mars that he hadn't seen in the security tape. A tattoo on the back of Mars's head that read: BURN IT.

'What can you tell me about Krupchek?'

'Not so much. He showed up one day looking for work when I needed a guy. He was well-spoken and polite; he's big and strong, you know, so I gave him a try.'

'Did he know the Rooneys before he came on the job?'

'No, I know that for a fact. I introduced them. You know, Mars this is Dennis, Dennis this is Mars. Like that. Mars just kinda stays by himself except for when he's with Dennis.'

Talley pointed out the tattoo.

'What's this mean, "Burn it"?'

'I dunno. It's just a tattoo.'

Talley glanced at Anders.

'Did you put out the tattoo as an identifier?'

'Yes, sir.'

Identities on the NCIC computer could be cross-checked by permanent identifiers like tattoos and scars. Talley turned back to Brad Dill.

'You know what he did before this?'

'No, sir. Nope.'

'Know where he's from?'

'He doesn't talk so much. You ask him, he doesn't say so much.'

'How does he get along with the other men?'

'Well enough, I guess. He never had much to do with anyone until Dennis came back. That was only a week or so ago. Before Dennis came back, he would just stay by himself and watch everyone else.'

'What do you mean, watch everyone else?'

'I don't know if I'm saying it right. When the guys go on a break, he doesn't sit with'm. He sits off by himself and watches them, kinda like he was keeping an eye on them. No, wait, that's not right. It was more like he's watching TV. Does that make sense? Sometimes it'd make me think he'd fallen asleep the way he'd do that. He was just, I dunno, staring.'

Talley didn't like what he was hearing about Krupchek, but he also didn't know what to make of it.

'Has he ever demonstrated violence or aggression toward the other men?'

'He just sits there.'

Talley handed the photograph back to Anders. Mars

Krupchek might be retarded or suffer from some other mental impairment, but Talley didn't know. He had no sense of who Mars Krupchek was, what he was capable of, or how he might act. This left Talley feeling anxious and wary. The unknown could kill you, and was often worse than you imagined.

'Mr. Dill, do you have an address for Krupchek?'

Dill pulled a tiny address book from his back pocket and read off an address and phone number. Anders copied them.

Talley thanked Brad Dill for his help, told him that Anders would bring him home, then took Anders aside out of earshot.

'Check that Krupchek's address matches with the billing address listed with the phone. If it does, call the Palmdale City Attorney's office and ask for a telephonic search warrant, then head to his residence. After you've got the warrant, go in and see what you find. Take someone with you.'

As Anders and Dill drove away, Talley tried to recall the things that he still needed to do. Mrs. Smith had to be found, his officers had to be fed, and he wanted to check the perimeter positions of the newly arrived Highway Patrol officers to make sure that Jorgenson hadn't placed them too close to the house. When he realized that he would have to call Rooney again soon, a swell of panic threatened to overwhelm him. He would have to call Rooney every hour throughout the night; interrupt his sleep, break down his resistance, wear him down. A hostage barricade was a war of attrition and nerves. Talley didn't know that his own nerves were enough to see it through.

Metzger's voice cut through his radio.

'Chief, Metzger.'

'Go, Leigh.'

'The Sheriffs are inbound. Ten minutes out.'

Talley slumped against his car and closed his eyes. Thank God.


DENNIS

Dennis tried not to look at Mars after his conversation with Talley, but he couldn't help himself. He thought about what Kevin had told him, about Mars wanting to shoot that cop who had come to the door, about Mars lying that the cop had pulled his weapon and Mars firing first. Maybe Talley had something; maybe Dennis could beat the rap if it was Mars who shot the officer, and not him. If Kevin backed him up, they might be able to cut a deal with the prosecutor for their testimony against Mars. Dennis felt a desperate hope, but then he remembered the money. If he cut a deal, he had to give up the money. He shoved the phone aside and turned back to the others. He wasn't ready to give up the cash.

Kevin looked at him anxiously.

'Are they giving us the helicopter?'

'No. We gotta find another way out of here. Let's start looking.'

The girl and her fat brother were still kneeling beside their father. She started on him right away.

'There's nothing to look for. You've got to do something to help my father.'

She still held the washcloth to her father's head, but now the ice was melted and the cloth was soaked. Dennis felt a flash of annoyance.

'Shut up, all right? I've got a situation here, in case you haven't noticed.'

Her face worked harder.

'All you're doing is watching yourself on TV. You hurt him. Look at him. He needs a doctor.'

'Shut up.'

'It's been hours!'

116

'Put more ice in the cloth.'

'Ice doesn't help!'

The fat boy started crying.

'He's in a coma!'

The girl surprised him. She lurched to her feet with the abrupt fury of a jack-in-the-box and stomped toward the door.

'I'm getting a doctor!'

Dennis felt outside of himself, as if the weight of the cops and his being trapped in this house were all suddenly real where they hadn't been before. He caught her in two steps, slapping her just the way his old man used to lay out the old lady, that shrill bitch. He caught the girl square on the side of the face with the weight of his hand, knocked her flat fucking down to the floor. The fat boy shouted her name and charged, pummeling Dennis like an angry midget. Dennis dug his fingers into the soft meat on the back of the boy's neck, and the fat boy squealed. Then Kevin was shoving him away.

'STOP IT!'

Kevin pushed the fat boy down with his sister, placing himself between them and Dennis.

'Just stop it, Dennis. Please!'

Dennis was in a blood fury. He wanted to beat Kevin down, to smash his face and kick him into a pulp. He wanted to beat the fat boy and the girl, then throw the cash in the Jaguar and crash out of the garage and shoot it out with the cops all the way down to Mexico.

Mars was staring at him, his face a shadow, his eyes tiny glints of strange light like ferrets peering from caves.

Dennis shouted, '*What?*'

Mars made the quiet smile and shook his head.

Dennis stepped back, breathing hard. Everything was coming apart. Dennis looked back at the television, half expecting to see the cops storming the house, but the scene outside was exactly as it had been minutes before. The girl was holding her face in her hands. The fat boy was glaring with hate-filled eyes like he wanted to cut Dennis's throat. Their father was breathing noisily through his nose. The pressure was making him crazy.

Dennis said, 'We gotta do something with them. I can't deal with this shit.'

Mars lumbered to his feet, large and gross.

'We should tie them up so we don't have to worry about them. We should have done that anyway.'

Dennis hooked his head toward the girl, speaking to Kevin.

'Mars is right. We can't leave these assholes running around like this, getting in the way. Find something to tie'm up with, and take them upstairs.'

'What do I use to tie them?'

'Look in the garage. Look in the kitchen. Mars, you find something, okay? You know what we need. This turd doesn't know anything.'

Mars disappeared toward the garage. Kevin took the girl's arm as if he was afraid that she would hit him, but she stood without resisting, her face working and the tears coming harder.

'What about my father? You can't just leave him like this.'

Her father was cold to the touch; every few seconds a tremor rippled through his body. Dennis took his pulse like he knew what he was doing, but he couldn't tell a goddamned thing. He didn't like how the man looked, but didn't say anything about it because there was nothing to say.

'We'll put him on the couch. That way he'll be more comfortable.'

'He needs a doctor.'

'He's just sleeping. You take a head shot, you gotta sleep it off, is all. My old man used to beat me worse than this.'

Dennis had Kevin help lift her father onto the couch. When Mars returned, Dennis told them to take the kids upstairs. He was tired of thinking about them. He was tired of thinking about everything except the money. He needed a way out.


JENNIFER

Mars opened the door to her room, then stepped aside so that she and Kevin could enter. He had come back from the garage with extension cords, duct tape, a hammer and nails. He gave two extension cords to Kevin.

'Put her in here. Tie her to the chair, and tie her *tight*. Tie her feet. I'll take care of the windows and the door when I finish with the boy.'

Mars looked at her with unfocused eyes, as if he were waking from a deep sleep and she was the memory of a dream.

'I'll check how you tie her when I come back.'

Mars pulled Thomas away as Kevin brought her into the room. The lights were on because she never turned them off; she fell asleep with them on, either talking on the phone or watching TV, and woke with them on, and never thought to turn them off when she left to start her day. The shades had been pulled and the phone was on the floor against the wall, its plug smashed so that it couldn't be used. Kevin dragged her desk chair into the middle of the floor. He avoided her eyes, nervous.

'Just let this happen and everything will be okay. You gotta pee or anything?'

She felt a flush of embarrassment. She had to use the bathroom so badly that she burned.

'It's in there.'

'Where? You got your own bathroom?'

'Uh-huh. It's right there.'

'Okay, come on.'

She didn't move.

'You can't come with me.'

He stood in the bathroom door, waiting.

'I'm not going to leave you alone.'

'I'm not going to the bathroom in front of you.'

'Would you rather pee on yourself?'

'I'm not letting you watch. I don't have guns or anything in there, if that's what you're worried about.'

He seemed annoyed, but she didn't care. He stepped into the bathroom to look around, then came back.

'Okay, I won't go in with you, but you can't close the door. I'll stand over here. That way I can't see you.'

'But you'll hear.'

'Look, piss or don't piss. I don't care. If you're not going to go, put your ass in the chair before Mars comes back.'

Jennifer had to pee so badly that she decided to go. She tried to pee quietly, but it seemed louder than ever. When she was finished, she returned to her room too embarrassed to make eye contact.

'You're disgusting.'

'Whatever. Sit here and put your hands behind the chair.'

'I don't see why you can't just lock me in. It's not like I can go anywhere.'

'Either I'm going to tie you or Mars will tie you.'

She perched on the chair, tense and wary.

Kevin had two long black extension cords. She cringed when he touched her, but he didn't treat her roughly or twist her arms.

'I don't want to make this too tight, but I got to tie you. Mars is going to check.'

His voice held a regret that surprised her. She knew that Kevin was scared, but now she wondered if he felt embarrassed at what they were doing. Maybe he even had a conscience. He finished with her wrists, then moved around in front of her to tie her ankles to the legs of the chair. She watched him, thinking that if there was a friend to be found among them it was him.

'Kevin?'

'What?'

She kept her voice soft, scared that Mars would hear.

'You're caught in this just like me.'

His face darkened.

'I've heard the three of you talking. You're the only one who seems to know that you're making it worse by being here. Dennis doesn't get that.'

'Don't talk about Dennis.'

'Why do you go along with him?'

'Things just happen, is all. Don't talk about it.'

'My father needs a doctor.'

'He's just knocked out. I've been knocked out.'

'You know it's worse than that. Think about what you're doing, Kevin, *please*. Make Dennis see. If my father dies they'll charge you with his murder, too. You know that.'

'There's nothing I can do.'

'You knew better than to rob that minimart, didn't you? I'll bet you tried to talk Dennis out of it, but he wouldn't listen and now you're all trapped in here and wanted for murder.'

He kept his face down, pulling at the extension cords.

'I'll bet that's true. You knew it was wrong, and it was. Now you know this is wrong, too. My daddy needs a doctor, but Dennis is just being stubborn. If you keep following Dennis and Mars, the police will kill you all.'

Kevin leaned back on his heels. He seemed tired, as if he had been worrying the problem for so long without solution that the worrying had worn him out. He shook his head.

'I'm sorry.'

A shadow moved behind Kevin, catching Jennifer's eye. Mars stood in the door, staring at them, his face blank. She didn't know how long he had been there, or what he had heard.

Mars didn't look at Kevin; he was staring at her.

'Never be sorry.'

Kevin stood so quickly that he almost fell.

'I tied her ankles too tight. I had to tie them again.'

Mars went to the windows. He hammered heavy nails into the sills so that the windows wouldn't open, then came back to stand in front of her. He stood very close, towering over her in a way that made him seem to reach the ceiling. He squatted between her legs, then tugged at the bindings on her ankles. The cord cut into her skin.

'This isn't tight enough. You tied her like a pussy.'

Mars wrapped the cord more tightly, then did the same at her wrists. The wire cut into her flesh so hard that she had to bite her tongue, but she was too scared to complain. He tore a strip of wide gray duct tape off the roll. He pressed it hard over her mouth.

Kevin worried his hands, fidgeting, clearly frightened of Mars.

'Make sure she can breathe, Mars. Don't put it so tight.'

Mars ran his fingers hard over the tape. She was so creeped out at his touch that she wanted to scream.

'Go downstairs, Kevin.'

Kevin hesitated at the door. Mars still knelt in front of her, pushing at the tape as if he wanted to work it into her pores. Pushing and pushing. Rhythmic. Pushing. Jennifer thought she might faint.

Kevin said, 'Aren't you coming?'

'I'll be along. Go.'

Jennifer looked at Kevin, pleading with him not to leave her alone with Mars.

Kevin left.

When she finally looked at Mars again, he was watching her. Mars brought his face level with hers, then leaned forward. She flinched, thinking he was going to kiss her, but he didn't. He didn't move for the longest time, staring first into her left eye, then into her right. He leaned closer, and sniffed. He was smelling her.

Mars straightened.

'I want to show you something.'

He pulled off his shirt, revealing a flabby body as pasty as an unwashed bedsheet. Tattooed across his chest in flowing script was:

*A Mother's Son.*

'You see? It cost two hundred forty dollars. That's how much I love my mom.'

Looking at him grossed her out. His chest and belly were specked with small gray knots as if he were diseased. She thought they might be warts.

She suddenly felt the weight of his eyes and glanced up to see him watching her. She realized that he knew she had been staring at the lumps. He touched one of them, a hard gray knot, then another, and the corner of his mouth curled into a smile that was almost too small to see.

'My mom burned me with cigarettes.'

Jennifer felt sick. They weren't lumps or warts; they were scars.

Mars pulled on his shirt, then leaned close, and this time she was certain that he would touch her. Her heart pounded. She wanted to turn away, but she couldn't.

He placed his hand on her shoulder.

Jennifer jerked against her binds, twisting her head, arching her back, feeling the bite of the extension cords in her wrists and ankles as she tried to scream through the tape.

Mars squeezed her shoulder once, firmly, as if he were testing the bone beneath her flesh, and then he drew away.

Mars made the little smile again, then went to the door. He paused there, staring at her with eyes so empty that she filled them with nightmares. He turned off the lights, stepped out, then pulled the door closed. The sound of his hammer was as loud as thunder, but not so loud as her fearful heart.

*

Dennis was at the window, watching the police, when he heard the pitch of the helicopters change. That was the first thing, the helicopters repositioning themselves. Then one of the patrol cars out front fired up. The lead car swung around in a tight arc, roaring away as a new Highway Patrol car arrived. He couldn't tell if Talley was still outside or not. The cops were up to something, which made Dennis feel queasy and scared. They would have to leave soon or they might not be able to leave at all.

Mars settled onto the couch by Walter Smith. He put his hand on Smith's head as if he was stroking the soft fur between a dog's ears.

'They didn't give you the helicopter because they don't believe you're serious.'

Dennis paced away from the window, irritated. He didn't like Mars's smug I-know-something-that-you-don't smile. Mars had egged him on about robbing the mini-mart, and Mars had shot the cop at the front door.

'You don't know what you're talking about. They've got rules about this stuff. Fuck them anyway. I never thought we'd get a helicopter. I just thought it would be worth a try.'

Mars stroked Smith's head, running his fingers slowly over the man's scalp as if he was probing the contours of his skull. Dennis thought it was weird.

'You don't see the big picture, Dennis.'

'You want a picture, Mars? Here it is: We've gotta find a way out of here with that cash.'

Mars patted Smith's head.

'Our way out is right here. You don't understand the power we have.'

'The hostages? Jesus, they're *all* we have. If we didn't have these people, the cops would be all over us.'

When Mars looked up again, Dennis thought his eyes were brighter, and somehow now watchful.

'What we have is the fear they feel. Their fear gives us power. The police will only take us seriously if they're scared we'll kill these people. It isn't the people that we have to trade, Dennis. It's their death.'

Dennis thought he was kidding.

'Okay, dude. Mars, you're creeping me out.'

'The police have no reason to deal with us unless they take us seriously. All they have to do is wait until we get tired, and then we'll give up. They know that, Dennis. They're counting on it.'

Dennis felt his chest expand against a tight pressure that filled the room. Mars continued to watch him, his eyes now focused into hard, dark beads. Dennis had the vague feeling that somehow the power between them was shifting, that Mars was leading him somewhere and waiting to see if Dennis would follow.

'So how do we convince them?'

'Tell them we're going to let the fat boy go as a sign of good faith.'

Dennis didn't move. He could see Kevin from the corner of his eye, and knew that Kevin was feeling the same awful pressure.

'We send the fat boy out the front door. We don't go with him, we just open it and tell him to go. He just has to walk across the yard here and out to the cars, and he'll be fine. Your pal, Talley, he'll probably call the kid over, saying something like, "C'mon, son, everything is fine." '

Dennis's back felt wet and cold.

'We wait until he's about halfway across the yard, then we shoot him.'

Dennis heard his own heartbeat. He heard his breath flow across his teeth, a faraway hiss.

Mars spread his hands at the simple beauty of it.

'Then they'll know we mean business, and we'll have something to trade.'

125

Dennis tried to tell himself that Mars was kidding, but he knew that Mars was serious. Mars meant every word.

'Mars. We couldn't do something like that.'

Mars looked curious.

'I could. I'll do it, if you want.'

Dennis didn't know what to say. Overhead, the helicopters beat louder. He went to the shutters and pretended to look out, but the truth was that he couldn't look at Mars any longer. Mars had scared him.

'I don't think so, dude.'

'You don't?'

'No. We couldn't do that.'

The bright intensity in Mars's eyes faded like a candle losing its flame, and Mars shrugged. Dennis felt relieved. He told them to watch out for the cops, then he once more walked through the house. He went into every downstairs room around the perimeter of the house, checking each window to see if he could use it to sneak out, but all of the windows were in plain view of the cops. Dennis knew that his time was running out. If he was going to get out, he had to do it soon, because more cops were on the way. He moved along the rear of the house, through the family room and into the garage. He hoped to find some kind of side door, but instead he came to a small utility bathroom at the end of a workshop off the garage. A sliding window with frosted glass was let into the wall above the sink. Dennis opened it, and saw the heavy leaves of an oleander bush, dark green and pointed, thick against the dusty screen. He pressed his face to the screen and peered out, but it was impossible to see very much in the growing darkness. The window was on the street side of the wall that enclosed the backyard, but was hidden by the oleander. If the oleander wasn't there the cops out front would be able to see him. Dennis pushed out the screen, taking care to do it quietly. He opened the window wider, crawled up onto the sink, and leaned out. He would never have done this in the daylight, but the darkness gave him confidence. The ground was four feet below. He worked his shoulders through the window. The row of oleanders followed the wall, but he couldn't tell how far. He was growing excited. He pushed himself back into the house, then turned around so that he could step through feet first, one leg and then another. He lowered himself to the ground. He was outside the house.

Dennis crouched on the ground beneath the oleander, his back pressed to the high stucco wall, listening. He could hear the police radios from the cars parked at the front of the house. He caught tiny glimpses of the two cars through the leaves, glinting in the streetlight. He couldn't see the cops, but he knew they would be watching the front of the house, not the row of shrubs along the side wall. Dennis lay down at the base of the wall and inched along its length. The oleanders were thicker in some places and thinner in others, but the police didn't see him. He came to the end of the wall and saw that the oleanders continued into the neighbor's front yard. Dennis grew more excited. They could bag the cash, drag it along behind the oleanders, then slip away while the cops were watching the house, right under their noses!

Dennis worked his way back to the window and climbed into the house. Dennis was pumped! He was going to beat this thing! He was going to beat Talley, beat the murder rap, and cruise south to TJ in style.

He ran back to the office to tell Kevin and Mars that he had found the way out.


MARION CLEWES

The planet Venus hung low in the blackening western sky, racing toward the ridge of mountains and the edge of Talley's roof. The stars were not yet out, but here in the high desert, away from the city, the sky would soon be washed with lights.

Talley's condominium was one of forty-eight stucco and stained-wood units spread over four buildings arranged like the letter H. Mature eucalyptus and podocarpus trees shouldered over the buildings like drunks leaning over a rail. Marion guessed that the condos had at one time been apartments, then converted and sold. Each unit had a small fenced patio at ground level, and centered between the four buildings was a very nice pool; small, unprotected parking lots were on either side of each building for the residents. It seemed like a pleasant place to live.

Marion walked through the grounds, hearing music and voices. Cars were turning into the parking lots, men and women still arriving from work; an older woman was methodically swimming laps, the pool's lone occupant; charcoal grills were smoking on several of the patios, filling the air with the smells of burning flesh.

Marion circled the building with Talley's unit. Because the buildings were of older construction (Marion guessed they had been built in the seventies), the gas meters, electric meters, and junction boxes for both telephones and cable TV were clustered together at an out-of-the-way spot opposite the parking lots. Any individual security systems would be junctioned with the telephone lines. Marion was pleased to see that the building had no alarms. Marion was neither surprised nor shocked; being a sleepy small town so far from LA, the greatest security the condo association might buy would be having a rent-a-cop cruise the parking lots every hour. If that.

Marion found Talley's unit, let himself through the gate to the front door. He clenched his jaw so as not to laugh; the patio and door were hidden by a six-foot privacy fence. He couldn't have asked for anything easier. He rang the bell twice, then knocked, already knowing that no one was home; the house was dark. He pulled on latex gloves, took out his pry bar and pick, then set to work. Four minutes later, the deadbolt slipped. Eighty seconds after that, he let himself in.

'Hello?'

He didn't expect an answer, and none came. Marion shut the door behind him, but did not lock it.

The kitchen was to the left, a small dining room to the right. Sliding glass doors offered a view of the patio. Directly ahead was a large living room with a fireplace. Marion looked for a desk or work space, but saw none. He unlatched the glass doors, then crossed the living room to open the largest window. He would relock everything if he left at his leisure, but for now he arranged fast exits. Howell did not want Talley dead, so Marion would try not to kill him even if Talley surprised him.

Marion climbed steep stairs to a second-floor landing with doors leading to a bathroom and two other rooms, the room to his right the master bedroom. He turned on the light. Marion expected to search every closet and drawer in the house for something that could be used as leverage, but there it was as soon as he entered, right there, waiting. It happened that way, sometimes.

A desk rested against the far wall, scattered with papers and bills and receipts, but that isn't what caught Marion's eye. Five photographs waited at the back of the desk, Talley with a woman and girl, the woman and Talley always the same, the girl at different ages.

Marion kneeled, brought the frame to his face.

A woman. A girl.

A wife. A daughter.

Marion considered the possibilities.

# CHAPTER 9

Friday, 8:06 P.M.

TALLEY

The Los Angeles County Sheriff's Department Crisis Response Team came around the corner like a military convoy. A plain Sheriff's sedan led the file, followed by a bulky Mobile Command Post vehicle that looked like a bread truck on steroids. The Sheriffs wouldn't need Mrs. Peña's home; the van contained its own power generator, a bathroom, uplinks for the Intelligence Officer's computers, and a communications center for command and control coordination. It also had a Mr. Coffee. The Sheriff's SWAT team followed in two large GMC Suburbans with a second van containing their weapons and support gear. As the convoy stopped, the SWAT cops unassed, already geared out in dark green tactical uniforms. They hustled to the second van, where a senior sergeant-supervisor passed out radios and firearms. Four radio cars followed the tactical vehicles with uniformed deputies who clustered around their own sergeant-supervisor. Talley heard a change in the helicopters' rotor turbulence as they repositioned to broadcast the Sheriffs' arrival. If Rooney was watching television, his stress level would soar. During periods like this the possibility of the subject panicking and taking action increased. Talley hurried to the lead car.

A tall, slender African-American officer climbed out from behind the wheel as a blond officer with thinning hair climbed from the passenger side.

Talley put out his hand.

'Jeff Talley. I'm the chief here. Are you the team commander?'

The tall man flashed a relaxed smile.

'Will Maddox. I'll be the primary negotiator. This is Chuck Ellison, my secondary. The commander would be Captain Martin. She's back in the van.'

As Talley shook their hands, Ellison winked.

'She likes to ride in the van instead of with us negotiators. Lots of pretty lights in there.'

'Chuck.'

Ellison looked innocent.

'Something I said?'

The energy on the street changed dramatically; Talley had felt that he was hanging from a ledge by his fingers, but now an organized military weight was settling over York Estates. A brilliant pool of white light swept over them on its way along the convoy. All three of them held up their hands to cut the glare. The different teams breaking up into their components with well-rehearsed efficency felt comforting. Talley no longer felt alone. In a matter of minutes, this man Will Maddox would take the responsibility of other lives from his shoulders.

Talley said, 'Mr. Maddox, I am damned glad to see you here.'

'Will. Mr. Maddox is my wife.'

Ellison laughed loudly.

Maddox smiled absently at the lame joke, glancing at the mouth of the cul-de-sac a half-block away.

'The barricade up there?'

'Up at the end. I've got two men directly out front, three men spread across the property on either side, and another three beyond the back wall on Flanders Road. We have two people on each entrance here into York and three with the media. We could use more with the media right away before they start leaking through the development.'

'You can brief the Captain on those kinds of things, but there are a couple of points that I need to hit before we get into all that.'

'Go.'

Talley walked with them back toward the control van to find the Captain. He knew from his own experience that Maddox and Ellison would want a virtual replay of his conversations with Rooney.

'It's you who's had direct contact with the subjects?'

'Yes. Only me.'

'Okay. Are the innocents under an immediate threat?'

'I don't believe so. The last contact I had with Rooney was about twenty minutes ago. Way I left it, he's in there thinking that he has outs both for Kim's murder and the attempt on the officer. You know about that?'

While inbound, the Sheriffs had received a radio briefing on the events leading up to the barricade situation. Maddox confirmed that they knew the bare bones.

'Okay. Turns out Kim had a gun, and more than one of the subjects besides Rooney fired upon the officer. I left him thinking that a sharp lawyer could cut a deal on both counts.'

'Has he made any demands?'

Talley told him about Rooney demanding that the perimeter be pulled back and the deal that they'd made, the hostage names for the pullback. Getting the first concession was often the most difficult, and how it was gotten could set the tone for everything that was to follow.

Maddox walked with his hands in his pockets, his expression knowing and thoughtful.

'Good job, Chief. Sounds like we're in pretty good shape. You used to be with LAPD SWAT, weren't you?'

Talley looked more closely at Maddox.

'That's right. Have we met?'

'I was on LAPD as a uniform before I went with the Sheriffs, which put us there about the same time. When we got the call here today, your name rang a bell. Talley. You did the nursery school.'

Talley felt uncomfortable whenever someone mentioned the nursery school.

'That was a long time ago.'

'That had to be something. I don't think I would've had the balls.'

'It wasn't balls. I just couldn't think of anything else.'

On a bright spring morning in the Fairfax area of Los Angeles, a lone gunman invaded a Jewish day-care center, taking an adult female teacher and three toddlers hostage. When Talley arrived, he found the gunman confused, incoherent, and rapidly dissociating. Fearing that the subject had suffered a psychotic break and the children were in imminent danger, Talley offered himself in trade for the children; this was against direct orders from his crisis team captain and in violation of LAPD policy. Talley approached the day-care center unarmed and unprotected, surrendering himself to the gunman, who simultaneously released the children. As the gunman stood in the door with one arm hooked around Talley's neck and a 9mm Smith & Wesson pistol pressed to Talley's head, Talley's best friend during those days, Neal Craimont, dropped the subject with a sixty-yard cortical brain shot, the 5.56mm hypervelocity bullet passing only four inches to the left of Talley's own brain stem. The newspapers had made Talley out to be a hero, but Talley had considered the events of that morning a failure. He had been the primary negotiator, and for a negotiator, it is always a failure when someone dies. Success only comes with life.

Maddox seemed to sense Talley's discomfort. He dropped the subject.

When they reached the rear of the command van, a woman wearing a green tactical uniform stepped from among a knot of sergeants to meet them. She had a cut jaw, smart black eyes, and short blond hair.

'Is this Chief Talley?'

Maddox nodded.

'This is him.'

She put out her hand. Now closer, Talley saw the captain's insignia on her collar. She had a tough grip.

'Laura Martin. Captain. I'm the field commander in charge of the crisis response team.'

Where Maddox and Ellison were relaxed and loose, Martin was as taut as a power cable, her manner clipped and humorless.

'I'm glad you've met our negotiators. Sergeant Maddox will take over as the primary.'

'We were just discussing that, Captain. I think we're in pretty good shape with that. The subjects seem calm.'

Martin keyed the radio transceiver strapped to her harness and called for a communications check of her supervisors in five minutes, then looked back at Talley.

'Do you have a perimeter in place around the house?'

'Yes, ma'am.'

'How many men?'

'Eleven. A mix of my people and the Highway Patrol. I put the men in close, then pulled them back to get things going with Rooney, so you'll have to be careful with that.'

As Talley spoke, Martin didn't seem to be paying attention. She glanced both ways along the street, leading Talley to think that she was measuring the scene and more than likely sizing up his officers. He found himself irritated. The command van was being repositioned farther down the block over an access point to the underground power and phone lines that ran under the streets. If they wanted to tap into the phone lines that ran to the house, they could do it from there. They could also tap power for the van. Talley had already called PacBell and the Department of Water and Power to the scene.

'I'll get my supervisors together so you can brief everyone at once. I want to rotate my tactical people into the perimeter as soon as we've stabilized the situation.'

Talley felt another flash of irritation; it was clear that the scene was stable. He suggested that Martin assemble her supervisors in Mrs. Peña's home, but Martin thought that would take too much time. As she called her people together under a streetlight, Talley radioed Metzger for copies of the floor plan. He passed them out as everyone assembled, and gave a fast overview of his conversations with Rooney, describing what he knew of the house and the people within it.

Martin stood next to him, arms crossed tightly, squinting at him with what Talley began to feel was a critical suspicion.

'Have you cut the power and phones?'

'We blocked the phones. I didn't see any reason to cut the power until we knew for sure what we were dealing with.'

Martin told her intelligence officer, a sergeant named Rojas, to have someone from the utility companies standing by if they needed to pull the plug.

Metzger pointed up the street.

'They're already standing by. See that guy in the Duke cap? That's him.'

The tactical team supervisor, a veteran sergeant named Carl Hicks, studied the floor plan sketches, and seemed irritated when Talley couldn't produce actual city floor plans.

'Do we know where they're keeping the hostages?'

'No.'

'How about the location of the subjects?'

'The room immediately to our right of the front door is the father's office. Rooney is usually in there when he talks to me, but I can't say if he sticks. I know he moves through the house to keep an eye on the perimeter, but he's buttoned up pretty well. The shades are down over every window except the French doors overlooking the pool in back. They don't have drapes back there, but he's got the lights off.'

Hicks frowned at Martin.

'Sucks for us, but what can you do? We might be able to get heat images.'

If they had to breach the house, it was safer for everyone if the breaching team knew the location of everyone in the environment.

Maddox tipped his chin toward Talley.

'The Chief here worked Rooney into admitting that all three perps are inside. I might be able to work him for the locations.'

Martin didn't look impressed with that.

'Hicks, float two men around the perimeter to find out exactly what we're dealing with here. Let's make sure this place is secure.'

Talley said, 'Captain, be advised that he's hinky about the perimeter. I pulled back the line to start the negotiation. That was part of the deal.'

Martin stepped away to stare up the street. Talley couldn't tell what she might be looking at.

'I understand that, Chief. Thank you. Now, will you be ready to hand off the phone to Maddox and Ellison as soon as we're in place?'

'I'm ready right now.'

She clicked her tongue curtly, then glanced at Maddox.

'Sounds good, Maddox. The three of you should get into position at the front of the house.'

Maddox's face was tight. Talley thought he was probably irritated with her manner, also.

'I'd like to spend some time going over the Chief's prior conversations with these guys.'

Martin checked her watch, impatient.

'You can do that while we rotate into the perimeter; I want to get the show on the road. Chief Talley, I have seven minutes after the hour. Do I now have command of the scene?'

'Yes, ma'am. It's yours.'

Martin checked her watch again. Just to be sure.

136

'Then log it. I now have command and control. Sergeant Maddox, get into position. Sergeant Hicks, you're with me.'

Martin and Hicks trotted away into the milling SWAT officers.

Maddox stared after her for a moment, then looked at Talley.

'She's wound kinda tight.'

Talley nodded, but said nothing. He had thought that he would feel relieved when he turned over command of the scene.

He didn't.

THOMAS

Alone in his dark room, Thomas held his breath, better to hear past the changing whup-whup-whup of the helicopters. He feared that Mars might pretend to leave, then creep back to see if he was trying to get untied. Thomas knew every squeak in the upstairs hall because Jennifer liked to spy on him; one squeaky spot was right outside his door, the other about halfway to Jennifer's room. So he listened.

Nothing.

Thomas was spread-eagle on his lower bunk, face up, his wrists and ankles tied so tightly to the corner bedposts that his feet felt numb. After Mars had finished tying him, he stood by the bed, towering over him like some kind of retard with his slack jaw hanging open like one of those public-bathroom perverts his mother always warned him about every time he went to the mall. Then Mars had taped over his mouth. Thomas was SCARED; sweat gushed from him like he was a lawn sprinkler and he thought he was going to suffocate. He struggled and pulled at the wires that held him, straining to get free until he felt Mars's breath on his cheek. Then he couldn't move at all, like his mind and body had disconnected and all he could do was just lie there like a turtle waiting for a car to squash it flat.

Mars placed a hand on his chest, and now the breath went to his ear. Warm and moist. Then, a whisper.

'I will eat your heart.'

Thomas's body burned from the inside out, a kind of wet heat that grew hotter and hotter. He messed his pants.

Mars went to the door, shut the lights, and left, pulling the door closed. Thomas waited, counting slowly to one hundred. Then he set about working his way free.

Thomas was good at working his way free. He was also good at sneaking out of his house, which he had done almost every night this summer. He would sneak out after his parents had gone to bed to hook up with Duane Fergus, who lived in a big pink house on King John Place. Sometimes they threw eggs and wads of wet toilet paper at the cars passing on Flanders Road. When that got old, they would sneak across Flanders to a development that was still under construction where teenagers parked to make out. Duane Fergus (who was a year older and claimed to shave) once threw a rock at a brand-new Beemer because (he said) the lucky turd behind the wheel was getting 'road head.' They both shit a brick when the car roared to life, bathing them in its lights. They ran so hard back across Flanders that a monster 18-wheeler had almost turned them into blacktop pie.

Thomas had perfected the art of moving through his home without being seen because he had changed some of the camera angles. Just a bit, just a nudge, so that his mom and dad couldn't see *everything*. He knew that most people didn't live in houses where every room was watched by a closed-circuit television system. His father explained that they had such a system because he handled other people's financial records and someone might want to steal them. It was a big responsibility, his father had said, and so they had to protect those records as best they could. His father often warned both Thomas and Jennifer to be careful of suspicious characters, and to never discuss the alarms and cameras with their friends. His mother was fond of saying that she thought the whole mess was nonsense and just their father's big toy. Duane thought they were da bomb.

The wire holding his left wrist was slack.

When Mars was tying Thomas's right wrist to the post, Thomas had scrunched away just enough so that now the cord held a little bit of play. Now he worked harder at it, pulling the knots tighter but creating enough slack to touch the knot that held him to the post. The knot was *tight*. Thomas dug at it so hard that the pain in his fingertips brought tears, but then the knot loosened. He worked frantically, terrified that Mars or one of the others would throw open the door, but then the knot gave and his left hand was free. The tape hurt coming off his mouth worse than getting a cavity filled. He untied his right hand, then his feet, and then he was free. Like Duane said, you had to risk being street pizza if you wanted to see a guy getting road head.

Thomas stayed on the bed, listening.

Nothing.

*I know where Daddy has a gun.*

Thomas felt calm and certain in what he needed to do. He knew exactly what the cameras could see and what they couldn't. He wanted to go to his bathroom to clean himself, but knew he would be visible on the monitor if he did. He pulled off his pants, used his underwear to clean off the poo as best he could, then balled the underwear and pushed them under the bed. He slipped to the floor and crawled along the wall toward his closet, passing under his desk. Someone had ripped his phone out of the wall, leaving the plug in the socket but tearing free the wires. Turds.

In *The Lion, the Witch, and the Wardrobe*, the children

found a secret door at the rear of their wardrobe that let them escape the real world into the magical land of Narnia. Thomas had his own secret door at the back of his closet: an access hatch to the attic crawl space that ran beneath the steep pitch of the roof. It was his own private clubhouse (his and Duane's), through which he could move along the eaves to the other access hatches dotted around the house.

Thomas pulled open the hatch and wiggled into the crawl space, being careful not to bump the rafters with his head. The heat in the closed space of the attic enveloped him like a gas. He found the flashlight that he kept just inside the hatch, turned it on, then pulled the hatch closed. The crawl space in this part of the house was a long triangular tunnel that followed the back edge of the roof. Where windows were cut into the roof, the triangle became a low rectangle, forcing Thomas to crawl on his belly. He worked his way along until he came to a second access hatch, this one in Jennifer's closet. He listened until he grew satisfied that the turds weren't in her room, then he pushed it open, knocking over a tumble of shoes.

The closet was dark, its door closed.

He eased his way out over the shoes and through a rack of her dresses, then turned off his flashlight. He listened at the closet door, and again heard nothing. He eased open the door. The lights in Jennifer's room were off; that was good because he knew that most of her room could be seen on the monitors. He opened the door so slowly that it seemed to take forever to get it open enough for him to stick out his head. The room was lit by pale blue moonlight. He could see Jennifer bound to the chair near the front of the room, her back to him.

'Jen?'

She lurched in the chair and mumbled. He called to her, his voice low.

'I'm in your closet. Just relax, okay? If they're watching, they can see you on the monitors.'

She stopped struggling.

Thomas tried to remember what the camera saw of Jennifer's room. He and Duane sometimes went into the security room when his parents were away so that Duane could see her naked. He was pretty confident that if he crept out of the closet on his belly, then hugged the wall beneath the windows where the shadows were darkest, he could get pretty close to the chair. If he heard Mars or those other turds coming, he could haul ass back into the crawl space, then go back to his room or run for the garage.

'Jen, listen up, okay? I'm going to come over there.'

She shook her head wildly, mumbling frantically into the tape.

'Be *QUIET!* I can untie you.'

He pushed open the closet a few inches wider, then edged forward on his elbows into the shadows. As he passed her desk, he saw that her phone had also been torn from the plug. Turds.

Thomas worked his way around the perimeter of the room, and soon he was stretched out beside her bed, using deep shadows as cover. He was about four feet from her now, and could see that her mouth was taped. He looked up at the corner of the ceiling where the camera was located. These cameras didn't hang down visible to anyone in the room; they were what his father called 'pinhole cameras,' set in the crawl space behind the wall where they peeked out through tiny holes. He slithered out to the chair and worked his way behind her. He figured that the camera could probably see her from the waist up, but not very well in the darkness. He decided to take a chance. He snaked his hand up behind her, then quickly yanked the tape from her mouth before ducking down to the floor again.

'Shit! Ow!'

'Be quiet! *Listen!*'

'They're going to catch you!'

'Shhhh! *Listen!*'

Thomas strained his ears again, concentrating past the helicopters and the sounds of the police outside.

Nothing.

'It's okay, Jen. They didn't see, and they can't see me now. Don't look around. Just listen.'

'How did you get in here?'

'I used the crawl space. Now *listen* and *hold still*. I'm going to untie you. They nailed the windows shut, but I think we can use the crawl space to get downstairs. If we sneak to the garage, we can open the garage door and run for it.'

'No!'

Thomas worked frantically at the knots binding her. The cords weren't that tight around her wrists and ankles, but the knots had been pulled *hard*.

'Thomas, *stop!* I mean it! Don't untie me.'

'Are you on dope? We might be able to get away!'

'But Daddy will still be in here! I'm not going to leave him.'

Thomas settled back on his heels, confused.

'But, Jen –'

'*No!* Thomas, if you can get out, then go, but I'm not leaving without my father.'

Thomas was so angry he wanted to punch. Here they were, locked in the dark with three psychokillers who probably drank human blood, one maniac who wanted to eat their hearts *for sure*, and she wouldn't leave. But then, as Thomas thought about it, he knew she was right. He couldn't leave their father, either.

'What are we gonna do, Jen?'

She didn't answer for a time.

'Call the police.'

'The house is surrounded by police.'

'Call them anyway! Maybe they have an idea. Maybe if we tell them exactly what's going on in here it will help them.'

Thomas glanced toward her desk, recalling the wires ripped from the plug.

'They broke the phones.'

Jennifer fell silent again.

'Then I don't know. Thomas, you should get out.'

'No!'

'I mean it. If you can get to the police, maybe you can help them. You know all about the alarms and the cameras. You know that Daddy is hurt. That asshole, Dennis, lied to them about Daddy. He's telling them we're all fine.'

'Let me untie you. We can hide in the walls.'

'No! They might hurt Daddy! Listen, if they find out that you're not in your room, I'm going to tell them that you got out. They won't know you're still in the walls. They'll never even think of that! But if both of us are gone, they'll take it out on Daddy. They might hurt him!'

Thomas thought about it.

'Okay, Jen.'

'Okay, *what?*'

'We're not going to leave him. I'm going to get us out of here.'

Jennifer jerked so hard against the cords that she almost tipped over the chair.

'You leave that gun alone! They'll kill you!'

'Not if I have the gun! We can hold them off long enough to let in the police, that's all we have to do.'

She twisted hard in the chair, trying to see him.

'Thomas, don't you dare! They're adults! They're criminals and they've got guns, too!'

'Don't talk so loud or they'll hear you!'

'I don't care! It's better than you getting killed!'

Thomas reached up, pulled the tape back over her mouth, and rubbed it hard so that it would stick. Jennifer squirmed, trying to shout through the tape. Thomas hated the thought of leaving her tied, but she just didn't see that he had no other choice.

143

'I'm sorry, Jen. I'll untie you when I get back. Then we can get Daddy out of here. You'll see. I won't let them hurt us.'

Jennifer was still struggling as Thomas worked his way back through the shadows. When he reached the closet he could still hear her trying to shout through the tape. She was shouting the same thing over and over. He could understand her, even though her words were muffled.

*They're going to kill you.*

*They're going to kill you.*

Thomas slipped back into the crawl space, working his way carefully through the dark.

### DENNIS

The little bathroom off the garage was as dark as a cave when Dennis showed them the window, telling Mars and Kevin that they could work their way into the neighbor's yard and then around the side of that house to slip past the cops. Mars seemed thoughtful, but Dennis couldn't be sure with all the dark shadows.

'This could work.'

'Fuckin' A, it could work.'

'But you never know what the police are doing or where they might be. We have to give them something to think about besides us.'

'They'll be watching this house. They got nothing else to do.'

Kevin said, 'I don't like any of it. We should give up.'

'Shut up.'

Mars went into the garage and stood by the Range Rover. Dennis was scared that Mars would suggest killing the kid again.

'C'mon, Mars, we've got to get goin' here. We don't have all the time in the world.'

Mars turned back to him, his face lit by the dim light from the kitchen.

'If you want to get away, we should burn the house.'

Dennis started to say no, but then he stopped. He had been thinking of putting the kids in the Jaguar and opening the garage door with the remote as a diversion, but a fire made better sense. The cops would shit their pants if the house started to burn.

'That's not a bad idea. We could start a fire on the other side of the house.'

Kevin raised his hands.

'You guys are crazy. That adds arson to the charges against us.'

'It makes sense, Kevin. All the cops will be watching the fire. They won't be looking at the neighbor's yard.'

'But what about these people?'

Kevin was talking about the Smiths.

Dennis was about to answer when Mars did it again. His voice was quiet and empty.

'They'll burn.'

The back of Dennis's neck tingled as if Mars had raked a nail across a blackboard.

'Jesus, Mars, nobody has to burn. We can put'm here in the garage before we take off. We'll figure somethin' out.'

They decided to use gasoline to start the fire. Dennis found a two-gallon plastic gas can that the family probably kept for emergencies, but it was almost empty. Mars used the plastic air hose from the family's aquarium to siphon gas from the Jaguar. He filled the two-gallon can, then a large plastic bucket that was stained by detergent. They were carrying the gasoline into the house when they heard the helicopters again change pitch and more cars pull into the cul-de-sac.

Dennis stopped with the bucket, listening, when suddenly the front of the house was bathed in light, framing the huge garage door and spilling into the bathroom window even through the oleanders.

'What the fuck?! What's going on?'

They hurried to the front of the house, gasoline splashing from the bucket.

'Kevin! Watch the French doors!'

Dennis and Mars left the gasoline in the entry, then ran into the office where Walter Smith still twitched on the couch. Spears of light cut through the shutters, painting them with zebra stripes. Dennis opened the shutters and saw that two more police cars filled the street. All four cars had trained their spotlights on the house and a great pool of light from the helicopters burned brilliantly on the front yard. More cars arrived.

'Holy shit.'

The television showed the L.A. County Sheriffs rolling through the dark streets of York Estates. Dennis watched a group of SWAT assholes trot through an oval of helicopter light as they deployed through the neighborhood. Snipers; stone-cold killers dressed in ninja suits with rifles equipped with night-vision scopes, laser sites, and – for all he knew – motherfucking death rays. Mars had been right; these bastards would drop them cold if they tried to drive away with the kids.

'This is *fucked*. Look at all those cops.'

Dennis peeked out the shutters again, but so many floodlights had been set up in the street that the glare was blinding; a thousand cops could be standing sixty feet away, and he wouldn't know.

'*Fuck!*'

Everything had once more changed. One minute he had a great plan to slip away, but now all sides of the house were lit up like the sun and an army of cops were filling the streets. Overhead, the helicopters sounded as if they were about to land on the house. Sneaking through the adjoining neighbor's yard would now be impossible. Dennis turned back to the television. Six patrol cars filled the cul-de-sac, washed in brilliant white light from the helicopter, as many as a dozen cops moving behind them.

Dennis went to Walter Smith, and inspected his wound. The bruising had followed his eye socket under the eye to his right cheek, and moved across most of his forehead above the eye. The eye had swollen closed. Dennis wished now that he hadn't hit the sonofabitch. He turned away and went to the door.

'I'm going to check the windows again, okay? I gotta make sure Kevin isn't falling asleep. Mars, you keep an eye on the TV. If anything happens, yell.'

Mars, leaning against the wall with his face to the shutters, didn't respond. Dennis wasn't sure if Mars heard him or not, but he didn't care. He trotted back to the family room to find Kevin.

'What's going on? Aren't we leaving?'

'The goddamned Sheriffs are here. They're crawling all over the goddamned neighborhood. They got *snipers* out there!'

Dennis was consumed with the sudden notion that he would be assassinated. These cops would want to pay back the bastard who had wounded one of their own, and that was him. If he passed a window or showed himself in the goddamned French doors, those sniper bastards would bust a cap and put one right through his head.

Kevin, of course, made it worse by putting on the pussy face.

'What are we going to do?'

'I don't know, Kevin! They got so many lights out there I can't see a goddamned thing. Maybe I can see better on those televisions back there in the safety room.'

Kevin suddenly turned toward the rear of the house.

'Did you hear that?'

Dennis listened, scared shitless that SWAT killers were even now slipping into the house like a tapeworm up a cat's ass.

'Hear what?'

'I thought I heard a bump from back there.'

147

Dennis held his breath to listen more closely, but there was nothing.

'Asshole. Just let me know if Mars is coming. I might be with the money.'

Dennis left Kevin at the mouth of the hall, then trotted back to the master bedroom, and into the safety room.

He hadn't checked the monitors since the sky was rimmed with red. Now he saw Mars standing by the shutters; the front entry with bullet holes in the door; and the girl tied to a chair in her upstairs room. He couldn't see the boy, but didn't think twice about it; Dennis searched the monitors for angles outside the house, but those views were shadowed and unreadable.

'Shit!'

He spun away from the monitors, frustrated and pissed. He jerked an armful of hangered jackets from the clothes rack and threw them at the far wall. If there was any way to get fucked, he could find it!

Dennis turned back to the monitors. He considered the buttons and switches beneath the monitors. Nothing was labeled, but he didn't have anything to lose. If it was up, he pushed it down; if it was out, he pushed it in. Suddenly a monitor that had shown nothing but shadows on the dark side of the house filled with a lighted view. He pushed a second button, and the pool area filled with light. A third, and the side of the house by the garage was lit. He saw the cops at the front of the house pointing at the lights that suddenly blazed at them.

Dennis pushed more buttons, and the wall at the rear of the property beyond the pool was bathed in light. Two SWAT cops with rifles were climbing over the wall.

'SHIT!!!'

Dennis sprinted back through the house, shouting.

'THEY'RE COMING!!! KEV, MARS!!! THEY'RE COMING!'

Dennis raced to the French doors in the dark beyond the kitchen. He couldn't see the cops past the blinding outside lights, but he knew they were there, and he knew they were coming.

Dennis fired two shots into the darkness, not even thinking about it, just pulling the trigger, *bam bam*. Two glass panes in the French doors shattered.

'The fuckin' cops are comin'! Talley, that fuck! That lying fuck!'

Dennis thought his world was about to explode: They would fire tear gas, then crash through the doors. They were probably rushing the house right now with battering rams.

'Mars! Kev, we gotta get those kids!'

Dennis ran for the stairs, Kevin shouting behind him.

'What're we gonna do with the kids?'

Dennis didn't answer. He hit the stairs three at a time, going up.


THOMAS

Three minutes before Dennis Rooney saw the SWAT officers and fired two rounds, Thomas lowered himself through the ceiling into the laundry room. It was so dark that he cupped his hand over the flashlight and risked turning on the light, using the dim red glow through his fingers to pick his footing. He let himself down onto the top of the hot-water heater, felt with his toe to find the washing machine, then slid to the floor.

He held still, listening to Kevin and Dennis. The laundry room turned a corner where it opened onto the kitchen; the pantry was off that little hall. He could hear them talking, though he couldn't understand what they were saying, and then the voices stopped.

Thomas crept through the laundry room to his father's tiny hobby room at the end opposite the kitchen. Both rooms were at the rear of the garage, though you could only get to the garage through the laundry. That's how everyone came into the house from their cars: through the laundry room and into the kitchen.

When Thomas reached the hobby room, he eased the door closed, then once more turned on his flashlight. His father's hobby was building plastic models of rocket ships from the early days of the space program. He bought the kits off eBay, built and painted them at a little workbench, then put them on shelves above the bench. His father also had a Sig Sauer 9mm pistol in a metal box on the top shelf. He had heard his mom and dad fighting about it: His dad used to keep it under the front seat of the Jaguar, but his mom raised such a stink that his father had taken it out of the car and put it in the box.

On the top shelf.

A long way up.

His hand cupped over the bell of the flashlight, Thomas spread his fingers enough to let out a shaft of light. He figured that he could use the stool to climb onto the bench, and, from there, he could probably reach the box.

He climbed. It was so quiet that every creak from the bench sounded like an earthquake. He turned on the flashlight again for a moment to fix the box in his mind's eye, then reached for it, but the box was too high. He stretched up onto his toes. His fingers grazed the box just enough for him to work it toward the edge of the shelf.

That's when he heard Dennis.

*'THEY'RE COMING!!! KEV, MARS!!! THEY'RE COMING!'*

Thomas didn't waste a moment thinking about the gun; he had come so close, but now he didn't have time. His only thought was to get back to his room before they discovered him. He jumped down from the bench and ran to the laundry as two fast gunshots exploded in the house, so loud that they made his ears ring.

He wasn't thinking about Jennifer's purse. It was on the folding table by the door to the garage, that convenient place where everyone in the family dropped their stuff when they came in from the garage. Jennifer's purse was there, a Kate Spade like every other girl in her high school owned. Thomas grabbed it.

He scrambled up onto the washing machine, from there to the top of the hot-water heater, then through the access hatch into the crawl space. The last thing that he heard before closing the hatch was Dennis shouting that they had to get the kids.

TALLEY

Handing off the role of primary negotiator was never easy. Talley had already forged a bond with Rooney, and now would pull away, replacing himself with Maddox. Rooney might resist, but the subject was never given a choice. Having a choice was having power, and the subject was never given power.

Talley brought Maddox and Ellison into the cul-de-sac where they hunkered behind their car. Talley wanted to go over his earlier conversations with Rooney in greater detail so that Maddox would have something with which to work, but they didn't have time. The gunshots from the house cracked through the summer air like a car backfiring in a distant canyon: *poppop*.

Almost instantly, a storm of transmissions crackled over their radios:

'*Shots fired! Shots fired! We are under fire from the house, west rear at the wall! Advise on response!*'

All three of them knew what had happened the instant they heard the calls.

'Damnit, she moved in too close! Rooney thinks he's being breached!'

Ellison said, 'We're fucked.'

Talley felt sick; this is the way it went bad, this is how people got dead, just this fast.

Maddox clawed for his radio as other voices checked off

positions and status. The tinny voice of Carl Hicks, the tactical supervisor, came back, calm over the strained voices of his men.

'Will advise, stand by while we assess.'

Talley didn't wait; he dialed the tactical team's frequency into his own transceiver.

'Pull back, pull back, pull back! Do NOT return fire!'

Martin's voice cut over his, short and clipped.

'Who is this?'

'Talley. I told you to respect that perimeter!'

'Talley, get off the freq.'

Maddox finally had his radio, cursing as he keyed the mike.

'One, Maddox. *Listen* to him, Captain. Do not breach that house. Pull back or we're going to have a mess!'

'Clear the frequency! Those people are in danger.'

'Do not breach that house! I can talk to him!'

Talley had his cell phone out. He punched redial to call the house, praying that Rooney would answer, then ran to Jorgenson's car, still there in the street, and turned on the public address system.


THOMAS

Thomas scrambled across the joists like a spider. He slammed his head into the low-hanging rafters so hard that his teeth snapped together, but he didn't stop or even think about the noise he was making. He scurried through the long straight tunnel of the crawl space past Jennifer's room, under her window, past her bathroom, past his, and then to the access hatch in his closet. He didn't pause to see if they were in his room, but scrambled through the hatch and ran to his bed. He wanted to retie himself; to pretend that he hadn't moved. He pulled the ropes back over his ankles, working frantically, his hands slick with sweat, as shouts and footsteps pounded toward him through the hall.

He looped the ropes and slipped his hands through, realized in a flash of fear that he had forgotten the tape that had covered his mouth, but then it was too late.


DENNIS

Dennis threw open the door. He saw that the boy had damn near untied himself, but he didn't care.

'C'mon, fat boy!'

'Get away from me!'

Dennis jammed his pistol into his waist, then pinned the fat boy with a knee to untie him. Outside, Talley's voice echoed over his P.A., but Dennis couldn't make out the words. He pulled the fat boy from his bed, hooked an arm around his neck, and dragged him back toward the stairs. If the cops crashed through the front door, he would hold his gun to the kid's head and threaten to kill him. He would hide behind the kid and make the cops back down. He had a chance. He had hope.

'Hurry up, Kevin! Jesus! Bring the girl!'

Dennis dragged the fat boy down the stairs and into the office where Mars was waiting by the window. Mars looked totally calm, as if he was killing time in a bar before going to work. He tipped his head when he saw Dennis, that stupid tiny smile on his calm face.

'They're not doing anything. They're just sitting there.'

Dennis dragged the kid to the shutters. Mars opened the shutters enough for Dennis to see. The cops weren't storming the house. They were hunkered behind their cars.

Dennis realized that the phone was ringing just as Talley's voice came over the P.A. again.

'Answer the phone, Dennis. It's me, Talley. Answer the phone so I can tell you what happened.'

Dennis scooped up the phone.

## TALLEY

Martin and Hicks ran into the cul-de-sac without waiting for a cover vehicle, Martin hitting the ground beside Talley so hard that she almost bowled him over, shouting, 'What in hell do you think you're doing, interfering with my deployment?'

'He's shooting at your people because he thinks they're assaulting the house, Martin. You're violating my agreement with him.'

'This scene now belongs to me. You handed off control.'

'Pull back your people, Martin. Just relax. Nothing is going on in there.'

Talley keyed the P.A. mike again.

'Dennis, take it easy in there. Please. Just pick up the phone.'

'Hicks!'

Hicks leaned into the car past Talley and jerked the mike plug from its jack.

Talley's head was throbbing. He felt caught in a vise.

'Let me talk to him, Captain. Order your people to stand down, and let me talk to him. If it's too far gone you can breach, but right now let me try. Tell her, Maddox.'

Martin glared at Maddox, who nodded at her. He looked embarrassed.

'He's right, Captain. Let's not get too aggressive here. If Talley made a deal, we have to honor it or this guy isn't going to trust me any further than a cat can shit a walnut.'

Martin glared at him so hard that she seemed to be trying to cook him with her eyes. She glanced at Hicks, then bit out the words.

'Pull back.'

Hicks, looking uncomfortable, plugged the P.A. mike back into its jack, then mumbled orders into his tactical mike.

Talley turned back to the house.

'Pick up the phone, Dennis. We made a screwup out here, but we are not coming into that house. Check it out. The perimeter is pulling back. Check it out and talk to me.'

Talley held the cell phone to his ear, counting the rings. It rang fourteen times, fifteen . . .

Finally, Rooney answered, screaming.

'You fuck! You fuckin' lied to me! I've got a fuckin' gun to this kid's head right here! We've got these people! We'll fuckin' kill'm, you fuck!'

Talley spoke over him, his voice loud and forceful so that Rooney would hear him, but not strident. It was important to appear in control even when you weren't.

'They're pulling back. They are pulling back, Dennis. Look. You see the officers pulling back?'

The sounds of movement came over the phone. Talley guessed that Rooney had a cordless and was watching the tactical team at the rear of the property.

'Yeah. I guess. They're going back over the wall.'

'I didn't lie to you, Dennis. It's over now, okay? Don't hurt anyone.'

'We'll burn this fuckin' place down, you try to come in here. We've got gasoline all good to go, Talley. You try to come in and this place is going to burn.'

Talley locked eyes with Maddox. Rooney booby-trapping the house with gasoline was a bad turn; if he was creating a situation dangerous to the hostages, it could justify a preemptive breach of the house.

'Don't do anything to endanger yourself or those children, Dennis. For your own sake and for the sake of the innocents in there. This kind of thing can create problems.'

'Then stay on the other side of that wall. You assholes try to come get us and this place is gonna burn.'

Talley muted the phone while Dennis answered to warn Maddox about the gasoline. Maddox relayed the information to the tactical team. If Rooney was telling the truth about the gasoline, firing tear gas or flash-bang grenades into the house could ignite an inferno.

'No one is coming in. We screwed up, is all. Some new guys came out and we got our wires crossed, but I didn't lie to you. I wouldn't do that.'

'You fuckin' well *did* screw up, dude! Jesus!'

The tension lessened in Rooney's voice, and, with it, Talley felt the vise ease its grip. If Rooney was talking, he wouldn't shoot.

'What's the status in there, Dennis? You didn't hurt anyone, did you?'

'Not yet.'

'Those shots you fired, they were out of the house?'

'I'm not saying I fired anything. You're saying that, not me. I know you're recording this.'

'No one needs a doctor?'

'*You're* gonna need a doctor, you try this shit again.'

Talley took a deep breath. It was done; they were past the crisis. Talley glanced at Martin. She looked irritated, but attentive.

Talley muted the receiver again.

'He's calming down. I think now would be a good time for the handoff.'

Martin glanced at Maddox.

'You ready?'

'I'm ready.'

Martin nodded at Talley.

'Go.'

Talley uncovered his phone.

'Dennis, have you been thinking about what we talked about earlier?'

'I got a lot on my mind.'

'I'm sure. It was good advice, what I said.'

'Whatever.'

Talley lowered his voice, trying to sound like what he was about to say was just between them, guy to guy.

'Can I tell you something of a personal nature?'

'What?'

'I gotta piss real bad.'

Rooney laughed. Just like that, and Talley knew that the handoff would work. He made his voice relaxed, putting a friendly spin on it, indicating that everything that was about to happen was the most natural thing in the world and beyond all objection. Rooney was just as relieved to be past this hump as Talley.

'Dennis, I'm going to take a break out here. You see all the new people we have?'

'You got a thousand guys out there. Of course, I see'm.'

'I'm going to put an officer named Will Maddox on the line. You scared me so bad that I've gotta go clean my shorts, you know? So Maddox will be here on the line if you want to talk or if you need anything.'

'You're a funny guy, Talley.'

'Here he is, Dennis. You stay cool in there.'

'I'm cool.'

Talley handed the phone to Maddox, who introduced himself with a warm, mellow voice.

'Hey, Dennis. You should've seen ol' Jeff out here. I think he crapped his pants.'

Talley didn't listen to any more. The rest of it would be up to Maddox. He slumped down onto the street and leaned against the car, feeling drained.

He glanced at Martin, and found her watching him. She duck-walked over, and hunkered on the pavement beside him, then searched his eyes for a moment as if she were trying to find the right words. Her face softened.

'You were right. I got in a hurry and screwed up.'

Talley admired her for saying it.

'We survived.'

'So far.'

After the screaming, after those frantic moments when Thomas thought that Dennis would shoot him in the head as he was threatening, Jennifer glared at him and said one word.

'Don't.'

No one heard but Thomas; Dennis was pacing and talking to himself, Kevin following Dennis with his eyes the way a nervous dog will watch its master. They were in the office, the TV on, just now reporting that shots had been fired in the house. Dennis stopped to watch, suddenly laughing.

'Jesus, but that was close. Jesus Christ.'

Kevin crossed his arms, rocking nervously.

'What are we going to do? We can't get away now. They're all around the house. They're even in the neighbor's yard.'

Dennis's face darkened, and he snapped.

'I don't know, Kevin. I don't know. We'll figure out something.'

'We should give up.'

'Shut up!'

Thomas rubbed his neck, thinking he might yak. Dennis had carried him down to the office by the neck, an arm hooked around his throat in a headlock, squeezing so hard that Thomas couldn't breathe. Jennifer came over and knelt by him, making as if to help him, but pinching his arm, instead, her whisper angry and frightened.

'You see? You see? You almost got caught!'

She went to their father.

Mars returned from elsewhere in the house, his arms filled with big white candles. Without saying a word, he lit one, dripped wax on the television, seated the base in the wax. He moved to the bookcase, did it again. Dennis and Kevin were coming apart, but Thomas thought that Mars looked content.

Dennis finally noticed.

'What the fuck are you doing?'

Mars answered as he lit another candle.

'They might cut the power. Here, take this.'

He stopped with the candles long enough to toss a flashlight to Dennis. It was the one from the kitchen utility drawer. He tossed a second to Kevin, who dropped it.

Dennis turned on the light, then turned it off.

'Those candles are a good idea.'

Soon, the office looked like an altar.

Thomas watched Dennis. Dennis seemed inside himself, following Mars with a kind of watchful wariness, as if Mars held something over him that he was trying to figure out. Thomas hated them all, thinking that if he only had the gun he could kill them, Mars with the candles, Dennis with his eyes on Mars, Kevin staring at Dennis, none of them looking at him, pull out the gun and shoot every one of them, bangbangbang.

Dennis suddenly said, 'We should stack pots and pans under the windows in case they try to sneak in, things that will fall, so we'll hear.'

Mars grunted.

'Mars, when you're back there, do that, okay? Set up some booby traps.'

Jennifer said, 'What about my father?'

'Jesus, not that again. Christ.'

Her voice rose.

'He needs a doctor, you asshole!'

'Kevin, take'm back upstairs. *Please*.'

Thomas didn't care. That was what he wanted.

'Do you want me to tie them again?'

Dennis started to answer, then squinched his face, thinking.

'It took too long to cut all that shit off, you and Mars tying them like a couple of fuckin' mummies. Just make sure they're locked in real good, not just with the nails.'

Mars finished with the candles.

'I can take care of that. Bring them up.'

Kevin brought them, holding Jennifer's arm, almost having to drag her, but Thomas walking in front, anxious to get back to his room though he tried to hide it. They waited at the top of the stairs until Mars rejoined them, now with a hammer and screwdriver. He trudged up the steps, thump thump thump, with the slow inevitability of a rising freight elevator, dark and dirty. Mars led them to Thomas's room first, the end of the hall. It was spooky without light.

'Get in there, fat boy. Pull your covers over your head.'

Mars pushed him inside hard, then knelt by the knob, the one Thomas would use to get out. He hammered the screwdriver under the base, popped it off, unfastened three screws, then pulled the knob free, leaving only a square hole. He looked at Jennifer then, no one else, Jennifer.

'You see? That's how you keep a child in its room.'

They left Thomas like that, pulling the door, then hammering the door closed. Thomas listened until he heard the crash of Jennifer's knob coming free and her door being nailed, and then he scrambled for his closet. He was thinking only of the gun, but as soon as he turned on his flashlight he saw Jennifer's purse. He had dropped it just inside the hatch when he scrambled back into the room. He clawed it open and upended it.

Out fell her cell phone.

# CHAPTER 10

## Palm Springs, California
Friday, 8:32 P.M.

SONNY BENZA

The three of them had Glen Howell on the speaker, Benza, Tuzee, and Salvetti, the TVs muted so they could hear. Benza, on his third pack of Gaviscom, nursed an upset stomach, his acid reflux acting up.

Howell, his voice crackling with the shitty cell connection, sitting in his car somewhere in the dark, said, 'He's got a wife and kid, a daughter. They're divorced or separated or something. The wife and kid live down in LA, but he sees the kid every two weeks or something.'

Tuzee, his face pasty beneath the tan, looking like a corpse from the strain, rubbed irritably at his face and interrupted.

'Stop it.'

'What?'

'Stop with the 'or something.' Don't end every sentence with 'or something.' It's pissing me off. You've got a college education.'

Benza reached out, patted Tuzee's leg, but didn't say anything.

Tuzee had his face in his hands, the flesh folded around his fingers like a man twice his age.

'He either sees them every two weeks or he doesn't; it's either a fact or it isn't. Find out the fucking facts before you call us.'

The connection popped and hissed, a background roar.

'Sorry.'

'Keep going.'

'He's seeing them this weekend. The wife is bringing up the daughter.'

Benza cleared his throat, phlegm from the Gaviscom.

'And you know this to be a fact?'

'Book it. We got that from his office, an older woman there who likes to talk, you know, how sad it is and all because the Chief's such a nice man.'

'Where are they now, the family I mean?'

'That, I don't know. I got people on that. They're due up tonight, though. That part I know for sure.'

Benza nodded.

'We've gotta think about this.'

Salvetti had already made up his mind. He leaned back, crossed his arms, his legs splayed and open.

'That shit just happened, that was too close. We've gotta move.'

'You mean the Sheriffs?'

'Yeah.'

'Yeah, that was close.'

They were silent for a time, each man lost in his own thoughts. Benza had dialed up Howell as soon as he saw the Sheriffs rolling into the neighborhood. Then, when the TV reported that shots were fired, he damn near tossed his soup, thinking this was it, SWAT was going in and they were cooked.

Howell said, 'There's more.'

'Okay.'

'They're looking into the building permits.'

'Why the fuck?'

'Something like this happens, some asshole barricades himself in a building, they want the floor plans. So now they're trying to find the people who built the house so they can get the plans.'

'Shit.'

Benza sighed and leaned back. Tuzee glanced at him,

shaking his head. Benza owned the construction companies that built the house and installed the security
systems. He didn't like where this was going. He stood.

'I'm going to walk, so if you can't hear me just say,
okay?'

'Sure, Sonny.'

'First thing first. Our records. I'm looking at this house
on the TV right now. There's a ring of cops around it like
they're about to hit the beach at Normandy, but let me
ask you something.'

'Okay.'

'Could we get our people in there?'

'In the house?'

'Yeah, in the house. Right now, right in front of the
cops, the TV cameras, everything; get a couple guys inside
the house?'

'No. I've got good people, Sonny, the best, but we can't
get in right now. Not the way it stands now. We'd have to
own the cops to do that. You give me a day, two days, I
could probably do it.'

Benza, irritated, glowered at the televisions, two pictures, one showing the house with a bunch of SWAT cops
out front, the other some blond dyke being interviewed,
short hair slicked back, dressed like a man.

'Could we get close? Now. Not owning the cops, but
now.'

Howell thought about it.

'Okay, look, I don't have a TV. I'm not seeing what
you're seeing right now, okay? But I know Smith's house
and I'm familiar with the neighborhood, so I'm going to
say yeah. We could probably get close.'

Benza looked at Tuzee and Salvetti.

'How about we burn it down? Right now, tonight. Get
some guys in there with some accelerant, everybody's
gonna know it's arson so who gives a shit what, torch the
place, burn it to the ground.'

He spread his hands, looking at them, hopeful.

Salvetti shrugged, unimpressed.

'No way to know the disks would be destroyed. Not for sure. I promise you this, if Smith has any of that stuff in his security room, it isn't gonna burn. Then we're fucked.'

Benza stared at the floor, ashamed of himself, thinking what a stupid idea, burn the place.

Tuzee leaned back now, crossing his arms, stared at the ceiling.

'Okay, look. Here it is the way I see it: If these kids were going to give up, they would've given up. Something's keeping them in that house, I don't know what, but they're sticking. The more cops pile up around that place, the more likely we are to have a breached entry.'

Salvetti sat forward, raising a hand like he was in class, interupting.

'Wait. Call me crazy, but how about this? Why don't we just call'm? Talk to these dicks ourselves, cut a deal.'

Howell's voice hissed from the speaker.

'The lines are blocked. The cops did that.'

'Smith's regular lines, maybe, but not our lines. We pay extra for those lines.'

Tuzee was saying, 'What do you mean, cut a deal?'

'We lay it out for these assholes who they're dealing with, say they think they're in trouble with the cops, they haven't seen the kinda trouble we can bring down. We cut a deal, pay'm something like fifty K to give up, we'll provide the lawyers, all of that.'

'No fuckin' way. Uh-uh.'

'Why?'

'You want to tell three punk assholes our business? Jesus, Sally.'

Salvetti fell silent, embarrassed.

Benza caught Tuzee looking at him, resigned.

'What, Phil?'

Tuzee slumped in his chair, more tired now than ever.

'Talley's family.'

'We've got a lot to think about with that.'

'I know. I'm thinking about it. Once we go down that road, no turning back.'

'You know where that ends, don't you?'

'You're the guy just suggested we burn the fucking house down, six people inside, the whole world watching.'

'I know.'

'We can't just sit. We came damned close with what happened tonight, and now they're looking at the building permits and God knows what else. That's bad enough, but I'm worried about New York. I'm thinking, how long can we keep the lid on this?'

'We've got the lid on. I trust the guys we have on the scene.'

'I trust our guys, too, but old man Castellano is going to find out sooner or later. It's bound to happen.'

'It's only been a few hours.'

'However long it's been, we need to get a handle on things before they find out. By the time that old man hears, we've gotta be able to tell him that we're no longer a threat to him. We've gotta laugh about this over schnapps and cigars, else he'll hand us our asses.'

Benza felt tired in his heart, but relieved, too. Comfort came with the decision.

'Glen?'

'I'm here, Sonny.'

'If we move on Talley like this, you got a man there who can handle it?'

'Yes, Sonny.'

'He can do whatever needs to be done? All the way?'

'Yes, Sonny. Can and will. I can handle the rest.'

Benza glanced at Phil Tuzee, Tuzee nodding, then Salvetti, Salvetti ducking his head one time.

'Okay, Glen. Get it done.'

# CHAPTER 11

**Eastern time**
Friday, 11:40 P.M.

**Pacific time, New York City**
8:40 P.M.

VIC CASTELLANO

His wife was a light sleeper, so Vittorio 'Vic' Castellano left their bedroom to take the call. He put on the thick terry-cloth bathrobe, the birthday present from his kids with *Don't Bug Me* embroidered on the back, and gimped alongside Jamie Beldone to the kitchen. Beldone held a cell phone. On the other end of it was a man they employed to keep an eye on things in California.

Vic, seventy-eight years old and two weeks away from a hip replacement, poured a small glass of orange juice, but couldn't bring himself to drink it. His stomach was already sour.

'You sure it's this bad?'

'The police have the house locked down with all Benza's records inside, including the books that link to us.'

'That sonofabitch. What's in his records?'

'They show how much he kicks to us. I don't know if it'll show business by business, but it's going to show something like that so he can keep track of where his money goes. If the Feds recover this, it will help them build an IRS case against you.'

Vic poured out the orange juice, then ran water in the glass. He sipped. Warm.

'It's been how long this is going on?'

'About five hours now.'

Castellano checked the time.

'Does Benza know that we know?'

'No, sir.'

'That chickenshit sonofabitch. Heaven forbid he call to warn me like a real man. He'd rather let me get caught cold than have time to fuckin' prepare.'

'He's a piece of shit, skipper. That's all there is to it.'

'What's he doing about it?'

'He sent in a team. You know Glen Howell?'

'No.'

'Benza's fixer. He's good.'

'Do we have our own guy there?'

Beldone tipped the phone, nodding.

'He's on the line now. I have to tell him what to do.'

Vic drank more of the warm water, then sighed. It was going to be a long night. He was already thinking of what he would say to his lawyers.

'Should we maybe get our own team in there?'

Beldone pursed his lips, then shook his head.

'We'd have to get the guys together, plus the five-hour plane flight; not enough time, Vic. It's Sonny's show. Sonny and Glen Howell.'

'I can't believe that chickenshit hasn't called me. What's he thinkin', back there?'

'He's thinking that if it goes south, he's going to run. He's probably more afraid of you than the Feds.'

'He should be.'

Vic sighed again, then went to the door. Forty years as the boss of the most powerful crime family on the East Coast had taught him to worry about the things he could control, and let other people worry about the things he couldn't.

He stopped in the door and turned back to Jamie Beldone.

'Sonny Benza is an incompetent asshole, and so was his fuckin' father.'

'The Mickey Mouse mob, Vic. Brain damage from all the tan.'

'If it goes south, Sonny Benza isn't goin' anywhere. You understand?'

'Yes, sir.'

'If they fuck this up, they gotta pay.'

'They'll pay for it, skipper.'

'I'm goin' to bed. You let me know if anything happens.'

'Yes, sir.'

Vic Castellano shuffled back to his bed, but could not sleep.

# CHAPTER 12

Friday, 8:43 P.M.

TALLEY

Talley was in Mrs. Peña's home with the Sheriffs, sipping her coffee, rich and heavy with brown sugar and cream though none of them had asked for it that way; she told them it was the Brazilian way. They were watching the security tape.

Talley pointed at the television with his cup.

'The first one inside is Rooney, this next guy is Krupchek. Kevin comes in last.'

Martin watched with the flat, uninvolved expression of an experienced officer. Talley found himself watching her instead of the tape, curious about her background and how she'd become a SWAT captain.

Martin nodded at the screen.

'What's that on his head, a tattoo? There, on the big one.'

'That's Krupchek.'

'Right, Krupchek.'

'It says 'burn it.' We're running it through the computer.'

Talley told them what he had learned from Brad Dill about Krupchek and the Rooney brothers, then filled them in on having dispatched Mikkelson and Dreyer to locate landlords and neighbors.

Ellison said, 'These guys have any family we can bring out? We had a guy once, he backed us off for twelve hours until his mama gets there. She gets on the phone, tells

169

him to get his ass out of that house, the guy comes out crying like a baby.'

Talley had worked with subjects like that, too.

'Rooney might have an aunt in Bakersfield, but Dill didn't know about Krupchek. If we can find their landlords or friends, we might get a line on the families. You want, I'll have Larry Anders, he's my senior officer here, put your Intelligence Officer in touch with whoever we find.'

Maddox nodded, his face creased with attention.

'I might want to talk to Dill and those people myself. You okay with that?'

'I know the job. Whatever you want. Tell Anders, and he'll arrange to bring them here.'

As the new primary negotiator, Maddox had the responsibility to form his own opinions on the behavior characteristics of a subject. Talley would have done the same thing.

Martin stepped closer to the television. They had reached the part of the tape where Krupchek leaned over the counter.

'What's he doing?'

'Watch.'

Maddox joined Martin at the TV. He crossed his arms in a way that Talley thought was protective.

'Jesus, he's watching that man die.'

Talley nodded.

'That's what I thought.'

'The sonofabitch is smiling.'

Talley finished his coffee and put down the cup. He didn't need to see it again.

'We told the Sheriff's investigators up at Kim's about the hand. See there on the counter? They should have a pretty good palm print from that, but I haven't heard.'

Martin glanced at Ellison.

'Run the prints for wants and warrants.'

'Yes, ma'am.'

Metzger came up behind Talley and touched his arm.

'Chief, see you a second?'

Talley excused himself from the Sheriffs and followed Metzger into the adjoining room. Metzger glanced back at the Sheriffs, then lowered her voice.

'Sarah wants you to call her right away. She's says it's important. She says I should knock you down and drag you to a phone, it's so important.'

'Why are you whispering?'

'She says it's *important*. You're supposed to call on your office line, not use a radio.'

'Why not the radio?'

'Because other people can *hear* on the radio. She says use the phone.'

Talley felt a hot burn of concern that something had happened to Jane and Amanda. He took out his cell phone, hitting the autodial for his office. Out by the television, Maddox was looking at him, concerned.

Sarah answered on the first ring.

'It's me, Sarah. What's up?'

'Oh, thank God. There's a little boy on the phone. He says that his name is Thomas Smith, and that he's calling from inside the house.'

'It's a crank. Forget it.'

Warren Kenner, who was Talley's personnel supervisor and one of only two Bristo sergeants, came on the line.

'Chief, I think we got something here. I checked the phone number the boy says he's calling from with the cell company. It's registered to the Smiths, all right.'

'Did you talk with the boy, or just Sarah?'

'No, I talked to him. He sounds real, saying things about the three guys in that house, and his sister and father. He says his dad's hurt in there, that he got knocked out.'

Talley worried his lip, thinking, getting just a little excited.

'Is he still on the phone?'

'Yes, sir. Sarah's talking to him right now on another line. They locked him in his room. He says he's on his sister's cell phone.'

'Stand by.'

Talley went to the door; several officers and Highway Patrolmen were milling near Mrs. Peña's kitchen, drinking coffee and eating cheese enchiladas. He called Martin, Maddox, and Ellison into the room, then led them as far from the others as possible.

'I think we've got something here. Kid on the phone, saying he's Thomas Smith from inside the house.'

Martin's face tightened, coming together in a kind of expectant question.

'Is this bogus or real?'

Talley went back to the phone.

'Warren? Who else knows about this?'

'Just us, Chief. Me and Sarah, and now you.'

'If this turns out to be real, I don't want the press finding out about this, you understand? Tell Sarah. That means you don't talk about this with anyone, not even the other police, not even off the record.'

Talley looked at Martin as he spoke. She nodded, agreeing.

'If Rooney and those other guys see the press talking about someone in the house calling out, I don't know what they might do.'

'I understand, Chief. I'll tell Sarah.'

'Put him on.'

A boy came on the line, his voice low and careful, but not frightened.

'Hello? Is this the Chief?'

'This is Chief Talley. Tell me your name, son.'

'Thomas Smith. I'm in the house that's on TV. Dennis hit my dad and now he won't wake up. You gotta come get him.'

An edge of fear crept into the boy's voice when he

mentioned his father, but Talley couldn't yet be sure the call wasn't a hoax.

'I have a couple of questions for you first, Thomas. Who's in the house with you?'

'These three guys, Dennis, Kevin, and Mars. Mars said he was going to eat my heart.'

'Besides them.'

'My father and sister. You gotta make Dennis send my dad to a doctor.'

The boy could have gotten all of this information off the news, but so far as Talley knew, no one had as yet reported, or knew, the whereabouts of the mother. They were still trying to locate her.

'What about your mother?'

The boy answered without hesitating.

'She's in Florida with my Aunt Kate.'

Talley felt a blossom of heat in his chest. This might be real. He made a scribbling gesture with his hand, telling Martin to get ready to write. She glanced at Ellison, who fumbled out his spiral notepad and a pen.

'What's your aunt's name, bud?'

'Kate Toepfer. She has blond hair.'

Talley repeated it, watching Ellison write.

'Where does she live?'

'West Palm Beach.'

Talley didn't bother to cover the phone.

'We got the boy. Get a number for this woman, Kate Toepfer in West Palm Beach, that's where the mother is.'

Maddox and Ellison exchanged words, Talley not hearing because he had already gone back to the boy. Martin stepped close, pulling at his arm to tip the phone so that she could hear.

'Where you are now, son, are you okay? Could they catch you talking to me?'

'They locked me in my room. I'm on my sister's cell phone.'

'Where's that, your room?'

'Upstairs.'

'Okay. Where's your dad and sister?'

'My dad's down in the office. They got him on the couch. He needs a doctor.'

'Was he shot?'

'Dennis hit him, and now he won't wake up. My sister says he needs a doctor, but Dennis won't listen.'

'Is he bleeding?'

'Not anymore. He just won't wake up. I'm really scared.'

'How about your sister? Is she okay?'

Maddox said, 'Ask him does he know the subject locations.'

Talley raised a hand, the boy still talking, saying something about his sister.

'What was that, Thomas? I missed that. Is she okay?'

'I said she won't leave. I tried to get her to leave, but she won't without our dad.'

Martin plucked at him.

'Can he get out? Ask him if he can get out.'

Talley nodded.

'Okay, Thomas, we're going to get you out of there as fast as we can, but I want to ask something. You're alone in your room on the second floor, right?'

'Yeah.'

'Could you let yourself out your window if we were down below to catch you?'

'They've got the windows nailed shut. But even if they didn't, they could see me.'

'They could see you climbing out the window even though you're alone?'

'We have security cameras. They could see on the monitors in my folks' room if they were looking. They would see you sneaking up to the house, too.'

'Okay, son, one more thing. Dennis told me that he had set up the house to burn with gasoline. Is that true?'

'They've got a bucket of gas in the entry hall. I saw it when they brought me downstairs. It really stinks.'

Talley heard brushing sounds on the phone, and the boy's voice dropped.

'They're coming.'

'Thomas? Thomas, are you all right?'

The boy was gone.

Martin said, 'What's happening?'

Talley listened, straining now, but the line was dead.

'He said they were coming, then he hung up.'

Martin took a deep breath, let it hiss out.

'You think they caught him?'

Talley closed the phone and put it away.

'I don't think so. He didn't sound panicked when he shut the phone, so I don't think he was discovered; he just had to end the call.'

'Was Rooney telling the truth about the gasoline?'

'Yes.'

'Shit. That's a problem. That's a fucking big problem. All we need is a goddamned barbecue.'

'He also said that there's a video security system. That's how he saw your people approaching the house.'

Martin turned to Ellison.

'Have the I.O. check the phone lines to see if there's a security feed. We might be able to back-trace it to the provider and find out what we're dealing with.'

Talley started to say that his people had already come up empty with that, but he let it go. If it was him, he'd double-check, too.

'He says the father is injured. That's why he called out, to say his father needs a doctor.'

Martin's expression turned grim. She hadn't heard that part.

'First the goddamned gas, and now this. If the man is in imminent danger, we might have to risk a breach.'

Maddox shifted, uncomfortable.

'How're we gonna breach knowing this guy can see it coming, him with gasoline ready to go? We'll get people killed.'

'If we have someone dying in there, we can't ignore it.'

Talley held up his hands like he was pushing them apart.

'The boy didn't say anyone is dying, he just said the man is hurt.'

He repeated Thomas's description of Walter Smith's condition. Martin listened, head down, but glancing at Maddox and Ellison from time to time as if to gauge their reactions. When Talley finished, she nodded.

'Well, that's not a lot of information.'

'No.'

'All right, at least we know we're not talking about a gunshot victim here. Smith's not in there bleeding to death.'

'Sounds like head trauma.'

'So we've got a possible concussion, but we can't be sure about that. We can't very well call Rooney back to ask about the father. He might get it in his head that one of those kids is calling out.'

Talley had to agree.

'We have to protect the boy. If he gets the chance to call again, I'm pretty sure he will.'

Maddox nodded.

'When I talk with Rooney again I'll push him to find out how everyone's doing. Maybe I can kick free some information about the father.'

They agreed that for now the best plan was to let Rooney and the others in the house calm down. Martin looked back at Talley.

'If the boy calls again, he'll call through your office.'

'I would guess so. He must've gotten the department's number from information.'

Talley knew what she wanted.

'I'll have someone in my office around the clock. If the boy calls, they'll page me and I'll bring you in.'

Martin checked her watch, then looked at Maddox.

'We've got to get to it. I want you and Ellison set up in front of that house so we can start breaking these assholes down.'

Talley knew what that meant: They would maintain a high noise level profile, phoning Rooney periodically throughout the night to keep him awake. They would try to wear him down by depriving him of sleep. Sometimes, if you got them tired enough, they gave up.

Martin turned back to Talley, and now her face softened. She put out her hand, and Talley took it. Her grip wasn't as hard as before.

'I appreciate your help, Chief. You've done a good job keeping this situation under control.'

'Thanks, Captain.'

Martin squeezed his hand, then let go.

'You want to relieve your people now, that's fine. I'd like four of your officers to liaison with the locals, but past that, we've got it. I know you have a slim department up here.'

'It's yours, Captain. You have my numbers. If you need me, call. Otherwise, I'll grab a few hours' sleep and see you in the morning.'

'We're good.'

Martin gave him an uncertain smile that almost looked pretty, then walked away. Talley thought that she probably had a hard time smiling, but people often did, and for reasons that surprised you. Maddox and Ellison followed her.

Talley brought his cup to the kitchen, thanked Mrs. Peña for her help, then went to his car. He brought Larry Anders up to speed, then checked the time, wondering if Jane and Amanda were still at dinner or were waiting at home.

He wondered why Martin had squeezed his hand.

*

The television crews wouldn't share their food, cheap pricks, big urns of Starbucks coffee that someone had brought, Krispy Kreme donuts, and pizza. Just as well, or Ken Seymore would have missed seeing Talley leave.

Rather than eating, Seymore was seated in his car, a Ford Explorer, near the gate. He told the two cops there, who had asked him what he was doing, that he was waiting for a pool photographer to arrive from Los Angeles. Going to snap some shots of the guys guarding the development, he had said. That had been enough. They'd left him alone.

When Seymore saw Talley drive out, he picked up his phone.

'He's leaving.'

That was all he needed to say.

# CHAPTER 13

Friday, 8:46 P.M.

JANE

Her heart pounding, her lips tingling from the kiss, his voice a whisper in her ear there in the dark, parked outside her house.

'We would be good together. I've thought that for weeks, the two of us, fitting together like pieces of a puzzle.'

He was a doctor at her hospital, newly divorced, two boys in high school, one a year older than Mandy, the other a year younger.

'You know it would be good.'

'It would.'

She loved the warm hardness of him, something that had been missing so long; this large male body, holding her, hers to hold. And a nice man. A nice man. They had the same sense of humor, wacky and sarcastic.

'Come home with me tonight. For a little while.'

Her first date with another man since Jeff moved out, almost a year; Jeff up there in Bristo, Jeff who had simply shut down on her, stopped feeling, pulled back, withdrawn, disappeared, whatever the hell. It felt like cheating.

'I don't know.'

'I don't want the night to end. We don't have to do anything. Not for at least five minutes.'

She laughed. Couldn't help herself.

He kissed her, and she kissed back, the sensuous play

of lips and tongues. She felt drunk with it, and so SO alive.

'I told Amanda I would be in by now.'

'I'll cry. Worse, I'll sulk. It's terrible when I sulk.'

Laughing, she put her hand over his face and pushed him away. Gently.

He sighed, and now they were serious.

'Okay. I had fun.'

'Me, too.'

'I'll see you at work tomorrow. I'll drop around the floor, find you.'

'I'm off tomorrow and the day after.'

'Thursday, then. That would be Thursday. I'll see you then.'

She kissed him a final time, a quick peck, though he wanted more, then hurried into the empty house. Amanda was sleeping over at her friend Connie's. She hadn't told Amanda that she was going out, let alone that she would be in by now. That had been a lie.

The next day, Jane changed her hair color, going with the dark red, the red that's almost black, wondering if it made her look younger, wondering what Jeff would think.

Everything that night, it had felt like cheating.


'Earth to Mom?'

Jane Talley focused on her daughter.

'Sorry.'

'What were you thinking?'

'If your father likes my hair.'

Amanda's face darkened.

'Like you should care. Please.'

'All right. I was wondering if that mess is going to blow up in his face. Is that better?'

They had stopped at *Le Chine*, a Vietnamese-Thai place

in a mall near the freeway, ordering *pho ga*, which was a rice noodle soup, and crispy shrimp, which was, well, crispy shrimp. They ate there often, sometimes with Jeff. Jane had toyed with the plain white rice, but that was it. She put down her fork.

'Let me tell you something.'

'Can't we just go home? I don't want to be here, anyway. I told him that.'

'Don't say "him." He's your father.'

'Whatever.'

'He's having a hard time.'

'A year ago it was a hard time, now it's just boring.'

Jane was so tired of keeping all the balls in the air, of being the supportive nurturing mother, of waiting for Jeff to come to his senses, that she wanted to scream. Some days, she did; she would press her face into the pillow and scream as hard as she could. A flash of anger shook her so deeply that if Mandy rolled her eyes one more time she would snatch up the fork and stab her.

'Let me tell you something. This has been hard on everybody; on you, on me, on him. He's not like this. It was that goddamned job.'

'Here we go with the job.'

Jane called for the check, so livid that she didn't trust herself to look at her daughter. As always, the owner, a woman named Po who knew they were Talley's family, insisted that there was no charge. As always, Jane paid, this time quickly, in cash, not waiting for change.

'Let's go.'

Jane walked out to the parking lot, still not looking at Amanda, her heels snapping like gunshots on the pavement. She got behind the wheel but did not start the car. Amanda slid in beside her, pulling the door. The night air smelled of sage and dust and garlic from the restaurant.

'Why aren't we moving?'

'I'm trying not to kill you.'

When Jane figured out what she needed to say, she said it.

'I am scared to death that your father is finally going to give up and call it quits. I could see it in him tonight. Your father, he knows what this is doing to us, he's not stupid. We talk, Amanda; he says he's empty, I don't know how to fill him; he says he's dead, I don't know how to bring him to life. You think I don't try? Here we are, split apart, time passing, him wallowing in his god-damned depression; your father will end it just to spare us. Well, little miss, let me tell you something: I don't want to be spared. I *choose* not to be spared. Your father used to be filled with life and strength, and I fell in love with that special man more deeply than you can know. You don't want to hear about the job, fine, but only a man as good as your father could be hurt the way that job hurt him. If that's me making excuses for him, fine. If you think I'm a loser by waiting for him, tough. I could have other men; I don't want them. I don't even know if he still loves me, but let me tell you something: I love him, I want this marriage, and I goddamned fucking well care whether or not he likes my hair.'

Jane, crying, saw that Amanda was crying, too, great honey drops inflating her eyes. She slumped back in the seat, bouncing her head on the headrest.

'Shit.'

Sharp rapping on the window startled her.

'Ma'am? Are you all right?'

Jane rolled down the window, just an inch, two. The man seemed embarrassed, leaning forward, one hand on the roof, the other on her door, his expression asking if there was anything he could do.

'I'm sorry, I know it's not my business. I heard crying.'

'That's all right. We're fine. Thank you.'

'Well, if you're sure.'

'Thank you.'

She was reaching for the key when he jerked open the

door, pushing her sideways into Amanda, the smell of donuts suddenly strong in the car.

Later, she would know that his name was Marion Clewes.

# CHAPTER 14

Friday, 9:12 P.M.

TALLEY

The sky was strange without red and green helicopter stars. Talley turned off his command radio and rolled down the windows, letting the silky air rush over him, still warm from the earth and smelling of yucca. It wasn't his show anymore, so he didn't need the radio. He needed to think.

Stretched out ahead and curving between the mountains, the street was bright with headlights rushing toward him. The past six hours had flicked past, one moment overtaking the next like a chain of car crashes, piling one atop the next with an intensity of experience that Talley hadn't known in a long time; part fear, part elation. Talley found himself working through the events of the day, and realized after a time that he was enjoying himself. That he would, or could, surprised him. It was as if some dormant part of himself was waking.

The hot night air brought a memory of Jane.

They had come to the desert for their honeymoon. Not when they first married; they didn't have enough money for that. But later, when his six-month probation was over, they had each taken two vacation days to make a long weekend, thinking they would drive to Las Vegas. The idea, the great plan, was to beat the summer heat by making the drive after sundown, but Vegas was a long way, four hours. They stopped at the halfway point for something to eat, a nothing little town at the edge of the

California desert, and went no farther. The honeymoon cottage that night was a twenty-dollar motel off the highway; dinner was a cheap steak at the Sizzler, after which they explored the town. Driving now, Talley remembered the desert heat of that night; Jane had scared him, Talley the tough young SWAT cop, by climbing out the car's window and sitting on the door as they raced along the back desert roads.

Talley hadn't recalled those memories in years, and now felt uneasy with their absence, as if they had been lost within himself. He wondered what else might be lost within himself.

Talley turned onto the condominium grounds. He found Jane's car parked in the first of the two spaces that were his, and pulled in beside it. He stared up the walk toward his condo, uneasy about the conversation they were about to have. She had finally called him out on their future, and now he had to deal with it. No more running, no more denial, no more excuses; he could keep her, or he could lose her. Tonight it was going to be as simple as that.

As Talley stepped from his car, he noticed that the parking lot was darker than usual; both security lights were out. Talley was locking his car as a woman stepped from the walk that led to his building.

'Chief Talley? Could I have a word with you?'

Talley thought she might be one of his neighbors. Most of the people in the complex knew he was the chief of police, often coming to him with complaints and problems.

'It's pretty late. Could this keep until tomorrow?'

She was attractive, but not pretty, with a clean, businesslike expression, and hair that cupped her face. He did not recognize her.

'I wish it could, Chief, but we have to discuss this tonight.'

Talley heard a single footstep behind him, the *shush* of

shoe on grit, then an arm hooked his throat from behind, lifting him backward and off his feet. Someone held a gun before his face.

'Do you see it? See the gun? Look at it.'

Talley clawed at the arm that was choking him, but only until he saw the pistol. Then he stopped struggling.

'That's better. We're only going to talk, that's all, but I will kill you if I have to.'

They lowered him, gave him his feet again. Someone opened his car again as someone else felt beneath his jacket and around his waist.

'Where's your gun?'

'I don't carry it.'

'Bullshit. Where is it?'

The hands went to his ankles.

'I don't carry it. I'm the Chief. I don't have to.'

They pushed him behind the wheel. Talley saw shapes; he wasn't sure how many; maybe three, could have been five. Someone in the backseat directly behind him smashed the ceiling light with the gun, then pushed the gun hard to his neck.

'Start the car. Back up. We're just going to talk to you.'

'Who are you?'

Talley tried to turn, but strong hands shoved his face forward. Two men wearing black knit ski masks and gloves were in the backseat.

'The car. Back up.'

Talley did as he was told, his headlights swinging across the walk. The woman was gone. Red taillights waited at the far end of the parking lot.

'See that car? Follow it. We won't go far.'

Talley pulled in tight on the car. It was a late-model Ford Mustang, dark green with a hard top and California plates. Talley worked at remembering the tag number, 2KLX561, then glanced in the rearview mirror as a second car tucked in tight behind his.

'Who are you?'

'Drive.'

'Is this about what's happening?'

'Just drive. Don't worry about it.'

The Mustang drove carefully, leading him back to the street, then out along Flanders Road to a minimall less than a mile away. All the shops were closed, the parking lot empty. Talley followed the Mustang into the alley behind the shops, where it stopped beside a Dumpster.

'Pull up closer. Closer. Bumper to bumper.'

He bumped the Mustang.

'Turn off the ignition. Give me the key.'

Talley had known a kind of fear when he had worked the tactical teams on SWAT before he was a negotiator; but that was an impersonal fear, a going-into-combat fear leavened by the armor you wore, the weapon you carried, and the support of your teammates. This was different, up close and personal. Men were assassinated like this, their bodies left in Dumpsters.

He turned off the ignition, but didn't take out the key. The second car came up so close that it was inches from his own, blocking him in. Talley told himself this was a good sign; they didn't want him to try to run. They wouldn't worry about it if they simply wanted to shoot him.

'Give me the damned key.'

He held it up; the hand snatched it away.

The passenger door opened. A third man slipped inside, also wearing a mask and gloves. He was wearing a black sport coat over a gray T-shirt and jeans. When his left sleeve hiked up, a gold Rolex flashed. He wasn't large, about Talley's size, maybe one-eighty, trim. The skin around his mouth and eyes was tan. He held a cell phone.

'Okay, Chief, I know you're scared, but trust me, unless you do something stupid, we're not here to hurt you. So you control that, okay? Do you understand?'

Talley tried to recall the Mustang's tag number. Was it KLX or KLS?

'Don't just stare at me, Chief. We've got to make some headway here.'

'What do you want?'

The third man gestured to the backseat with the phone, giving Talley another glimpse of the watch. Talley thought of the third man as the Watchman.

'The man behind you is going to reach around and get hold of you. Don't freak out. That's for your own good. Okay? He's just going to hold you.'

The arm looped around his neck again; a hand took his left wrist, twisted it behind his back; another took his right; the second man in the back was helping. Talley could barely breathe.

'What is this?'

'Listen.'

The Watchman put the phone to Talley's ear.

'Say hello.'

Talley couldn't imagine what they wanted or who they were. His mouth felt stuffed with cotton batting. The phone was cold against his ear.

'Who is this?'

Jane's voice, shaky and frightened.

'Jeff? Is that you?'

Talley tried to buck away from the arm crossing his throat; he strained to pull his arms free, but couldn't. Seconds passed before Talley realized the Watchman was talking to him.

'Take it easy, Chief; I know, I know. But just listen, okay? She's all right. Your kid, she's all right, too. Now just relax, breathe deep, listen. You ready to listen? Remember: Right now, from this point on, you're in control. You. You control what happens to them. You want to hear her again? You want to talk to her, see that she's okay?'

Talley nodded against the pressure of the arm, finally managed to croak.

'You sonofabitch.'

'Bad start, Chief, but I understand. I'm married myself. Me, I *wish* somebody would take my old lady, but that's just me. Anyway, here.'

The Watchman held the phone to Talley's ear again.

'Jane?'

'What's going on, Jeff? Who are these people?'

'I don't know. Are you all right? Is Mandy?'

'Jeff, I'm scared.'

Jane was crying.

The Watchman took back the phone.

'That's enough.'

'Who the hell are you?'

'Can we let you go? You past your shock and all that, we can turn you loose and you won't do something stupid?'

'You can let go.'

The Watchman glanced at the backseat, and Talley was released. The Watchman leaned toward Talley, going eye to eye and doing it with purpose.

'Walter Smith has two computer disks in his house that belong to us. Don't worry about why we want those disks. More important, don't care. But we want them, and you're going to see that we get them.'

Talley didn't know what the Watchman was talking about; he shook his head.

'What does that mean? What?'

'You're going to control the scene.'

'The Sheriffs control the scene.'

'Not anymore. It's your scene. You'll take it back or whatever it is you have to do, because no one – let me repeat that – *no one* is going into that house until *my* people go in that house.'

'You don't know what you're talking about. I can't control that.'

The Watchman raised his finger, as if he was offering a lesson.

'I know exactly what I'm talking about. You have a

189

coordinated mixed scene now with your people – the Bristo Police Department – and the Sheriffs. In a couple of hours, a group of my people are going to arrive at York Estates. You will tell everyone involved that they are an FBI tactical team. They'll look the part, and they know how to act the part. You see where I'm going with this?'

'I don't have any idea what you're talking about. I can't control any of this. I can't control what happens in that house.'

'You better get up to speed fast, then. Your wife and kid are counting on you.'

Talley didn't know what to say. He worked his fingers under his thighs, trying to think.

'What do you want me to do?'

'You get my people set up, then you stand by and wait to hear from me.'

The Watchman handed Talley the cell phone.

'When this phone rings, you answer. It'll be me. I'll tell you what to do.'

Talley stared at the phone.

'When it comes time to go in the house, my people will be the first in. Nothing, and I mean *nothing*, will be removed from that house except by my people. Do you get that?'

'I can't control what those kids do. They could be giving up right now. They could start shooting. The Sheriffs might be going inside right now.'

The Watchman slapped him, a hard straight push hitting him square in the forehead with his open palm. Talley's head rocked back.

'Don't panic, Talley. You should *know*. SWAT guys *know*. Panic kills.'

Talley gripped the phone with both hands.

'Okay. All right.'

'You're going to be thinking, What can I do? Here you are, a policeman, you're going to think about calling the FBI or bringing the Sheriffs in, about getting me before something happens to your wife and child, but, Chief, think about this: I have people right there in York Estates, right under your nose, reporting everything that happens. If you bring anyone in, if you do *anything* other than what I am telling you to do, you'll get your wife and kid back in the mail. Are we clear on that?'

'Yes.'

'When I have what I want, your wife and daughter will be released. We're cool with that. They don't know who has them just like you don't know who we are. Ignorance is bliss.'

'What is it you want? Disks? Like computer disks? Where are they, where in the house?'

'Two disks, bigger than normal disks. They're called Zip disks, labeled Disk One and Disk Two. We won't know where they are until we find them, but Smith will know.'

The Watchman opened the door, paused before leaving, his glance flicking to the phone.

'Answer when it rings, Chief.'

The keys were dropped into Talley's lap. Doors opened, closed, and Talley was alone there in the alley behind the minimall in the middle of nowhere. The Mustang pulled away. The second car roared away, backwards. Talley sat behind the wheel, breathing, unable to move, feeling apart from his own body as if this had just happened to someone else.

He clawed for the keys, started his car, and spun the wheel hard, flooring it, fishtailing gravel. He hit his lights and siren, rolling code three, blasting straight back to his condo, never bothered to pull into a spot, just left the car like that in the parking lot, lights popping, and ran inside, almost as if they might be sitting there, all of this some hallucination.

The condo was empty, the silence of it outrageously loud. He called them anyway, not knowing what else to do.

'Jane! Amanda!'

Their only sign was the keys to Jane's car, sitting plainly on the dining room table, small and hard, left there as a threat.

Talley put Jane's keys in his pocket. He went upstairs to the little desk in his bedroom where he stared at the photographs. Jane and Amanda, much younger then, stared back in a picture taken at Disneyland, Jane sitting at one of those outdoor restaurants in Adventureland, her arms wrapped around Amanda, both of them showing more white teeth than a piano. They had eaten tostadas or tacos, one, with some salsa that was so mild that they'd laughed about it, the three native Angelenos, salsa with all the kick of Campbell's tomato soup, something that only people from Minnesota or Wisconsin would find spicy. Talley choked a sob in his chest. He took the picture from the frame, put it in his pocket with the keys. He went to his closet for the blue nylon gym bag on the top shelf, and brought the bag to his bed. He took out the pistol that he had carried during his SWAT days, a Colt .45 Model 1911 that had been tuned by the SWAT armorer for accuracy and reliability. It was big, ugly, and supremely dangerous. It held only seven bullets, but SWAT used the .45 as their combat pistol because just one of those big heavy bullets could knock a large man off his feet. A .38 or a 9mm couldn't promise that, but the .45 could. It was a killer.

Talley ejected the empty magazine, filled it with seven bullets, then reseated it. He dug through the gym bag for the black ballistic nylon holster. He took off his uniform, then put on blue jeans and tennis shoes. He fitted the holster onto his belt at his side, then covered it with a black sweatshirt. He clipped his badge to his belt.

The cell phone that the Watchman gave him was sitting on his desk. Talley stared at it. What if it rang?

What if the Watchman ordered him into Walter Smith's house right now and the people inside that house were killed? What if he answered that phone to hear Jane and Amanda screaming as they were murdered?

Talley sat on the edge of the bed thinking that he was a fool. He should go directly to both the Sheriff's Detective Bureau and the FBI; even the Watchman knew it. That would be the smart way to play this mess, and that was what he would have done except that he believed that the Watchman was telling the truth about having someone at York Estates, and would kill his family. Talley was scared; it's easy to say what someone should do when they're not you; when it's you, it's a nightmare. He told himself to be careful. The Watchman was right about something else, too: Panic kills. That same message had hung on the wall at the Special Weapons and Tactics School: Panic kills. The instructors had hammered it into them. It didn't matter how urgent the situation, you had to think; act quickly but efficiently. A mind is a terrible thing to waste, and nothing wastes your mind faster than getting your ass shot off. Think.

Talley put the Watchman's phone in his pocket and drove to his office.

The Bristo Camino Police Department was a two-story space in the mall that used to be a toy store. Talley's officers jokingly called it 'the crib.' This time of night, the mall parking lot was empty; only one radio car was out front, along with the personal cars belonging to his officers. Talley left his car at the curb. The second floor contained a single holding cell, a ready room for briefings, a bathroom, and a locker room. The most serious criminals it had held were two sixteen-year-old car thieves who had driven a stolen Porsche up from Santa Monica only to wrap it around a palm tree; mostly, the cell was used to let drunk drivers sleep off their buzz. Office space for Sarah filled most of the ground floor, with the front desk being designated for the duty officer of the watch, though Sarah, herself not a sworn officer, served that post whenever she wasn't ensconced in the communications bay. Talley's office sat in the rear, but his own computer wasn't tied into the National Law Enforcement Telecommunication System; only one computer in the office could access the NLETS, and that was up front by Sarah.

Kenner, sitting at the front desk, raised his eyebrows in surprise when Talley entered.

'Hey, Chief. I thought you went seven.'

Seven was the code for taking a meal break, but it was also slang for going off duty. Talley let himself through the gate that separated the public space from the desks without making eye contact. He didn't want conversation.

'I've got more to do.'

'What's happening out at the house?'

'The Sheriffs have it.'

Sarah waved from the communications bay. She was a retired public school teacher with bright red hair who worked the job because she enjoyed it. Talley nodded at her, but didn't stop to chat the way he ordinarily would. He went straight to the NLETS computer.

Sarah called, 'I thought you went home?'

'More to do.'

'Isn't that sad about that little boy? What happened with that?'

'I just stopped by to look up something. I've got to get back to the house.'

He made his manner brusque to discourage her.

Talley typed in the Mustang's license number, 2KLX561, and requested a California Department of Motor Vehicles search.

'Ah, Chief, I'd like to get some time out there. You know, at the house.'

Kenner had come up behind him, looking hopeful. Talley leaned forward to block the computer's screen.

'Call Anders. Tell him I said to rotate you out there at the shift change.'

Talley turned back to the computer.

'Ah, Chief? You think I could work the perimeter?'

Talley blocked the screen again, letting his annoyance show.

'You want some trigger time? That it, Kenner?'

Kenner shrugged.

'Well, yes, sir.'

'See Anders.'

Talley stared at Kenner until he returned to the front desk. The DMV search came back, showing that license plate 2KLX561 was currently an unregistered listing. Next, he typed in the name *Walter Smith* and ran it through the National Crime Information Center, limiting the search to white males in the Southwest within a ten-year time frame. The NCIC search kicked back one hundred twenty-eight hits. That was too many. Talley could have limited the search if he had Smith's middle name, but he didn't. He cut the frame to five years, tried again, and this time got thirty-one hits. He skimmed the results. Twenty-one of the thirty-two arrestees were currently incarcerated, and the remaining ten were too young. As far as the law enforcement computer network knew, the Walter Smith who lived in York Estates was just another upstanding American with something in his house that men were willing to kill for.

Talley deleted the screen, then tried to recall as many details as possible about the three men and the woman who kidnapped him. The woman: short dark hair that cupped her face, five-five, slender, light-colored blouse and skirt; it had been too dark to see any more. The three men had worn nicely tailored sport coats, gloves, and masks; he had noticed no identifying characteristics. He tried to remember background noise from when he spoke with Jane, some telling sound that could identify her location, but there had been none.

Talley took out the Watchman's phone, wondering if a print could be lifted. It was a new black Nokia. The phone's battery indicator showed a full charge. Talley felt a sudden fear that the battery would fail, and he would never hear from Jane and Amanda again. He trembled as the panic grew, then forced those thoughts down. *Think.* The cell phone was his link to the people who had Jane and Amanda, a link that might lead back to them. If the Watchman had called Jane's location, that number would be in the memory. Talley's heart pounded. He pressed redial. No number came up. Talley checked the phone's stored memory, but no numbers were listed. *Think!!!* If the people holding Jane had phoned the Watchman, Talley might be able to reverse-dial the number with the star 69 feature. He pressed star 69. Nothing happened. Talley's heart pounded harder; he wanted to smash the fucking phone. He wanted to throw it against the wall, then stomp it to splinters. *Goddamnit, THINK!!!* Someone had paid for the phone and was paying for its service. Talley turned off the phone, then turned it back on. As the view screen lit, the phone's number appeared. 555–1367. Talley wanted to jump up and pump his fist. He copied the number, his only lead.

Then Talley realized he had another lead: Walter Smith. Smith could identify these people, Smith had what they wanted, and Smith might even be able to tell him where they had taken Jane and Amanda. Smith had answers. All Talley had to do was reach him.

And get him out of that house.


Talley called Larry Anders when he was five minutes from the development, saying to meet him inside the south entrance, and to wait there alone. The traffic passing the development was less than it had been earlier, but a long line of gawkers still made the going slow once Talley turned off Flanders Road. He burped his siren to make them pull to the side, then waved himself through the blockade.

Anders was parked on the side of the road. Talley pulled up behind him and flicked his lights. Anders walked back to Talley's window, looking nervous.

'What's up, Chief?'

'Where's Metzger?'

'Up with the Sheriffs in case they need something. Did I do something?'

'Get in.'

Talley waited as Anders walked around the front of the car and climbed in. Anders wasn't the oldest person on his department, but he was the senior officer in years served, and Talley respected him. He thought again that the man in the ski mask had someone here, and wondered if that person was Larry Anders. Talley recalled a photograph that had appeared in the *Los Angeles Times*, one taken at the day-care center that showed Spencer Morgan, the man who had held the children hostage, holding a gun to Talley's head. Talley thought of the trust it had taken for him to stand there while his friend Neal Craimont lined up the crosshairs.

Anders squirmed.

'Jesus, Chief, why are you staring at me like that?'

'I have something for you to do. You're not to tell anyone else what you're doing, not Metzger, not the other guys, not the Sheriffs, no one; just tell them that I want you to run down some background info, but don't tell them what. You understand me, Larry?'

Anders replied slowly.

'I guess so.'

'I can't have you guessing. Either you can keep your mouth shut or you can't. This is important.'

'This isn't something illegal, is it, Chief? I really like being a cop. I couldn't do something illegal.'

'It's police work, the real thing. I want you to find out as much as you can about Walter Smith.'

'The guy in the house?'

'I believe he's involved in illegal activity or associates with people who are. I need to find out what that is. Talk to the neighbors, but don't be obvious about it. Don't tell anyone what you're doing or what you suspect. Try to find out whatever you can about him, where he's from, stuff like that; his business, his clients, anything that will give us a handle on him. It will help if you can learn his middle name. When you've finished here, go back to the office and run him through the FBI and the NLETS database. I went back five years, but you go back twenty.'

Anders cleared his throat. He was uncomfortable with all this.

'What's the problem with telling our guys? I mean, why not?'

'Because that's the way I want it, Larry. I have a good reason, I just can't tell you right now, but I'm trusting that you'll keep your word.'

'I will, Chief. Yes, sir, I will.'

Talley gave him the Nokia's cell phone number.

'Before you do any of that, I want you to trace this cell phone number. You can do this by phone from here. Find out who it's billed to. If you need a court order, call the Palmdale District Court. They have a judge on page for night work. Sarah has the number.'

Anders looked at the slip of paper.

'The judge, he'll want to know why, won't he?'

'Tell him we believe this number will provide life-or-death information about one of the men in the house.'

Anders nodded dully, knowing it was a lie.

'All right.'

Talley thought, trying to remember if there was something else, something that might give him a line to find out who he was dealing with.

'When you get back to the office, run a DMV stolen-vehicle search for a green Mustang, this year's model. It would be a recent theft, maybe even today.'

Anders took out his pad to make notes.

'Ah, you got a tag?'

'It's running a dead plate. If you get a hit, note where it was stolen. Who was checking into the building permits?'

'Ah, that was Cooper.'

'I want you to stay on that.'

'It's midnight.'

'If you have to get the city supervisors out of bed, do it. Tell them the Sheriffs are desperate for the house plans, it's life or death, whatever you have to say, but find out who built that house.'

'Yes, sir.'

'You're going to have to work all night, Larry. It's important.'

'That's okay.'

'Update me with everything you find out, whatever time it is. Don't use the radio. Call my cell. You got the number?'

'Yes, sir.'

'Get to it.'

Talley watched Anders drive away. He told himself that Anders could be trusted; he had just placed the lives of his family in Larry Anders's hands.

Talley parked outside Mrs. Peña's house and went to the Sheriff's command van. The back gate was open, glowing crimson from the soft red lights within. Martin, Hicks, and the I.O. supervisor were clumped around the coffee machine.

Talley rapped on the side of the van as he climbed inside. When Martin glanced over, she smiled with a warmth that surprised him.

'I thought you left.'

'I'm taking back command of the scene.'

It took a moment for his statement to register, then Martin's brow furrowed. The warmth was gone.

'I don't understand. *You* requested our help. You couldn't wait to hand off to me.'

Talley had readied the lie.

'I know I did, Captain, but it's a liability issue. The city supervisors want a representative of Bristo to be in charge. I'm sorry, but that's the way it has to be. As of now, I'm resuming command of the scene.'

Hicks put his fists on his hips.

'What kind of half-assed hicktown crap is this?'

Talley pointedly looked at Hicks.

'No tactical action is to be taken without my approval. Is that clear?'

Martin stalked across the van, stopping only inches away. She was almost as tall as Talley.

'Outside. I want to talk about this.'

Talley didn't move. He knew that the Sheriffs regularly worked under local restraints when they functioned in advisory and support roles; Martin would still be in direct control of her people, though Talley would command the operation. Martin would go along.

'There's nothing to talk about, Captain. I'm not going to tell you how to do your job; I need you, and I appreciate your being here. But I have to sign off on any action we take, and right now I'm saying that there will be no tactical action.'

Martin started to say something, then stopped. She seemed to search his eyes. Talley met her gaze and did not look away, though he felt embarrassed and frightened. He wondered if she could see that he was lying.

'What if those assholes lose it in there, Chief? You want me to track you down and waste time asking your permission to save those kids?'

Talley could barely answer.

'It won't come to that.'

'You don't know that. That house could go to hell in a second.'

Talley stepped back. He wanted to get out of the van.

'I want to talk to Maddox. Is he still at the house?'

Martin continued to search his eyes, and now she lowered her voice.

'What's wrong, Chief? You look like something's bothering you.'

Talley looked away.

'It has to be this way, that's all. I have this city council.'

Martin considered him again, then lowered her voice still more as if she didn't want Hicks and the Intelligence Officer to hear.

'Maddox told me a little about you. You were pretty hot stuff down there in Los Angeles.'

'That was a long time ago.'

Martin shrugged, then smiled, though not so warmly as before.

'Not so long.'

'I want to see Maddox.'

'He's in the cul-de-sac. I'll tell him you're on the way.'

'Thanks, Martin. For not making this worse.'

She stared at him, but turned away without answering.

Talley found Maddox and Ellison waiting at their car in the mouth of the cul-de-sac.

Ellison looked curious.

'Can't get too much of a good thing, huh, Chief?'

'Guess not. Has he made any more demands?'

Maddox shook his head.

'Nothing. We've been phoning every fifteen or twenty minutes to keep him awake, but other than that, there's nothing.'

'All right. I want to move up by the house.'

Maddox opened his driver's-side door.

'You taking back the phone?'

'That's it. Let's go.'

Talley checked the Watchman's cell phone, making sure it was on. They eased the car into the cul-de-sac and returned to the house.

*

Jennifer nodded in and out of a light drowse, never quite sleeping, listening to the helicopters and the squawk of police voices that she could not understand. She thought they might be dreams. Jennifer couldn't get comfortable with her wrists taped, lying in her bed, on top of the covers, the room so hot it left her sweaty and gross. Every time she felt herself falling asleep, the phone rang, distant from downstairs, and left her head filled with thoughts she could not stop: Her father; her brother, thinking that he might be creeping through the walls to do something stupid.

Jennifer jerked upright when the door opened. She saw Mars framed in dim light. Her skin crawled, being on the bed with him there, him and his toad eyes. She scrambled to her feet.

Mars said, 'We can't make the microwave work.'

'What?'

'We're hungry. You're going to cook.'

'I'm not going to cook for you. You're out of your mind.'

'You'll cook.'

'Fuck yourself!'

The words came before she could stop them.

Mars stepped close, then searched her eyes the way he had when she was tied to the chair, first one eye, then the other. She tried to step back, but he laced his fingers in her hair, holding her close. He spoke so softly that she could barely hear.

'I told you, that's a bad thing.'

'Leave go of me.'

He bunched his fist, pulling her hair.

'Stop.'

He twisted his fist, pulling tighter. His face held no expression except for a mild curiosity. The pain was enormous. Jennifer's entire body was rigid and clammy.

'I can do anything I want to you, bad girl. Remember that. Think about it.'

Mars pushed her through the door, then roughly along the hall and down the stairs. The kitchen lights were on, bright and blinding after so long in the black of her room. Mars cut the tape at her wrists, then peeled it away. She had not seen his knife before. It was curved and wicked. When he turned to the refrigerator, she glanced at the French doors, and fought the urge to run even though Thomas had given her that chance. Two frozen pizzas were sitting on the counter and the microwave oven was open.

'Heat the pizza.'

Mars turned away from her and went to the refrigerator, his back wide and threatening. Jennifer remembered the paring knife, pushed behind the food processor when they first invaded her home. She glanced toward the food processor, looking for it. When she looked back at Mars, he was watching her, holding a carton of eggs. It was like he could see inside her.

'I want scrambled eggs and hot dogs on mine.'

'On the pizza?'

'I like it with hot sauce and butter.'

As Jennifer got a frying pan and a bowl and the other things she would need, Dennis appeared from the entry. His eyes were dark and hollow.

'Is she cooking?'

'She's making eggs.'

Dennis grunted listlessly, then turned away without another word. She found herself wishing that he would die.

'When are you going to let us go?'

'Shut up. All you have to do is make the pizza.'

She broke all nine eggs into a glass bowl, then put the frying pan on to heat. She didn't bother with salt and pepper. She wanted the eggs to taste nasty.

Mars stood in the family room, staring at her.

203

'Stop watching me. I'm going to burn the eggs.'

Mars went to the French doors.

Him walking away was like a weight being lifted. She could breathe again. Jennifer beat the eggs, sprayed the pan with PAM, then poured in the eggs. She got hot sauce from the refrigerator, then glanced at Mars. He was standing by the French doors, staring at nothing, with his right hand on the glass. She shook hot sauce into the eggs until the eggs were orange, hoping it would poison them, then she thought that she might be able to poison them for real. Her mother had sleeping pills, there was probably rat poison or weedkiller in the garage, there was Drāno. She thought that Thomas might be able to get the sleeping pills. Then, if they made her cook again, she could put it in the food.

She glanced over at Mars again, expecting that he had read her mind again and would be watching her, but he had moved deeper into the family room. She looked at the paring knife. The handle was sticking out from behind the food processor, directly beneath the cabinet with the plates. She glanced at Mars again. She couldn't see his face, only the shadow of his bulk. He might have been looking at her, but she couldn't tell. She walked directly to the cabinets, took down some plates, and picked up the knife. She fought the urge to glance at Mars, knowing that if their eyes locked he would know, he could tell. She pushed the knife under her shirt into the waist of her shorts and into the bottom of her bathing suit, horizontally so that it lay against the flat of her belly.

'What are you doing?'

'Getting plates.'

'You're burning the eggs. I can smell'm.'

She brought the plates to the stove, feeling the hard shape of the knife low on her belly, thinking that now if they turned their backs, she could kill them.

Across the house in the office, the telephone rang.

# CHAPTER 15

Friday, 11:02 P.M.

TALLEY

The Sheriffs had set up a dedicated phone for Maddox and Ellison. It was looped by a cell link from Maddox's radio car to the command van, where it was hardwired into the Smith's phone line beneath the street. It provided the negotiators with a cell phone's freedom of movement while allowing all conversations to be recorded in the van. Martin, Hicks, and everyone else in the van would be listening to every word. Talley didn't want that.

Talley took out his cell phone, but he had forgotten Smith's number and had to ask for it.

Maddox, watching him, said, 'We've got the hard line.'

Talley ignored him.

'I'm more comfortable with this. You got the number?'

Unless the Sheriffs had changed the phone block, the Smiths' phone should still accept Talley's calls. Ellison read off the number as Maddox watched Talley. Talley knew they thought this was odd, but he didn't care.

'Why are you doing this?'

'What?'

'Out of the blue, you're back, you're calling the house. Every call has to have a point. Why?'

Talley stopped dialing the number and tried to order his thoughts. He had developed a certain amount of respect for Maddox and wanted to tell him the truth, but his fear wouldn't allow it. He wanted Smith. That's all he knew. Smith was his link to the people who had his wife and daughter. He considered the house and what might be on the other side of its door, then looked back at Maddox. He needed to say something that would bring Maddox onto his side.

'I'm scared that Smith is dead. I think I can push Rooney into telling us without tipping him off that the boy called.'

'If he's dead, Rooney isn't going to say shit and the boy would've told us.'

'So what do we do, Maddox? You want to breach the house?'

Maddox held his gaze, then looked back at the house and nodded.

'All right, then.'

Talley redialed the number, then waited for the ring. The front and sides of the house glowed from the banks of white lights that the Sheriffs had erected, the glare so hot that the house seemed washed out and pale. Exaggerated black shadows stretched across the lawn like grave markers. The phone rang four long times before Rooney picked up.

'That you, Talley? I saw you come back.'

For the space of three heartbeats, Talley said nothing. That had never happened before, but it took that time for Talley to push aside the anxiety that he knew would be in his voice. He could have nothing weak in his voice. Nothing that might warn Rooney or put him on guard.

'Talley?'

'Hello, Dennis. You there in the office, watching us?'

The shutters flicked open, then closed.

'I guess you are. Did you miss me?'

'I don't like that new guy, Maddox. He thinks I'm stupid, calling every fifteen minutes, pretending he wants to make sure we're all right, but it's to keep us awake. I'm not stupid.'

Talley felt himself grow calm now that he was back on the phone. He had hated it earlier today, but now the familiarity of it strengthened him, just him and the phone and the subject, a small self-contained world where he played a game against the voice on the other end. It surprised him that he felt a confidence that he hadn't known in years, a deep sense that he could control this world if not the larger one. He glanced up at the helicopters. Red and green angels.

'I came back tonight because we've got a big problem out here.'

Rooney hesitated as Talley knew he would; thinking. Talley knew that what he was about to say would surprise Maddox and Ellison, so he glanced at them and touched his lips. Then he filled the silence that Rooney left, firming his voice to show that he was serious and concerned.

'I need you to let me talk to Mr. Smith.'

'We been through that, Talley. Forget it.'

'I can't forget it this time, Dennis. These people out here, the Sheriffs, they think you won't let me talk to Mr. Smith or his children because they're dead. They think you've murdered them.'

'That's bullshit!'

Maddox and Ellison shifted next to him, staring. Talley felt the weight of their eyes but ignored them.

'If you don't let me speak with Mr. Smith, they are going to assume that he is in fact dead, and they are going to breach the house.'

Rooney started cursing and shouting that everyone was going to die and that the house would burn. Talley expected his reaction and let him vent.

Maddox gripped Talley's arm.

'What the hell are you saying? You can't say somethin' like that!'

Talley held up a hand, telling him to back off. He waited for a break in Dennis's rant.

'Dennis? Dennis, I'm telling you right now that I

207

believe you, but they don't. This isn't up to me, son. I believe you. But unless you give me something to convince them, they're going in. Let me speak to him, Dennis.'

Talley was taking a big chance. If Smith was conscious and able to speak, Rooney might very well put him on the phone. If that happened, Talley would still try to get the information about the men in the car, but he knew the odds of that would be slim. Talley's only hope was that Smith was still unconscious. If Rooney would admit his condition, Talley had a shot at getting Smith released.

Rooney said, 'Fuck you and fuck them! If you try to come in here, these kids are gonna die!'

'Let me speak to him, Dennis. Please. They think he's dead, and they are going to come in.'

Rooney screamed, 'SHIT!'

Talley could hear the frustration in Rooney's voice. He waited. Rooney was silent and that meant he was thinking; he couldn't put Smith on the phone, but he was scared to admit that Smith was injured. Talley felt a surge of excitement, but hid it. He softened his voice, made it understanding and sympathetic. *We're both in this together, pal.*

'Is something wrong in there, Dennis? Is there a reason you can't put Smith on the phone?'

Rooney didn't answer.

'Talk to me, Dennis.'

Rooney took almost a full minute before he finally answered.

'He got knocked out. He won't wake up.'

Talley knew better than to ask how; it would put Rooney on the defensive, and Talley didn't want to do that. He had Smith's situation out in the open, so now he could try to get Smith. Maddox, still watching, raised his eyebrows in a question. Talley nodded, getting there; he repeated the admission for Maddox.

'So you're saying that Mr. Smith is unconscious. Okay, okay, I'm glad you're telling me this, Dennis. That explains things. Now we can deal with it.'

'They better not try to come in here.'

*They*, not *you*.

'I think we can work with this, Dennis. Are we talking about a head injury here? I'm not asking how this happened, but is that what's wrong with him?'

'It was an accident.'

'Is he breathing?'

'Yeah, but he's out cold. He can't talk.'

Now Talley had to move it to the next level. Now he had to get in the house, or get Smith out.

'Dennis, now I understand why you couldn't put him on, but you've got a guy in there who needs to be in the hospital. Let me come get him.'

'Fuck that! I know what you bastards will do, you'll rush the house.'

Rooney was scared. He was flat-out terrified.

'No. No, we wouldn't do that.'

'Fuck yourself, Talley. You ain't comin' in!'

Talley pressed harder. He knew that he could have suggested sending in a paramedic or a doctor, but he didn't want anyone going in; he wanted Walter Smith coming out.

'If you won't let us come in, then all you have to do is put him outside, right outside the front door.'

'I'm not stupid! I'm not gonna walk out the door with all the snipers you have out there!'

Talley saw movement to his side, Maddox and Ellison. He heard Maddox key his radio, telling someone to have the ambulance brought up.

'No one is going to shoot you. Just put him outside and we'll come get him. If you save his life, Dennis, it will help you when you get to court.'

'No!'

'That's all it takes, Dennis. Put him outside.'

Rooney's voice rose.

'No!'

'Save him.'

Rooney shouted again.

'No!'

'Help me help you.'

Rooney slammed down the phone.

'Dennis?'

Nothing. Rooney was gone.

'DENNIS?!'

Maddox and Ellison stared at him, motionless, waiting.

'What?'

Talley had been so close, but he had wanted it too much. He had pressed too hard. He had lost.


DENNIS

Dennis slammed down the phone, then picked it up and smashed it on Smith's desk.

'That fuck! That fuck wants me dead!'

He was so angry that his head felt swollen and thick. Kevin paced in front of the television with his arms crossed, a nervous wreck. Kevin went to the couch and stared down at Walter Smith.

'We should let them have him. He's a lot worse.'

'*Fuck* them! They didn't give us a helicopter, did they?'

'What does that matter? Look at him, Dennis! I think he's having seizures.'

Smith would be still as a corpse, then he would suddenly jerk, his whole body twitching. Dennis couldn't look at him.

'You wouldn't know a seizure if it bit you on the ass.'

'*Look* at him. Maybe it's brain damage.'

Dennis went to the shutters. Nothing had changed

since he'd looked the time before, or from the time before that: The cul-de-sac was filled with cops and cop cars, and more seemed to be coming. Dennis wouldn't admit it to Kevin, but he was scared. He was hungry and tired, and the smell of the gasoline in the entry was making him sick. His pockets bulged with the money he had stuffed in them.

Kevin came over to him.

'Dennis, he's dying. It's bad enough we got the Chinaman and that cop, this guy dies they'll add another murder charge.'

'Shut up, Kevin. Jesus.'

'We should talk to a lawyer like that cop said. We need a lawyer to cut us a deal. We can blame Mars.'

'Don't let him hear you!'

'I don't care if he hears!'

'Just calm down, Kevin. I'm working on it. I just need some food, is all. Some food and some time. We'll think of something. The girl is in there cooking.'

'How can you even think about eating? I'm about to puke.'

'I saw some Gaviscom in the bathroom. Eat that.'

'I want to sleep.'

'Would you shut the fuck up?! The cops will put you in jail, where you can sleep every night for the rest of your life!'

Dennis knew Kevin was right, but he tried not to think about it. Every plan he hatched had holes big enough to hide a house, and now the cops were threatening to break down the doors. Walter Smith twitched and trembled again. It looked like he was freezing to death, the way you'd shiver if you were sleeping on a block of ice. Dennis felt tears well in his eyes because he was so scared. Here he was, sitting on a million bucks, and he didn't know what to do.

Mars and the girl came in with the pizzas, Dennis

thinking that maybe the food would help, but when the girl saw her father, she dropped the pizza and ran straight to her father.

'What's wrong with him? *Daddy?!*'

Dennis thought his head would burst.

She dropped down to her knees, leaning over her father but not touching him.

'Look at the way he's shaking. Why is he shaking like this? Aren't you going to do something?'

Kevin put on the pussy face.

'Dennis, he needs a doctor.'

Dennis wanted to smash him.

'No.'

The girl glared at him, screaming.

'He's ice-cold! Can't you see this? Don't you know he's dying?!'

Kevin stepped closer, in Dennis's face now, pleading.

'*Please*, Dennis. If he dies, we got another murder charge. We're fucked up bad enough.'

Dennis was scared. He didn't want the sonofabitch to die. He didn't want another murder charge.

Kevin picked up the phone.

'Call them. Let them have him.'

'No.'

'They'll like it that you're trying to help. They might even cut us some slack. Think about it, Dennis. *Think*.'

Kevin stepped closer, his whisper more than a plea.

'If those SWAT guys come in here, you'll never keep the money.'

Dennis glanced at Mars, who sat on the floor with a plate of eggs and pizza, eating. Mars met Dennis's eyes, then made a little smile like he knew it all along, like Dennis didn't have the balls to play it hard.

Fuck Mars.

Dennis wanted the money.

He took the phone and punched in Talley's number.

★

Talley was charging his phone off the cigarette lighter in Maddox's car when the phone rang. He tensed, a jag of fear jolting him because he thought it was the Watchman's Nokia.

Maddox said, 'That's your phone.'

Talley opened his phone.

'Talley.'

It was Rooney.

'Okay, Talley. If you want him, come get him. But just you.'

Talley had thought it was over, thought he had completely blown any chance at getting to Smith, but here was Rooney delivering him. Talley was dead, but now he lived again. He had a chance at Jane and Amanda!

Talley rolled to his knees and peered over the car's hood. He muted the phone to hiss at Maddox.

'Ambulance. He's coming out.'

Ellison said, 'Sonofabitch.'

Maddox went back on the hard line as Talley un-muted his phone.

'Okay, Dennis. I'm here. I'm with you. Let's figure this out.'

'There's nothing to figure out, goddamnit. Come get him. But you better keep SWAT outta here. That's the deal.'

'I can't carry him by myself. I'll have to bring someone else.'

'Fuckin' liar! You're going to try to kill me!'

'That won't happen, Dennis. You can trust me. Me and one other person and a stretcher. That's it.'

'Fuck you, Talley, *fuck you!* All right! You and one other guy, but that's it! You gotta strip down! I want you stripped! I gotta know you aren't carrying guns!'

Talley looked at Maddox and twirled his finger, telling Maddox to have the ambulance get here fast.

'Okay, Dennis. If that's what you want, that's what we'll do.'

'You'll keep'm outta here. That's the deal, right? We have a deal?'

'That's the deal.'

'I swear to Christ if those bastards try something these kids are gonna die! Everybody's gonna die.'

'Just take it easy. Work with me and no one has to die.'

'Fuck you!'

The connection popped in Talley's ear. Rooney was gone.

Talley stared at the house. Several moments passed before he lowered the phone; his hand was okay, but his ear hurt from the pressure. His sweatshirt was soaked, and the Colt cut into his belly. He felt numb.

Maddox stared at him, and Ellison smiled.

'Sonofa*bitch*. You kicked one free. That was great work, man. That was a *clinic*.'

Talley left them without a word. He climbed into the backseat, stripped off his clothes except for his underwear and shoes, and waited for the ambulance. In an earlier life Talley would have felt proud, but now he wasn't. He hadn't done it for Walter Smith. He was risking Smith's life, his own, and likely the children's in the house. He had done it for himself, and for Amanda and Jane.

# CHAPTER 16

Friday, 11:19 P.M.

TALLEY

Martin buzzed around him like an angry wasp. She had ridden up in the ambulance with an ER doctor named Klaus from Canyon Country Emergency.

'Wear a vest. Just strap it over your chest, he'll be able to see you're not armed.'

'The deal was that we would be stripped. I don't want to spook him.'

Klaus was a young, thin man in black-framed glasses. He introduced himself as he shook Talley's hand.

'I was told that we have a head trauma and possible gunshot wounds.'

'Let's hope not, Doctor.'

Klaus smiled awkwardly, embarrassed.

'I guess they sent me because I did two years at Martin Luther King down in South Central. You see everything down there.'

One of the paramedics, an overweight man named Bigelow, volunteered to go with Talley. Here was Bigelow, walking over from the ambulance in the dim light behind the front line, wearing only striped boxers with his clunky paramedic shoes and black socks up to his knees. Bigelow's partner, a woman named Colby, brought the stretcher.

Talley said, 'You ready?'

'Yes, sir. Good to go.'

Martin seemed irritated.

'You know it's stupid to agree to something like this. You were SWAT. You know you never expose yourself without protection. We could end up with two bodies out there.'

'I know.'

Talley didn't mention the day-care center. He folded his Colt into his sweatshirt, left it on Maddox's backseat with his clothes, then joined Bigelow. He wanted this thing to happen before Rooney changed his mind.

Talley called the house on his cell phone. Rooney answered on the first ring.

'Okay, Dennis. Put him outside. We're stripped, so you can see we're unarmed. We'll wait in the drive. We won't approach the house until after you've closed the door.'

Rooney hung up without answering.

Martin said, 'I don't like this. Tactical people should recover this man.'

Talley ignored her, and glanced at Bigelow.

'Here we go. I'll walk in front of you going up to the door. Once we have him on the stretcher, I'll take the rear position coming out. Okay?'

'You don't have to do that.'

'It'll be fine.'

Talley and Bigelow went around the car and stepped in front of the lights. It was like passing into a world of glare. Stick-figure shadows moved into the mouth of the drive, then stopped, waiting. Talley could tell that Bigelow was frightened; he was probably worried because of what Martin had said.

'It's going to be all right.'

'Oh, sure. I know.'

'We'd look pretty silly if they put our picture in the paper.'

Bigelow smiled nervously.

Talley watched the house. First, the shutters opened like a narrowed eye. That would be Rooney, looking them over for weapons. Smith's front door opened, a crack at

216

first, then wider. Talley sensed the difference in the line of officers behind him; their shuffling stopped, no one cleared their throat or coughed. The sound from one of the helicopters changed in pitch and a light swept to the door, offering nothing against the glare of the floodlights. It wasn't Dennis Rooney. Kevin and Mars Krupchek waddled out with Smith between them, put him on the front entry about six feet from the door, then returned to the house.

'Okay, let's do it.'

Talley went directly to Walter Smith. Here was this middle-aged man wearing a Polo shirt, stonewashed jeans, and sneakers, and men were willing to murder Jane and Amanda for something in his house. The contusion on the side of his head was visible even from the mouth of the drive.

Bigelow said, 'Let me set down by his head.'

Talley stepped away, letting the paramedic open the stretcher and lock out the frame. Talley kept his eyes averted from the shutters and did not try to look into the house. He watched Smith. He wanted to see some sign that Smith was waking, but the depth of Smith's sleep scared him. Smith trembled from the center of his body, and Talley grew frightened that the man might be in a coma.

'How's he look?'

Bigelow peeled back an eyelid, flashed a penlight in Smith's eye, and grunted.

'Pretty bad concussion for sure.'

Bigelow fingered Smith's neck, probing for a cervical injury, and seemed satisfied by what he found.

'Okay. We're good. We don't need a brace. I'll support his head and shoulders. You lift beneath his hips and knees. He's going to be heavier than you think, so be ready. On three. Three.'

They slid Smith onto the stretcher. Bigelow started

fastening a strap across Smith's chest, but Talley stopped him.

'Don't bother with it. Let's get him out of here while we can.'

They moved straight down the sidewalk to the street and into the lights, where they were immediately surrounded by Hicks's tactical team. Klaus ran up alongside the stretcher, snapping at Bigelow.

'Why isn't this man's neck braced?'

'I didn't see any sign of cervical injury.'

'Goddamnit, he should've been braced anyway.'

Colby took over from Talley to help Bigelow. Ellison brought over Talley's clothes, and Talley pulled on his pants while they loaded Smith into the ambulance. Talley followed Klaus inside.

'I have to talk to him.'

'Hang on.'

If Klaus was shy and awkward before, now he was focused and intense. He peeled back Smith's eyelid and flashed a penlight in his eye just as Bigelow had done. Then he did the same with the other eye.

'We've got unequal pupilation. At best it's a severe concussion, but it could mean brain damage. We'll have to do plates and a CT scan at the hospital to know for sure.'

'Wake him. I need to talk to him.'

Klaus kept working. He checked Smith's pulse.

'I'm not going to wake this man.'

'I just need him for a few minutes. That's why I got him.'

Klaus pressed his stethoscope to Smith's neck.

'He's going to the hospital. He could have an intracranial hematoma or a fracture, or both. You get a pressure buildup in the brain, it can be bad.'

Talley leaned past Klaus. He took Smith by the face and shook him.

'Smith! Wake up!'

Klaus grabbed Talley's hand, trying to pull it away.

'What the fuck are you doing? Get away from him!'

Talley shook Smith harder.

'Wake up, goddamnit!'

Smith's eyes fluttered, one open more than the other. He didn't seem to be looking at Talley, so Talley leaned closer. The eyes seemed to focus.

Talley said, 'Who are you?'

Klaus pushed at him now.

'Let go of him. I'll have you brought up on charges, you sonofabitch.'

Smith's eyes lost their focus and closed. Talley took Klaus by the arm, trying to make him see.

'Use smelling salts, give him a shot, whatever. I just need a minute.'

Colby cranked the engine, and Talley slapped at the wall, shouting.

'*Don't move this van!*'

Klaus and Bigelow both stared at him. Klaus slowly looked at Talley's hand gripping his arm.

'I'm not going to wake him. I don't even know that I can. Now let go of me.'

'We're talking about lives here. Innocent lives. I just need to ask him a few questions.'

'Let go of me.'

Talley stared into the hard, angry eyes. Tension knotted his face and neck. He held tight to Klaus's arm and thought about the Colt folded in his sweatshirt.

'Just one question. Please.'

The hard little eyes showed no mercy.

'*He can't answer you.*'

Talley stared at Smith's still form. So close. So close. Klaus looked down at his arm again, Talley still squeezing tight.

'Let go of me, goddamnit. We're taking this man to the hospital.'

Martin was watching him from the door, Ellison and Metzger behind her. Talley released the doctor's arm.

'When is he going to wake up?'

'I don't know if he'll ever wake up. You get bleeding between the skull and brain, the pressure can build to such a degree that brain death can result. I don't know. Now stay in or get out, but just let us go.'

Talley looked at Smith again, feeling helpless. He climbed out of the ambulance and pulled Metzger aside.

'Who's still here? Which of our guys is still here?'

'Jorgy. I think Campbell is still – '

'Then Jorgenson stays here. I want you waiting in this guy's lap. I want to know the *second*, and I mean the second, that he wakes up.'

Metzger turned away, keying her shoulder mike for Jorgenson.

Talley walked back to Maddox's car for the rest of his gear. His chest heaved. He felt angry and closed. He had put everyone at risk, and Smith was beyond him. Smith couldn't talk. He stared at the house, wanting to do something, but there was nothing to do.

Talley felt himself hating Dennis Rooney, and wanted to kill him.

He turned away and saw Martin watching him. He didn't care.


DENNIS


None of it looked real: Talley and the other guy in their underwear, carrying Smith away; Smith being loaded into the ambulance; the search-lights from the helicopters crisscrossing each other over the ground like light sabers. The pools of light were so bright that all the color was washed from the picture; the cops were gray shadows, the ambulance pink, the street blue. Dennis watched the ambulance work its way from the cul-de-sac, thinking only then that the ambulance could have been his ride out, that he could have made it a part of the deal, grab the suitcase with the money, tape his hand to a gun and the gun to Smith, then take over the ambulance and make them drive him south to the border. Why did all the best ideas come when it was too late?

Mars stepped up beside him with the same look he had for the Mexicans at work: I can see inside you; I know what you're thinking; you have no secrets from me.

'They would have killed you as soon as you got into the ambulance. Better to stay in here.'

Dennis glanced at Mars, then walked away, pissed that Mars found him so obvious. Mars was getting to be a pain in the ass. Dennis sat at Smith's desk and put up his feet.

'Staying here sucks, Mars. You might like it, but I want to get the hell out. I bought us some time, now we've got to figure this out. Any ideas?'

He looked from Mars to Kevin, but neither of them answered.

'Great. That's just fucking great. If anyone decides to help, just speak up.'

Dennis turned to the girl and spread his hands.

'All right. Your old man's out. You happy now?'

'Thank you.'

'I'm fuckin' starving. Go back in the kitchen and fix something else. This time don't throw it on the floor. And make some coffee. Make it strong. We're gonna be up all night.'

Mars took the girl back to the kitchen.

When they were gone, Dennis noticed that Kevin was staring at him.

'What?'

'We're not going to get out of here.'

'For chrissake! *Please!*'

'Mars and I don't care about the money. You won't let go of it and that's why we're still here. There's no way to get away with it, Dennis. We're surrounded. We're on fucking television. We're *fucked*.'

Dennis pushed out of the chair so quickly that Kevin jumped back. He was sick of dealing with their negativity.

'We're fucked until we think of a way out, asshole. Then we're not fucked, we're rich.'

Dennis stalked around the desk and went to the den. The smell of gasoline was strong there, drifting in from the hall, but he wanted a drink, and he wanted to be in the den. The den was his favorite room. The dark wood paneling and plush leather furniture made Dennis feel rich, like he was in the lobby of a fine hotel. And the bar itself was beautiful: beaten copper that looked bright and shiny and a thousand years old, bar cabinets inlaid with frosted glass, and stainless steel fixtures gleaming with the overhead light. Dennis selected a bottle of Stolichnaya vodka, then found ice in a small refrigerator and glasses on a smoked glass shelf. He poured a short one, then went back around the bar to sit on a stool. Dennis peeled a hundred-dollar bill from the roll in his pocket and tossed it on the bar.

'Keep the change, m'man.'

Dennis drank most of the vodka, loving the way it raked his throat, a stiff belt that pushed its way into his head. He refilled his glass. The clean cold vodka burned his nose and made his eyes water. He rubbed his eyes, but couldn't make the water stop.

*They lived in a one-bedroom apartment above an Exxon station, Dennis, age eleven, Kevin, two years younger, and their mother, Flo Rooney. Dennis didn't know her age then or now; their father was long gone, a pothead named Frank Rooney who fixed transmissions and didn't pay child support. Well, fuckit, they weren't married anyway; common-law.*

*Dennis shoved Kevin toward the bedroom, Kevin with big bug eyes like they were gonna pop from his head,*

scrambling backwards because he was scared. They were
supposed to be sleeping; the world was dark.
'They're doing it.'
'Nuh-uh. Stop saying that.'
'Can't ya hear'm? They're doin' the nasty. Let's go see.'
They had lived in more apartments than Dennis could
remember, some for just a week or two, once for almost a
year; dingy places with stained ceilings and toilets that
ran. Flo Rooney usually worked a job, once she worked
two, and more than once she had none. There was never
enough money. Flo was a short woman with a body like a
bowling ball, Q-Tip legs, and bad skin. She liked her gin
and smelled of Noxzema. When she got in her mopes and
had too much gin, she would bitch to the boys that she
didn't have enough money to keep them, that she would
have to put them in a home. Kevin would cry, but Dennis
would pray: *Please, please, put me in the fuckin' home. It
was always about money.*

Dennis shoved Kevin toward their mother's bedroom
door. Both boys were trying to be quiet because she was
with a man she had brought home from the bar. This
month she was working as a barmaid, next month it
would be something else, but there was always a man.
She called them her 'little pleasures.' Dennis called them
drunks.
'Don't ya want to see'm doin' it?'
'No!'
'You said you did! Listen to what he's doin' to her!'
'Dennis, stop! I'm scared!'
The scent of sweat and sex hung sharp in the air, and
Dennis hated her for it. He was jealous of the time she
gave them, and humiliated by what she let them do, and
by what she did to them. He was ashamed, but at the
same time excited. Her gasping, grunting curses drew
him.
He pushed Kevin again, this time more gently.
'Go on. Then you'll know.'

223

*This time Kevin went, creeping to the door. Dennis stayed on their sleeper couch, watching. He wasn't sure why he was pushing Kevin so hard to see; maybe he wanted Kevin to hate her as much as he did. With their father on the bum and Flo working, Dennis usually had to see after his younger brother, making their breakfast and getting them to school, seeing that Kevin got home okay and making dinner. If Dennis had to be Kevin's father and mother, there wasn't room for another. Maybe that was it, or maybe he just wanted to punish her.*

*Kevin reached the door and peeked inside. Dennis knew that something nasty was going on because he could hear the man telling her what to do. She hadn't even bothered to close the door.*

*Kevin watched for the longest time, and then he stepped into the door, right out in the open where their mother could see.*

*Dennis whispered loudly.*

*'Kev!'*

*Kevin sobbed, then began to cry.*

*Inside the room, the man yelled, 'Sonofabitch! Get the hell outta here!'*

*Kevin stumbled backward as the man came lurching through the door, naked and with a huge glistening erection. He was carrying his jeans.*

*'I'll teach you to watch, you little shit!'*

*He was a big man, his body white and arms dark, coarse and hairy with tattoos on his shoulders and a loose flabby gut. His eyes glowed bright red from booze and pot. He stripped a thick leather belt from the jeans, then chased after Kevin, swinging the belt. Its buckle was a great brass oval inlaid with turquoise. The belt came down, cracking across Kevin's back, and Kevin screamed.*

*Dennis drove into the man as hard as he could, flinging punches that had no effect, and now the belt was his,*

*snapping across him over and over and over until all his
tears were gone.*

*She never came out, and after a while the man went
back into the room. Her little pleasure.*

'Dennis?'

Dennis cleared his eyes, then slid off the bar stool.

'Be quiet, Kevin. I'm not leaving here until I can take
that cash.'

Dennis went back to the office and unplugged the
phone. There was no point in talking to the cops until he
knew what to say. He wanted the money.


KEN SEYMORE


The Channel Eight news van was parked at the edge of
the empty lot. The reporter was a pretty boy, couldn't
have been more than twenty-five, twenty-six, something
like that, who got off telling everyone he went to USC.
Trojan this, Trojan that, God's a Trojan. A Trojan was a
fuckin' rubber, but Seymore didn't say that. The reporter
pool complained all evening because there were no
toilets; the local cops promised that a honeywagon was
coming out, but so far, zip.

Seymore asked the guy if it would be all right to step
behind their van, take the lizard for a walk.

The pretty boy laughed, sure, but watch where you
step, they got a regular lizard trail back there. Dick.
Seymore thought he was the kind of guy who ordered
chocolate martinis.

Seymore stepped behind the van where no one could
see him and did two spoons of crank. It hit the top of his
head like a blast of cold air and made his eyes burn, but it
kept him awake. It was after two and all of them were
fighting the hours. Seymore noted that the Asian chick
with the hot ass kept ducking into her SUV and had a fine

set of the sniffles to show for it. A regular one-woman Hoover convention.

Coming out from behind the van, Seymore saw the Channel Eight reporter conferring with his producer and cameraperson, a man with hugely muscled arms. They looked excited.

Seymore said, 'Thanks, buddy.'

'No problem. You hear? They're getting one out of the house.'

Seymore stopped.

'They are?'

'I think it's the father. He's hurt.'

A siren spooled up, and they all knew it was the ambulance. Every camera crew in the lot hustled to the street in hopes of a shot, but the ambulance left from a different exit; the siren grew louder, peaked, then faded.

Seymore's phone rang as the siren dopplered away. He answered as he walked away, lowering his voice but unable to hide his irritation. He knew who it was; he started right in.

'Why the fuck I gotta hear this from a reporter? Fuckin' Smith comes out, forchrissake, and I gotta learn about it *last*?'

'Do you think I can get to a phone any time I want? I'm right out front in this; I have to be careful.'

'All right, all right. So tell me, was he talking? The guy here says he was hurt.'

'I don't know. I couldn't get close enough.'

'Did he have the disks? Maybe he had the disks.'

'I don't know.'

Seymore felt himself losing it. Fuckups like this could cost him his ass.

'If anyone should know, it's you, goddamnit. What the fuck are we paying you for?'

'They're taking him to Canyon Country Hospital. Go fuck yourself.'

226

The line went dead.

Seymore didn't have time to get pissed about it. He called Glen Howell.

# Part Three
## THE HEAD

# CHAPTER 17

**Pearblossom, California**
Friday, 11:36 P.M.

MIKKELSON AND DREYER

It was late when Mikkelson and Dreyer found Krupchek's trailer, a thirty-foot Caravan split at the seams, waiting for them at the end of a paved road in Pearblossom, a farm community of fruit orchards and day workers in the low foothills at the base of the Antelope Valley. That was Mikkelson's notion when they finally found the damned place, that it was waiting, wide, flat, and dusty, the way a desert toad waits for a bug.

Dreyer swiveled the passenger-side floodlight and lit up the place. Somewhere under the dust, it was pale blue going to rust.

Dreyer, more cautious by nature, said, 'You think we should wait for Palmdale?'

Mikkelson, anxious to get inside, said, 'Why'd we go to the trouble of getting the warrant, if we're gonna wait? We don't have to wait. Leave the light.'

Krupchek's road ran the gut of a shallow canyon between two low ridges. No streetlights, no cable TV, no nothing out here; they had phone service and power, but that was about it; the sun went down, it was *black*.

Mikkelson, tall and athletic, behind the wheel because she got carsick when Dreyer drove, got out first. Dreyer, short and square, came up beside her, the rocky soil crunching. Both had their Maglites. They stood there, staring at the trailer, both a little bit nervous.

'You think anyone is home?'

'We'll find out.'

'You think that's his car?'

'We'll run the tag when we finish inside.'

An eighties-era Toyota Camry, itself dusty and speckled with rust, sat outside the darkened trailer.

They were late getting here, having gone to the Rooneys' apartment first, where they'd had to dick around with his landlord and the goofy woman who lived above them, the stupid cow asking over and over if she was going to be on the news. Mikkelson had wanted to slap her. When they had finally come up to Pearblossom, finding the trailer had been a bitch because it was dark and these little roads weren't marked, most of them, so they'd had to stop to ask directions three times. The last stop, a Mexican up from Zacatecas who worked for rich women as a stable groom, turned out to live next door. Here's the Mexican, a small man with his small wife and six or seven small children, saying that Krupchek kept to himself, never any sounds, never any trouble, had only spoken with Krupchek the one time someone had left a heart carved of bone on their step, the Mexican walking over that evening to ask if it was Krupchek, Krupchek saying no, then closing the door. No help there.

Mikkelson said, 'Let's go.'

They approached the trailer, then walked from end to end, just looking. It was like they didn't want to touch it, these creepy feelings you get.

Dreyer said, 'How do we get in? We look for a key or something?'

'I don't know.'

Here they had the warrant, but how did they get in? They hadn't thought of that.

Mikkelson rapped on the door with her Maglite, calling, 'Anyone in there? This is the police.'

She did that twice, getting no answer, then tried the

door, one of those flimsy knobs that was tougher than it looked. It was locked.

'We could jimmy it, I guess.'

'Maybe we should try to find the landlord, have him open it.'

The Mexican had told them that all the land along the road was owned by a man named Brennert, who rented out the properties, mostly to migrant farmworkers.

'Shit, that'll take forever. We'll just pop the damned thing.'

Dreyer made a dogged face, unhappy.

'I don't want to pay for breaking it.'

'We've got the warrant, we're not going to have to pay.'

'You know the bastard might sue, not Krupchek but Brennert. You know how people are.'

'Oh, hell.'

Dreyer could be like that. He was terrified of getting sued. They talked about it all the time, how police officers were sued right and left these days just for doing their jobs, Dreyer hatching plans to put everything in his wife's name to protect it from the lawyers.

Mikkelson got the tire iron from their trunk, wedged it in the jamb by the knob, and popped the door. She put her back into it because these damned things were always stronger than they looked.

A smell like simmering mustard greens rolled out at them.

'Jesus, does this guy ever wash?'

Mikkelson leaned inside, feeling full of herself because this was the first time she had ever broken into a property with the full force of the law behind her and it felt pretty damned cool.

'Anyone home? Knock, knock, knock, it's your friendly neighborhood police.'

'Cut the crap.'

'Relax. There's no one in here.'

Mikkelson found the light switch and stepped inside. The interior of the trailer was dingy and cramped with tattered furniture in listless colors, stifling with accumulated heat.

Dreyer said, 'Well, okay, now what?'

But it was Dreyer who saw them first, having turned to the kitchen, Dreyer saying, 'Jesus, look at *that*.'

It would have been funny except there were so many of them; five or six boxes, maybe, or even ten or twelve, and Mikkelson would have laughed, making a joke, but the overwhelming sight of so many screamed insanity in a way that made her cringe. Later, the Sheriff's forensics people would count: seven hundred sixteen Count Chocula boxes, empty, flattened, and folded, all neatly bound with cord, stacked against the walls and on the kitchen counters and in the cupboards in great teetering towers, each box mutilated in exactly the same way, a single cigarette burn, charred and black, on the point of Count Chocula's nose. They would understand the burns later, too.

Dreyer, not getting the same creepy read as Mikkelson, went for the joke.

'You think he got something good for all these box tops?'

'Put on your gloves.'

'What?'

'The gloves. Let's be careful here.'

'It's cereal, for chrissake.'

'Just put on the gloves.'

'You think he ate it?'

'What?'

'All this cereal. You think he eats it? Maybe he just scrounges for the boxes. There must be a giveaway, you know, a contest.'

The Caravan was cut into three sections, the kitchen to their right, the living room where they entered, the

bedroom to their left, all of it cramped and claustropho-
bic, littered with free newspapers, Jack-in-the-Box wrap-
pers, soiled clothes, and beer cans; the little kitchen with
a tiny sink, an electric range, a half-size refrigerator.

Mikkelson, ignoring Dreyer's speculations, moved left
to the bedroom, pulling on the vinyl disposable gloves,
wondering about the smell. At the door, she lit up the bed
with her Maglite, saw stained sheets in a rumpled mess,
paper and clothes on the floor, and the jars.

'Dreyer. I think we should call.'

Dreyer stepped up behind, his own light beam dancing
into the room.

'Shit. What is that?' Dreyer's voice was hushed.

Mikkelson stepped in, holding out her light. Gallon-
sized glass jars lined the walls, jars that you get when you
buy the big pickles in one of those discount stores, lining
the walls, stacked to windows that were latched tight to
hold out the air. Shapes floated in the jars, suspended in
yellow fluid. Some of the jars were so jammed with fleshy
shapes there was almost no fluid.

'Goddamn. I think it's rats.'

'Jesus.'

Mikkelson squatted for a better look, wanting to cover
her mouth, maybe put on a gas mask or something so she
wouldn't have to breathe the fetid air.

'Shit, it's squirrels. He's got squirrels in here.'

'Fuck this. I'm calling.'

Dreyer left, keying his radio as he fled to the safer night
air.

Mikkelson backed out of the room, stood in the door,
thinking what to do. She knew she should go through
Krupchek's things, look for identifying information, family phone numbers, things like that which might help
Talley at the scene. She went back to the kitchen, looking
for the phone, figuring to find what she needed there.

Mikkelson, thoroughly creeped out, stood by the phone
but stared at the oven. She had this creepy feeling, she

would later say, that's all there was to it; the smell, the squirrels, all those mutilated boxes. She took a deep breath as if she were about to plunge into cold water and jerked open the oven.

More Count Chocula.

Mikkelson laughed at herself. Ha ha, like what else did she expect to find?

Tension now gone, she opened the cupboards, one after the other, all with Count Chocula, bound and burned. She returned to the phone, but hesitated again, then found herself standing at the refrigerator.

Outside, Dreyer called, 'You coming out?'

'I'm okay.'

'Wait out here. The Sheriffs are sending detectives.'

'Dreyer?'

'What?'

'You ever notice, a refrigerator is like a white coffin standing on end?'

'Jesus, would you just come out?'

The refrigerator came open without effort, empty and strangely clean against the squalor of the trailer, no soda, no beer, no leftovers, just white enamel that had been lovingly polished. This refrigerator, Mikkelson would later testify, was the cleanest thing in the trailer.

A thin metal door was set in the top of the box; the freezer. Her hand had a mind of its own, reaching out, pulling the door. Her first thought was that it was a cabbage, wrapped in foil and Saran Wrap. She stared at it, stared hard, then closed the doors, never once, not once, tempted to touch that thing in the freezer.

Mikkelson left the trailer to wait with Dreyer in the hot night air, the two of them saying nothing, waiting for the Sheriffs, Mikkelson thinking, *Let them touch it.*

# CHAPTER 18

## Santa Clarita, California
Friday, 11:40 P.M.

GLEN HOWELL

Howell took three rooms in the Comfort Inn, all at the rear of the motel with outside entrances. Marion Clewes had the woman and the girl bound hand and foot in one room, tape over their eyes and mouths. Howell had checked to make sure they were secure, then went back to his own room even though the place smelled of cleaning products and new carpets. He didn't like being around Clewes.

Howell was sitting on his bed when he received the call from Ken Seymore, his heart trying to jump out of his nose as he heard that Walter Smith had been removed from the house.

'Did the cops go in? What the fuck is happenin' out there?'

'No one went in, it was just Smith coming out.'

'He just walked out?'

'They carried him. He's fucked up. One of the pricks in there must've beaten him. They took him out in an ambulance.'

Howell sat silent for a moment, thinking. Smith out while his kids were still inside was a problem. Smith in the hospital where they'd pop him full of dope, get him high, that was a problem, too.

'Did anything else come out of that house?'

'Nothing they're telling the news pool.'

Howell hung up and immediately phoned information for the Canyon Country Hospital's phone number and address, then called the hospital for directions off the freeway. He found the location in his *Thomas Guide* to double-check the directions, then he used his cell phone to call Palm Springs.

Phil Tuzee answered. Howell filled him in, then waited as Tuzee talked it over with the others. It was Sonny Benza who came back on the line.

'This is fuckin' bad, Glen.'

'I know.'

'He have the disks on him?'

'I don't know, Sonny. I just heard about this two minutes ago. It just happened. I'm going to send someone over.'

'Find out if he has the disks and see if he's been talking to anyone. That won't be good if he's talking. His kids are still in that house?'

'Yeah.'

'Sonofabitch.'

Howell knew they were all thinking the same thing; a man desperate to save his kids might say anything. Howell tried to sound hopeful.

'They say he's fucked up pretty bad. I don't know that for sure, Sonny, but if he's unconscious he can't be talking. The press pool out there is talking a concussion with possible brain injury. They make it sound like the guy's in a coma.'

'Listen, don't tell me anything you don't know for sure. I wipe my ass with rumors. You just hold your shit tight out there and take care of this.'

'It's tight.'

'That's why those pricks let him out, he's hurt? Maybe we'll get lucky and the fucker will die.'

'Talley talked them into letting him out.'

'You know something, Glen? That doesn't sound like

238

your shit is tight. That sounds like the fuckin' wheels are comin' off. Do I have to come out there myself?'

'No way, Sonny. I got it.'

'I want those goddamned disks.'

'Yes, sir.'

'I don't want Smith talking, not to anyone, you understand?'

'I understand.'

'You know what I'm saying?'

'I know.'

'Okay.'

Benza hung up. It was their call; they had made it. Howell picked up the hotel phone and called two rooms down.

'Come over here. I got something for you to do.'

# CHAPTER 19

## Friday, 11:52 P.M.

### TALLEY

Talley checked the time, then took out the Watchman's Nokia and checked its charge. Crazy thoughts of holding a gun to the doctor's head flashed like pinwheels through his mind. Smith knew who was behind this. Smith knew who had his family. Talley paced the mouth of the cul-de-sac, his thoughts kaleidoscoping between Amanda and Jane, and Dennis Rooney. Maddox and Ellison had the phone again, but Dennis refused to answer their calls and had taken his own phone off the hook. Talley sensed that Dennis was working through something, but Talley didn't know what.

When the phone rang Talley again thought it was the Nokia, but it was his private line.

Larry Anders said, 'Chief? Can you talk?'

Anders's voice was low, as if he were trying to keep his words private. Talley lowered his own voice even though no one was near.

'Go, Larry.'

'I'm with Cooper here in the city planner's office. Man, that guy was pissed. He didn't want to get up.'

Talley took out his notepad.

'First tell me about the cell number. You run that yet?'

'I had to get a telephone for that. It's unlisted, so the cell company didn't want to release.'

'Telephone' meant that Anders had to get a telephonic search warrant.

'Okay.'

'The number is registered to Rohiprani Bakmanifelsu and Associates. It's a jewelry company in Beverly Hills. You want me to try to contact them?'

'Forget it. It's a dead end.'

Talley knew without hearing more that the cell number had been cloned and stolen. Since Bakmanifelsu hadn't yet deactivated it, he hadn't yet discovered the pirated activity on his account; the number had probably been cloned within his past billing period.

'What about the Mustang?'

'There's nothing, Chief. I ran wants for the past two model years. We got sixteen hits for cars that were still unrecovered, but nothing green came up.'

'Were any of them stolen today?'

'No, sir. Not even in the past month.'

Talley let it go.

'Okay. What about the building permits?'

'We can't find any of that, but we might not need'm. The planner knew the developer who opened York Estates, a man named Clive Briggs. It used to be nothing but avocado orchards out there.'

'Okay.'

'I just got off the phone with him. He says that the contractor who built the Smiths' house is probably at Terminal Island.'

Terminal Island was the federal prison in San Pedro.

'What do you mean, probably?'

'Briggs didn't know for sure, but he remembered the contractor. The guy's name was Lloyd Cunz. Briggs remembers because he liked the guy's work so much that he tried to hire him for another development he had goin', but Cunz turned him down. He was based in Palm Springs, he said, and they didn't want to take any more long-range jobs.'

'The contractor came all the way from Palm Springs?'

'Not just the contractor. He brought his crew: the

carpenters, the cement people, plumbers, electricians, everybody. He didn't hire anyone locally. He said it was to keep up the quality of the work. Three or four years later, Briggs tried to hire Cunz again and learned that he'd been indicted on racketeering and hijacking charges. He was out of business.'

Talley knew that a builder wouldn't bring an entire construction crew that far unless he was building something he didn't want the locals to know about. Talley already had a sense of where this was going. Organized crime.

'Did you run Cunz through the computer yet?'

'Well, I'm still here at the planner.'

'When you get back to the office, run him and see what you get.'

'You're thinking these guys are in organized crime, aren't you?'

'Yeah, Larry. That's what I'm thinking. Let me know what you find.'

'I won't tell anyone.'

'No. Don't.'

Talley closed his phone and stared at the cul-de-sac. Walter Smith was almost certainly a member of organized crime. The Watchman was probably his partner, and the disks probably contained evidence that could put them away. The pressure he felt was like an inflating balloon in his head and chest. Talley knew that he was losing control of the scene, and of the events that would soon happen. When the Watchman's phony FBI agents arrived, he would have even less control, and that would put the people in the house in even greater jeopardy. The Watchman didn't care who died; he just wanted the disks.

Talley wanted the disks, too. He wanted to know what was on them. These people would never have taken Talley's family if the disks in Smith's house didn't pose a terrible threat to them. They feared those disks being discovered more than they feared the investigation that would come from having kidnapped Talley's family. They figured they could survive the investigation, but they knew the disks would make them fall. That meant the disks named names.

Talley believed that he and his family would not survive the night. The men in the car, they could not afford to trust that the police couldn't build a case against them for what was happening here. They would not take that chance. Talley was absolutely certain that as soon as the Watchman had the disks, he would murder all three of them. Talley wanted the disks first. He thought he knew how to get them.

Talley trotted into the cul-de-sac to join Maddox and Ellison at their car.

'He answer your calls yet?'

Ellison sipped black coffee from a Styrofoam cup.

'Negative. Phone company says he's still got it unplugged.'

'You guys have a P.A. in this car?'

'No. What're you thinking?'

Talley duck-walked to the lone Bristo car that remained in the street. He grabbed the mike, then flipped on the public address system. Maddox had followed him over, curious.

'What are you doing?'

'Sending a message.'

Talley keyed the mike.

'This is Talley. I need you to call me.'

His voice echoed over the neighborhood. The officers around the perimeter glanced at him.

'If it's safe, call me.'

Talley didn't expect Rooney to call. He wasn't talking to Rooney.

Rooney's voice answered from the house.

'Fuck you!'

Ellison laughed.

'It was a good try.'

Maddox said, 'What was that about being safe?'

Talley didn't answer. He tossed the microphone into the car, then crept to the far side of the cul-de-sac, where he sat on the curb behind the patrol cars. He wanted the boy. He hoped that Thomas would understand that Talley had been asking him to call.

His phone rang almost at once.

'Talley.'

It was Sarah, sounding excited.

'Chief, it's the little boy again.'

Talley's heart raced. If Smith couldn't tell him who had his family, maybe the disks could.

'Thomas? You okay, son?'

The boy sounded calm.

'I wasn't sure you were talking to me. Is my daddy okay?'

This time Thomas sounded even more hushed than before, his voice a whisper. Talley turned up the volume on his phone, but still could barely hear him.

'He's in the hospital over in Canyon Country. What about you and your sister? Are you all right?'

'Yeah. She's not in her room anymore. They took her downstairs. I thought they were doing something bad to her, but they didn't know how to use the microwave.'

'Are you in any danger right now?'

'Uh-uh.'

Talley stared out of the cul-de-sac. The Sheriff's tactical units were in their positions behind the radio cars. Hicks and Martin would be in the command van, waiting for something to happen. Talley remembered his first day with SWAT, how a sergeant-supervisor told him that SWAT stood for Sit, Wait, and Talk. Talley's eyes welled as he fought to control his fear. He put his thoughts on the children in the house. If Talley thought either Thomas or Jennifer was in immediate mortal danger, he would launch the breach. He would launch without hesitation. He believed that they were not.

244

'How's your battery on that cell phone?'

'Ah, it's showing half a charge, maybe a little less. I turn it off when I'm not using it.'

'Good. Can you plug it into a charger when you're not using it?'

'Uh-uh. All the chargers are downstairs. My mom does that 'cause everyone else forgets.'

Talley worried that if the boy's battery failed, they would lose communication, but all he could do was press ahead and move fast.

'Okay, Thomas, turn it off when we're not talking and conserve as much power as possible, okay?'

'Okay.'

'Your dad has business partners. Do you know who they are?'

'Uh-uh.'

'He ever mention names?'

'I don't remember.'

'Was he working in his office today?'

'Uh-huh. He was trying to finish something because a client was coming to pick it up.'

Talley had trouble taking it to the next level, but he knew that this boy was his wife's and daughter's only chance.

'Thomas, I need your help with something. It might be easy or it might be dangerous. If you think those guys in there could find out and hurt you, then I don't want you to do it, okay?'

'Sure!'

The boy was excited. He was a boy. He didn't understand risk.

'Your dad has a couple of computer disks. I'm not sure, but they're probably on his desk or in his briefcase. He was probably working with them today. They're called Zip disks. You know what that is?'

Thomas made a derisive snort.

'I've had a Zip drive for years, Chief. Jeez. Zip disks are

245

big and thick. They hold more information than regular disks.'

'These disks are labeled disk one and disk two. When you're downstairs in the office again, could you get to your dad's desk? Could you find those disks and try to see whose files they are?'

'No, they wouldn't let me go to the desk. Dennis makes me sit on the floor.'

The slim hope that Talley had felt only moments before withered. Then Thomas went on.

'But I might be able to sneak into the office if they're not around. Then I could just swipe the disks and open them on my computer up here in my room.'

'I thought they locked you in your room.'

'They do, but I can get out.'

'You can?'

Talley listened as Thomas described being able to move through the crawl space in the eaves and attic, and how he was able to emerge in different parts of the house through access hatches.

'Thomas, could you get to his office that way, through the crawl space?'

'Not into his office, but I can get into the den. There's a service door in the wine cellar behind the bar. It's right across from my dad's office. My mom says she can always tell when he sneaks across one time too many.'

Talley's hope surfaced again, but it was dampened by the knowledge that he could not allow this child to risk his life.

'That sounds too dangerous.'

'It won't be if they don't see me. Mars spends most of his time in the office, but Kevin is back by the French doors. Dennis walks around a lot. He stays in the safety room sometimes, the one where all the monitors are. But once I'm in the den, all I have to do is sneak across the entry and go to my dad's desk. That wouldn't take any time at all.'

246

Talley thought it through, trying not to let the need he felt cloud his judgment. He would have to get all three subjects away from that area of the house. He would have to blind the cameras in case one or all of the subjects were in the safety room with the monitors.

'If I could get Rooney and the others away from the office, do you think you could get the disks without being caught?'

'No problemo.'

'Could you do it in the dark?'

'I do stuff like that almost every night.'

Thomas laughed when he said it. Talley didn't laugh. He was supposed to help this child; now he wanted this child to help him. He felt as much a hostage as Thomas or Jane, and hoped that he could forgive himself for what he was about to do.

'All right, son. Let's figure this out.'

The night air was so clear that the houses and cars and cops in the street all seemed etched in glass. House lights, street lamps, and the red flares of cigarettes were hard sharp points of glare; overhead, the helicopters floated against the star field like nighthawks balanced on the sky, waiting for something to die. Talley checked his watch and knew the Watchman would call again soon. Thomas was still up in his room and the sister was still cooking, but that could change at any moment. Talley didn't have much time.

Talley found Jorgenson and brought him to the Department of Water and Power truck. The DWP technician, a young guy with a shaved head and a braided chin beard, was stretched across the bench seat of his truck, sleeping. Talley shook his foot.

'Can you cut the power to the house?'

The service tech rubbed at his face, blotchy with sleep. 'I could do that, yeah. Good to go.'

'Not now. You turn it off, that means all the power in the house goes off, not just in part of the house?'

Talley couldn't afford a mistake, and neither could Thomas.

The tech slid out of his truck. The manhole was open. A short aluminum fence circled it as a warning.

'Not just the one house, the entire cul-de-sac. I control the branch line from here. I cut the juice, it's all going dead. If I set up there in the cul-de-sac I could cut it just to a single house, but they told me out here.'

'Out here is fine. How long does that take, to cut the power?'

'On-off, like flipping a switch.'

'The phones won't be affected?'

'I got nothin' to do with that.'

Talley left Jorgenson with the technician, then radioed Martin to have Hicks and Maddox meet him at the command van. Martin answered stiffly.

'Listen, I appreciate that you talked Rooney into releasing Mr. Smith, but then you walked away without a word. You want command, you have to stay available. We might have needed to clear an action, but you weren't here.'

Talley felt defensive, but also resentful that she was calling him on this and wasting time.

'I didn't walk away. I was with Maddox and Ellison, and then I made some calls.'

He didn't tell her that he had spoken with Thomas.

'You have command of this action, but please don't try any more stunts without including me in the loop. If you want my cooperation, then you have to keep me informed.'

'What are you talking about?'

'I heard you on the public address, ordering Rooney to call you. That's why we have negotiators.'

'Maddox was right beside me.'

'He claims you did that without consulting him.'

'Can we talk about this later, Captain? Right now I want to deal with Rooney.'

Martin agreed to have Hicks and Maddox meet him in the command van. When Talley arrived, he still did not tell them that he had spoken with Thomas again, nor the true reasons for everything he was about to do.

'We know that Rooney is sensitive to the perimeter. I want to cut the power to the house, then shake him up with a Starflash to make him start talking.'

A Starflash was a shotgun-fired grenade built of seven to twelve submunitions that exploded like a string of powerful firecrackers. It was used to disorient armed subjects during a breach.

Hicks crossed his arms.

'You're going to fire into the house with the gas in there?'

'No, outside. We need to get his attention. The last time I pushed the perimeter, we didn't have to call him because he called us.'

Martin glanced at Maddox. Maddox nodded. So did Hicks.

Martin shrugged, then looked back at Talley.

'I guess you're in command.'

They were on.


THOMAS

Thomas listened at his door. The hall was quiet. He edged back along the walls to his closet, and then into the crawl space. He stopped to listen at each vent. Jennifer was still in the kitchen, but he couldn't hear anyone else. All he needed was a laugh or cough or sneeze to fix their locations, but he heard nothing.

Thomas's house was shaped like a short, wide U with the wide base of it facing the cul-de-sac and the stubby arms reaching toward the pool. Most of the crawl space followed the inside of the U except for a branch into a dead space above the wine cellar. Thomas had always thought it weird that they called it a cellar when it was just a little room behind the bar in the den.

It wasn't easy to reach. The wine cellar had its own air-conditioning system, a single compressor that hung in the dead space, suspended from the rafters by four chains and filling the crawl space with its width. Thomas had to wiggle under the compressor to reach the hatch on the far side; there was no way around. Thomas had squeezed under it before, but not often, and he was smaller then. He lay on his back and inched under. Flat like that, his nose still scraped the compressor's smooth flat bottom. It smelled damp.

When he reached the hatch side of the compressor he was wet with sweat. The dust that covered him turned to slick mud. It had taken a lot longer to get under it than he thought.

Thomas listened at the access hatch. After a few seconds, he slowly lifted the hatch. The wine cellar was empty and dark. It was a long narrow room lined with floor-to-ceiling wine racks, kept at a chilly fifty-two degrees. Thomas clicked on his flashlight, wedged it in the rack against one of the bottles, then turned himself around to dangle his feet and feel for footing. In a few moments he had reached the floor.

He eased open the door. The den beyond was bright with light. He could hear the TV in his father's office across the hall and Jennifer in the kitchen. He heard a male voice, but he couldn't tell if it was Dennis or Mars; he was pretty sure it wasn't Kevin.

The den was a cozy, wood-paneled room that his father used for business meetings and smoking cigars. Two dark leather couches faced each other across a coffee table, and the shelves were filled with books that his dad liked to read for fun, old books about hunting in Africa and science fiction novels that his father told him were worth a lot of money to collectors. A bar lined by four leather stools filled one side of the room. It was the one room in the house where Thomas's mom let his father smoke, though she made him close the doors when he had the stogies fired up. Thomas's father liked calling them 'stogies.' It made him smile.

All Thomas had to do to reach the office was cross the den to the double doors, then run across the hall. To his right would be the front door; to his left, the entry hall that led to the kitchen and back of the house.

Thomas took out his cell phone and turned it on.

He called Chief Talley.


TALLEY

Talley checked his radio.

'Jorgenson?'

'Here, Chief.'

'Stand by.'

Talley was at the rear of Smith's property with a Sheriff's tac officer named Hobbs. Hobbs had a Remington Model 700 sniper rifle fitted with a night-vision scope. The chamber was clear and the magazine empty. Talley carried a shotgun fixed with the Starflash grenade.

'Let me see.'

Talley took the rifle from Hobbs and focused the scope on the French doors. He had been peering over the top of the wall for almost six minutes, waiting for Thomas to call. Jennifer and Krupchek were in the kitchen. He thought Kevin was in the family room, but he wasn't sure. Dennis passed through the kitchen twice. He had exited toward the master bedroom three minutes earlier and had not returned. Talley thought he was probably in the safety room, watching the perimeter on the monitors.

Talley's phone rang. He was expecting it, but he wasn't ready for it. He jumped, startled.

Hobbs whispered, 'Easy.'

Talley handed the rifle back to Hobbs, then answered, his voice low.

'Talley.'

Thomas whispered back at him.

'Hi, Chief. I'm in the den.'

Talley watched the shadows play on the French doors.

'Okay, bud. You ready? Just like we said?'

'Yeah. I won't get caught.'

'If there's any chance – '*any!* – 'you get back up to your room.'

Talley felt like a liar even saying it. The whole thing was a chance.

'Here we go.'

Talley keyed his shoulder mike.

'Kill the lights.'

The house plunged into darkness.


DENNIS

Dennis sat at Walter Smith's desk, watching television. Kevin was back by the French doors, and Mars had the girl in the kitchen. All but two of the local stations had resumed regular programming, breaking in every few minutes with an aerial shot of York Estates, but the national cable channels didn't bother. Dennis felt slighted. He watched MTV with the sound low, black guys with blond hair pretending to be gangsters. He pointed his pistol at them, try this, motherfuckers.

Dennis had progressed from vodka on the rocks to vodka from the bottle, racking his brain for a way he could escape with the money. He was pissed off and frustrated, and grew scared that Kevin was right: that he

252

wouldn't be able to get away with the cash, and that he would go back to being just another shitbag in a cell. Dennis took another hit of the vodka, thinking that he'd rather be dead. Maybe he should just run. Stuff his pockets with as much cash as possible, torch the friggin' house like Mars said, then duck through the little window into the oleander and run like a bat out of hell. They would probably machine-gun him before he got ten feet, but what the hell, it was better than being a turd.

'Shit.'

Dennis left the office, went back to the bedroom, and put the suitcase on the bed. He stared at the cash. He touched the worn bills, silky smooth and soft. He wanted it so badly that his body trembled. Cars, women, clothes, dope, copper bars, Rolex watches, fine food, boats, homes, freedom, happiness. Everybody wanted to be rich. Didn't matter who you were or where you came from or how much money you had; everyone wanted more. It was the American Dream. Money.

The notion came to Dennis like a rush of Ecstasy as he stared at the money: Cops are poor. Cops wanted to be rich like everyone else. Maybe he could split the loot with Talley, trade cash for safe passage to Mexico, work out a scam so that the other cops wouldn't know, something like pretending to swap the hostages for Talley so that the two of them could drive down to TJ together, laughing all the way because the other cops wouldn't dare try to assassinate him if they thought Talley's life hung in the balance. He would even toss in Kevin and Mars; let'm have someone to swing for the Chinaman. Dennis grew excited as he spun through the possibilities. Everyone knew that cops didn't make shit for a living. How far would Talley go for a hundred thousand dollars? Two hundred thousand? A half a million?

Dennis decided to call Talley right away. He was halfway back to the office, thinking how best to persuade

Talley that he could be a wealthy man, when the house died. The lights went out, the TV stopped, the background hum that fills all living homes vanished.

Kevin shouted from the other side of the house.

'Dennis? What happened?'

'It's the cops! Get those fuckin' kids!'

Blind in the darkness, Dennis rushed forward, following the wall. He expected to hear the doors crashing open at any second, and knew his only chance was to reach the girl or her fat brother.

'Kevin! Mars! Get those kids!'

Milky light from the French doors filled the family room. Kevin was behind the sofa; Mars was in the kitchen, holding the girl by her hair. Mars was smiling, the crazy bastard. Like this was fun.

'Told you they'd cut the power.'

Talley's amplified voice echoed through the house, not from the street this time, but from the backyard.

'Dennis? Dennis Rooney?'

Dennis wondered why Talley was behind the house.

'Dennis, it's time to talk.'

Then the backyard erupted: Explosions jumped and careened over the surface of the water like automatic gunfire. Star-bright flashes lit the backyard like a Chinese New Year parade. The world was going to hell.

Dennis threw himself behind the kitchen counter, waiting for it to end.


THOMAS


Thomas pushed out of the wine cellar as soon as the lights went off, slipped around the end of the bar, and scurried to the double doors. Dennis and Kevin were shouting, their voices coming from the family room. He knew he wouldn't have much time.

Thomas got down on his hands and knees, and peeked through the doorway. Across the hall, his father's office flickered with light from the candles. Thomas leaned farther out into the entry to see if anyone was coming. The hall was empty.

*No guts, no glory.*

Thomas ran across the hall into his father's office just as Chief Talley's voice boomed through the house. He knew that something loud was going to go off, so he tried to ignore all that. He concentrated on listening for footsteps.

Thomas went directly to the computer on his father's desk. He had brought his flashlight, but the candles gave enough light so that he didn't need it. The desk was scattered with papers, but he didn't see any disks. He checked the computer's Zip drive. It was empty. He lifted the papers around the computer and keyboard, but he didn't see any disks there, either.

A series of explosions cut through the house like a giant string of firecrackers. Thomas thought Dennis was shooting. Kevin shouted something, but Thomas didn't understand him. He was scared that they were on their way. He ran to the door to go back into the den, but stopped at the hall, listening. His heart pounded so loud he could barely hear, but he didn't think they were coming.

Chief Talley had told him not to spend more than a minute or two. He didn't have much time. He had used too much already.

Thomas looked across the entry hall to the safety of the den, then glanced back at the desk. A picture flashed in Thomas's memory: Earlier that day, after all the shooting, his father had tried to talk Dennis into getting a lawyer and giving up; he had gone to his desk, placed the disks in a black case, and put the case into the drawer. The disks were in the drawer!

Thomas went back to the desk.

*

## DENNIS

The back of the house exploded with noise and light as if the Marines were hitting the beach. Dennis saw cops at the wall, lit by the glare from their lights, but they didn't rush the house.

Dennis thought, *What the fuck?*

Talley's voice echoed from the backyard.

'It's time to talk, Dennis. Me and you. Face-to-face. I want you to come out, just you, I'll meet you and we'll talk.'

Kevin scrambled into the kitchen on all fours, fast, like a cartoon.

'What are they doing? What's going on?'

Dennis didn't know. He was confused and suspicious, and then suddenly very afraid.

'Mars! Those fuckers are trying to blindside us! See what they're doing in front!'

Dennis grabbed the girl from Mars, who lurched to his feet and went down the hall.


## THOMAS

The black leather case was a soft black leather folder about the size of a compact disk. The candlelight behind the desk was too dim to see into the drawer, so Thomas turned on his flashlight, cupping the lens to hide most of the light.

The case was in the top drawer.

It opened like a book. Each side had pockets to hold disks. Two disks were in the right pockets, labeled just as Chief Talley had described, disk one and disk two. Thomas was closing the drawer when he heard footsteps coming fast down the hall.

Thomas wanted to run, but it was too late.

The footsteps came *fast!*

They were coming to the office!

They were at the door!

Thomas turned off his flashlight and ducked under the desk. He pulled himself into a tight ball, hugging his knees, and he tried not to breathe.

Someone was in the room.

His father's desk was a great oak monster, heavy and ancient and as big as a boat (his dad jokingly called it the *Lexington*, after the aircraft carrier). It sat on curvy legs that left a small gap between the desk and the floor. Thomas saw feet. He thought it was Mars, but he couldn't be sure.

The feet went to the window.

Thomas heard the shutters snap open. Light from outside poured into the room. The shutters snapped closed.

The feet stayed at the shutters. Thomas imagined he must be peeking through the cracks.

Dennis shouted from the back of the house.

'What in hell's going on out there?'

It was Mars in the room. He stood at the shutters without moving.

'Goddamnit, Mars!'

The feet stepped away from the window, but Mars didn't leave. The feet turned toward the desk. Thomas tried to squeeze himself smaller. He hugged his legs so tight that his arms hurt.

The feet took a step toward the desk.

'Mars! What the fuck are they doin'?'

The feet walked to the end of the desk. Thomas tried to close his eyes; he tried to look away, but he couldn't. He watched the feet as if they were snakes.

'*Mars!*'

The feet turned and left. Thomas followed them with his ears, down the hall, away, gone.

Thomas scrambled from under the desk and went to the door. He peeked down the hall, then ran across to the den.

He heard Chief Talley talking over the public address system as he pushed into the wine cellar, climbed the racks, and found the safety of the crawl space.


## TALLEY

Talley knew that Rooney and the others would be panicked. They would believe that Talley had launched a breach and Dennis or one of the others would probably run to the front of the house to see what the Sheriffs were doing. Talley had to keep their attention focused here at the back of the house. On him.

'Is he still in the kitchen?'

Hobbs was peering through the night-vision scope.

'Yeah, him and the girl. He's trying to see us, but he can't see past the lights. The big one went down the hall. I don't see the brother.'

Talley keyed the portable P.A.

'We are *not* breaching the house, Dennis. We need to talk. Me and you. Face-to-face. I'm coming out to the pool.'

Martin and Hicks hustled toward him through the shadows. Martin wasn't happy.

'What face-to-face? We didn't discuss that.'

'I'm going out.'

Talley dropped the P.A. and heaved himself over the wall before she could say anything more. He wanted to draw Rooney's attention away from the front of the house even if it meant offering himself up to do it.

Martin's voice followed him over the wall.

'Damnit, Talley, all you'll do is make yourself a target.'

Talley walked to the edge of the pool and raised his voice.

'I'm unarmed. I'm not going to strip for you this time, so take my word for it. I'm unarmed, and I'm coming alone.'

Talley held his hands out from his sides, open palms forward, and walked toward the house along the side of the pool. A dark raft floated effortlessly on the water. A towel was spread on the deck, the radio that had played earlier silent, its batteries dead.

He reached the end of the pool nearest the house and stopped. A flashlight lay on the kitchen floor, its beam cutting a white slash that bounced off the counters. Talley raised his hands higher. Again, the bright lights behind him cast his shadow toward the house. It looked like a crucifix.

'Come out, Dennis. Talk to me.'

Dennis shouted from the house, his voice muffled through the closed French doors.

'You're fucking crazy!'

'No, Dennis. I'm tired.'

Talley walked closer.

'No one's going to hurt you. Not unless you hurt those kids.'

Talley stopped outside the French doors. He could see Dennis and Jennifer plainly now. Dennis held the girl with one hand, a pistol with the other. A shadow moved to Talley's left, deep in the family room, and Talley saw a slender figure. Kevin. He looked like a child. On the other side of the kitchen, opposite the family room, a hall disappeared into the house. Talley saw a flickering glow from a door. A large shape blocked the light, growing in the shadows. That would be Krupchek. Talley felt a well of relief; wherever the boy was, they didn't have him. He had to keep them focused. He spread his hands wider. He went closer.

'I'm standing here, Dennis. I'm looking at you. Come out and let's talk.'

Talley heard them talking, Dennis calling Kevin into the kitchen. Krupchek stood at the mouth of the hall now, floating in the darkness. He held something in his hands, a flashlight, a gun, Talley couldn't tell.

Dennis got to his feet and came to the French doors. He looked out past Talley, then tried to see the sides of the house, probably thinking he would be rushed if he opened the doors. Talley spoke calmly.

'No one here but me, Dennis. You have my word.'

Dennis placed his gun on the floor, then pushed open the door and stepped out. Talley knew that people always looked heavier in pictures, but Rooney was shorter and thinner than Talley would have guessed from the video-tape, and younger.

Talley smiled, but Rooney didn't smile back.

'How ya doin', Dennis?'

'Had better days.'

'This has been a long one, I'll hand you that.'

Dennis tipped his head toward the far wall.

'You got a sniper out there, gonna shoot me?'

'If you tried to grab me, they probably would. Otherwise, no. We could have shot you from the wall if we wanted to do that.'

Dennis seemed to accept that.

'Can I come out there, closer to you?'

'Sure. It's all right.'

Dennis stepped away from the door and joined Talley out by the foot of the pool. Dennis took a deep breath, looking up at the stars as he let it out.

'Good to be outside.'

'I guess.'

Talley said, 'I'm going to lower my arms, okay?'

'Sure.'

Talley could see Kevin still with the girl in the kitchen and Krupchek still in the hall. The boy was inside somewhere, getting the disks. Talley hoped it wouldn't take long.

Talley said, 'We've been at this a long time now. What are you waiting for?'

'Would you be in a hurry to go to prison for the rest of your life?'

'I'd be doing everything I can to get the best deal possible. I'd let these people go, I'd cooperate, I'd let a lawyer do my talking. I'd be smart enough to realize that I'm surrounded by police officers and I'm not getting out of here except through their good graces.'

'I want that helicopter.'

Talley shook his head.

'It's what I said before, where's it going to land? I can't give you a helicopter. That's not going to happen.'

'Then a car. I want a car to take me to Mexico, a car and an escort and a free pass south of the border.'

'We've been through that.'

Rooney seemed to be working himself up to something. He waved his arm in a flash of anger.

'Then what fuckin' good are you?'

'I'm trying to save your life.'

Dennis glanced back into the house. Talley watched him, thinking that Rooney showed the day's strain. Finally, Rooney faced him again and lowered his voice still more.

'Are you a rich man?'

Talley didn't answer. He didn't know where Rooney was taking this. He had learned to let them get wherever they were going on their own.

Rooney patted his pocket.

'Can I reach in here, show you something?'

Talley nodded.

Rooney stepped closer. Talley couldn't make out what Rooney took from his pocket at first, but then he saw that it was money. Rooney seemed to be trying to shield it so that only Talley could see.

'That's fifty one-hundred-dollar bills, Chief. Five thousand dollars. I got a whole suitcase of this stuff in the house.'

Rooney pushed the bills back into his pocket.

'How much would it be worth to you, getting me out of here? A hundred thousand dollars? You could drive me down to Mexico, just me and you, no one the wiser, just tell the others that was the deal we made without mentioning any money. I wouldn't tell. They got money in this house, Chief. More money than you've ever seen in your life. We could carve it up.'

Talley shook his head.

'You picked a bad house to hole up in, Dennis.'

'Two hundred thousand, cash, hundred-dollar bills, right in your pocket, no one needs to know.'

Talley didn't answer. He wondered about Smith, what he did here in the middle of nowhere, here in the safe, anonymous community of Bristo Camino, with so much cash and information in his house that this kid was willing to die for it and the men in the car were willing to kill for it. Do you ever really know your neighbors?

'Give up, Dennis.'

Rooney wet his lips. His eyes flicked past Talley again, then back.

'You tryin' to drive up the price? Okay, three hundred. Three hundred thousand dollars. Could you ever earn that much? You can have Mars and Kevin. Fuckin' bust *them*. Make that part of the deal.'

'You don't know what you're dealing with. You can't buy your way out of this.'

'Everybody wants money! Everybody! I'm not giving this up!'

Talley stared at him, wondering how far to go. If Rooney quit now, Amanda and Jane might pay for it. But if Rooney quit now, walked out right now, Talley would have the disks. Once the Watchman's people arrived, Talley might not have the chance.

'This house isn't what you think it is. You believe some guy has this kind of cash just laying around in his house?'

'There's a million bucks in there, maybe *two* million! I'll give you half!'

'The man you sent to the hospital, Walter Smith, he's a criminal. That money belongs to him.'

Rooney laughed.

'You're lying. What a crock of shit.'

'He has partners, Dennis. This is their house, and they want it. The way I'm offering is the only way out for you.'

Rooney stared at him, then rubbed at his face.

'Fuck you, Talley. Just fuck you. You think I'm an idiot.'

'I'm telling you the truth. Give up. Work with me here, and at least you'll have your life.'

Rooney sighed, and Talley could see the sadness settle over him like a cloak.

'And what's that worth?'

'Whatever you make of it.'

'I'll go back in now. I'll think about it and give you my answer tomorrow.'

Talley knew that Dennis was lying. Talley had a sense for when they would give up and when they wouldn't, and Rooney had hold of something he couldn't turn loose.

'Please, Dennis.'

'Fuck off.'

Rooney backed to the door, then stepped inside and pulled it closed. The darkness inside swallowed him like dirty water.

Talley turned back to the officers lining the wall and walked away, praying that Thomas had the disks and was safe. Rooney wasn't the only one holding onto something he couldn't turn loose.

# CHAPTER 20

Saturday, 12:04 A.M.

THOMAS

Thomas dripped with sweat. His knees were cut from the rafters, and, where streaks of sweat washed the cuts, they burned. Thomas didn't care. He was excited and happy – dude, he was *pumped!*; this was the best sneak ever, better than any he'd made with Duane Fergus!

With the power off, Thomas didn't have to worry about being seen on the monitors. He pushed through the hatch into his closet, and crossed the room to his computer. He took the computer apart and lugged it to the floor at the foot of his bed so that he wouldn't be seen by the camera when the power returned. His hands were so sweaty that he almost dropped the screen and caught it on his knee.

The lights came on without warning. Thomas worried that the turds would probably come upstairs to check on him, so he hurried to load the first disk.

The file icon that appeared was unnamed. He double-clicked on the icon to open it. A list of corporate names appeared that Thomas didn't know anything about. He opened a random file, but saw only tables and numbers. Thomas felt a stab of fear that he had snatched the wrong disks even though these were the *only* disks. Nothing that he saw made sense to him, but these were the disks Chief Talley wanted, so maybe the Chief would understand.

Thomas stopped in his work to listen for squeaks. The hall was quiet.

Thomas turned on his phone again, but this time the power indicator showed that less than half the power remained. He was down to almost a quarter of a charge.

Thomas pushed his redial button to call Chief Talley.

## TALLEY

Talley climbed back over the wall where Martin and Hicks were waiting for him. Martin was angry.

'That was really dumb. What do you think you accomplished?'

Talley hurried away without answering her. He didn't want her around when Thomas called. He radioed Maddox to recount his conversation with Rooney as he walked around the side of the neighbor's house, and kept it short. He left out that Rooney had told him about the enormous store of cash in the house, as that would raise too many questions, and felt terrible about it. Talley was a negotiator. Another negotiator was depending on him, and Talley was lying by omission. Maybe that was why he kept the call short; he couldn't stand himself for doing it.

His phone rang as he reached the cul-de-sac. He hurried into a neighboring drive, out of sight of the house, and stood by himself.

'I got'm!'

Talley forced himself to stay calm. He didn't have anything yet.

'Good work, son. You're back in your room now, right? You're safe?'

'That big guy, Mars, he almost caught me, but I hid. What was that thing you blew up in the backyard? That was so *cool!*'

'Thomas, when we're done with this, I'll let you blow up one of those things yourself, you want. But not now, okay? I need to know what's on those disks.'

'Numbers. I think it's somebody's taxes.'

'You've opened them?'

'I told you I could.'

Martin and Hicks came out of the neighboring drive and joined the other officers behind the police vehicles that filled the cul-de-sac, Martin working her way to Maddox. Talley moved farther away.

'You sure did, Thomas. Are those disks labeled?'

'Uh-huh. Just like you said, disk one and disk two.'

'Tell me what you got when you opened them.'

'I got one open right now.'

'Okay, tell me what you see.'

Talley patted himself down for his pad and pen in case he had to write.

Thomas described a list of files named for companies that Talley didn't recognize, anonymous names like Southgate Holdings and Desert Entertainment. Then Thomas mentioned two more companies: Palm Springs Ventures and The Springs Winery. There was the Palm Springs connection: Smith's home had been built by a Palm Springs contractor. Talley had Thomas open the Palm Springs Ventures file, but from Thomas's descriptions it sounded like a balance sheet or some kind of profit-and-loss statement without identifying the individuals involved. Talley scratched down the names on his pad.

'Open the files and see if there are any names.'

After a second, Thomas said, 'All I see is numbers. It's money.'

'Okay. Open the other disk. Tell me what that one says.'

Even the few seconds that it took Thomas to change the disks seemed to take forever, Talley sweating every moment of it that the boy would be discovered. But then Thomas read off file names and Talley knew that this was the one: Black, White, Up Money, Down Money, Transfers, Source, Cash Receipts, and others. Thomas was still reading file names when Talley stopped him.

'That's enough. The file named Black. Open that one.'

'It's more files.'

'Named what?'

'I think it's states. CA, AZ, NV, FL. Is NV Nevada?'

'Yeah, that's Nevada. Open California.'

Thomas described a long table that went on for pages listing names that Talley didn't recognize, along with dates and payments received. Talley grew antsy. This was taking too much time.

'Read off more of the file names.'

Thomas read off six or seven more names when Talley stopped him again.

'Open that one. Corporate Taxes.'

'Now there's more numbers, but I think they're years. Ninety-two, ninety-three, ninety-four, like that.'

'Open this year.'

'It's a tax form that my dad makes up to send to the government.'

'Up at the top of the page, does it say whose tax it is, maybe a company name?'

The boy didn't answer.

'Thomas?'

'I'm looking.'

Talley glanced toward the cul-de-sac. Martin was watching him. She held his eye for a moment, then said something to Hicks and came toward him, hunched over to stay under cover of the cars.

'It says Family Enterprises.'

'But there's no one's name?'

'Uh-uh.'

Talley wanted to look at the disks himself; if he could see them he knew he could find what he needed instead of depending on a ten-year-old boy.

'Look for something like Officers or Executive Compensation, something like that.'

Martin had cleared the line of police vehicles and was

out of the line of fire from the house. She straightened and came toward him. He held up his hand to warn her off, but she frowned and kept coming.

Martin said, 'I want to talk to you.'

'In a minute.'

'It's important.'

Talley moved away from her, annoyed.

*'When I'm off the phone.'*

His tone stopped her. Martin's eyes hardened angrily, but she kept her distance.

Thomas said, 'Here it is.'

'You found the name?'

'Yeah, there's a place called Compensation to Officers, but there's only one guy listed.'

'Who?'

'Charles G. Benza.'

Talley stared at the ground. The cool night air suddenly felt close. Talley looked at the house, then glanced at Martin. Talley had been wrong. Walter Smith wasn't a mobster with something valuable in his house. The boy's father kept Sonny Benza's books. That's what it had to be: Smith was Benza's accountant, and he had Benza's financial records. It was all right there in Smith's house, enough to put Benza away and his organization out of business. Right here in Bristo Camino.

Talley sighed deeply, the breath venting from his core in a way that seemed to carry his strength with it. This was why people were willing to kidnap and murder. Smith could put them out of business. Smith knew their secrets and could put them away. The mob. The men in the car were the mob. The head of the largest crime family on the West Coast had Jane and Amanda.

Thomas's voice suddenly came fast and thin.

'Someone's coming. I gotta go.'

The line went dead.

Martin put her hands on her hips.

'Are you going to talk to me now?'

'No.'

Talley ran for his car. If the disks could put Benza away, so could Walter Smith. He radioed Metzger at the hospital as he ran.


THOMAS

Thomas heard the nail being pried from his door. He jerked the computer's plug from the wall, then vaulted onto his bed, shoving the cell phone under the covers as the door opened. Kevin stepped inside, carrying a paper plate with two slices of pizza and a Diet Coke.

'I brought you something to eat.'

Thomas pushed his hands between his crossed legs, trying to hide the fact that he wasn't tied, but the tape he'd stripped from his wrists was in plain sight on the floor. Kevin stopped when he saw it, then glared.

'You little shit. I oughta kick your ass.'

'It hurt my wrists.'

'Fuckit, I don't guess it matters anyway.'

Thomas was relieved that he didn't seem too upset. Kevin handed over the pizza and soda, then checked the nails that held the windows closed. Thomas worried that he would notice that the computer was in a different spot, but Kevin seemed inside himself.

Kevin made sure that the windows were secure, then leaned against the wall as if he needed the support to keep his feet. His eyes seemed to find everything in the room, every toy and book, every piece of furniture, the clothes strewn in the corner, the posters on the walls, the smashed phone thrown on the floor, the TV, the CD player, even the computer against the wall, all with an expression that seemed empty.

Kevin's gaze finally settled on Thomas.

'You're fucking lucky.'

Kevin pushed off the wall and went to the door.

269

Thomas said, 'When are you leaving my house?'

'Never.'

Kevin left without looking back and pulled the door closed.

Thomas waited.

The nail was hammered back into the doorjamb. The floor squeaked as Kevin moved away.

Thomas tried to count to one hundred, but stopped at fifty and once more made his way to the closet. He wanted to know what they were planning. He also wanted the gun.

# CHAPTER 21

## Canyon Country, California
Saturday, 12:02 A.M.

MARION CLEWES

The Canyon Country Hospital sat between two mountain ridges in a pool of blue light. It was modern and low, not more than three stories at its tallest, and sprawled across the parking lot. Marion thought it looked like one of those overnight dot-com think tanks you see in the middle of nowhere, sprung up overnight at a freeway off-ramp, all earth-colored stone and mirrored glass.

Marion cruised around the hospital, finding the emergency room entrance at the rear. Friday night, a little after midnight, and the place was virtually deserted. Marion knew hospitals that saw so much action on Friday nights they ran double ER staffs and you could hear screams from a block away. The Santa Clarita Valley must be a very nice place to live, he thought. He was liking everything he found about it.

The small parking area outside the ER showed only three cars and a couple of ambulances, but four news vehicles were parked off to the side. Marion expected this, so he wasn't put off. He parked close to the entrance with the nose of his car facing the drive, then went into the hospital.

The newspeople were clumped together at the admitting desk, talking to a harried woman in a white coat. Marion listened enough to gather that she was the senior emergency room physician, Dr. Reese, and that tests were currently being run on Walter Smith. Two young nurses, both pretty with dark Toltec eyes, stood behind the admitting counter, watching with interest. Marion thought that this was probably very exciting for them, having the newspeople here.

Marion went to a coffee machine in the small waiting area and bought a cup of black coffee. A female police officer sat watching the interview. A young Latino man sat across from her, rocking a small baby while an older child slept half in his lap, half on the seat next to him. The man looked frightened in a way that let Marion think that his wife was probably the reason they were here. Marion's heart went out to him.

'It's like they've forgotten you, isn't it?'

The man glanced up without comprehension. Marion smiled, thinking he probably didn't speak English.

'That's so sad,' he said.

Marion turned away and went back to the admitting area. A gate opened to a short hall, beyond which was a kind of communal room with several beds partitioned by blue curtains, and another hall with swinging doors at the end. Marion waited at the gate until an orderly appeared, then he smiled shyly.

'Excuse me. Dr. Reese said someone would help me.'

The orderly glanced at Reese, who was still busy with the reporters across the room.

'I'm Walter Smith's next-door neighbor. They told me to pick up his clothes and personal effects.'

'That the guy who was the hostage?'

'Oh, yes. Isn't that terrible?'

'Man, the stuff that happens, huh?'

'You never know. We're worried sick. Those children are still in there.'

'Man.'

'I'm supposed to bring his things home.'

'Okay, let me see what I can do.'

'How's he doing?'

'The doctor's checking the CT results now. They should know soon.'

Marion watched as the orderly disappeared into one of the doors farther up the hall, then he stepped through the gate and walked up the hall just far enough so that the nurses at the admitting desk could no longer see him. He waited there until the orderly returned with a green paper bag.

'Here you go. They had to cut his clothes off, but there isn't anything we can do about that.'

Marion took the bag. He could feel shoes in the bottom.

'Do I have to sign?'

'No, that's all right. We're not that formal around here. I used to work for County-USC; man, you had to sign for everything. Here, it's not like that. These small towns are great.'

'Listen, thank you. Is there another way out of here? I don't want to leave past the reporters. They were asking so many questions before.'

The orderly pointed to the swinging doors at the far end of the hall.

'Through there, then take a left. You'll see a red exit sign at the end. That'll bring you out the front.'

'Thanks again.'

Marion put the bag on the floor to go through Smith's things. He did it right there. The bag contained jeans, a belt, a black leather wallet, white Calvin Klein briefs, a Polo shirt, gray socks, black Reebok tennis shoes, and a Seiko wristwatch. The clothes had all been split along the centerline. Marion felt the pants pockets, but found only a white handkerchief. There were no computer disks. Mr. Howell would be disappointed.

Marion tucked the bag under his arm and walked down the hall past the beds in the communal room. The beds were empty. Marion wondered about the Latino man's wife, but stopped thinking about it when he found Smith in a room at the end of the hall. Smith's left temple was covered in a fresh white bandage, and an oxygen cannula was clipped to his nose. Two nurses, one red-haired and one dark, were setting up monitor machines that Marion took to be an EEG and an EKG. That the nurses were only now setting up the monitors told Marion that the tests had just finished but the doctors were still waiting for results. That gave him time. When the doctors knew Smith's true condition, they would either proceed with some additional intervention or move Smith into the main body of the hospital. A room there would make things easier, but surgery would make Marion's job impossible. He decided not to take the chance.

Marion found a quiet spot farther down the hall where a gurney was resting against the wall. He put the bag on the gurney, then put a syringe pack and a glass vial of a drug called lidocaine into the bag. Both the syringe and the lidocaine were Marion's, brought in from the car.

A tall young man pushed an empty wheelchair around a corner. He looked sleepy.

Marion smiled pleasantly.

'I used to tell myself I would get used to these hours, but you never do.'

The man smiled back, sharing the tragedy of late hours. 'You're telling me.'

When the man was gone, Marion worked inside the bag so no one could see. He tore open the syringe pack, twisted off the needle guard, and pierced the top of the vial. He drew deep at the lidocaine, filling the syringe. Lidocaine was one of his favorite drugs. When injected into a person with a normal healthy heart, it induced heart failure. Marion placed the syringe on top of Smith's torn clothes so that it would be easy to reach, then closed the bag and waited.

After a few minutes, the dark-haired nurse left Smith's room. Shortly after that, the second nurse left.

Marion let himself into the room. He knew that he didn't have much time, but he didn't need much. He put the bag on the bed. Smith's eyes fluttered, opening partway, then closing, as if he was struggling to wake. Marion slapped him.

'Wake up.'

Marion slapped him again.

'Walter?'

Smith's eyes opened, not quite making it all the way. Marion wasn't sure if Smith could see him or not. Marion slapped him a third time, leaving a bright red mark on his cheek.

'Are the disks still in your house?'

Smith made a murmuring sound that Marion could not understand. Marion gripped his face again and shook it violently.

'Speak to me, Walter. Have you told anyone who you are?'

Smith's eyes fluttered again, then focused. The eyes tracked to Marion.

'Walter?'

The eyes dulled and once more closed.

'Okay, Walter. If that's the way you want it.'

Marion decided it was time. He felt confident that he could report that the disks were still in the house and that Smith hadn't been able to speak since his release from the house. The people in Palm Springs would be pleased. They would also be pleased that Walter Smith was dead.

'This won't hurt, Walter. I promise.'

Marion smiled, and suppressed a laugh.

'Well, that's not exactly true. Heart attacks hurt like a motherfucker.'

Marion opened the bag and reached in for the syringe.

'What are you doing?'

The red-haired nurse stood in the door. She stared at Marion, clearly suspicious, then came directly to the bed.

'You're not supposed to be in here.'

Marion smiled at her. She was a small woman with a thin neck. His hands still in the bag, Marion let go of the syringe and lifted the clothes so that the syringe would fall to the bottom. He never took his eyes from the nurse or stopped smiling. Marion had a fine smile. Sweet, his mother always said.

'I know. I came for his belongings, but I got the idea of leaving something from home, you know, like a good-luck piece, and there was no one to ask.'

Marion took out the wallet and opened it. He took out a worn picture of Walter with his wife and children. He showed it to the nurse.

'Could I leave it? Please? I'm sure it will help him.'

'It might get lost.'

Marion looked past her. No one was in the hall. He glanced at the far side of the room. Another door; maybe to a bathroom, maybe a closet or a hall. He could cover her mouth, lift her, it would only take seconds.

'I know, but . . . '

'Well, just tuck it under the pillow, then. You're not supposed to be here.'

The dark-haired nurse stepped through the door and went to one of the monitors. Marion closed the bag.

The red-haired nurse said, 'Is it okay if he leaves this picture? It belongs to Mr. Smith.'

'No. It'll get lost and someone will bitch. That always happens.'

Marion put the picture into his pocket and smiled at the red-haired nurse.

'Well, thanks anyway.'

Marion was patient. He was content to wait until Smith was once more alone, but he heard sirens as he walked back to the admitting room where he saw the female police officer outside the entrance. Marion thought that she was talking to herself, but then realized she was talking into her radio. The sirens grew closer. The reporters trickled outside, joining her, asking questions, but she suddenly broke away from them and ran back into the hospital. Marion decided not to wait.

Marion went out to his car, feeling dispirited by the way things had worked out. Palm Springs was not going to like his report after all, but there was nothing to be done about it. Not yet.

Then two police cars arrived. Marion watched the officers run through the shouting reporters into the hospital, and then he phoned Glen Howell.

TALLEY

Running for his car, Talley radioed Metzger at the hospital. He told her that there had been a threat to Smith's life, and to put her ass outside Smith's door. He grabbed Jorgenson and Campbell from Mrs. Peña's home and told them to follow him.

Talley rolled code three, full lights and siren. He knew that Benza's people would learn what he was doing, and that this might jeopardize himself and his family, but he couldn't let them simply kill the man. He didn't know what else to do.

When they reached the hospital, Talley saw the knot of reporters coming toward him from the entrance. Talley hurried out of his car to meet Jorgenson and Campbell.

'Don't say a word. Everything is no comment. You got that?'

Their eyes were confused and overwhelmed as the reporters surrounded them.

'Let's get in there.'

As they entered the hospital, Talley glanced from face to face, from hands to bodies, hoping for a glimpse of a deep tan, a heavy Rolex watch, and for clothes similar to those worn by the men and woman he had seen in his parking lot. Everyone was a suspect. Everyone was a potential killer. Anyone could lead him back to his Amanda and Jane.

The hospital security chief, an overweight man named

277

Jobs, met them at the admitting desk with Klaus and the ER supervisor, an older woman who introduced herself as Dr. Reese. Talley asked that they speak somewhere more private, and followed them past the admitting desk through a gate and around a corner into a hall. Talley saw Metzger standing outside a door not far away. Talley went directly to her, telling Reese and the others to wait.

'Is everything okay?'

'Yeah. It's fine. What's going on?'

Talley stood in the door. Smith was alone in the room. His head lolled to the side, then righted. Talley glanced back at Metzger.

'I'll be right back.'

Talley told Jorgenson and Campbell to wait with Metzger, then explained to the doctors.

'We have reason to believe that there could be an attempt made on Mr. Smith's life. I'm going to post a guard outside his room and have police here on the premises.'

Klaus made his face into a pinched, sulky frown.

'An attempt on his life? Like what you did in the ambulance?'

Reese ignored him.

'We work at an ER pace here, Sheriff. Things move quickly. I can't have that disrupted.'

'I'm the chief of police in Bristo. I'm not a sheriff.'

'I understand. Are my staff in danger?'

'Not with my officers here, no, ma'am.'

Klaus said, 'This is bullshit. Who would want to kill this guy?'

Talley didn't want to lie. He was tired of lying. He shrugged.

'We have to take the threat seriously.'

Jobs, the security chief, nodded.

'The world is filled with nuts.'

Talley worked it out that his officers would remain the primary guard outside Smith's room with Jobs's security personnel as supplement; if Smith was moved to another part of the hospital, the Bristo police would accompany him. They were still talking about it when Metzger called from her post.

'Hey. He's waking up.'

Klaus pushed past them and hurried into the room, Talley following. Smith's eyes were open and focused, though still vague. He mumbled something, then spoke again, more clearly.

'Where am I?'

The words were slurred, but Talley understood them.

Klaus drew out the penlight, peeled open Smith's eyes, then passed the light, first over one, then the other.

'My name is Klaus. I'm a doctor at Canyon Country Hospital. That's where you are. Do you know your name?'

It took Smith a few moments to answer, as if it took him a while to understand the question, then figure out the answer. He wet his lips.

'Smith. Walter Smith. What's wrong?'

Klaus glanced at the monitors.

'Don't you know?'

Smith seemed to think again, but then his eyes widened and he tried to sit up. Klaus pushed him down.

'Easy. Stay down or you'll faint.'

'Where are my chilren?'

Klaus glanced at Talley.

Talley said, 'They're still in the house.'

Smith's eyes tracked vaguely over. Talley lifted his sweatshirt so that Smith could see his badge.

'I'm Jeff Talley, the Bristo chief of police. Do you know what happened to you?'

'People came into my house. Three men. What about my children?'

'They're still in the house. So far as we know, they're okay. We're trying to get them out.'

Klaus grudged a nod.

'Chief Talley is the one who got you out.'

Smith looked up at him.

'Thank you.'

His voice was soft and fading. Smith settled back, his eyes closed. Talley thought they were losing him again.

Klaus didn't like what he saw on the monitors. His face pulled into the pinched frown again.

'I don't want him to overdo it.'

Talley brought Klaus aside and lowered his voice.

'I should have a word with him now. About what we talked about.'

'I don't see as it would do any good. It will only upset him.'

Talley stared at Smith, knowing he could punch the right button because he could read Klaus as easily as he read a subject behind a barricade.

'He has a right to know, Doctor. You know he does. I'll only be a moment. Now, please.'

Klaus scowled some more, but he left.

'Smith.'

Smith opened his eyes, not quite as wide as before. Talley watched as they flagged closed. He bent close.

'I know who you are.'

The eyes opened again.

'Sonny Benza has my wife and daughter.'

Smith stared up at him, as blank as a plate, showing no surprise or shock, revealing nothing. But Talley knew. He could sense it.

'He wants his financial records. He's taken my wife and daughter to make sure I cooperate. I need your help, Smith. I need to know where he has them. I need to know how to get to him.'

Something wet dripped on Smith's shoulder. Talley's eyes blurred, and he realized that he was crying.

'Help me.'

Smith wet his lips. He shook his head.

'I don't know what you're talking about.'

The eyes closed.

Talley leaned closer, his voice raspy.

'He's going to kill you, you sonofabitch.'

Klaus came back into the room.

'That's enough.'

'Let me speak to him a few more minutes.'

'I said, *That's enough*.'

Talley posted the guards, then left. He drove again with the windows down, frustrated and angry. He punched at the steering wheel and shouted. He wanted to race back to the house; he didn't want to go back to the house. He wanted to crash through doors and keep crashing until he found Amanda and Jane. It was impotent rage. He pulled the Nokia from his pocket and set it on the seat. He knew it would ring. He knew the Watchman would call. He had no other choice.

It rang.

Talley swerved to the shoulder of the road. He was in the middle of nowhere, on the stretch of highway between Canyon Country and Bristo, nothing but rocks and road and truckers trying to make it to Palmdale before dawn. Talley skidded to a stop and answered the call, the Watchman shouting before Talley spoke.

'You fucked up, you dumb fucking cop, you fucked up bad!'

Talley was shouting back, shouting over the Watchman's words.

'*No, YOU fucked up, you sonofabitch!* Do you think I'm going to let you just murder someone?!'

'*You wanna hear them scream?* That it? You want a blowtorch on your daughter's pretty face?!'

Talley punched the dash over and over, never felt the blows.

'I got YOU, you motherfucker! *I got YOU!* You touch them, you harm one fucking hair, and I'll go in that house right fucking now, I'll get those disks, and I'll see what's on them. You want them in the newspaper? You want the

281

*real* FBI to have'm? I don't think you want that, you COCKSUCKINGMOTHERFUCKER! And I've got *Smith!* Don't you fucking forget that! *I've got Smith!'*

Talley's hands shook with rage. It was the way he felt in the minutes after a SWAT entry when shots had been fired, his blood running so hot that only more blood could cool it.

When the Watchman spoke again, his voice was measured.

'I guess we each have something the other wants.'

Talley forced himself to be calm. He had bought himself time.

'Remember that. You fucking remember that.'

'All right. You have a guard on Smith. Fair enough. We'll deal with Smith when we deal with Smith. Right now we want our property.'

'Not one fucking hair. One hair and you bastards are mine.'

'We're off that, Talley. Move on. You still have to make sure that I get those disks. If I don't, more than hair will be harmed.'

'So what's next?'

'My people are good to go. You know who I mean?'

'The FBI.'

'Six in two vans. If there's any fuckup, if you do anything other than what I tell you to do, you'll get your family back in the mail.'

'I'm doing what I can, goddamnit. Tell me what you want.'

'Whatever they say they need, you give it to them. Whatever they want you to do, you do it. Remember, Talley, I get those disks, you get your family.'

'Jesus, man, we can't have an assassination squad out here. The neighborhood is full of professional police officers. They're not stupid.'

'I'm not stupid, either, Talley. My guys know how to walk the walk and talk the talk. They will behave in a professional manner. Use the Sheriffs for your perimeter, but have their tactical team stand down. My guy, the team leader, he'll cover that with the Sheriffs. They were in the area on a joint training mission with the Customs Service and the U.S. Marshals. They called you, offered their assistance, and you accepted.'

Talley knew that Martin would never buy that. He saw the whole thing blowing up in his face.

'No one will believe that. Why would I accept with the Sheriffs already here?'

'Because the Feds told you that Walter Smith is part of their witness protection program.'

'Is he?'

'Don't be stupid, Talley. My man will cover it with the Sheriffs when he gets there. He knows what to say so they'll go along. Do you want to hear your wife again?'

'Yes.'

The line was empty for a time, then Talley heard voices, and then Jane screamed.

'*Jane?!*'

Talley clutched the phone with both hands. He shouted, forgetting where he was, what he was doing.

'*JANE!*'

The Watchman came back on the line.

'You heard her, Talley. Now take care of my people and get them set up.'

The line went dead. Talley was left shaking and sweating. He pressed star 69, trying to call back, but nothing happened. Jane was gone. The Watchman was gone. Talley shook so badly he felt drunk. He got himself together. He put away the phone. He drove back to the house.

# CHAPTER 22

Saturday, 12:03 A.M.

DENNIS

When Dennis went back into the house, Mars didn't say anything, but Kevin started on him right away.

'What did he say? Did he offer a deal?'

Dennis felt dull, not desperate anymore, or even very frightened. He was confused. He didn't understand how Talley could turn down so much money unless Talley didn't believe him. Maybe Talley thought he was lying about how much money was in the house just as Talley had lied to him about the house belonging to mobsters.

'What *happened*, Dennis? Did he give us an ultimatum?'

The girl was on her hands and knees on the kitchen floor, staring at him.

'Is your old man in the mob?'

'What are you talking about?'

He could tell that the girl didn't know a goddamned thing. It was all stupid. He was stupid just for asking.

'Mars. Get her out of here. Take her back to her room.'

Dennis went to the office for the vodka, then brought it to the den, drinking on the way. The lights came on as he dropped onto the thick leather couch.

Kevin stopped in the door.

'Are you going to tell me what happened?'

'I shouldn't have told him about the money. Now he's gonna keep it all for himself.'

'He said that?'

'I tried to cut him in. What the fuck, it's a lot of cash, I thought we could buy our way out. See, that was my mistake. Once I told him how much money we had, he probably started thinking he could keep it for himself. Fuck that. If we don't escape, I'm telling everybody. All three of us will tell them about the cash, so if Talley tries to keep it they'll nail his ass.'

Dennis pulled deeper at the bottle, his mouth numb to it, angry at that bastard, Talley, for stealing his money.

'He's gonna kill us, Kev. We're fucked.'

'That's crazy. He's not going to kill us.'

Kevin was so fuckin' stupid.

'He's got to kill us, you idiot. He can't let us tell people about the money. The only way he can keep it is if nobody knows about it. He's probably gonna cap all three of us before they even read our rights. He's probably plannin' how to do it right now.'

Kevin came over and stood by the couch, crowding him.

'It's over, Dennis. We have to give up.'

'Fuck it's over! That money is *mine!*'

Dennis felt his anger building, and drank more of the vodka. That had always been Kevin's role in life, to hold him back, dragging behind him like an anchor, keeping him down.

Kevin stepped closer.

'You're going to get us all killed for that money. Talley's not playing games. The cops are going to get tired of waiting for us to give up, then we'll all be fuckin' killed!'

Dennis raised the bottle, and shrugged.

'Then we might as well die rich.'

'No!'

Kevin slapped the bottle from his hand, and then Dennis was off the couch. Dennis felt out of himself, his head a red blur of rage and frustration. He shoved Kevin over the coffee table and followed him down. Kevin grunted with the impact and tried to cover his face, but

Dennis held him with his left hand and punched with his right, hitting his brother again and again.

'Dennis, stop!'

He hit Kevin as hard as he could.

'Stop crying, goddamnit!'

He hit Kevin harder.

'*Stop crying!*'

Kevin rolled into a ball, his face blotched red, sobbing. Dennis hated him. He hated their father and their mother, hated all the rathole apartments and the brutal assholes their mother had brought home, hated his shitty job and the Ant Farm and every day of their failed lives, but most of all he hated Kevin for reminding him of these things every time he looked at him.

'You're fuckin' pathetic.'

Dennis climbed to his feet, breathless and spent.

'That money is mine. I'm not leaving without it, Kevin. Get that in your head. *We're not giving up.*'

Kevin crawled away, whimpering like a beaten dog.

Dennis picked up the bottle, and saw Mars standing in the door, watching without expression. Dennis wanted to hit Mars, too, the sonofabitch.

'What? You got something to say?'

Mars did not respond, the shadows in the dim light masking his eyes.

'*What?*'

Mars responded somberly.

'I like it here, Dennis. We're not going to leave.'

'Fuckin' A we're not.'

The vague smile flickered at Mars's lips, the only part of him that Dennis could see.

'We're going to be fine, Dennis. I'll take care of everything.'

Dennis turned away and sucked down another belt of the vodka.

'You do that, Mars.'

Mars melted into the darkness and disappeared.

286

Dennis burped.

Creepy bastard.

Quiet settled over York Estates. The traffic on Flanders Road had thinned; the line of cars filled with the morbid gawkers who wanted a brush with crime was gone, leaving the California Highway Patrol motor officers who were manning the barricades with nothing to do. Inside the development, the Sheriffs sat in their cars or at their posts. No one talked. Everyone waited.

Talley pulled his car to the curb outside Mrs. Peña's home and cut the engine. He looked at the command van. With nothing going on at the house, Maddox and Ellison would have pulled back to the van to alternate shifts on the phone, the off negotiator catching a catnap in the van's bunk or the backseat of a car. Talley was tired. The center of his back between his shoulder blades was knotted with a pronounced pain that cut into his spine. His head felt cloudy from more than fatigue, leaving him to mistrust his thinking. He wasn't a kid anymore.

Talley went inside for a cup of black coffee, but returned to his car. Three of the CHiPs and two sheriffs were in Mrs. Peña's kitchen, but he didn't want to talk. He sat on the curb with the Nokia and his own phone beside him. He sipped the coffee, thinking about Amanda and Jane, seeing them seated together on a couch in the anonymous room where they were held, seeing them alive, seeing them unharmed, seeing them safe. Imagining them that way helped.

Talley's radio popped at his waist.

'Chief, Cooper.'

'Go, Coop.'

'Ah, I'm here at the south gate. We got some FBI guys asking for you.'

Talley didn't answer. He worked at breathing. He stared at the Sheriff's command van and the line of police cars lining the street and the officers moving among them, feeling frightened and unsure. He was about to lie to them. It would be like letting the enemy into the camp. It would be lying to these people who were here to help him and help the people in that house.

'Chief? They say you're expecting them.'

'Let them in.'

Talley walked up the street to the corner. He didn't know what to expect and wanted to meet them alone, away from everyone else. He stood beneath a street lamp so they would stop in its light. He wanted to see them.

Two gray Econoline vans eased to the corner, four men in the lead van, two in the rear. Talley raised his hand, stopping them. Both vans pulled to the curb and cut their engines. The men inside had short haircuts and were wearing black tactical fatigues, standard issue for FBI tactical units. One of the men in the back wore a ball cap that read FBI.

The driver said, 'You Talley?'

'Yes.'

The man on the passenger side of the lead van got out and came around the nose of the van. He was taller than Talley and muscular. He looked the part: black tac fatigues, jump boots, buzzed hair. A black pistol hung beneath his left arm in a ballistic holster.

He stopped in front of Talley, glanced up the street at the Sheriffs, then turned back to Talley.

'Okay, Chief, let me see some ID. I want to be sure who I'm talking to.'

Talley lifted his sweatshirt enough to show his badge.

'I don't give a shit about that. Show me a picture.'

Talley took out his wallet and showed the photo ID. When he was satisfied, he took out his own badge case and opened it for Talley to see.

'Okay, here's mine. My name is Special Agent Jones.'

Talley inspected an FBI credential that identified the man as William F. Jones, Special Agent of the Federal Bureau of Investigation. It showed a photograph of Jones. It looked real.

'Don't sweat anyone asking for our papers. Every man in my group has the ID.'

'Are you all named Jones?'

Jones snapped the case closed and put it away.

'Don't be funny, Chief. You can't afford it.'

He slapped the nose of the lead van, nodding at the driver. The doors of both vans opened. The remaining five men stepped out, moving to the rear of the second van. Like Jones, they looked the part down to the haircuts. They strapped into armored vests with FBI emblazoned on the back.

Jones said, 'In a few minutes your phone is going to ring. You know the phone I mean. So let's get some stuff straight before that. Are you paying attention?'

Talley was watching the men. They strapped on the vests, then snapped on new thigh guards with practiced efficiency. Someone at the rear of the second van passed out black knit masks, flash-bang grenades, and helmets. Each man folded the mask twice and tucked it under his left shoulder strap where he could reach it easily later. They clipped the grenades to their harnesses without fumbling and tossed their helmets into the seats or balanced them atop the van. Talley knew the moves, because he had practiced them himself when he worked SWAT Tactical. These men had done this before.

'I'm paying attention. You used to be a cop.'

'Don't worry about what I used to be. You've got other stuff to worry about.'

Talley looked at him.

'How can you people expect this to work? The Sheriffs have a full crisis response team here. They're going to be pissed off and they're going to have questions.'

'I can handle the Sheriffs and anything else that comes up. What's my name?'

Talley didn't know what in hell he wanted.

'What?'

'I asked you my name. You just saw my commission slip. What's my fucking name?'

'Jones.'

'All right. I'm Special Agent Jones. Think of me that way and you won't fuck up. I can lift my end, you got a wife and kid praying you can lift yours.'

Talley's head throbbed. His neck was so tight that it burned, but he managed a nod.

Jones turned so that they both faced the line of vehicles.

'Who's in charge there?'

'Martin. She's a captain.'

'You told her about us yet?'

'No. I didn't know what to say.'

'Good, that's better for us. The less time she has to ask questions, the better. Now, the man on the phone, you know who I mean, did he tell you how we're going to cover this?'

'Smith is in witness protection.'

'Right, Smith is in the program so we have a proprietary interest. What's my name again?'

Talley flashed with anger and fought to control it. Everything seemed out of control and surreal, standing there in the purple street light, moths ticking and snapping into the glass, with these cops who weren't cops.

'Jones. Your name is Jones. I wish I knew your fucking real name.'

'Keep it tight, Chief. We gotta work together here. I'm in charge of a special operations unit that was working training exercises on the border with the Customs Service when Washington learned what was happening here. The D.C. office called you, explained the situation, and asked for your cooperation. We owe Smith, we're obligated to protect him and his cover, so you agreed. I'm going to explain all this to Captain Martin, and all you're going to do is sit there and nod. You got that?'

'I've got it.'

'Martin won't like it, having us here, but she'll go along because what we're telling her makes sense.'

'What if she checks? What if she knows people in the LA office?'

'It's after midnight on a Friday night. She phones LA, all she'll get is a duty agent, and he'll have to check with someone else, which he won't want to do. Even if she calls the agent in charge in Los Angeles and wakes him, he'll wait until tomorrow to call D.C., because none of these people, not one, will have any reason to doubt us. We're not gonna be here that long.'

Jones handed Talley a white business card with the FBI seal pressed into the left corner and a phone number with a Washington, D.C., area code.

'If she gets it into her head to call someone, tell her that this is the guy back there who called you. She can talk to him until she's blue.'

Talley put the card in his pocket, wondering if the name on the card was a real agent, and thought that he probably was. Thinking that scared him. It was like a warning, this is how much power we have.

Talley glanced at the men. They were geared up now. A man in the second van was passing out MP5s, CAR-15s, and loaded magazines.

'What are you people going to do?'

'You and I are going to straighten this out with the Sheriffs. Two of my people are going to reconnoiter the house, see what we have. After that, we'll deploy in a secure position and wait for the man to call. You've got your phone, I have mine. When he gives the word, we move. If something happens in the house that provokes a launch beforehand, we'll do it. But we will control the scene until we've recovered our target. After that, the house is yours.'

Talley thought about the man's words, thought he might have done this in the military, for the Rangers or Special Forces.

'I won't be able to keep the others out. You know that. The Sheriffs will come in, and I'm going, too.'

Jones met Talley's eyes and shook his head.

'Listen, man, if it helps you get through this, we don't want to kill anyone, not even the three dicks who started this mess. We just want the stuff in the house. But we know what's required when we breach that house. We'll have to secure the scene before we can recover what we want. We'll do that, Talley. We're professionals.'

The phone in Talley's pocket chirped. He had a phone in his left pocket and a phone in his right, and didn't remember which was which. Talley pulled out the phone in his left pocket. It was the Nokia. It chirped again.

'Answer it, Chief.'

Talley pressed the button to answer the call.

'Talley.'

'Is Mr. Jones with you?'

'Yes, he's here.'

'Put him on.'

Talley passed the Nokia to Jones without a word. Jones put it to his ear, saying his name to let the caller know he was on. Talley watched Jones. His eyes were pale blue or gray, Talley couldn't tell which in the dim light. A man in his mid-forties, maybe, who kept himself in good shape and could be hard when he had to be. As Jones spoke, his eyes flicked nervously to the Sheriffs in the distance. Talley thought that he was probably scared. Any sane man would be scared, doing what he was doing. Talley wondered what the Watchman had on this man, or if Jones was doing it for money.

Jones ended the call and passed the phone back to Talley.

'Let's go, Chief. Time to get it done.'

'What does he have on you?'

Jones stared at him, then looked away without answering.

'I know why I'm doing this. What does he have on you?'

Jones cinched down his vest, tighter than necessary, so tight the straps cut.

'You don't know shit.'

Jones started up the street.

Talley followed him.


## KEVIN

The stink of gasoline was so thick in the closed space of the entry hall that it burned Kevin's eyes and filled his throat with the taste of metal. He gagged, acid washing the back of his throat, then he couldn't hold back and vomited, puke splashing the wall. Dennis, in the den with his vodka, was too far gone to have heard.

They were going to die.

Kevin remembered a story from elementary school that explained how coastal Africans caught the tiny monkeys that lived at the edge of the water. The Africans would bore a hole in a coconut just big enough so that the monkey could squeeze its hand inside. They would put a peanut touched with honey into the coconut. The monkey would reach inside to grab the peanut, only with the peanut in its hand and its hand balled into a fist, the monkey's hand would no longer fit through the hole. As long as it held onto the peanut, the monkey couldn't take its hand out of the coconut. These monkeys wanted the honey-coated peanuts so badly that they would not let go even as the monkey-hunters walked up to cover them with nets. Dennis was the monkey in this house, surrounded by police but unwilling to let go of his peanut.

Kevin stumbled into the little bathroom off the entry

and splashed his face with water. His lip and eye were swelling from the beating Dennis had given him. He washed out his mouth, then washed his face, rubbing the water through his hair and around his neck. After the shootings, the fear, the running, the nightmare terror of the day, he finally knew what he had to do, and why: He was not willing to die with his brother; no matter their childhood, no matter Dennis taking the old man's belt for him, no matter the horrors they had endured. Dennis was willing to die for money he couldn't have, and Kevin refused to die with him. He would take the girl and her brother, and the three of them would get the hell out of here. Let Dennis and Mars do what they want.

Kevin dried his face, then went back to the den to see if Dennis was still there. Kevin expected that Dennis and Mars would try to stop him from leaving. He knew that they could, so he wanted to get the kids out of the house without being seen. Dennis's feet sprouted up over the end of the couch, still flat on his back. Kevin peeked into the office, checking for Mars, but Mars wasn't there. Kevin thought that he might be back in the family room by the French doors, but suddenly he had the prickly feeling that Mars was watching him on the monitors. Kevin slipped past the den back along the hall to the master bedroom. If Mars was in the security room, he was going to tell Mars that Dennis wanted him to watch the front of the house again, but the master bedroom was empty and so were the closets and security room. Kevin stared at the monitors, seeing the police outside, seeing his brother in the den and the girl in her room, but he didn't see Mars. He thought maybe he should break the monitors or figure out a way to turn off the security system, but if he moved quickly enough it wouldn't matter; once he had the kids, they would be out of the house in seconds or they wouldn't be out at all.

Kevin hurried back through the house to the entry, and then up the stairs. He knocked twice softly on the girl's door, pulled the nail from the door, and let himself inside. The girl was curled into a ball on her bed, her eyes open, the lights full on. She swung her feet out and stood as the door opened.

'What do you want?'

'Shh. Keep your voice down.'

Kevin was scared. Here he was a grown man, and he felt like a child whenever he crossed wills with his brother. Sometimes he felt such a strong mix of fear and a desperate need to please Dennis that he couldn't move.

'We're going to get out of here.'

She seemed confused, her eyes flicking to the door, then back to him.

'Where are you taking me?'

'Not with them. I don't mean with Dennis and Mars. I'm taking you and your brother. We're going to leave them here.'

The marks on his face registered with her for the first time, and Kevin felt himself flush.

'What happened to you?'

'Don't worry about it. Dennis isn't going to give up. He's going to stay here no matter what, but we're not.'

'They're letting us leave?'

'Mars and Dennis don't know I'm doing this. They would stop us, so we have to be careful, but we're getting out of here and they can do what they want.'

Uncertainty played across her face. She glanced at the door again.

Kevin said, 'Do you want to go or not? I'm offering you a way out of here.'

'I can't go without Thomas.'

'I know that. All three of us will go, but we have to be careful and move fast. Now do you want to go or not?'

'I want to go!'

'Stay here and pretend like nothing's happening. I'll get Thomas and come back for you. When the three of us are together, we'll go straight downstairs and out the front door. Do you have a white pillowcase?'

'We're going to walk out the door? Just like that?'

'Yes! We need a white flag or something so the cops don't shoot us.'

He could tell she was scared, but excited, too, anxious to get out of the house.

'All right, okay. I have a pillowcase.'

'Get it while I'm getting your brother. When I get back, don't say a word. Just follow me and try to be quiet, but be ready to *move*. We're going to walk fast.'

She nodded, her head bouncing.

'I will.'

Kevin eased the door open and peered into the hall. Dim light glowed at the stairwell, coming from below. The hall seemed darker than before, masked in a blackness that made him wish for a flashlight. He heard voices and grew even more worried. If Mars and Kevin were in the office, they would see the three of them coming down the stairs.

Kevin pulled the door shut behind him and crept back along the hall to the stairwell, listening. Twice the hall creaked, making Kevin cringe. When he reached the top of the stairs, he listened harder, then felt a well of relief. The voices were coming from the television.

He turned back toward the boy's room, telling himself to hurry, to do this quickly without noise, to do it *now* or else the moment would pass and he would never do it; he would be trapped in this house with Dennis and Mars, and he would die. Kevin was so frightened that it was difficult to think. The boy, the girl, out. He repeated it to himself like a chant.

Something moved in the darkness ahead of him.

Kevin froze, his senses straining, his heart pounding. The girl must have come out of her room. He whispered.

'Stay in your room.'

A black shadow drifted against the darkness outside her

door, but the shadow did not answer. Kevin strained to see into the bottomless grave of the hall, but saw nothing.

The floor creaked behind him. Kevin spun around.

Mars stood inches away, backlit by the light from the stairs. Kevin jerked backwards. They were screwed unless he could keep Mars away from the front door. He thought of the security room, as far from the front door as it was possible to get in this house.

'Jesus, Mars, you scared the shit out of me. I was looking for you. Dennis wants you to watch those monitors back in the bedroom.'

Mars stepped closer, his pale face empty.

'I heard you with the girl, Kevin. You're going to leave.'

Kevin stepped back. Mars followed him, staying uncomfortably close.

'That's bullshit, Mars. I don't know what you're talking about.'

'Don't ruin a good thing, Kevin. You'll regret it later.'

Kevin felt a stab of anger that shook him. Fuck it. Mars had heard; let him hear it all. Kevin stopped backing up.

'Then you can stay! I've had enough of this, Mars. We're trapped. It's over! If we stay, the cops will kill us. Don't you get that?'

Mars stared down at him, his pasty face thoughtful. Then he stepped aside.

'I get it, Kevin. If you want to go, go.'

Kevin waited for more, thinking that Mars was upset or angry, or would drag him downstairs to Dennis, but Mars only raised his hand, offering the way to the stairs. His voice was soft and encouraging.

'Go.'

Kevin glanced toward Thomas's room.

'I'm going to take these kids.'

Mars nodded.

'That's okay. Go.'

Kevin stared up at Mars, then turned and stepped into darkness.

*

After Talley and Jones had spoken with Martin, Jones moved his two vans to the mouth of the cul-de-sac. Talley returned to his car, where he sat by himself, watching the two vans. Jones and one of his men, a blond guy with a crew cut and wire-rimmed glasses, left the vans to scout the perimeter.

Talley felt like a traitor and a coward. He had returned to his car so that he could avoid the Sheriffs and his own men. When he and Jones were in the command van with Martin, he couldn't bring himself to look at her. He let Jones do the talking.

When Jones and his man disappeared into the cul-de-sac, the street was still.

Martin climbed down from the command van, saw Talley in his car, and walked over. She had taken off the flak vest and all the crap SWAT cops clip to themselves, and was wearing only the black fatigues and a cap. The cap read BOSS. Talley watched her approach, hoping that she would continue into Mrs. Peña's, but she came to his side of the car.

Martin stopped a few feet away, took out a pack of cigarettes, and offered one to Talley.

'Don't smoke.'

Martin lit up without a word. She drew the smoke in deep, then blew a plume that gassed into the night air like a shroud of fog. Talley didn't know many SWAT cops who smoked. Bad for the wind.

When she spoke, her voice was calm and reasonable.

'You gonna tell me what's going on?'

Talley watched the smoke.

'What do you mean?'

'I'm not stupid.'

Talley didn't answer.

'All the phone calls. That scene in the ambulance between you and the doctor, wanting him to wake Smith;

I thought you were going to shoot the guy. Whatever you were talking about with that kid, then charging off to the hospital. I had my I.O. call over there, Talley; if someone phoned in a death threat, it's news to everybody else out here, including the people back at your office.'

She drew more smoke, then appraised him.

'Now we got the FBI with this bullshit about Smith being in witness protection. What's going on, Chief? Who is Walter Smith?'

Talley glanced over. Her eyes were steady and cool, meeting his without guile. He liked her measured attitude, and her direct manner. He thought he would probably like her, given the time for it; she was probably a pretty good cop. The weight of the day suddenly pressed down on him with an intensity that left him numb. There were too many things to control and too many lies to tell. It was all too complicated, and he couldn't afford to mess this up. Like a juggler with a hundred balls in the air, he was going to drop one sooner or later. A ball would hit the ground and someone would die. He couldn't let that happen. He couldn't fail Amanda and Jane or the kids in that house or even Walter Smith.

'I need help.'

'That's why we rolled out, Chief.'

'Do you know the name Sonny Benza?'

She searched his face, Talley thinking that she couldn't place the name, but then she did.

'That's the mob guy, right?'

'Smith works for him. Smith has something in that house that can put Benza away, and Benza wants it.'

'Jesus.'

Talley looked at her, and felt his eyes go wet.

'He has my wife and daughter.'

Martin looked away.

Talley told her about the disks, the Watchman, and Jones. He told her how he had played it, and how he intended to play it. She listened without question or comment until he was finished, then she crushed her cigarette beneath her heel and stared at the two vans where Jones's people waited.

'You have to bring this to the Bureau.'

'I can't do that.'

'Turn it over to Organized Crime. With what you have they could move on Benza right now, pull him straight out of bed and hang him by his thumbs. We breach into that house, get these disks he wants, and that's all she wrote. That's how you save your family.'

'It's not your family.'

She considered the dead cigarette, and sighed.

'No, I guess not.'

'All I have is a voice on a phone, Martin. I don't know where they are, I don't know who has them. Benza has people out here; he knows what we're doing. He could make Jane and Amanda vanish even before we read him his rights, and what do I have? Three men I can't identify in cars I can't identify, and Jones over there. I don't give a shit about making a case. I just want my family.'

Martin stared at the two vans, and sighed again. It was getting to be a long night for all of them.

'I am not going to let murder happen out here, Talley. I can't do that.'

'Me neither. Jesus.'

'Then what are you going to do?'

'I can't let those disks go into evidence. They're the only leverage I have.'

'What do you want from me?'

'Help me. Keep it between us, but help me get those disks. I can't let Jones go into that house alone.'

Talley watched her, hoping that she would go along. He couldn't stop her from going upstairs. All he could do was trust her. She looked back at him, and nodded.

'I'll do what I can. You keep me informed, Talley. I don't want to get shot in the back. I can't let my people get hurt, either.'

Talley felt better, the load lessened because now she helped bear it.

'All I need are those damned disks. I get those disks, and then I'll have something to trade.'

She considered him, then put her cigarettes back into her jumpsuit. Talley knew what she was going to say before she said it.

'You need more than that. You know too much for Benza to leave you alive. You realize that, don't you? You, your family, Smith; he can't leave any of you alive. What are you going to do about that?'

'I'll deal with it when I have the disks.'

Talley's cell phone rang, loud in the silence of the night. Martin jumped.

'Shit.'

Talley thought it might be Thomas, but it was Mikkelson, sounding far away and strange.

'Chief, Dreyer and I are still out here at Krupchek's trailer with detectives from the Sheriff's Bureau. We got some stuff to report.'

Talley had forgotten about Mikkelson and Dreyer. It took a moment for him to gather his thoughts.

'Go, Mikkelson.'

'Krupchek isn't Krupchek. His real name is Alvin Marshall Bonnier. His mother's head is in the freezer.'

# Part Four
TACTICS

# CHAPTER 23

Saturday, 12:52 A.M.

Alvin Marshall Bonnier, age twenty-seven, also known as Mars Krupchek, was wanted in connection with four counts of homicide in Tigard, Oregon. The local authorities theorized the following chain of events based on witness interviews and forensic evidence: Bonnier, who lived alone with his mother at the time of the murders, abducted and raped his next-door neighbor, Helene Getty, age seventeen, and disposed of her body in a wooded streambed near their homes. She had been strangled and repeatedly stabbed in the chest, abdomen, and vaginal area. Mrs. Bonnier, an invalid suffering from crippling arthritis, subsequently discovered Getty's bloodstained panties and left Reebok tennis shoe, also splattered with blood, in her son's bedroom. She confronted her son, at which time Alvin stabbed his mother to death in the living room, then carried her body to the bathroom, where he dismembered it. Bonnier wrapped the limbs and torso in newspapers and plastic trash bags, then buried these remains in Mrs. Bonnier's rosebed. Neighbors stated that when the boy was young, Mrs. Bonnier made switches from the thorny rose branches with which she beat the boy. Bonnier kept his mother's head in the refrigerator, but transferred the head to the trunk of the family car several days later. With his mother's head along for company, he befriended sixteen-year-old Stephen Stilwell at a local shopping mall and enticed the boy to take a drive, probably offering cigarettes and beer. Instead, Bonnier drove Stilwell to a nearby abandoned drive-in movie theater, where he sodomized the boy, then stabbed him repeatedly. He placed Stilwell in the trunk with his mother's head, then drove to the same area where he had disposed of Helene Getty's body. Upon arrival at that location, he discovered that Stilwell was still alive, whereupon he cut the young man's throat, mutilated his genitals, and abandoned the body without attempting to conceal it. Witnesses at the shopping mall were able to provide a description of Bonnier and his automobile. Twelve days later, an eighteen-year-old high school senior named Anita Brooks hitched a ride with Bonnier after missing her bus. Instead of bringing her to school, Bonnier drove to a nearby lake, where he strangled her before branding the victim's breasts and vagina with her own cigarettes. Evidence gathered at the scene indicated that he had placed his mother's head on a nearby picnic table, probably so that she could watch the mutilation. Bonnier immediately returned home, parked his car in its usual spot, then, so far as the police know, departed the area. Authorities discovered Anita Brooks's body first. Alvin Marshall Bonnier was not identified as the suspect until two days later when neighbors investigated the foul smell coming from the Bonnier residence and summoned the police, who located his mother's body between the roses. Stilwell and Getty were found within the following week.

Talley listened to Mikkelson's recitation of the facts with a growing sense of urgency that Martin read in his expression.

'What in hell is happening?'

Talley raised his hand, telling her to wait.

'Mikki, they're positive that Bonnier and Krupchek are the same person?'

'That's affirm, Chief. The palm print he left in Kim's matched dead on, and the Bureau guys brought a copy of

306

the warrants fax from Oregon. I saw the photo. It's Krupchek.'

'What's happening out there now?'

'The VICAP hit automatically notified the FBI. The detectives here have locked down the scene to wait for a team from the LA field office.'

Talley checked his watch.

'What's their ETA?'

'I dunno. You want me to check?'

'Yeah.'

Talley filled in Martin while he waited for Mikkelson. As Martin listened, her face grew closed and uncertain, but Mikkelson was back on the line before she could respond.

'Chief?'

'Go, Mikki.'

'The Feds should be here within a couple of hours. You want us to wait for them or come back to York?'

Talley told her to come back, then snapped the phone shut. He ran his hand across his head and stared toward the cul-de-sac.

'This is fucking great. I've got the mafia outside and fucking Freddy Krueger in the house.'

Martin watched him calmly.

'This changes things.'

'I *know* it changes things, Captain! I'm trying to save my wife and daughter, but I have to get those kids out of that house.'

'Because of Krupchek? They've been in there all day with him, Talley. Another few hours won't matter.'

'It matters. All of this matters.'

Talley left Martin at the command van and found Jones briefing his people at their vans. Jones saw Talley approaching, and separated from the others. Talley noted that Jones appeared apprehensive, resting a hand on the MP5 slung from his shoulder.

'What's up, Chief?'

'We have a problem. One of the three subjects in the house isn't who we thought. Krupchek. His true name is Alvin Marshall Bonnier. He's wanted for multiple homicides in Oregon.'

Jones smiled tightly, like Talley was making an unfunny joke.

'You're shittin' me.'

'You're going to be swimmin' in shit when you hear this: The real FBI are on their way. This isn't bullshit, Jones or whatever your name is. The Sheriffs pulled a palm print from the minimart these assholes robbed. They got a VICAP hit. You know what that is?'

Jones wasn't smiling anymore, but he didn't look concerned, either.

'I know.'

Talley explained that detectives from the Sheriff's Homicide Bureau were presently at Krupchek's home awaiting the arrival of FBI agents from the LA field office.

'They'll visit that house, then they'll come here, and they won't leave. By morning, this place is going to be covered with FBI, including a *real* FBI SWAT team.'

'We'll be gone by then. We're breaching the house as soon as I hear back from the man.'

'I want to go in now.'

Jones shook his head.

'Not until I get the call.'

Talley couldn't tell if Jones was suspicious or simply didn't understand.

'Listen to me. It's different now. This isn't just three turds holding a family hostage anymore. Those kids are in there with a lunatic.'

'It'll be fine, Talley.'

'We're talking about a man wanted for multiple homicide, Jones. He cut off his own mother's head and keeps it in the freezer.'

'I don't give a shit.'

'He's psychotic. Psychotics decompensate in stressful

situations, and this guy has been in a pressure cooker all day. If that happens, he might do anything.'

Jones was unmoved.

'We'll breach when I get the call. It won't be long.'

'Fuck you.'

'After the call.'

Talley walked away. He saw Martin watching from the command van, but didn't know what to say to her. He recalled his conversations with Rooney, and decided that Rooney did not know that Krupchek was really Alvin Marshall Bonnier. If Rooney was knowingly associating with a serial killer, it would mean he derived a vicarious pleasure from Bonnier's company. Rooney's need to be seen as special would have forced him to drop hints of Bonnier's identity in hopes of impressing Talley, but Rooney had not done that. Rooney didn't know, which meant that Rooney might as easily end up Bonnier's victim as the rest of them.

Talley glanced back at Jones. He and his men were waiting together at the rear of their van. Waiting for the call.

Talley decided that he couldn't wait any longer. He had to warn Rooney and Thomas, and he had to get those kids out of there.

Then he heard screaming from the house.


DENNIS

Dennis reached for the Stoli bottle and fell off the couch, landing on his face and knees in a pool of vodka. His ass was in the air, pointing toward the front of the house, toward the cops who filled the cul-de-sac.

Dennis patted his ass, and giggled.

'Too bad you cops can't see this! You can kiss my skinny white ass right here.'

Dennis collected the bottle and pushed to his feet. He

caught himself on the sofa arm to keep from tipping over, then took his pistol from his waist. Holding it made him feel better. The television showed a woman on her knees, pushing a rolling platform back and forth on the floor. Her abdominal muscles were so beautifully defined that she looked like an anatomy chart. Dennis watched her with a sense of profound loss, then raised the pistol to his own head.

'Bang.'

He lowered the gun.

'Shit.'

Dennis dropped his gun onto the couch, then considered the money. Stacks of hundred-dollar bills lined the coffee table. He fished the remaining packs of cash from his pockets and fanned the bills like a deck of cards. He had tried every way he could think of to keep the money, but failed. He had tried to get a car and a helicopter, and he had tried to buy Talley, and all of that had failed. He had tried to find a route out of the house, but the cops had him locked down. Dennis Rooney had run out of ideas, and now he was thinking that maybe his parents and teachers had been right all along: He was stupid. He was a small-time loser, who would always be a loser, living on dreams. A panicked urge to run with a bag of cash, sprinting through the shadows in a final lame attempt to get away swept over him, but he believed in his heart that the cops would kill him and he did not want to die. He didn't have the balls for it. As much as he wanted this money, Dennis Rooney admitted to himself that he was a chickenshit. His eyes filled with tears of regret and shame. Kevin was right. It was time to quit.

Dennis wiped the snot from his nose, and pulled himself together.

'I guess that's it, then.'

He tossed the money into the air, watched the fluttering green bills fall around him, then called Kevin.

'Kev!'

Kevin didn't answer.

'Mars!'

Nothing.

'Shit!'

Dennis lurched to the hall and made his way to the kitchen. It was still wrapped in shadows, lit only by the glare from the police lights shining in through the French doors. He wanted a glass of water, and then he would call Talley. He thought he might be able to trade one of the kids for a conversation with an attorney, then see what kind of deal he could cut for himself before surrendering.

'Kevin, goddamnit, where are you?!'

Here the sonofabitch had begged to surrender, and now that Dennis was ready, the wimpy puss wasn't around.

'Mars!'

The voice from the other side of the kitchen startled him.

'What are you doing, Dennis?'

Dennis wheeled around like a tall ship under sail, squinting into the shadows.

'Where's Kevin?'

'He's not here.'

'Where is he? I need to see him.'

Dennis wanted to get things straight with Kevin before telling Mars. Part of him was afraid that Mars might try to stop him.

Mars took shape in the light. Dennis thought he must have been in the pantry, or maybe the garage.

'Kevin left.'

Dennis grew irritated, not understanding.

'That doesn't help me, Mars. Is he in the security room, the office, what? I've got to talk to him.'

'He didn't want to stay here anymore. He left.'

Dennis stared at Mars, understanding, but not believing it, telling himself that Kevin could not have deserted him.

'Waitaminute. Are you telling me that he *left*, as in went out the door and surrendered to the cops?'

'I overheard him talking to the girl.'

'SHIT! That *FUCK*!'

'I'm sorry, Dennis. I came down to find you.'

Dennis felt sick. If Kevin had surrendered and taken the kids with him, he had taken Dennis's last chance to cut a deal with Talley.

'Did he take those kids with him?'

'I don't know.'

'Jesus, Mars! Get upstairs and see! If he took those kids, we're fucked!'

Mars went for the stairs without another word, and Dennis raged at the top of his lungs.

'KEVIN!! You ASSHOLE!'

Dennis threw the vodka bottle at the Sub-Zero so hard that his shoulder flashed with pain. He stalked back to the den for a fresh bottle. Even when he wanted to surrender, things got fucked up.


THOMAS

Thomas heard Dennis and Kevin fighting through the air-conditioning vent. Kevin wanted them to give up, but Dennis wouldn't. Thomas knew what that meant: If Dennis wouldn't give up, the three turds might stay here for days, and one of them might try to do something to his sister. Thomas had seen the way Mars watched her.

The shouting died quickly. Thomas waited for someone to come upstairs, but the hall remained silent. He decided that they were trying to sleep.

Thomas slipped back into his closet and returned to the crawl space. He thought about stopping in Jennifer's room to tell her what he was doing, but he knew she didn't want him to mess with the gun. He worked his way across the house, stopping at the air vents to listen, but all he heard was the television playing in the den. The rest of the house was silent.

Thomas let himself down through the ceiling hatch into the laundry room, climbing down from the hot-water heater to the washer to the floor. It was dark, lit only by some slight dim light filtering from the kitchen through the pantry. He had to use his flashlight.

Just as he reached the floor he heard Dennis shouting for Kevin and Mars. Dennis was close, just on the other side of the kitchen or maybe in the family room. Thomas panicked. He started climbing back to the ceiling, but then Mars answered Dennis, and Thomas stopped. They were talking. Thomas was still scared, but he was so close to the gun that he didn't want to once more leave without it. He strained to listen. Dennis was cursing Kevin; they weren't coming this way, they weren't looking for him.

Thomas hurried into the utility room. He cupped his hand over the flashlight and flicked it on again, just long enough to mark the spot in his mind where the gun box waited on the highest shelf. He rested the flashlight on the bench, then climbed onto the bench.

He went up onto his toes, stretching as tall as he could, but the box was still out of reach. He flicked on the light again, and spotted a gallon metal paint can at the edge of the bench. He pulled it into position, put one foot on it, and stepped up. The paint can creaked, but held. He stretched high again, and this time his hands found the gun box. He had it! Thomas pulled the box from the shelf, then lowered himself from the can and climbed down from the bench. His heart pounded with excitement. The box was a lot heavier than he had imagined! It felt as if a cannon were inside!

Thomas opened the box and lifted out the gun. It felt as heavy as a brick, way too big for his hand. Thomas didn't know its caliber or anything about it, even though his

313

father had let him fire it once when they had gone to the pistol range. It had kicked so hard that his hand stung!

Thomas would need his hands free to climb, so he pushed it into his pants. The gun made him feel powerful, but scared at the same time; he was buoyant with confidence that he could protect himself and Jennifer, and that now they could get out, but he didn't want to hurt anyone. He hoped he wouldn't have to use it.

Thomas was on his way back to the laundry room when his foot slipped from under him. He almost fell, catching himself on the bench just in time. He explored the floor with his foot, and found something slippery and wet. He lifted his foot. His shoe came free with a tacky sound. Thomas turned on his light. A dark liquid like oil was spreading on the floor. He followed it with his light. It was coming from the broom closet. Thomas opened his fingers to let out more light. The oil was red.

The closet door zoomed close in Thomas's mind's eye as if he had telephoto vision. The cramped space in the utility room shrank as the door grew larger. The gun was forgotten, leaving only the door and the viscous red liquid seeping out from beneath.

Thomas stared at the door. He wanted to open it. He wanted to run.

He stepped across the red pool, reached for the knob, but couldn't touch it. His fingers hovered an inch away.

Open it!

Thomas gripped the knob carefully, terrified that whatever was on the other side of the door might try to hold it closed. He slowly pulled open the door.

Kevin fell out, collapsing in a lifeless heap at Thomas's feet, his dead arms thrown around Thomas's legs.

His throat was slashed, his head lolling on white bone; the horrible second smile was locked in silent laughter.

His eyes were open.

Thomas screamed.

*

nnifer listened at her door, pressing her ear to the cold
ood, hoping to hear Kevin return. He only had to go
own the hall to reach Thomas, but he was taking so long
at she feared Mars or Dennis had interfered. Her
omach knotted and she pressed her fists into her belly in
useless attempt to make it stop. The knife hidden in the
aist of her pants pricked her skin, making her gasp. She
arranged the blade to make it more comfortable.

The hall outside her door creaked.

*Kevin!*

She heard the nail being pulled from the doorjamb. She
as excited and happy and ready to run. She wanted to
e her father again! She wanted to hug Thomas so tight
at he squirmed! She wanted her Mommy!

The door swung open, and Mars stepped inside, tall,
ide, and massive as a bear. She jumped back so fast that
e almost fell.

His smile made her think of bad boys burning ants.

He said, 'Were you expecting someone else?'

She backed away from the door, wishing that Kevin
ould come back right now because Mars was so awful
d gross.

She forced herself to meet his eyes without looking
way.

'I'm not expecting anyone except the police.'

Mars nodded agreeably.

'They'll be here soon. You probably don't have long to
ait.'

She cursed her smart mouth; she didn't like anything
e said or how he said it or his expressions. She just
anted him to leave.

Mars stepped into the room and pushed the door shut.
e held the big nail that they used to wedge the door. He
pped it absently on his leg, tap-tap, tap-tap. Jennifer

didn't like that he closed the door. She didn't like that he tapped the nail. She crossed her arms protectively over her breasts.

'What do you *want*?'

Mars watched her with bright nervous eyes that didn't match with his slack-jawed expression. It was as if he wasn't in the room with her, but was on the other side a glass wall, here but not here, outside looking in, in his own horrible world.

'What do you want?'

'Kevin left without you.'

She felt herself flush. Her arms tightened so fiercely that her nails dug into her flesh, and she wanted to scream.

'He wanted me to tell you. He thought about it and decided it was just too risky to sneak past Dennis with you and your brother, so he went by himself. He said to tell you he was sorry.'

Jennifer shook her head, not knowing what was real and what wasn't, what he knew or what he didn't, or if her only hope of getting out of here had slipped out the door without her.

'I don't know what you're talking about.'

Mars came closer.

'No? Well, it doesn't matter. All the lights are almost off.'

'What are you talking about?'

Mars seemed to grow as he got closer, filling the room. Jennifer backed away.

'Good boys turn off the lights so that no one can see them doing bad things in the dark. My mother told me that.'

Jennifer's rear end bumped into her desk. She had gone as far as she could and now Mars was very close. He touched the nail to her chest, tap-tap.

'Don't touch me.'

Tap-tap.

'Stop it.'

Tap.

'Kevin's gone. Dennis is gone. Your father is gone. The little fat boy, he's gone, too. Now we can have fun.'

He pressed the nail onto her chest, a steady pressure that hurt but did not break her skin. Jennifer tried to lean away, but there was nowhere to go. Mars raked the nail slowly down between her breasts. Jennifer stared into his eyes, watching him watch her, her vision blurred with tears. His eyes were black pools, their surface rippled by secret winds. He knew he was doing something bad; he knew he was being naughty. He didn't watch the nail; she sensed that his pleasure came in seeing her fear. Jennifer slid her hand down along her belly. She worked her fingers beneath the waist of her pants, searching for the knife. He pushed the nail harder. He was breathing harder. She wanted to scream.

'Do you like this?'

Jennifer jerked the knife free and stabbed, striking out blindly, trying to force him away. The stiff short blade struck something hard. Mars grunted in surprised pain, like a dog coughing, as they both looked down. The knife was buried high on his chest in his left shoulder.

Mars whimpered, a pathetic moan, his face knotted with pain.

Jennifer pushed at him, screaming, trying to get away, but he didn't move. He grabbed her throat, squeezing hard, pressing his hips into hers to pin her to the desk.

He grabbed the knife with his free hand, whimpered again, then pulled out the blade. A crimson flower blossomed from the wound.

He looked back into her eyes, then brought the knife to her face. He squeezed harder, cutting off her breath.

'You're going to enjoy this.'

Jennifer felt herself fainting.

*

The scream from the rear of the house cut through the alcohol, surprising Dennis more than startling him. It was high-pitched like a girl shrieking, followed by bumping, slamming noises that came from the far side of the kitchen near the garage. Dennis pulled out his gun, shouting.

'What the fuck was that? Who is that?'

It couldn't be Mars, who had just left, or the two kids, who were both upstairs unless that chickenshit Kevin had taken them. Maybe Kevin had returned.

'Kev? Is that you, you asshole?'

Dennis turned on his flashlight and swept the light beam across the kitchen. No one answered and nothing moved.

'Goddamnit, who's there?'

No one answered.

Dennis flashed the light toward the French doors, paranoid with the notion that the police were tricking him.

'Talley?'

Nothing.

Dennis pushed the gun ahead of him and eased through the kitchen toward the garage.

'Is that you, fat boy?'

Nothing.

'Kevin, if that's you, say something, goddamnit. Mars said you left.'

Nothing.

Dennis stepped into the pantry, shining the light through into the laundry room beyond. The floor was covered with a growing red stain that oozed toward him. Dennis frowned, not understanding. He took a step closer, then another. He saw his brother on the floor. Dennis lowered the gun, and straightened.

'Kevin, what the fuck? Get up.'

A deep trembling started at his center, filling him, growing until his entire body shook and the light beam danced mindlessly around the small room.

'Kevin, get up.'

Dennis walked on mile-long legs without feeling. It was hard to keep his balance. He stopped at the edge of the pool of blood and shined the light on his brother. He saw the open neck, the grotesque white bone within the flesh, the wide, staring eyes. Dennis turned off the light.

The fat boy and the girl could not have done this.

Mars.

Mars lied.

Mars killed Kevin.

Dennis backed out of the pantry into the kitchen, then ran for the stairs.

'Mars!'

He took the stairs two at a time, intent only on finding Mars, killing him. Halfway up, he heard the girl scream.

'*MARS!*'

Dennis slammed into the girl's door, shoving it open so hard that it crashed against the wall. Mars had the girl by her throat, pinned against her desk. Dennis aimed his gun.

'You're dead, you fuck.'

Mars calmly pulled the girl in front of him, blocking Dennis's aim. Dennis saw the knife and the growing bloodstain on Mars's left shoulder.

Mars smiled at Dennis with wide-eyed innocence.

'What's wrong, dude? What are you so pissed off about?'

Dennis could see the terror on the girl's face, her eyes swollen and red. She managed a word.

'Please.'

Dennis raised his gun. He didn't want to shoot past her, but he wanted that fucker Mars square between the eyes. He wanted to make Mars scream.

'This fuck killed Kevin. He cut his damned throat. There's blood everywhere.'

Like he needed her absolution.

The girl closed her eyes and cried harder.

Dennis should have been ready, but he wasn't. H
should have pulled the trigger, but he didn't.

And then it was too late.

Mars lifted the girl by the neck and rushed forward
charging Dennis, crossing the short space in no time a
all. Dennis hesitated only a heartbeat because he didn'
want to shoot the girl, but that was too long. The gir
crashed into him, the full force of Mars's weight behin
her, knocking Dennis backwards into the hall. Then th
girl was cast aside, Mars was on top of him, and Denni
saw a glint off the knife as it came down.

THOMAS

Rational thought was beyond him; he was filled with
suffocating fear that drove him to run, to get out, to *move*
Thomas did not know that he screamed. He slipped in th
blood, falling hard into the red pool, then slipped again a
he climbed onto the washer. He clambered up into th
crawl space, cutting his hands and knees as he scramble
across the rafters. He couldn't move fast enough, onc
banging his head so hard that he saw bright flashes. H
had the gun now. He could save himself. His only though
was to reach Jennifer. The two of them would ru
downstairs and out the door, and neither Mars nor Denni
could stop them. *He had the gun!*

Thomas heard Jennifer's door crash open as he squeeze
through the hatch into her closet. He froze, listening, an
heard voices. Dennis was shouting at Mars. Mars wa
holding Jennifer as Dennis faced him, shouting that Mar
had cut Kevin's throat. Thomas drew the gun from hi
pants, big and heavy and awkward, but he didn't know
what to do. Dennis had a gun, too!

Then Mars pushed Jennifer into Dennis, and all three o

320

them sprawled into the hall. Thomas crept into the room. Mars grunted like a pig when it eats, drool streaming from his mouth as he stabbed Dennis over and over. Jennifer was crawling away, splattered with blood.

'Jen! C'mon!'

Thomas darted past Mars into the hall, and grabbed Jennifer's arm. He pulled her toward the stair.

'Run!'

The two of them stumbled away as Mars heaved to his feet. His eyes were wild and darting. He was bigger, stronger, faster; Thomas knew that he would catch them.

Thomas whirled around and jerked up the pistol with both hands.

'I'll shoot you!'

Mars stopped. He was streaked with blood, and breathing hard. Blood dripped from his face. Even more blood painted the walls and floor. Dennis bubbled like a fountain and moaned.

The pistol was heavy and hard to hold. It wobbled, even though Thomas held it with both hands. Jennifer pulled at his shoulder, her voice a frightened whisper.

'Keep going. Let's get out of here.'

They backed away, Thomas trying to hold the gun steady.

Mars walked after them, matching them step for step.

Thomas pushed the gun at him.

'Stay away! I'll shoot you!'

Mars spread his arms as if to embrace them. He continued walking.

'Remember what I told you when I tied you to your bed?'

Thomas remembered: *I'm going to eat your heart.*

They reached the landing. Jennifer started down the stairs.

Mars walked faster.

'I'm going to cut out your heart. But I'm going to cut out your sister's heart first, so you can watch.'

'Stay away!'

Fear amped through Thomas like electric current. His body shook with it, and his bladder let go. He didn't want to shoot; he was scared to shoot, scared that it would be wrong even though he feared for his life, scared that he would be punished for it and would burn in hell and branded a bad person who had made a terrible awful mistake, but Mars came on and he was too scared not to shoot, too scared of that awful knife and the blood that dripped and ran over everything and that Mars really would do it, would cut out his heart, and Jennifer's, and eat them both.

Thomas pulled the trigger.

*Click!*

Mars stopped, frozen at the sharp sound.

*Click!*

The gun didn't fire.

All the things that his father had showed him at the pistol range came flooding back. He gripped the slide hard and pulled back to load a bullet into the chamber, but the slide locked open and did not close. Thomas glanced down into the open action. The magazine was empty. The pistol was unloaded. There were no bullets. *There were no bullets!*

When Thomas looked up again, Mars smiled.

'Welcome to my nightmare.'

Jennifer screamed, 'Run!'

Thomas threw the gun at Mars and ran, following Jennifer down the stairs. The air was thick with the smell of gasoline and vomit. Jennifer reached the front door first, and clawed at the handle, but the door would not open.

'Open it!'

'The deadbolt is locked! Where's the key?'

The key wasn't in the lock. Thomas knew with certain dread that it was probably upstairs in Dennis's bloody pocket.

Mars pounded down the stairs, closing the ground between them. He would be on them in seconds. They would never reach the French doors or garage before he caught them.

Jennifer grabbed his arm and pulled.

'This way! *Run!*'

She pulled him toward their parents' room. Thomas realized that she was taking him to the safest place in the house, but Mars was getting closer, off the stairs now and out of the entry and right behind them.

Thomas raced after his sister down the hall, through their parents' bedroom, and into the security room. They slammed the steel door and threw the bolt in the same moment that Mars crashed into the other side of the door.

The world was silent.

Thomas and Jennifer held each other, shaking and scared. All that Thomas could hear was his own heavying breath.

Then Mars pounded on the door; slow, rhythmic thuds that echoed through the tiny room . . . boom . . . boom . . . boom.

Jennifer squeezed Thomas, whispering.

'Don't move. He can't reach us in here.'

'I know.'

'We're safe.'

'Shut up!'

His father had told him that the door could stop *anything*.

The pounding stopped.

Mars cupped his hands to the door and shouted to make himself heard. His muffled voice came through the steel.

'You're bad. You're bad. You're bad. Now I'm going to punish you.'

Mars hit the door once more, then walked out of the room.

Thomas remembered the cell phone.

He clawed it out of his pocket, and turned it on.

323

The cell phone chimed as it came to life.

'Thomas! Look!'

Jennifer was watching Mars on the monitors. He was in the entry by the front door. He picked up the two containers of gasoline, then walked through the house splashing gasoline on the walls. He smiled as he worked.

Jennifer said, 'Ohmigod, he's going to burn us.'

The cell phone chimed again, and Thomas glanced at the display. The battery indicator flickered.

The cell phone was going dead.

'Here! It's working!'

Thomas punched in Talley's number, then glanced up at the monitors. Mars was staring into the camera as if he saw directly into their eyes and hearts. Then Thomas saw his lips move.

'What's he saying?'

Jennifer grabbed Thomas and pulled him away from the door.

'He's saying good-bye.'

Mars tossed the match.

The room erupted in flame.


## TALLEY

When Talley heard the first scream from the house, he took a position behind a Highway Patrol car. The CHiPs in the cul-de-sac shifted uncomfortably because they heard it, too. Talley couldn't tell if the voice was male or female, but there had only been the one scream. Now the house was still.

Talley moved to the nearest Highway Patrol officer.

'You on the command frequency?'

'Yes, sir. You heard that in the house? I think something's going on.'

'Give me your radio.'

Talley radioed Martin, who acknowledged his call without comment. Talley moved down the line of patrol cars, listening hard for something more from the house, but it was silent.

Then, room by room, the lights went off.

Talley saw Martin approaching, and moved out to meet her. The scream had scared him, but the silence now scared him more. Jones was too far away to have heard.

Martin huffed up, excited.

'What's going on? Why is the house so dark?'

Talley was starting to explain when they saw a dull

orange glow move inside the house at the edges of the window shades. He thought it was a flashlight.

His phone rang.

'Talley.'

It was Thomas, incoherent from shouting and from a weak connection.

'I can't understand you! Slow down, Thomas; *I can't understand you!*'

'Mars killed Kevin and Dennis, and now he's burning the house! We're in the security room, me and Jennifer! We're trapped!'

The cell connection faltered again. Talley knew that the boy must be getting low on power.

'Okay, son. Okay. I'm coming to get you! How much power doy you have?'

'It's dying.'

Talley checked his watch.

'Turn it off, son. Turn it off, but turn it on again in two minutes. I'm on my way in!'

Talley felt strangely distant from himself, as if his feelings were bound in cotton. He had no choice now; he would act to save these children. It didn't matter what the Watchman wanted, or Jones, or even if it put Jane and Amanda at risk. He pulled Martin by the arm, taking her with him as he ran back along the street toward Jones, shouting instructions as they ran.

'Krupchek's torching the house! Get the fire truck up here!'

'What about Jones?'

'I'm getting him now. We're going in!'

'What about your wife?'

'Get the fire truck, and tell your people to stand by; if Jones won't move, we'll go in without him!'

Martin fell behind to use her radio. Talley ran toward Jones.

'Krupchek's torching the house. We have to go in.'

Jones glanced toward the house without expression

328

Talley could see that Jones didn't believe him.

'We're waiting to hear from the man.'

Talley grabbed Jones's arm, and felt him stiffen. Behind them, the fire engine rumbled to life and swung around the corner.

'The house is burning, goddamnit. Krupchek has those kids trapped in the security room. We can't wait.'

'That's bullshit.'

'Look at it!'

Talley shoved Jones toward the house.

Flames were visible in the den window. Police radios crackled as the perimeter guards reported the fire, and the officers in the cul-de-sac openly milled behind their cars, waiting for someone to do something. Hicks and the Sheriff's tactical team trotted toward Martin.

Jones seemed frozen in place, anchored by his expectation of the Watchman's call.

Talley jerked his arm again, pulling him around.

'I'm breaching that house, Jones. Are you coming or not?'

'We go when the man says. Not before.'

'We can't wait for the man!'

'They'll fuckin' kill your family.'

'*Those kids are trapped!*'

Jones gripped his MP5. Talley slipped his hand under his sweatshirt and touched the .45.

'What? You want to shoot it out with the chief of police here in the street? You think you'll get the disks that way?'

Jones glanced at the house again, then grimaced. None of this was in the game plan. Everything had suddenly grown beyond their control, and Jones, like Talley, was being swept forward by the storm.

Jones decided.

'All right, goddamnit, but it's just us going into that house. We'll secure the structure, then retrieve the disks.'

'If you don't get your people on the hump, the firemen will get there first.'

They made their assault plan as they ran to the house.

*

MARS

The flames built slowly, growing up the doors and the walls like flowers on a trellis. Mars followed the flames as they crept along the trail of gas he had made through the house. He thought that the fire would spread with a whoosh, but it moved with surprising lethargy. The air clouded with smoke that smelled of tar.

Mars wanted music.

He went to the den, where he remembered a nice Denon sound system. He tuned to a local hip-hop station, and cranked the speakers to distortion. He helped himself to a bottle of scotch, then returned to the bedroom.

The bed was a raging inferno. Fire covered the doors and walls, and a layer of smoke roiled at the ceiling. The heat made him squint. A layer of smoke roiled at the ceiling. Mars took off his shirt and drank. He checked the Chinaman's gun, saw that there were still plenty of bullets, then took out his knife.

Mars crouched at the far side of the room, far from the flames and below the smoke. He watched the door. He hoped that if the security room grew hot enough, and the children grew frightened enough, the kids would open the door to escape.

Then he would have his way.

TALLEY

Two men would breach the front door, two the French doors; Talley and Jones would breach through a window to enter a guest bedroom located next to the master. Once inside, Jones would radio the sixth man, who would shatter the sliding doors in the master bedroom to distract Krupchek from the bedroom door, which would be the point of egress for the assault. All of them would carry fire extinguishers to suppress the flames.

Talley didn't have time to get his own vest from his car. He borrowed a vest from one of the CHiPs, strapping it over his sweatshirt, then slung a fire extinguisher over his shoulder. The firemen ran out their hoses, remaining under cover until word would come down that the hostiles had been neutralized.

When they agreed on the assault plan, Talley phoned Thomas. The connection was even weaker than before, and this time Talley told him to keep the phone on. Powering up the system probably cost more power than it saved. If Jones thought anything of Talley and the boy talking, he did not comment.

Martin edged close to Talley as Jones deployed his men.

'What do you want me to do?'

'I don't know.'

'You just going to let them leave with the disks?'

'I don't know what I'm going to do, Martin. I don't know. I just gotta get those kids.'

Talley finished strapping on the vest and adjusted his radio. Everything moved quickly and efficiently, without wasted moves or words. When he was set, he looked over at Jones.

'You ready?'

Jones seated his helmet, then shook himself a last time to settle his equipment.

'Remember, Talley.'

'Let's just do this damned thing.'

Jones set off for the house. Talley let him get a step ahead, then turned back to Martin.

'If I don't get out, don't let him leave. Bring in the detectives and try to save my family.'

'Just make it your business to get out.'

She turned away before he could answer and shouted at her SWAT team to remain in place.

Talley caught up to Jones at the corner of the house outside the guest bedroom window. They heard music, loud and throbbing within the burning house. Talley was thankful for it, because the noise of the music and the fire would cover their entrance. They pulled away the screen, then Jones used a crowbar to wedge open the window. He pushed aside the shade, then gave Talley a thumbs-up, saying the room was clear. They lifted the fire extinguishers into the room, then they waited. They would not enter the house until the others were in position. Talley took the phone from his pocket and checked in with Thomas.

'Thomas?'

'I'm here, Chief.'

The boy's voice broke up, salty with static.

'We're almost there. Three minutes, maybe four. As soon as we get Krupchek, the firemen will come in.'

'It's getting hot.'

'I know. Is Krupchek still in the bedroom?'

Talley wanted to keep the boy talking. If he was talking, he wouldn't have time to think about how scared he was. Neither would Talley.

'He's sitting on the floor by the – '

The cell line went dead.

'Thomas? *Thomas?*'

Nothing.

The boy's phone had finally failed.

Jones glanced over his shoulder at Talley, and twirled his finger. They were spooling up, getting ready to launch.

'Let's go, goddamnit.'

Jones jabbed his finger at the window.

'Go!'

Jones went first, Talley giving him a boost up, then scrambling inside after him. The room was lit only by the low wall of flame that barred the door to the hall. The master bedroom door was only ten feet away. Jones shot the bolt on his MP5; Talley popped the slide on his pistol. They turned on their flashlights, then met each other's eyes. Talley nodded. Jones keyed his mike.

'Now.'

332

Talley heard the sliding glass doors in the master bedroom shatter at the same time that the front door blew inward off its hinges.

Two fast shots came from the master bedroom. Talley and Jones charged down the hall as a third shot cracked in the bedroom, then they were through the door.

The bedroom was an inferno. The man who had shattered the glass doors was down, writhing in agony. Talley glimpsed a flash of movement from his right and saw Krupchek heave up from behind a Morris chair, chest bare and glistening, an angry, strictured smile on his face. Krupchek screamed, a high-pitched screech, as he swung his pistol, pumping out shots even as Talley and Jones fired. Krupchek stumbled backwards, arms windmilling as he fell into the flames, thrashing and still screaming. Jones fired two short bursts into him and he was still.

They unstrapped their fire extinguishers as Jones's other men cleared through the door, covering the room with their weapons.

Talley shouted, 'We're clear!'

Jones pointed at the first two, then the fallen man.

'You and you, him, out to the van.'

Talley blasted gouts of $CO_2$ at the burning security door, and shouted for Jones to help.

'Jones! The kids are in here.'

Jones shoved the next man toward the door.

'The office is at the front of the house. Make sure the hall is clear.'

'Help me get these kids!'

Jones and the last man joined Talley at the wall. Their $CO_2$ extinguishers hissed like dragons. The red walls turned black as the flames engulfing them died. Talley banged at the door with his fire extinguisher.

'Thomas! It's me!'

The fire on the walls licked to life again, eating away the paint.

'Thomas!'

Talley fogged the door as it opened. The boy and his sister stood back, wary of the heat. Jones grabbed Talley's arm.

'They're yours, Talley. We're getting the disks.'

Talley let them go. He blasted the walls around the door again to beat back the flames, then stepped through and took the boy's hand.

'We're going to move fast. Stay behind me.'

Jennifer crowded next to him, nervously peering around him into the room.

'Is he dead?'

Talley ached when he saw her. Jennifer and Amanda were close to the same age. They wore their hair in the same cut. He wondered where Amanda was now. He wondered if she was looking for her own monster.

'He's dead, Jennifer. Come on. You guys did great.'

Talley hurried them along the hall, using the fire extinguisher whenever the flames crowded too close. He paused only long enough to switch his radio to the Bristo frequency, and called Mikkelson.

'Mikki!'

'Go, Chief!'

'The kids are coming out the front. Take care of them.'

When they reached the entry, Talley could see into the office. Jones and his men were searching Smith's desk. Talley pulled Thomas aside out of their view, knowing that these were his last few moments to save his own family. The Watchman would know that they had entered the house. He would be calling Jones for a report, and he would be expecting the disks.

Talley bent close to the boy.

'Are the disks still up in your room?'

'Yeah. With my computer.'

Talley pointed at Mikkelson waiting in the cul-de-sac and pushed the kids through the door.

'Go to her. Go!'

Talley waited to see that both kids ran toward the cars

then he slipped up the stairs. The air on the second floor was dense with smoke so thick that it choked the beam from his flashlight to a dull glow. He couldn't see more than a few feet. He worked his way along the wall and found Rooney lying outside the first door. Red bubbles clustered on Rooney's chest and mouth like glass mushrooms. Talley couldn't tell if he was dead or alive, and didn't take the time to check. He kicked Rooney's pistol away, then looked in the first room long enough to realize that it belonged to Jennifer. He moved down the hall. The second room belonged to the boy. Talley found his computer on the floor at the far side of the bed. One disk sat on the floor, the other in a disk drive beside the keyboard. Talley held the light close to read their labels, his heart pounding, and saw that he had them – disk one and disk two; the only leverage he had that could save his family!

'Talley!'

Talley jerked at the voice, then saw that Martin was standing in the door. Her helmet was cinched tight and her pistol was at her side.

'Did you find them?'

He joined her. The smoke was heavier now. Talley saw flames at the end of the hall.

'Where's Jones?'

'They're tearing up the office. They haven't found the disks.'

'The boy had them in his room.'

Talley showed her the disks. He wanted to find a way out without seeing Jones and started for the stairs. Martin grabbed his arm. She brought up her gun.

'Give them to me.'

He was startled by her tone. He glanced at the gun, then saw that Martin was watching him with anxious eyes.

'What are you talking about?'

'Give me the disks.'

He glanced at the gun again, and knew with certainty that Benza owned her.

Talley shook his head.

'When did they get to you?'

She thumbed off the safety lever.

'Give me the disks, Talley. You'll get your family.'

He knew that he wouldn't. He knew that once Benza was safe, anyone who knew anything about Smith's relationship to Sonny Benza would die.

Talley stepped back, holding the disks at his side. Once she had the disks she would kill him. It would be easier that way.

'Where's Jones?'

'Still downstairs. He doesn't even know.'

'What are you going to do, Martin? Tell them I was shot in the confusion? You going to blame Krupchek and Rooney?'

'If I have to.'

'How much are they paying you?'

'More than you'll ever know.'

She raised the gun higher.

'Now give me the disks.'

The flames crept up the stairwell at the end of the hall. Talley saw their twisting red glow through the smoke, and something moving in the glow.

'Give me the disks, Talley. It's the only way to get out of this alive.'

A shadow lifted itself from the floor.

'Rooney's alive.'

Her eyes flicked once to the side, then came back to him. She didn't believe him.

'*Give me the disks!*'

Dennis Rooney lurched into the light, eyes glassy and dripping with blood. He had found his gun.

'*Martin!*'

She turned, but not in time. Rooney fired before she could swing her gun to him. Something hard slapped

336

Talley in the chest. The next bullet caught Martin in the thigh, and the third in the cheek beneath her right eye.

Martin spun slowly into the smoke as Talley drew his weapon and fired.

# CHAPTER 25

Saturday, 2:41 A.M.

TALLEY

The heavy bullet from Talley's combat pistol bounced Dennis Rooney off the wall, leaving a gory smear of blood. Talley planted a knee in Rooney's chest and knocked away his gun, but this time Rooney was dead. Talley listened for the sound of Jones's team coming up the stairs, but he couldn't hear anything over the crackling, snapping sound of the fire.

He radioed Mikkelson.

'You got the kids?'

'We heard shots!'

'*Do you have the kids?*'

'Yes, sir. They're safe.'

'The FBI agents took out a wounded man. Three of them went to their van.'

'Ah, roger. We saw that.'

Talley's mind raced. He had taken the offensive, and now he had to finish the assault. Time was his enemy. He had to take the fight to the Watchman and press his advantage.

'Get Jorgenson and Cooper. If Larry's back, get him, too. Arrest them. Strip their radios and cell phones, cuff them, and don't let them communicate with anyone.'

'Ah, arrest the FBI?'

'They're not FBI. Arrest them, Mikki. They are armed and dangerous, so you watch your ass. Have someone bring them to the jail, but do not – I repeat, do *not* – le them talk to anyone: no phone calls, no press, no lawyers, nothing. Don't tell anyone about this. Do you understand?'

'Ah, sure, Chief.'

'Stand by.'

Everything now depended on speed. The Watchman might learn that his people were being arrested, but his information would be spotty and incomplete; he wouldn't know what had happened or why, so he wouldn't act against Jane and Amanda until he knew the details. Talley was counting on that. He was betting his family on it. If Talley had any hope of saving his family, he had to do it before the Watchman knew what he was doing.

Talley pushed the disks under his vest and ran to the stairwell. The fire in the entry had jumped to the stairs and was climbing the walls. The smoke was a twisting orange haze. Talley crept down the stairs with his eyes on the office, then crossed to the door just as one of Jones's men stepped out. Talley aimed at his face, touching his own lips to motion the man quiet, then stripped his pistol and MP5. Talley handcuffed him and pushed him into the office.

Jones was frantically searching the floor around the desk, his flashlight beam dim in the haze; the drawers had been pulled, their contents scattered. The second man was stripping books from the shelves. They both looked up when Talley pushed the first man to the floor.

Talley trained his gun on them. He no longer felt the fire's heat; he was so amped on adrenaline and fear that he was totally focused on the two men in front of him.

'Hands on your heads, lace your fingers, turn around with your backs to me.'

Jones said, 'What the fuck are you doing?'

The second man swung his MP5, but Talley squared him with a round, the heavy .45 punching through his vest. Talley had fired ten thousand practice rounds a year every year on the LAPD's combat training range when he was with SWAT. He didn't have to think about it.

Talley brought his gun back to Jones.

'Lace your fingers. *Now!*'

Jones raised his hands, then slowly turned. He laced his fingers over the top of his head.

'You're fucking up, Talley. They've got your family.'

Talley stripped the second man of his weapons, never taking his gun from Jones. He tossed the weapons to the side, checked the pulse in the man's neck, then went to Jones. He took his pistol and MP5, tossed them with the others, then ripped the power cord from Smith's computer. He forced Jones onto his belly, then pulled his hands behind his back. He pressed the gun to Jones's neck.

'Move, I'll fucking kill you.'

Talley planted his knee in the small of Jones's back, then tied his wrists. He wanted to get Jones out of the house, but he didn't want to do it on television. He keyed his radio.

'Mikki?'

'Jesus, Chief, are you all right? We heard more shots.'

'Have the firemen move in, then roll your car to the back of the house on Flanders Road. Meet me there.'

Talley knew that the television cameras would be trained on the firefighters. He wanted everyone's attention on the front of the house, not the rear. He didn't want the Watchman seeing this on television.

'What's going on?'

'*Do it!*'

Talley pushed Jones and the surviving man to the rear of the house. The fire was consuming the house; wallpaper was peeling off the walls and chunks of drywall fell from the hall ceiling. When they reached the French doors, Talley changed his radio to the Sheriff's command frequency and told the officers on the back wall to kill their lights. The backyard plunged into darkness. Talley pushed the two men outside and hustled them straight to the wall. When the Sheriff's sergeant-supervisor saw that Talley had two FBI agents bound, he said, 'What the fuck's going on?'

'Help me get these guys over.'

Mikkelson and Dreyer were climbing out of their car by the time Talley jumped to the ground.

The SWAT officers stared at Jones and the other man. Here they were, the backs of their vests blazoned with a huge white FBI, cuffed and dragged over the wall. The sergeant again asked Talley what was happening, but Talley ignored him.

'Martin's inside. The second floor. She's been shot.'

Talley got the response he wanted. The SWAT cops poured over the wall and rushed toward the house.

Talley shoved his prisoners toward Mikkelson's car.

Jones said, 'You're finished, Talley.'

'I'm not the guy with his hands tied.'

'You know what he's going to do, don't you? You understand that?'

'I've got the disks, you motherfucker. We'll see how much your boss wants them now.'

When Mikkelson saw the two FBI agents, she pooched out her lips in confusion.

'Jesus. Did I miss something here?'

'These people aren't FBI.'

Talley pushed the first man into the backseat of their car, then shoved Jones against the fender.

'Where are they?'

'I don't know. I'm not part of that.'

'Then where is *he?*'

'I don't know.'

'What's his name?'

'It doesn't work like that, Talley. He's a voice on the phone.'

Talley searched Jones's pockets as he spoke, and found Jones's cell phone. He pressed star 69, but nothing happened.

341

'Shit!'

He pushed the cell phone in Jones's face.

'What's his number?'

'I don't know any more than you.'

Talley kneed him in the stomach.

Dreyer said, 'Holy shit.'

Talley slammed Jones into the car.

'You fucking well know his number!'

'I want to talk to an attorney.'

Talley kneed him again, doubling Jones over. Mikkelson and Dreyer squirmed uneasily.

'Ah, Chief . . .'

'These bastards have my family.'

Talley cocked the .45 and pressed it into Jones's cheek.

'We're talking about my wife and daughter, you sonofabitch. You think I won't kill you?'

Talley wasn't on Flanders Road anymore; he had stepped into the Zone. It was a place of white noise where emotions reigned and reason was meager. Anger and rage were nonstop tickets; panic was an express. He had been all day coming to this, and here he was: The SWAT guys used to talk about it. You went to the Zone, you lost your edge. You'd lose your career; you'd get yourself killed, or, worse, somebody else.

Talley bent Jones backwards across the trunk of the car. He had to reach the Watchman, and this man knew how. He didn't have time to wait for the Watchman to call. He needed the Watchman off guard. Time was his enemy.

'He calls me. Just like with you.'

Talley's head throbbed. He told himself to shoot the sonofabitch, put one in his shoulder joint and make him scream. Mikkelson's voice came from far away.

'Chief?'

The white noise cleared and Talley stepped back from the Zone. He lowered his gun. He wasn't like them.

Jones glanced away. Talley thought he seemed embarrassed.

'I don't call him. He calls me, just like with you. That's how they stay safe. Just hang on to the phone. He'll call.'

Talley stared at Jones's phone, then dropped it to the street and crushed it. He had the Nokia, but if it rang, he would not answer it. If the Watchman placed the call, the Watchman would expect him to answer. Talley didn't want to do what the Watchman expected.

'Put him in a cell with the others.'

Everything seemed like it was ending even before it began. He couldn't stop now. Once you breached the structure, you pressed on until the end. If you stopped, you died.

Smith would know. They trusted Smith with their closest secrets. It had all come back to Smith again.

'Where are the kids?'

'Cooper has them with the paramedics. They're okay. We finally got the mother, Chief. She's flying back from Florida.'

'Tell Cooper to meet me at the hospital. Tell him to bring the children.'

Talley wiped the smoke from his eyes as he looked back at the house. The fire was eating its way through the roof. Tongues of flame lapped beneath the eaves even as silver rainbows of water arced over the house. Talley could smell the fire on his skin and in his clothes. He smelled like a funeral pyre.

### KEN SEYMORE

Seymore was trading Adderall for cold dim sum with a news crew from Los Angeles when a string of dull pops snapped from the direction of the house. The Los Angeles remote producer, a skinny kid with a goatee and no life experience, stopped his discourse on news selection as a political vehicle.

'What was that?'

Ken Seymore recognized the sound right away: gunfire.

Seymore knew that Howell hadn't launched the breach, because Howell would have told him. He trotted to the nearest news van to find out what was happening. The tech there monitored a police scanner tuned to the Sheriff's tactical frequency.

'You guys get anything on that?'

The tech waved him silent. He listened to the scanner with a bug in his ear, because their news director didn't want anyone else to hear.

'They called up the fire company. The goddamned house is on fire.'

'What was the shooting?'

'That was gunfire?'

'Hell, yes.'

The tech waved Seymore quiet again and tuned his receiver, working through the frequencies.

'The SWAT team went in. Shit, they got casualties. It sounds like they got the kids. Yeah, the kids are coming out.'

The technician pulled the plug from his ear and shouted for his producer.

A heavy column of smoke rose into the light from the helicopters, and then another string of pops echoed over the neighborhood.

Seymore took out his phone.


GLEN HOWELL


The local stations resumed live coverage because of the fire. Flames lapped from the windows on the left side of the house, but the fire at the rear, back by the pool, was going pretty good. Fire crews hosed the roof and shadows ran along the perimeter, but the aerial shot was so murky that Howell couldn't tell who was who or what was happening, just that everything was going to hell.

'You sure Jones's people got hit?'

'They said it was FBI, so it hadda be Jones's guys. We're getting this shit off the scanner.'

'They get the disks?'

'I don't know. It's happening right now; no one's talking to us.'

'Why the fuck did they go in?'

'I thought you gave'm the green light.'

'It wasn't me.'

'Hang on a sec; there's more traffic on the scanner. Okay, they're saying two FBI agents came out and both kids. The kids are out.'

Howell tried to stay calm.

'Who's in the fuckin' house?'

'I don't know.'

'Is Jones still in the goddamned house?'

'I don't know.'

'Where's Talley?'

'I don't know.'

'You're paid to know, goddamnit. That's why you're there.'

Howell broke the connection, then punched in Jones's number. The phone rang once, then a computer voice came on telling him that the user had left the service area or turned off his phone. Howell called Martin. He let her phone ring fifteen times, and finally hung up.

'Fuck!'

He dialed Talley's number and listened to the Nokia ring. He let it ring twenty times, and then he snapped his phone shut so hard he thought he might have broken it.

TALLEY

Talley rolled code three all the way to the hospital. He beat Cooper, arriving a few minutes after three A.M. The parking lot was almost deserted; the remaining press camped by the emergency room entrance. Talley parked at the side of the hospital to avoid them, but got out of the car because sitting was difficult. He leaned against the door with his arms crossed, watching the street, then realized he was still wearing the bullet-resistant vest and the radio. He took them off and tossed them into the backseat. He found the Nokia, and dropped it onto the front seat.

The Nokia rang.

Talley hesitated in the door of the car, thinking the Watchman had finally heard about the house. He stared at the ringing phone as if he was hiding from it, as if any movement might draw the Watchman's eye and the Watchman would somehow know that Talley was there. Talley should have turned the goddamned thing off. He wanted the Watchman to wonder.

Talley felt his chest tighten, and realized that he had stopped breathing. The phone stopped ringing as Cooper turned into the parking lot. Talley took a breath, then raised his hand, but Cooper was already turning toward him.

Talley watched carefully as Thomas and Jennifer got out of Cooper's car. They looked pale and tired, and their eyes were anxious with apprehension. Talley knew that they might seem fine now in the initial elation of being released, but later there could be nightmares, flashbacks, and other symptoms of post-traumatic stress disorder. Jennifer reminded him of Amanda all over again. Talley felt himself lifted by such a swell of feeling that he wanted to both cry and hug them, but he only let himself smile.

Jennifer said, 'Are we going to see our father?'

'That's right. Did Officer Cooper tell you about your mother? We spoke with her in Florida. She's flying back now.'

They beamed. Jennifer actually said, 'Yay.'

Talley put out his hand.

346

'We didn't really meet before. My name is Jeff Talley.'

'I'm Jennifer Smith. Thank you for what you did.'

She shook his hand firmly, her smile blinding. Thomas shook his hand as if it were serious business. They stood so close together that their arms touched, and both children stood very close to him. He knew that this was normal. He was the man who had saved them.

'It's good to finally meet you, Thomas. You were a big help. You were very brave. You both were.'

'Thank you, Chief. You're really dirty.'

Jennifer rolled her eyes, and Cooper laughed.

Talley glanced at his hands. They were streaked with soot and sweat, as was his face.

'I guess I am. I haven't had time to clean up.'

Jennifer said, 'He can be so rude. You should look at yourself, Thomas. You've got ash on your nose.'

Thomas rubbed at his nose, but his eyes never left Talley.

'Is our daddy okay?'

'He's doing better. Let's go see him.'

Talley brought them through the side entrance. He held their hands, letting go only to badge an orderly who led them through the hospital to the emergency room. Everyone they passed stared at them. Talley knew that it was only a matter of time before word spread to the press that the chief of police had brought the hostage children to their father. When the press knew, the Watchman would know.

Talley refused to bring the children through the ER admitting area. The orderly led them past the hospital laboratory along a hall that the ER personnel used to bring samples to the lab. Klaus and Reese were no longer present, but a nurse that Talley recognized from before stopped them.

'You're the Chief, aren't you? May I help you?'

'I'm bringing the Smith children to see their father.'

'I'd better get Dr. Reese.'

'Fine, you go get her. We'll be in the room.'

Talley found Smith's room without waiting. He thought that Smith would be sleeping, but Smith was staring at the ceiling, his eyes blinking. He was still wired to the monitors.

Jennifer said, 'Daddy?'

Smith lifted his head enough to see, and then his face registered surprise and elation.

The kids ran to him, both to the side of the bed without wires, and hugged their father. Talley waited in the door, giving them a moment, then entered and stood at the end of the bed. Jennifer cried, her face buried in her father's chest. The little boy wiped at his eyes and asked if it hurt.

Talley watched. Smith wrapped his arm around Jennifer and held Thomas's arm. He looked up past them, met Talley's eyes, then hugged his children tighter.

'Thank God you're all right. You're all right, aren't you? You're okay?'

'Mommy's coming home.'

Talley stepped up behind Jennifer.

'We reached your wife. She's in the air now.'

Smith met Talley's eyes again, then looked away.

Talley said, 'Your family is safe.'

Smith nodded, still not looking at him.

'What happened to the three men?'

'They're dead.'

Thomas pulled at his father's arm.

'Daddy, our *house* is on fire. We almost *burned*.'

Thomas jerked his father's arm again, then coughed a great shuddering sob and buried his face in his father's stomach. It was all coming out now, all of Thomas's tension and fear. Smith stroked his son's hair.

'It's okay, partner. It's okay. You're safe. That's all that's important.'

Talley waited until the boy had calmed, then squeezed Jennifer's shoulder.

'Could you guys wait in the hall for a second? I need to talk to your dad.'

Smith glanced up, then nodded to send his children to the hall. Jennifer took Thomas's hand and led him outside. Smith took a deep breath, let it out, then looked up.

'Thank you.'

Talley took out the two disks.

Smith stared at them, then looked away again.

'Did you tell my kids?'

'No. They'll have questions. Thomas helped me get them. He opened them on his computer.'

'It wouldn't mean anything to him.'

'He'll wonder. He's going to ask sooner or later.'

Smith sighed again.

'Shit.'

'Those are good kids you got there. That little boy, Thomas, he's something else.'

Smith closed his eyes.

Talley watched Smith, wondering if there was anything he could say to get this man to help him. He had negotiated with hundreds of subjects, and that was the game: Figure out what they needed to hear and say it; find their buttons and push them. All of that seemed beyond Talley now. He didn't know what to say. He glanced over at Thomas and Jennifer standing in the hall, and felt a pain so deep and pure that he thought it might break him. If he could just get Jane and Amanda back, he would never let them go.

He patted Smith's arm.

'I don't know where you come from or what you've done in your life, but you'd better do right by those kids. You've got your family now, Smith. They're safe. Help me get mine.'

Smith blinked hard at the ceiling. He shook his head, then closed his eyes tight. He took another deep breath, then looked past Talley to his own children.

'Shit.'

'Yeah. Shit.'

Smith looked at him. Smith's eyes were wet.

'If you've got the disks, you've got everything. You can put them all away.'

'Who has my family?'

'That would be Glen Howell. He was coming to the house today. He's Benza's man on the scene.'

Talley touched his wrist.

'Gold Rolex here? Dark tan?'

Smith nodded.

Talley was getting excited. He had something now. He was close by the door and ready to breach.

'Okay, Smith. Okay. Glen Howell. He's been calling me, but now I need to call him. How do I reach him?'

Smith gave him Howell's phone number.

# CHAPTER 26

Saturday, 3:09 A.M.

TALLEY

alley doubled the guards on Smith and his children, then
urried back to his car. He closed his eyes and tried to
nd focus. He was a crisis negotiator; Howell was a
bject; Amanda and Jane were hostages. He had done
is before; he could do it again. It was just him and the
one.

*I'm going to kill this dog!*

The overhead lights made the world purple. Talley
oked up at the sky, but could see only a few stars past
e bright lights. A few stars were enough; Jane and
manda were under these same stars. So was Howell.

When his breathing was even and his shoulders relaxed,
alley got into the car. His task was to sound confident
d controlled. His task was to assume control.

Talley punched Howell's number into the Nokia. His
dy began to shake with tension, but he fought it. He
osed his eyes again. He breathed.

The Watchman answered on the second ring, sounding
rupt and irritated.

'What?'

Talley made his voice soft.

'Guess who.'

Howell recognized his voice. Talley heard it in the
uality of the silence even before Howell answered.

'How'd you get this number?'

'Here are two words for you: Glen Howell.'

'Fuck yourself.'

'I think Sonny Benza is going to fuck *you*. I have h financial records. I have your SWAT team. I have Captai Martin. I have you. And I have Walter Smith.'

Howell's voice rose.

'I have your fucking family. Don't forget that.'

Talley kept his voice even. He knew that if he remaine calm, Howell would grow more frightened. Howell woul suspect that Talley was up to something, and, by suspec ing it, he would believe that it was true. Howell's onl way out now was through Talley. Talley had to make hii see this.

'You know where you screwed up? If you had sat tigh and let this thing play out, if you hadn't brought me int it or sent in your fucking animals, I would never hav known. The disks would have slipped through the crack and Benza would be safe. Now you have to deal with me

'You're drowning in deep water, Talley. You're jus some fuckin' cop who doesn't have a clue. You're killin your family. You're committing suicide.'

'I'll give you five minutes. Call Benza. Ask him if h wants to spend the rest of his life in prison.'

'I'll ask him how many times he wants me to fuck you daughter.'

'Ask him if I can keep the money.'

All Talley heard was the hiss of the cell connection.

'I have something else that belongs to you. I foun some money in the house. Looks like almost a millio dollars.'

Talley had learned from a hundred negotiations that al liars think everyone lies, all thieves think everyon steals, crooked people think everyone is crooked. Th strain in the silence was the sound of Howell trying t read Talley just as Talley was reading Howell. He woul be scared and suspicious, but he would also want t believe. His belief was everything.

Howell answered slowly.

'What do you want, Talley?'

'How much money did I find?'

'One-point-two million.'

'I'll sell you a pass. My wife and daughter, and the money, for the disks. If you hurt them, the disks go straight to the FBI and I'll keep the money anyway.'

Talley knew that Howell would never consider a straight-up trade, his family for the disks, because there was no reason for Talley to keep his word. But the money changed things. Howell would understand greed. He would see himself in Talley and believe that a cop might think he could get away with that.

Talley didn't wait for Howell to answer.

'I'll tell you how this is going to work. I'll bring the disks to the north entrance of the mall by the freeway. You bring my family. If they're okay, we'll trade. If I don't make it home tonight, my officers will still have Smith and your phony FBI SWAT team.'

'You make it home, you'll cut them loose?'

'I'll cut them loose.'

'Okay, Talley, I think we can do this.'

'I thought we might.'

'But not at the mall. We'll do this where I want to do this.'

'As long as it's not in the middle of nowhere.'

'The Comfort Inn west of Bristo.'

'I know it.'

'Be there in ten minutes. Someone will be waiting in the parking lot. One minute late, there won't be anyone there to find.'

Talley ended the call. He placed the Nokia carefully on the seat, then closed his eyes. The Comfort Inn was less than a mile away. He got out of the car, stripped off his sweatshirt, then strapped on the vest. He pulled the sweatshirt over it. He checked his pistol; one in the chamber, safety on. He left his radio on, but turned the speaker volume down to zero. He got back into the car.

He still had much to do.

### GLEN HOWELL

Howell was shaking when he put down the phone. Talley had caught him off guard and jammed him into making a deal that might be a setup, but he didn't see what other choice he'd had. His job was to recover the disks.

Howell picked up the house phone. Duane Manelli was sitting in a room two doors down with LJ Ruiz.

'I need you and LJ outside. Talley's coming here.'

'What the fuck!'

'I don't know if he's coming alone. Get your ass outside and set up to watch the area.'

'What happened to Jones?'

'Jones is down.'

Howell hung up. He checked his watch. He didn't want to make his next call, but he didn't have a choice about that, either. Making the next call scared him more than waiting for Talley.

He dialed Sonny Benza.

### PALM SPRINGS

'Sonny? Sonny, wake up.'

Benza opened his eyes, and saw Phil Tuzee. Charles Salvetti was pacing by the desk, looking upset. Benza was stretched out on the couch, the three of them still in his office at four in the morning. Benza's back ached like a sonofabitch. Another fuckin' trip to the chiropractor.

'What?'

'Glen Howell's on the phone. We got a friggin' mess here. Look.'

Benza sat up and squinted at the television. Smith's house was in flames.

'Jesus Christ. What happened?'

'It's a fuckin' bloodbath. Howell's team went in, and everything went to hell. Now they're pulling bodies out of the place.'

'Did we get the disks?'

Benza knew the answer from Tuzee's expression. Acid flooded his stomach.

'No, skipper. Talley has the disks.'

Salvetti called from the desk.

'C'mon. Howell's on the speaker. He says we don't have much time.'

Benza went to the phone, trying to control his anger.

'What the fuck are you doing down there?'

Howell cleared his throat, leaving Benza to conclude that the man was rattled. Benza didn't like that. Glen Howell wasn't a man to rattle.

'It isn't working out the way we planned.'

'I guess it fuckin' well isn't.'

Howell explained the situation. Talley not only had the disks; he had Smith, Jones, and Jones's team. Benza saw himself killing Glen Howell. He saw himself driving Howell to the desert and chopping him into sausage with a machete.

'Sonny?'

Benza's rage cleared, and he saw Salvetti and Tuzee watching him. Howell was still talking. Sonny Benza was more frightened now than he had ever been in his life. He interrupted.

'Glen? Listen to me, Glen.'

He spoke softly, trying to keep his voice from shaking. Salvetti and Tuzee watched him.

'I want to tell you something here, Glen, before you go any further. I trusted you to handle this, and you've ucked it up. You're letting me down here, Glen.'

'Sonny, Talley has the disks, but we can still get this settled.'

Howell's voice shook.

'It's good you've got a plan for that.'

'He wants the money that Smith was holding for us, the one-point-two. He gets his family and the money, he says he'll give us the disks and cut loose our guys.'

Salvetti said, 'Waitaminute. Are you saying that this asshole wants to be paid off? He's *extorting* us?'

'One-point-two is a lot of money.'

Tuzee shook his head, looking at Benza but speaking to Howell.

'It's a setup. He's baiting you to get the wife.'

'What other choice do we have?'

Benza answered, softly again, without waiting for Tuzee's or Salvetti's opinion.

'You don't have any other choice.'

Howell didn't answer for several seconds.

'I understand.'

'Hang on.'

Benza muted the phone. He stretched his back, trying to lessen the ache, but it only hurt worse. He tried to figure out which way to jump; either Talley was really trying to scam the cash or he wasn't. If Talley was setting up Howell, the next few hours would be a shit storm. Federal agents might already be pouring over the disks and petitioning for warrants. Benza knew that he should warn New York, but the thought of it made his bowels clench.

'Phil, call the airport and have the jet prepped. Just in case.'

Tuzee went to the other phone.

Benza took the speakerphone off mute. He didn't want to accept defeat yet; there might still be a way out.

'Okay, Glen, listen: I don't care about the money. If I gotta lose the cash to buy some time, so be it.'

'That's what I figured.'

'If Talley is setting you up, we're fucked anyway.'

'I'll give you fair warning.'

'Fuck you and your fair warning. Get the disks, then get rid of him. If you don't get the disks, you're gonna have a problem, Glen. You understand that?'

'Our guys will still be in custody. He's not going to cut them free until after he has his family.'

Benza glanced at Tuzee again. He didn't like the idea of killing his own employees, but he had done it before. He had to get rid of Smith, Talley, Jones and his crew, and anyone else who was vulnerable after tonight. That was the only way he would be safe.

'After Talley is dead, we'll take care of Smith and Jones and his people. That's the best way to do this. Everyone has to die.'

'I understand.'

Benza pressed the button to end the call, then went back to the couch.

Salvetti came over and sat next to him.

'This thing is goin' south, Sonny. We gotta think about that. We should warn New York. We let'm know what's comin', old man Castellano might cut us some slack.'

Benza considered that, then shook his head.

'Fuck New York. I'm not that anxious to die.'

'You sure about that, Sonny? We still got a few minutes here.'

'We lose those disks, the last thing I want is a conversation with that old man. Even prison looks good by comparison.'

Salvetti frowned.

'That old man has long arms. He'll reach us even in prison.'

Benza looked at him.

'Jesus, Sally, always the cheery word.'

Tuzee crossed his arms, and shrugged.

'What the fuck, we get those disks, we'll beat the Feds and Castellano will never know this happened. Things could still work out.'

Benza decided to pack. In case things didn't.

# CHAPTER 27

## Santa Clarita, California
Saturday, 3:37 A.M.

TALLEY

Talley drove without lights, swerving far onto the shoulder whenever he passed an oncoming vehicle. He pulled off the road a hundred yards before the motel and left his car in the weeds, thankful for the black sweatshirt he had pulled on earlier. He tied a roll of duct tape to a belt loop, then shoved a handful of plastic restraints into his pocket. He rubbed dirt on his face and hands to kill their shine, then drew his pistol and trotted toward the motel. The moon was up, bright like a blue pearl, giving him light.

Talley guessed that Howell would post observers to warn him if the police were approaching. He worked his way to the edge of the motel property and froze beside a spiky-leafed manzanita bush, searching the shadows at the edge of the light for some bit of movement or blackness that did not fit. Talley had approached a thousand armed houses when he was on SWAT; this time was no different. The motel was a long two-story barn surrounded by a parking lot. A smattering of cars were sleeping outside the ground-floor rooms. Two huge tractor-trailer trucks sat at the rear; a third was parked near the street. Talley worked his way around the perimeter of the grounds, moving outside the field of light, pausing every two paces to look and listen.

He spotted one observer on the east side parking lot, sitting between the wheels of an eighteen-wheeler that had been docked for the night. A few minutes later, he found the second man hunkered beneath a pepper tree across the street on the west side. Talley looked carefully for others, but only two men were posted.

### DUANE MANELLI

Manelli lay belly-down in the hard dirt at the base of a pepper tree, watching LJ Ruiz move between the wheels of the eighteen-wheeler. They were hooked up by cell phone. If either saw an oncoming vehicle or anything suspicious, they could alert the other, and then Glen Howell. Manelli didn't like it that he could see movement. This meant that LJ was bored, and bored men made mistakes.

He whispered into his phone.

'LJ, you in position?'

'Yeah, I'm here.'

'Settle in and stop moving around.'

'Fuck yourself. I'm not moving.'

Manelli didn't respond. LJ had stopped moving, so Manelli let it go. Duane Manelli had spent enough time on night recon training exercises when he was in the army to respect radio silence.

Manelli settled into the dirt.

Ruiz said something, but Manelli didn't understand.

'Say again.'

Ruiz didn't answer.

'I didn't hear you, LJ. What'd you say?'

Nothing came back.

'LJ?'

Manelli heard the rocks crunch behind him, then his head exploded with rainbow light.

Talley bound Manelli's wrists behind the man's back with the plastic restraints, pulling the leads tight. He secured Manelli's ankles the same way, then rolled the man over.

Talley slapped Manelli's face.

'Wake up.'

Talley slapped harder.

'Wake up, goddamnit. You're under arrest.'

Manelli's eyes fluttered. Talley waited until the eyes focused, then pressed the gun into Manelli's neck.

'You know who I am?'

'Talley.'

'Which room are they in?'

'They're not. Howell sent them away.'

Talley cursed under his breath. He didn't expect that Howell would have kept them with him, but he had hoped.

'All right. Where are they?'

'I don't know. Clewes took them.'

Talley had not heard that name before, Clewes, but it didn't matter. He had not heard of any of these people.

'Where did Clewes take them?'

'I don't know. In the car. Howell is gonna call him. I don't know what they're gonna do. That was between Clewes and Howell.'

Talley glanced at the motel, fighting down his panic. The passing seconds loaded onto his back like bags of sand. He was wasting time, and he needed a plan. He told himself to think. He chanted the SWAT mantra: Panic kills. If Jane and Amanda were being held somewhere else, he would have to force Howell to bring them back.

He looked back at Manelli.

'How many people does Howell have?'

'Five here at the motel, plus Clewes.'

'You and the asshole at the truck, leaves three inside?'

'That's right, plus Clewes. He has more people, but

lon't know where they are. They could show up here anytime.'

Talley thought it through. Three in the room. Three against one, with more on the way. None of it mattered. He had no other choice.

'Which room?'

Manelli hesitated.

Talley pushed the .45 harder into Manelli's throat. The sweat and dirt from his face dripped onto Manelli like muddy rain.

'Which room?'

Manelli sighed.

'One twenty-four. Let me ask you a question, Talley?'

Talley hesitated. He didn't have time for questions.

'What?'

'You're not just some hick cop?'

'No. No, I'm not.'

Talley covered Manelli's mouth with duct tape, then slipped across the road and returned to the parking lot, searching for room 124. He found the green Mustang on the far side of the motel, parked one parking place down from 124. A man in a blue knit shirt was standing by it, smoking. This man outside left two more men in the room. Talley saw a silver wristwatch on his left arm; this man wasn't Glen Howell.

Talley worked his way as close to the Mustang as possible. The man finished his cigarette, then leaned against the car. He was less than fifteen yards away. Forty-five feet. Talley told himself that it wasn't very far.

The door to room 124 opened, and a man with a dark tan stepped out.

'Keep your eyes open. He should've been here.'

Talley saw a gold Rolex on his wrist, and recognized the voice. Howell.

Talley released the safety on his pistol, and readied himself to move.

The Mustang man complained to Howell.

'This is bullshit. That chickenfuck ain't gonna come. We should get outta this shithole while we still can.'

'He'll come. There's nothing else he can do.'

Howell went back into the room, closing the door.

The Mustang man lit a fresh cigarette. When he turned away, Talley rushed forward.

The Mustang man startled at the sound, but he was too late. Talley hit him hard on the side of the head, using the .45 as a club. The Mustang man staggered sideways. Talley grabbed him around the neck from behind in a choke hold, and pushed him toward the room. He didn't want the Mustang man unconscious; he wanted him as a shield.

Talley moved fast now; he kicked the door next to the knob, busting the jamb, and shoved the Mustang man through, screaming his identification.

*'Police! You're under arrest!'*

Talley didn't think they would shoot him until they had the disks. He was counting on that.

Glen Howell brought up a pistol as he dropped into a crouch, shouting at a man with a big head seated by the window. The man rolled out of his chair and also came up with a gun, aiming from the floor in a two-handed grip as Howell shouted not to fire.

'Don't shoot him! Don't shoot!'

Talley shifted his aim between the two men, making himself as small as possible behind the Mustang man. Insects spiraled in from the night, hungry for the light.

Talley shouted, 'Where's my family?'

They sucked air like freight engines. No one was shooting, but if one person fired, everyone would fire. They each had something the other wanted. Talley knew it. He knew that Howell knew it. It was the only thing holding them back.

Howell abruptly released his gun, letting it swing free on his finger.

'Just take it easy. Take it easy. We're here to do business.'

'*Where are they?*'

'Do you have the disks?'

Talley shifted his aim to the man with the big head. He felt as if he was at the day-care center again, held hostage by men with guns.

'You know I have the disks, you sonofabitch. Where's my family?'

Howell slowly stood, hands out, letting his gun hang.

'Let's just take it easy. They're all right. Can I take a phone from my pocket?'

'They were supposed to be here.'

'Let me get the phone. You can talk to them, see they're okay.'

Talley shifted his aim from the big-headed man to Howell, then back again. Howell took out a cell phone and pressed in a number. Someone on the other end answered, and Howell told them to put the woman on. He held out the phone.

'Here. Talk to her. She's all right.'

Talley jammed his gun under the Mustang man's jaw, and warned him not to move. Howell brought the phone over, holding it with two fingers like a teacup. Talley took it with his free hand, and Howell stepped back.

'Jane?'

'Jeff! We're –'

The line went dead.

'SHIT!'

Howell shrugged, reasonably.

'You see? They're alive. Whether they stay that way depends on you.'

Talley tossed the phone back to Howell, then took out a single disk. This was where everything could go bad. This was where he took his biggest chance, and risked everything.

'One disk. You'll get the other when I have my girls.

Not talk to them on the phone, but *have* them. I get my girls, you get the disks. You don't like it, tough. You kill me, everyone still goes to jail.'

He tossed the disk onto the bed.

Talley could read that Howell wasn't happy with just the one disk, but Talley was counting on that. He wanted Howell off-balance and worried. It was a negotiation. Talley knew that Howell would be weighing his options just as Talley weighed his; Howell would be wondering if Talley had the second disk with him, thinking that if Talley had both disks, Howell could simply shoot him and take the disks and this would be over. But Howell couldn't be sure. If he killed Talley, and Talley didn't have both disks, then Howell would be fucked. So Howell wouldn't shoot him. Not yet. And that gave Talley a chance to jam him into revealing Amanda and Jane.

Talley watched the tension play over Howell's face. Talley offered nothing.

Howell picked up the disk.

'I have to see if it's real.'

'It's real.'

'I have to make sure.'

An IBM ThinkPad with a Zip drive attached was set up on the nightstand. Howell sat on the edge of the bed as he opened the disk, then grunted at the contents.

'All right. This is one of them. Where's the other?'

'First my girls. I see my girls, you get the disks. That's the way it works.'

Sweat leaked from Talley's hair and ran down his neck. It felt like crawling ants. Howell would either take the chance or he wouldn't. Neither of them had any other choice. It had all come down to which one would break first.

It was a face-off.

Talley waited as Howell considered his options. Talley

364

already knew what he would decide. Talley had left Howell no other choice.

Howell picked up his phone.

GLEN HOWELL

Talley wasn't acting like a has-been cop who had been broken by the job and come to nowhereland to hide; he was carrying on like a full-blown SWAT tactical street-monster. But Talley was also scared. Howell knew that he had to use that fear; he had to make Talley so frightened of losing his wife and daughter that he stopped thinking. Howell figured that Talley had the second disk on him, but the only way he could find out was to kill him. If he killed Talley, and Talley didn't have the disk, Howell would be fucked. Sonny Benza's message was clear; Benza would kill him.

The phone at the other end rang once before Marion Clewes answered.

'Yes?'

Howell spoke clearly, never taking his eyes from Talley. He wanted Talley to know that Glen Howell held the lives of his wife and child in his hands.

'Bring them. Stop the car outside the room, but don't get out. I want to show him that they're all right.'

'Okey-doke.'

Howell watched Talley closely, and noticed that Talley tensed when Howell told Clewes to stay in the car. Talley didn't like that, but tried not to show it. Howell felt encouraged. He felt as if he had played a winning card.

'Don't hang up. It's very important that you stay on the line. I'll want to talk to you again.'

'All right.'

Howell lowered the phone. Clewes was parked behind a Mobil station down the street. He would be here in seconds.

'Okay, Talley, they're on the way.'

'I want more than just seeing them. I won't give you the disk until I have them.'

'I understand.'

Howell heard the car before he saw it. Clewes wheeled to a stop in the empty space next to the Mustang, the nose of his car framed dead-center in the open door. The woman, Jane, was in the passenger seat. The daughter was in the rear. They were both tied, their mouths taped.

Howell saw Talley move slightly toward the door and his wife, then catch himself before looking back at Howell.

'Tell him to get out of the car.'

Howell raised the phone.

'Marion?'

Outside, Clewes lifted his own phone. They could see each other clearly through the open door.

'Yes, sir?'

'Aim your gun at the woman's head.'


MARION CLEWES


The world was comfortable here within Marion's car, which still held that yummy new-car smell; with the windows up, the engine idling, and the air-conditioning blowing softly, Marion could hear only the two women crying and the voice in his ear. He took no pleasure in their tears.

'Yes, sir.'

Marion had his orders. Just as Glen Howell's job was to recover the disks, Marion knew exactly what he was supposed to do and when he was supposed to do it. It was all about doing your job, being rewarded if you succeeded, being punished if you failed. Success or failure were defined by the disks.

Marion raised his gun to the mother's head. She

trembled, and clenched her eyes. Behind her, in the backseat, the daughter moaned loudly.

Marion smiled warmly, trying to lend comfort, even as he watched the events within the motel.

'Don't worry, ladies. You'll be fine.'

His gun did not waver from its mark.

## TALLEY

The world collapsed to an automobile only ten steps away. Talley saw everything happening inside the car with a clarity so great it seemed unreal: The man behind the wheel touched a small black pistol to Jane's temple. Glistening tears spilled from Jane's eyes. In the backseat, Amanda rocked from side to side, also crying.

Talley screamed, 'NO!'

Howell kept the phone to his mouth, speaking to Talley but also the man in the car.

'Give me the second disk or he'll kill your wife.'

'NO!'

Talley jerked his gun to the man in the car but was scared that the angle of the windshield would deflect his shot. This wasn't like when Neil Craimont had killed the man holding a gun to Talley's head at the day-care center; the man in the car was surrounded by glass. An accurate shot could not be guaranteed. Talley jerked his aim back at Howell. Everything was suddenly wrong; everything that he was trying to do had gone to hell.

Howell was winning.

'I'll kill you, Howell! You'll never get the disk!'

'He'll kill your wife, but your daughter will still be alive. Are you listening to this, Marion?'

Talley saw the man behind the wheel nod. Talley shifted his aim again, back to the man in the car.

'I'll fucking kill you! Can you hear *that*, you sonofabitch?!'

The man in the car smiled.

Howell spoke reasonably.

'I'll still have your daughter. Your wife will be dead, but your daughter will be alive. Do you see her there in the car, Talley? But if you shoot me, then he'll kill your daughter, too. Do you want to lose both of them?'

Talley aimed at the man in the car again. His breath was coming so hard that his gun shook. If he shot low, the bullet would deflect high, but he didn't know how much; anything short of a perfect shot would cost Jane's life. If Talley shot at the man in the car, Howell or the man with the big head would shoot him, and then all of them would be dead.

Howell said, 'The negotiation is over, Talley. I won.'

Talley glanced at Howell. He measured the shots; first the man in the car, then Howell, lastly the man on the floor. He would have to make all three to save his family. He didn't think that he could make them.

Howell said, 'Drop your gun, and give me the second disk. Give me the disk or he'll put her brain on the window.'

Talley's eyes filled because he thought they would all die anyway, but he still had one chance left. One small chance, because Howell and Benza still wanted the disks.

Talley dropped his gun.

The Mustang man jumped out of the way. Howell and the big-headed man charged forward. They scooped up Talley's gun and shoved him against the wall, pinning him like an insect to a board. Howell searched him even as Talley told him about the second disk.

'It's in my left front pocket.'

Talley felt numb. Defeated. Outside, the man behind the wheel climbed out of the car and came to the door. Talley watched Amanda and Jane in the car. Jane met his eye, and in that moment he felt buoyed by a tide of love that felt as if it could carry him away.

Howell loaded the disk into the ThinkPad.

Talley watched him open the disk, and took a grim pleasure in watching Howell's face darken and grow fierce.

'You sonofabitch. This isn't the disk. This isn't the second disk! It's a goddamned blank!'

Talley felt strangely removed from this room and these people. He glanced at Jane again. He smiled at her, the same small smile they had often shared at night when they were alone in bed, and then he turned back to Howell.

'I don't have the second disk anymore. I gave it to the Sheriffs, and they're giving it to the FBI. Benza's over. You're over. There's nothing either of us can do.'

Talley watched the disbelief float to the surface of Howell's face like a great slow bubble.

'You're lying.'

'I'm not lying. We're done here, Howell. Let us go. Let us go and save yourself the murder charge.'

Howell stood stiffly, like a mechanical man. He lumbered around the bed as if he was in shock, picked up his gun from the floor, and aimed it at Talley.

'Are you out of your mind?'

'I just want to take my family home.'

Howell shook his head as if he still couldn't believe that this was happening, and then he blinked numbly at the man in the door, the man who had been in the car.

'Kill every one of these people.'


MARION CLEWES

Marion watched as Glen Howell opened the second disk. He was disappointed to see that Talley had tried to fake them out with a false disk, but he had expected as much. Talley was a policeman, after all; Marion had never expected that he would let a man like Sonny Benza walk away, not even with his family being held. In the end,

369

turning over the disk to the proper authorities had been the right thing to do.

'Kill every one of these people.'

It was all about doing your job, being rewarded if you succeeded, being punished if you failed. Success or failure was defined by the disks, and Glen Howell had not recovered the disks.

Marion felt sad about that; he had always liked Glen Howell even though Mr. Howell hadn't liked him.

Marion had his orders.

Marion lifted his gun.


### TALLEY


The man in the door whom Howell had called Marion raised his gun and aimed it squarely at Talley's face. Marion was a small man, ordinary in appearance, the type of anonymous man who would be invisible in a mall and impossible for witnesses to describe. An Everyman; average height, average weight, brown, brown.

Talley stared into the black hole of the muzzle and braced for the bullet.

'I'm sorry, Jane.'

Marion shifted his gun hard to the side and fired. He adjusted his aim, and fired again, then again. The first bullet took Howell above the right eye, the second the Mustang man dead-center in the left eye, and the third caught the man with the big head in the temple.

Marion lowered his gun.

Talley stood motionless against the wall, watching Marion the way a bird watches a snake.

Marion shrugged.

'Life is unforgiving.'

Marion crossed the room to retrieve the one good disk, pocketed it, then went to the car. He helped Jane out, then opened the back door and helped Amanda. He walked around the car, climbed in behind the wheel, and drove away without another word. Talley saw him using his cell phone even before he was out of the parking lot.

The motel was quiet.

A dark wind had blown through Bristo Camino, something beyond Talley's control, beyond his pain and his loss, and now it was gone. Now, only the three of them were left.

'Jane?'

Talley stumbled out of the room and ran to his wife. He hugged her with frantic desperation, then pulled his daughter close, squeezing them to him as the tears spilled down his face. He held them and knew then that he would never let them go, that he had lost them once and now had almost lost them this second time, lost them forever, and that he could and would never allow that to happen again.

It was over.

# CHAPTER 28

## Palm Springs
Saturday, 4:36 A.M.

SONNY BENZA

Sonny Benza didn't try to sleep again after they got off the phone with Glen Howell. He popped twenty milligrams of Adderall and snorted two lines of crank to prop himself up, then the three of them sat down to wait.

The first time the phone rang, he damn near jumped off the couch.

Tuzee looked at him, asking if Sonny wanted him to answer the phone. Benza nodded, saying, Yeah, answer it.

Tuzee answered.

'It's the airport. They wanna know where you want to go. They gotta file a flight plan.'

'Tell them Rio. We'll change it in the air.'

As Tuzee hung up, Salvetti said, 'They're still gonna know where we go. These jets fly so high that air-traffic control watches them all the way.'

'Don't worry about it, Sally. We'll take care of it.'

'I'm just saying.'

'Don't worry about it.'

The second time the phone rang, Tuzee answered without asking. Benza could tell from Tuzee's expression that this was the word.

Salvetti said, 'Shit.'

Tuzee punched on the speaker, saying, 'It's Ken Seymore. Ken, Sonny and Charlie are here. What do you have down there?'

'It's gone to shit. All of it's gone to shit. I'm still here at the development, but – '

Benza shouted over him. The fear in Seymore's voice infuriated him.

'I don't give a shit where you are. Do we have the goddamned disks or not?'

'No! They got the disks. Glen Howell and two more of our guys are dead. They got Manelli and Ruiz and I don't know who else. It's a goddamned clusterfuck down here. I don't know what happened.'

'Who killed Howell? Talley?'

'I don't know! Yeah, I think it was Talley. I don't know. Man, I'm hearing all kinds of things.'

Sonny Benza closed his eyes. Just like that it was gone, everything was gone, three low-class assholes break into a house and everything that he had worked for his entire life was about to end.

Tuzee said, 'You *sure* they got the disks?'

'Talley gave the disks to the Sheriffs. That much I know for sure. Then I don't know what happened. Glen got jammed up at the motel, they had a big fuckin' firefight or somethin', and now the FBI just rolled up, the *real* FBI. What do you want me to do?'

Benza shook his head; there wasn't anything Ken Seymore or anyone else could do.

Tuzee said, 'Vanish. Anyone who isn't in custody, take off. You're done.'

The line went dead without another word. Ken Seymore was gone.

Benza stood without a word and went to the great glass windows overlooking Palm Springs. He was going to miss the view.

Salvetti came up behind him.

'What do you want us to do, Boss?'

'How long do you figure we have before the Feds get here?'

He had a pretty good idea, but he wanted to hear it.

Salvetti and Tuzee traded a shrug.

Tuzee said, 'Talley will tell them what's on the disk then they'll probably talk to Smith. I don't know if he' corroborate or not.'

'He'll talk.'

'Okay, they'll want to detain you as a flight risk to giv themselves time to write the true counts, so they'll get warrant based on our alleged involvement with th killings and kidnaps in Bristo. Say they get a telephoni warrant and coordinate with the state cops out her through the substation . . . I'd say two hours.'

'Two hours.'

'Yeah, I don't think they can get here before that.'

Benza sighed.

'Okay, guys. I want to be in the air in an hour.'

'You got it, Sonny.'

Salvetti said, 'You gonna tell New York?'

Benza wouldn't tell New York. He was more frightene of their reaction than he was of battling the Feds.

'Fuck'm. Go get your families. Don't bother packing we'll buy new when we get there. Meet me at the airpor as soon as you can. Forty-five minutes tops.'

The three of them stood mute for a time. They were i deep shit, and all three of them knew it. Benza shook eacl man's hand. They were good and dear friends. Sonny Benza loved them both.

'We had a good thing here, guys.'

Charlie Salvetti started to cry. He turned away an hurried from the office without another word.

Tuzee stared at the floor until Salvetti was gone, ther offered his hand again. Benza took it.

'All this will blow over, Sonny. You'll see. We'll ge this straight with New York, and we'll be fine.'

Benza knew that was bullshit, but he appreciated Tuzee trying to cheer him. He even found it within himself to smile.

374

'Philly, we're gonna be looking over our shoulders the rest of our lives. Fuck it. It's all part of the game.'

Tuzee smiled tiredly.

'Yeah, I guess so. See you at the airport.'

'You bet.'

Tuzee hurried away.

Sonny Benza turned back to the window. He admired the lights in the desert below, glittering like fallen dreams, and remembered how proud his father had been, how much the old man had bragged, *Only in America, Sonny, only in America; right down the fuckin' street from Francis Albert!*

Frank Sinatra had been dead for years.

Benza went to wake his wife.


**New York City**
Saturday, 7:49 A.M., Eastern time

VIC CASTELLANO

Vic Castellano sat on his terrace overlooking the Upper West Side of Manhattan. It was a beautiful morning, clear and pleasant, though it would be hotter than a sonofabitch before noon. He still wore the white terry-cloth bathrobe with *Don't Bug Me* on the back. He liked that sonofabitch so much he'd probably wear it until it was threads. He put down his coffee.

'I can tell by your expression it ain't good.'

Jamie Beldone had just come out to see him.

'It's not. The police have the disks. They have Benza's accountant, and several of his people. Once the Feds develop the information, we're going to have a fight on our hands.'

'But we'll survive it.'

Jamie nodded.

'We'll take a few shots, but we'll survive. Benza, that's something else.'

'That sonofabitch still hasn't had the decency to call. You imagine that?'

'It shows a lack of class.'

Castellano settled back in his chair, thinking out loud. He and Jamie had gone over this a hundred times last night, but it never hurt to go over such things again.

'We'll survive, but because of this Mickey Mouse West Coast asshole we're exposed to serious heat from the federal prosecutor. This means we've got just cause to seek redress.'

'The other families will see it that way.'

'And since the Feds are going to put Benza out of business, no one can beef if we take care of it for them.'

'It's a fair trade.'

Castellano nodded.

'All in all, it's probably good for everyone that all this happened. We can send somebody out west, take over Benza's end of things, and cut ourselves a bigger piece of the pie.'

'The silver lining that everyone will enjoy. What are you going to do, skipper?'

Castellano had known what he was going do for the past six hours. He took no pleasure in it, but he had it all arranged.

'Make the call.'

Beldone started back into the house.

'Jamie!'

'Yes, sir?'

'I want to be sure about this. That guy Clewes, Marion Clewes, he's kinda flaky. I don't want to just take his word that Benza fucked up. I want to know for sure.'

'I'm sure, Vic. I double-checked. I just hung up with Phil Tuzee.'

Castellano felt better. He knew that Phil Tuzee wouldn't steer him wrong.

'That's good enough. Make the call and finish this.'

## Palm Springs, California
Saturday, 4:53 A.M., Pacific time

SONNY BENZA

Benza's wife moved so slowly that he wanted to stuff a cattle prod up her ass. The kids were even worse.

'Would ya hurry it up, for chrissakes? We gotta get outta here.'

'I can't leave my things!'

'I'll buy you new things!'

'We can't leave our pictures! What about our wedding album? How can you buy a new wedding album?'

'Five minutes, you got *five minutes!* Get the kids and meet me out front or I'll leave your ass here.'

Benza trotted back through the house to the garage. All he carried was a blue nylon gym bag with one hundred thousand in cash, his blood pressure meds, and his .357. Anything else he needed he could buy when they landed; Benza had over thirty million dollars stashed in foreign accounts.

Benza hit the button to open the garage door. He tossed the nylon bag into the backseat of his Mercedes, then slid behind the wheel. He started the car, threw it into reverse, then hit the gas hard, backing in a wide arc toward the front door. He was moving so fast that he almost broadsided the nondescript sedan that blocked his path.

Flashes of light speckled the air around the sedan, exploding Benza's rear window. The bullets knocked him into the steering wheel, then sideways onto the seat. Sonny Benza tried to get the .357 out of his bag, but he didn't have time. Someone pulled open the driver's-side door and shot Sonny Benza in the head.

# Part Five
## THE AVOCADO ORCHARD

# CHAPTER 29

Sunday, 2:16 P.M.
Two weeks later

TALLEY

The fantasy was always the same: On the days that Jeff
Talley visited the avocado orchard, he imagined Brendan
Malik playing in the trees. He saw the boy laughing,
kicking up dust as he ran, then climbing into the branches
where he swung by his knees. Brendan was always happy
and laughing in these daydreams, even with his skin
mottled in death and blood pulsing from his neck. Talley
had never been able to imagine the boy any other way.

Jane said, 'What are you thinking?'

The two of them were slouched down in the front seat
of his patrol car, watching red-tailed hawks float above
the trees. Amanda had stayed in Los Angeles, but Jane had
come up for the weekend.

'Brendan Malik. Remember? That boy.'

'I don't remember.'

Talley realized that he had never told her. He had not
mentioned Brendan Malik to anyone after that night he
left the boy's house, not even the police psychologist.

'I guess I never told you.'

'Who was he?'

'A victim in one of the negotiations. It's not important
anymore.'

Jane took his hand. She turned sideways so that she
faced him.

'It's important if you're thinking about it.'

Talley considered that.

'He was a little boy, nine, ten, something like that About Thomas's age. I think about him sometimes.'

'You've never mentioned him.'

'I guess not.'

Talley found himself telling her about the night with Brendan Malik, of holding the boy's hand, of staring into his eyes as the little boy died, of the overwhelming feelings of failure and shame.

Listening, she cried, and he cried, too.

'I was trying to see his face right now, but I can't. don't know whether to feel happy or sad about that. You think that's bad?'

Jane squeezed his hand.

'I think it's good we're talking about these things. It's a sign that you're healing.'

Talley shrugged, then smiled at her.

'About goddamned time.'

Jane smiled in that way she had, the smile that was encouraging and pleased.

'Did you find out about Thomas?'

'I tried, but they won't tell me anything. I guess it's best this way.'

Walter Smith and his family had entered the U.S. Marshals' witness protection program. They had simply vanished; one day here, the next gone, hidden by the system. Talley hoped that Thomas would one day contact him, but he didn't think it likely. It was safer that way.

Jane said, 'How much time before you have to get back?'

'I've got time. I'm the Chief.'

Jane smiled wider.

'Let's walk.'

They walked from sunlight to shade to sun, bees swirling sluggishly around them, lazy in the midday heat It was good to walk. It was peaceful. Talley had been away for a very long time, hiding inside himself, but now he was back. He was on the way back.

The orchard, as always, was as still as a church.

'I'm glad you're here, Jane.'

Jane squeezed his hand. Talley knew, then, that though a church was a place to bury the dead, it was also a place to celebrate the living. Their lives could begin again.

All Orion/Phoenix titles are available at your local bookshop or from the following address:

Mail Order Department
Littlehampton Book Services
FREEPOST BR535
Worthing, West Sussex, BN13 3BR
*telephone* 01903 828503, *facsimile* 01903 828802
*e-mail* MailOrders@lbsltd.co.uk
(Please ensure that you include full postal address details)

Payment can be made either by credit/debit card (Visa, Mastercard, Access and Switch accepted) or by sending a £ Sterling cheque or postal order made payable to *Littlehampton Book Services*.
DO NOT SEND CASH OR CURRENCY.

Please add the following to cover postage and packing

*UK and BFPO*
£1.50 for the first book, and 50p for each additional book to a maximum of £3.50

*Overseas and Eire*
£2.50 for the first book plus £1.00 for the second book and 50p for each additional book ordered

---

BLOCK CAPITALS PLEASE

name of cardholder ........................        delivery address
................................        *(if different from cardholder)*

address of cardholder ......................        ................................

................................        ................................

................................        ................................

................................        ................................

postcode ....................        postcode ....................

☐ I enclose my remittance for £ ........................

☐ please debit my Mastercard/Visa/Access/Switch (delete as appropriate)

card number ☐☐☐☐☐☐☐☐☐☐☐☐☐☐☐☐

expiry date ☐☐☐☐        Switch issue no. ☐☐

signature ........................................................

*prices and availability are subject to change without notice*